# Bound

I0665918

## Thaddeus Nowak

www.ThaddeusNowak.com

Published by Mountain Pass Publishing, LLC.

ISBN: 978-0-9863946-2-1

First Printing: February 2020


Set in Adobe Garamond Pro

# Dedication

This book is dedicated to Chad, Trey, and Glenn for all campaigns and D&D sessions we had growing up. Those early years of gaming had a huge impact on me, and has led in no small way to the books I have written, and will write.

This book is also for Ed, and all the people at Pawn & Pint, who convinced me to try 5th edition. And last, but not least, to those who took the time to join my campaigns at Pawn & Pint. Dave, you will be missed.

# Acknowledgements

I would like to thank the many people who helped make this story possible: my wife Sherri, my best friend Chad, my parents, and my editor Judy Reveal. Any errors left in the work are entirely mine.

# Chapter 1

Kyrie wiped her brow, smearing the dirt that had accumulated on her face and in her hair. The wind blowing down the mountain made the fifty-degree temperature a bit cold, but her aggressive use of the hoe in the rocky soil helped to compensate for her lack of a coat. *Though the clouds sure aren't helping,* she thought. The wispy white streaks were just thick enough to block the sun. She frowned. March had been far too dry; so far April did not look to change that trend. The prospect of carrying buckets of water up the slope to soak the seeds her mother was planting made her back ache even more.

She tried to rub away some of the dirt on her face with her shoulder, but the old shirt needed cleaning more than she did. She just had not cared to do the laundry when she also had to clean the dishes, tend the fire, do her homework, and look after her mother. *Get better,* she wished her mother. *We just can't find what is wrong.*

Kyrie hefted the hoe. "Come on me, the sooner this is done, the sooner you can lug up the water." She forced a laugh; her father would have fainted at hearing her desire to rush into more work. She sniffed back the emotion that threatened to weaken her as she resumed digging into the remnants of the prior year's peas; the earthy scent of turned soil filling her nose. She remained determined to not think about having allowed her father to die last June. *However, you should have known something was wrong with him,* still slipped through her thoughts. She wiped away a trail of tears and redoubled her work with the hoe.

Kyrie finished the furrow and turned around to work back the other direction. She looked for her mother but did not see her. The curve of the mountain and the steep slope hid their cabin, as well as the road and the lower valley, from her view. After scratching her dirty scalp, she trudged back through the dead vines she had yet to remove. A drink of water and a late lunch filled her thought as she walked back toward home.

As the larger valley came into view, she looked down at what had been her home for her whole life. The aged and weather-worn cabin was a quarter mile down the steep slope. It sat nestled next to a large boulder and a grove of pine trees. Her father had fixed the slate roof several years before and she could barely tell the differences in the lichen and moss that covered the stone.

A lone dirt road descended back and forth from the cabin into the lower valley. Its passing was barely visible from her position, betrayed only by a slight gap in the trees. The road's haphazard path was in contrast to the scar that cut straight up the slope, bringing a pair of power lines to the cabin. The clearing under the lines had not been tended in ages and small trees fought the grasses for growing space.

No smoke came from the cabin's stone chimney, *which means no hot lunch.* She knew the hope had been an unlikely one. It would not take that long to rekindle the fire, but the longer she delayed the work in the field, the later she would be outside working. *And that would mean we won't finish the next part of the adventure tonight.* The thought of having to wait another night for her character to escape the city in her mother's Dungeons & Dragons campaign motivated her action.

With her hoe in hand, she walked along the rows of furrows toward the cabin. Her father would have chapped her hide if she left tools sitting out and unattended. After a dozen steps, she slowed. She noticed her mother sitting in a furrow thirty feet away. Panic washed over her and she opened her mind further, but she could still feel no one near her, not even her mother.

"Mom!" Kyrie shouted, the hoe fell from her hand, and she sprinted the distance to her mother's slumped form. Desperate to disbelieve her senses, she shouted again as she skidded to a stop and dropped to her knees. She grabbed her mother's shoulders. "Mom!" she wailed as her mother's limp form fell back against the ground.

"No, Mom, don't leave me," Kyrie pleaded and pulled her mother against her. Their precious seeds scattered across the ground as the bucket tumbled down the slope.

Kyrie forced herself to calm down and breathe. She reached out again, searching for the signs of nearby threats, but she only felt a scattering of animals. She looked over her mother's body, searching for signs of injury. She had not heard any gunfire and she found no blood or bleeding wounds.

Kyrie refused to acknowledge the cold feel of her mother's body and reached deep within herself. She pulled at the energy that had grown in her over the years and tried to force the power into her mother. She tasted the salt of the tears running down her face as she searched for her mother's subconscious mind. However, her mother did not respond, and no matter how much she pleaded, she could feel no life in the body that had cared for her every day. "No, Mom." She wiped her face, smearing the dirt that became streaked by her tears.

Desperation ran through her and Kyrie looked around at what had been her world. She jumped to her feet and raced down the slope, absorbing more and more energy with every stride. Her parents had always told her if anything happened to them, her first priority was to get to safety, but she could not bring herself to abandon her mother. She fundamentally knew that resurrection spells did not exist. They were merely a construct in Dungeons & Dragons, but when her father had died, her mother had sobbed that if someone had only gotten him to a hospital sooner, he might have lived. *We won't fail!* Kyrie swore as she leaped over a log and landed nimbly without slowing. She sprinted past the cabin and raced along the rutted and decaying road.

The seldom used road zigzagged back and forth down the mountain; the switchbacks evening out the slope to something reasonable for a four-wheel-drive. However, the winding road spanned four and a half miles to reach Ms. Conner's house and Kyrie felt the press of time on her. At the first switchback, Kyrie leaped into the pine forest and continued to run down the steep slope. Loose soil, rocks, and debris followed her instinctual foot falls, leaving a mini landslide trailing in her wake.

She burst through a wall of pine branches, crossed the road, charged back into the forest, and within fifty paces, emerged into the clearing under the electric lines. She ran like a gazelle through the open space, using the power in her body to leap over fallen trees, rocks, and other debris. The energy continued to flow, burning nerve endings and bringing her pain, but she ignored the discomfort.

Her heart pounded in her chest, but her body responded easily to the physical effort. Since she turned six, her parents had made her run down and back up the road every day. Coupled with living her whole life on the mountain, the thin air did not bother her, but fear for her mother pushed her much harder than normal. Soon the energy draw became too painful, and as it slowed, her breathing turned into ragged panting, leaving the taste of blood on her breath.

She knew the distance to Ms. Conner's house on the road, but she reduced her run to under two miles by going straight down the mountain. *You just need to get Mom to a hospital.* She did not really know what one was, but she remembered the word from when her father had died.

Nearing exhaustion, Kyrie stumbled over a ridge and emerged into the clearing around Megan Conner's mobile home. Rusting cars, old refrigerators, and debris generated by humans filled the yard. Kyrie ran up the metal steps and banged on the door as she bent over to catch her breath. Blood dripped on the dirty welcome mat and she wiped her face, smearing blood, sweat, and dirt. Scrapes and cuts from her hasty descent covered her exposed skin.

Kyrie pounded on the door again; she felt Ms. Conner taking her time to emerge from deeper within the old building.

"What in the hell is all this racket?" demanded a gravelly voice.

"Ms. Conner!" Kyrie shouted before she gulped down another breath. "My mother! I couldn't heal her. Something's wrong."

The door opened revealing an old woman with thinning hair and a weathered appearance only achieved through lots of sun and smoking. The woman's face dropped. "Dearie, what sick bastard did that to you?"

"Please Ms. Conner, my mother needs a hospital!"

The old woman stepped back. "I'll call Sheriff Sawyer, he'll be able to get an ambulance, but the nearest hospital is three hours away."

Kyrie brushed passed the word ambulance, uncertain of what it meant, but she knew three-hours seemed like far too long to wait and her parents dislike for law enforcement made her bite her lip. "Do we need the sheriff? I just need a doctor to help my mother."

"Dearie, you need Sheriff Sawyer. Let me make this call and then I'll go with you back to your cabin." Megan Conner removed a rounded yellow rectangle from the wall and started pressing buttons on what Kyrie guessed was a phone. "Was your mother bleeding? Did she fall or hurt herself?"

Kyrie shook her head; her breathing already normalizing. She felt a sense of mistrust coming from Ms. Conner and it made her uncomfortable. "No. I found my mother slumped over in the field. She felt cold and didn't respond to me."

Kyrie sensed a sudden change in Ms. Conner's demeanor, as if the urgency of her mother's condition had diminished.

"Sheriff Sawyer. It's me, Megan Conner. It seems Rachel Smith may have had a heart attack or something. I've got her girl with me now. Oh, I don't know, I've not gone up the slope yet. The girl is covered in cuts, but I think she ran down the slope. Yeah, I'll keep an eye on things." Ms. Conner started tapping her foot. "Look, can you call Paul's boy and get him up here just in case there is something he can do? I've got to take Kyrie back up to Stan's cabin. Yeah, thanks, see you shortly."

Kyrie had tried to hear what the sheriff had said, but her heart still pounded in her ears and she felt herself growing physically weak.

"Here, let me get you a soda," Ms. Conner said, "then we'll take my truck to your parent's cabin. Hopefully my old wreck can make it." The older woman opened the off-white refrigerator, pulled out a cylinder like ones Kyrie had seen littering the ground along some streams on the outskirts of the valley. She took the cold metal container from Ms. Conner. The older woman then grabbed her keys from a wooden bowl nestled between several piles of disorganized papers covering the small kitchen table. Kyrie peered at the oddly shaped container in her hand. She could feel the sloshing of a liquid inside, but where she had seen an opening before in the cans littering the streams, this one only had lines etched into the metal.

"Come on," Ms. Conner said, ushering Kyrie from the house as the woman slid into a heavy coat. The older lady closed the door behind them and nodded her head toward a truck whose original color could barely be determined as green. The fact that it had inflated tires was the only visible difference from the other vehicles in the yard.

Kyrie pulled at the latch and climbed into the passenger side of the truck. She had only been out of the valley four times that she could remember. She had seen the exteriors of cars and trucks and had seen how people opened the doors, but she had never been inside one and no vehicle had ever made it all the way to the cabin since she had been young. That was in great part because her parents had carefully damaged the road to make it look like rains had caused deep ruts.

Ms. Conner climbed into the other side of the truck, fidgeted with something near the steering wheel, and pressed on something on the floor. After a bit of growling, the metal beast came to life. Kyrie would have watched more carefully, but her thoughts kept returning to her mother laying in the fields above their cabin.

Ms. Conner manipulated some levers and turned the wheel as the truck lurched into motion. "Don't you know how to open a soda can?" The older woman reached one hand over and tapped on a bit of metal attached to the top of the can. "Pull that forward to open it." The woman shook her head and made the engine roar as they bounced over a small rut in the gravel road. "I respect those that home school their kids. Best way to ensure you don't grow up with socialist ideas, but have mercy, someone your age should have at least seen a soda can."

Kyrie closed her mind; not only did her head hurt from the energy she used, but she knew the disapproval Ms. Conner felt was not with her and she did not want to feel someone thinking badly of her parents. Kyrie looked down at the top of the can and noticed words she had missed earlier. She used her dirty fingernail to pry up the metal tab before pulling it forward. Foam and liquid erupted from within the metal container, flowing over the top and spilling down her hand and onto her pants.

"Keep it off the seats! Someone your age should know not to open them so fast on a rough road."

Kyrie looked down at the sticky brown liquid. "What do I do with it?"

Ms. Conner shook her head. "Drink it."

Although it was mumbled, Kyrie clearly heard Ms. Conner say, "Daft Girl." Feeling obligated, Kyrie took a sip of the liquid, trying to hold the can steady as the truck bounced and lurched over the road that had as little maintenance as the clearing under the power lines. The sweetness made her sick, and she simply held the can away from her as they made their way slowly up the mountain side. The slow progress made Kyrie wish teleport spells existed in reality.

The truck took them close, but not all the way to the cabin. The deep ruts her parents cut across the road prevented even the most robust vehicles from getting within five-hundred feet of the structure. The distance provided a delay where her parents could take action to deal with an unwanted or unexpected visitor.

Ms. Conner parked at the last switchback; the only space wide enough for a vehicle to turn around. They got out of the truck and Kyrie set the soda on the ground, then bounded ahead of Ms. Conner, and raced up the slope to her mother's side. The older woman struggled to navigate the rocky ground and it took Ms. Conner a long time to arrive. Kyrie felt tears again falling from her face, knowing that her mother's condition had not changed and fearing how long it would take for anyone else to get here.

"Dearie, let's wait inside and out of this wind. Sheriff Sawyer will send over Paul's boy. He's a paramedic. The closest thing the likes of us have to a hospital or doctor."

Kyrie felt no life in her mother's body and the hollowness seeped into her. She ignored the unfamiliar word and allowed herself to be led back down to the aged cabin. She opened the door with mechanical movement and let Ms. Conner inside.

"Wow," the older woman said. I expected you to live in filth. I mean, look at your clothing and hair. But this is—"

"Clean," Kyrie said, not quite removing the acid from her voice. Compared to Ms. Conner's home, the interior of the cabin was neat and organized, with everything in its proper place. The building featured a combined kitchen and family room. Bookshelves lined all the walls. A large table sat in the middle of the space. Its surface empty except for two neatly organized stacks of papers that represented the schoolwork her mother would have taught her this evening. Three doors branched off the main room. Two led to bedrooms and a third to a single bathroom.

"Well, I'd guess your mother has you around to make sure things get done. My worthless daughter left at seventeen and might bother to call if she is drunk enough."

Kyrie bowed her head, knowing she had intentionally insulted an elder. "I'm sorry for my comment."

Ms. Conner pulled a small box from one of her pockets and removed a narrow stick. Kyrie watched her then remove a lighter and ignite the stick she had placed in her mouth. "Forget it, Dearie, you just lost your mother, I don't hold grudges."

Kyrie blinked her eyes as smoke issued from the stick and Ms. Conner's mouth. The odor made her sick, but she did not want to insult the woman a second time.

Ms. Conner walked over to a set of bookshelves and started looking at the titles. "So, this must be all those books your mother had me order for you over the years. I confess, none of these titles mean anything to me."

"Those books cover physics and the next shelf is mathematics."

Ms. Conner turned toward the distant sound of sirens. "Wait here, Dearie." She started walking toward the door and then paused to turn back to Kyrie. "You might want to wash your face and change your cloths…if you have a clean pair."

Kyrie did not have to feel a sense of compulsion to know Ms. Conner had not phrased that as a suggestion. Before the older lady had closed the outer door, Kyrie had already moved to the sink. She turned the old taps and allowed the water to become lukewarm before she splashed it against her face. She used the soap and scrubbed her arms, washing away the dirt and dried blood. With the grime removed, she realized she had allowed all the cuts and scrapes to heal to mere pink lines. Her parents had warned her constantly not to allow others to know she could do that, but in her worry for her mother, she had forgotten to fight back the instinct.

Kyrie grabbed the hand towel next to the sink and used it to dry her face and arms as she hurried into her bedroom. *I can't fix it now,* she thought with a frown, knowing her face would have healed even more than her arms because of how sensitive that skin was.

She stripped out of her dirty work cloths and slid on a clean shirt and a long sleeve sweater that would hide her arms. Her second pair of jeans lay on the floor and they were no cleaner than those she wore, but that pair lacked the rips she had created while running down the slope.

She recalled the look of pride in her mother's eyes when the package with the new clothing had arrived and fresh tears came unbidden. "I failed you as well, Mother." She did not have to wait to be told too much time had passed. She sensed it in Ms. Conner as well as in her own heart. "I should have run. I should not have gone for help, but I'm not ready to be alone."

She felt several people approaching the front door of the cabin and wiped her eyes with the back of her hands. Her mother had warned her that one day she would find herself on her own. When they had been alive, her parents had told her what to do if that ever happened. *You're just not ready.*

The approaching people pushed Kyrie into action, she pulled on her other pair of jeans and then slid her feet back into her worn shoes. She moved to the bookshelf on the other side of her bed and pulled out a dusty copy of Isaac Asimov's Foundation. She flipped through the book to find a small slip of paper securely tucked between the pages. She folded the strip of paper with a handwritten number on it, lifted her shirt and sweater, and slid it into her bra.

She replaced the book and went to two others, retrieving four twenty-dollar bills. She slid the money in her pants' pocket as the front door to the cabin opened and a man's voice called out her name. She straightened her clothing and then exited her small bedroom. She knew she would have to retrieve the rest of the cash her father had buried after everyone left.

"There you are," said a dark-haired man in a dark blue uniform. A heavy coat went to his waist, and beneath the coat, he had a bulk to his upper body that did not appear natural to Kyrie. "Can you tell me what happened?" he asked.

Kyrie looked from the man to Ms. Conner and then back. "We were planting seeds. When I looked back to find where my mother was, she was slumped against the seed bucket. I ran down to Ms. Conner for help."

The man crossed the room and tried to put a hand on her shoulder, but she moved a step away. "I won't hurt you, Kyrie. I'm Sheriff Sawyer." He glanced around the room and pulled a chair away from the table. "Please sit. What I have to tell you won't be pleasant."

Kyrie felt more tears falling from her eyes. She moved to the chair and sat.

"Young Lady, I'm afraid your mother has passed away. We don't know why yet, but I've asked Mike Douglas to examine her. His first thought is likely she had a heart attack or a stroke. Likely she didn't suffer."

Kyrie bit her lower lip. She could feel the unease coming from the man and Ms. Conner. "Will you bury her like my father?"

The man glanced as Ms. Conner. "Well, I wasn't involved with burying your father. That would have been your mother's doing." He shifted, pulled out a second chair, and sat down facing her. "How old are you?"

"I'm sixteen."

"And do you have any other family?"

Kyrie shook her head. "I do not. Just my mother and father." The man frowned and Kyrie wondered what she should have said. Her parents told her to trust no one, but now that she faced an official asking questions, she did not know when to lie and when to tell the truth. She had not expected that truth to cause her trouble. *You definitely do not want to be compelled to tell the truth.*

"And your mother's name was Rachel Smith? Your father Robert Smith?"

Kyrie nodded her head. She could feel the congestion in her sinuses and did not trust her voice.

"Do you know if they have any identification? I didn't see a driver's license on your mother."

"Oliver," Ms. Conner said, moving away from the door and closer to the conversation. "I don't believe either of them ever drove. They never had a car of their own—not that the road is in any condition either. When he worked odd jobs, her father always had someone pick him up near my house and Rachel would walk down and pick up packages at my place from time to time." She frowned and sat down at the table.

"Really?" the sheriff asked. "I'd never heard that."

"They always paid me a little extra for the hassle, but I didn't mind. It was mostly books and clothing they had delivered. Nothing illegal," she added hastily.

The sheriff nodded his head. "I believe you Megan. It's just a bit odd." He turned back to Kyrie. "Any identification?"

"I'm not sure what you mean," she replied softly.

"She's been cooped up here for years. I don't know if she's ever been out of the valley," Ms. Conner said and Kyrie bit back a response to the disapproval she felt.

"Is that true, you have never left the valley?" the sheriff asked her.

"I have not had much need to," Kyrie responded without answering. "We've had everything we need."

"You're still a minor and all the adults living here are dead. I'll need to look around for some form of ID. Something with a picture and details about your parents. Have you seen anything like that?"

Kyrie shook her head.

"That room is your bedroom I assume."

Kyrie nodded her head as he pointed to the room she had come out of to meet him.

"Your parents' bedroom?" he asked, pointing to the room beside hers.

"Yes, Sir."

"Okay, just sit here for a moment." He rose to his feet, went to the door, and entered her parents' bedroom.

Kyrie sat in the chair and stared at the floor. She felt Ms. Conner watching her as she heard the sheriff rifling through her parents' drawers and possessions.

After a while, Sheriff Sawyer returned to the main room overburdened with so many things that they obscured his face. He managed to make it to the table and dumped a rifle, two swords, a dagger, an unstrung long bow, a handful of books, and an old shoe box onto the wooden surface. "Well, I can't find an ID. I can't even find a single picture in your house, but care to explain these?" The sheriff pushed the weapons away from her. "I saw some dings in the blades like they had been used."

Kyrie glanced to the swords and dagger, which were all still in their scabbards. "They are my father's." She refrained from saying he had practiced with her at least every other day up to the point he died.

"And these books?" He set them on the table next to her. "Dungeons & Dragons? Your parents worship the Devil?"

Kyrie narrowed her eyes. The venom in the man's voice ate at her composure. *What have you done? Mother said never to trust anyone.* Aloud, she spoke evenly. "D&D is a role-playing game."

The sheriff glared at her. "Well, I've been all through your parents' drawers, though they could have hid who knows what in all of those papers and books. But I've not found any ID of any type. No official documents at all." He lifted the shoe box in his other hand. "But I did find this. Can you to tell me what is in it?"

"I assume you already know," Kyrie said. "It has no lock."

He slammed the box on the table causing Ms. Conner to jump. "Don't get smart with me, Little Girl. Where does your mother get over eight-hundred dollars in cash to stuff into a shoe box? Where does she get the money for rent and all these books and the ability to keep this place clean?"

Kyrie swallowed. "I'm sorry for upsetting you. I did not understand what you meant when you asked the question. It is the money left from my father when he worked. He would bring all of it home and we'd save it."

"Oliver," Ms. Conner said, leaning forward toward the sheriff. "They home schooled the girl her whole life. I think she may be autistic or something. Perhaps a little slow. Don't yell at her, she just lost her mother."

The sheriff sighed and then sat down on the chair he had used earlier. "Did your parents treat you right? Did they abuse you?"

Kyrie cocked her head to the side. "My parents loved me. Why would they harm me?"

"Some people do things," the sheriff said. "Sometimes young girls don't know what is right and what is wrong."

Kyrie did not know where he planned to take his line of inquiry, but both Ms. Conner and the sheriff looked at her very expectantly, as if they hoped she would say a certain thing. "My parents were good to me."

The sheriff nodded his head. "And you don't have any cousins or grandparents? No family. No one we can call about you?"

Kyrie's thoughts went to the number she had secreted in her bra, but she would not reveal that number to anyone. "No one. I only knew my parents and Ms. Conner."

"And you never asked about your grandparents?" His disbelief filled the room.

Kyrie wanted the conversation to end so she could leave and find a phone, but she did not know how to make these people go away. *You should have just run like Mother said.* "Why would I ask?"

"Oliver, remember, simple." Ms. Conner tapped her finger against her temple.

The brown-haired man exhaled and shrunk in size. "I'll have to take her in. Likely all the way to Fort Collins. Just not looking forward to the drive." He raised his eyebrows at Ms. Conner's expression. "I can't leave her here alone. She's just sixteen and…" He let his statement trail off with a glance at Kyrie.

Kyrie felt her heartbeat rise. *You can't let them take you.*

"She can stay with me tonight, Oliver. She just lost her mother and I'm the only one she knows." Ms. Conner lowered her voice. "You can see how frightened she is. Imagine her in custody."

The sheriff shook his head and then shrugged. "Save me almost five hours driving… Fine, but I'll have to call in the Staters. They'll end up taking her to be placed in a home. God knows there aren't enough resources in Gould or Walden to deal with an orphan."

"Can't I just stay here?" Kyrie asked, starting to feel her panic building.

"Dearie, Oliver can't leave you by yourself, you're not old enough." Ms. Conner stood up. "You know me. I can help you take care of things until Oliver finds a place where you can live."

The sheriff nodded his head. "I'll know more once I run some prints and do some background checks. Perhaps there are some estranged relatives that can step in." He raised a finger, "but child services will be out here tomorrow."

# Chapter 2

The day slipped into night before Kyrie realized the passage of time. Her head throbbed. She knew the aftereffects of using too much energy far too well, but when combined with the overwhelming odor of smoke in the trailer, she felt distinctly unwell. Not having the mental, or physical strength to protest, she let Ms. Conner tuck a blanket around her as she lay on the older woman's hard sofa. The makeshift bed had been cleared of clothing and magazines to make room for her. The mobile home only had one real bedroom, and that belonged to Ms. Conner. What had originally been the other bedroom now acted as a large repository for boxes and random possessions piled several feet high.

"I am so sorry for your loss, Dearie. I wish I could make it better." The older lady stood up. "Do you want another soda?"

Kyrie shook her head and tried to fight back her tears. The loss of her father less than a year ago had been hard, but this woman's patronizing tone made her miss her mother so much more. Kyrie kept from glancing at the phone on the wall. *Once you use the phone, she'll never see us again.*

"Well, if you need anything, just let me know. Otherwise, try to sleep. Oliver will look to see if you have any additional family somewhere."

Kyrie nodded her head and let Ms. Conner move away from the sofa. The older woman had not left her alone and she knew she could not disappear while under observation. She needed time to get supplies and leave the valley before Ms. Conner could call the sheriff or someone else to look for her. *You'll need at least an extra hour to get the money father hid. And now the weapons are gone and the sheriff has mother's cash.* She sighed; the thought of leaving all the things she could not carry weighed on her and she started to cry. However, she knew that could not deter her.

*You know the instructions. Get to immediate safety. When safe, call Lars and follow his instructions. Trust no one except for Lars. Retrieve resources only when safe to do so, and when no one will be aware of you doing it. Find a new place to hide.* She wanted the next part to be true as well: *We will come to you if we can.*

She closed her eyes. Neither of her parents would come to her now. Her mother had promised to never leave her alone. To never abandon her. However, Kyrie knew what dead felt like. She hunted animals to put food on their plates and her mother had felt just like those animals: devoid of life. *Don't let that be the last memory of your mother. Think of the good times.*

The sounds of Ms. Conner closing her bedroom door echoed through the mobile home. Despite the pain, she opened her mind to monitor the older woman. She felt Ms. Conner moving around her bedroom and Kyrie wondered how long it would be before the older lady went to sleep. She did not want anyone to catch her and ask questions.

As time passed, Kyrie periodically concentrated on the older lady's presence and she eventually felt the woman lay down. However, the older woman remained awake and Kyrie felt herself fighting to keep her eyes open. Only the drive to honor her parents' commandments kept her awake long enough so she could call the number on the paper.

After Ms. Conner's mental state finally shifted into a deep sleep, Kyrie slid out from under the blanket. She carefully crept across the worn floor, flinching at each squeak that came, but the older lady did not stir.

Kyrie swallowed. She had observed Ms. Conner using the phone earlier, and that matched her parents' description of the function, but she had never actually used one. She lifted the part Ms. Conner had spoken into and flipped it over. A strange sound emitted from the device and white buttons with numbers glowed on their own.

Kyrie fished the slip of paper from her bra and unfolded it. She visualized the Fibonacci sequence, left off the leading zero, and mentally combined the first eight terms into a long series of numbers. She added that number to the value on the paper, making eleven digits. Mimicking Ms. Conner's actions earlier in the day, she pressed the buttons that matched the new number. With each button she pressed, she noted the change in the noise the phone emitted. When she had finished, as if by magic, the device started making a new sound. *Magic would be easier to understand,* she thought as she placed the device against her face.

Suddenly the ringing sound stopped and silence filled the device. She wondered if she had done something wrong and started pulling the phone away as a male voice spoke into her ear.

"My God, what's wrong?" Worry and concern mixed together with an initial slurring of the man's words. "Rachel, has something happened?"

"Hello. Are you Lars? My name is Kyrie. My mother said I had to call this number the first moment I could."

"Kyrie." The sounds of movement and shuffling came through the phone. "Are you safe? Is your mother safe?"

Kyrie felt tears welling up. "I'm in Ms. Conner's home. My mother died in the field today. I'm safe for now, but the authorities are involved, and my parents always said to avoid them."

"Kyrie, where are you exactly? Do you have an address?"

"Address? I don't know."

The voice on the phone grew firmer. "Are you calling from this Ms. Conner's home?"

"Yes. I'm using her phone. She is…" Kyrie reached out with her mind and confirmed the older woman still slept. "Sleeping in the other room."

"Okay, I will do a reverse phone number lookup and find out where you are. Do you think you are in danger? Do you know how your mother died?"

"No. The sheriff said it might be a heart-attack, like my father. My father died almost a year ago. I need to get my supplies. Mother told me you would tell me where to go and what to do."

"I know." Something shuffled. "Kyrie, I will attempt to find a way to get you someplace safe, but since the police are already involved, if you run now, they would pursue you. Based on what I know, your parents have shielded you from the outside world for far too long. You would get caught because you don't know how things work and that would just put you back in custody, but with suspicion on you." The man on the phone sighed.

Kyrie felt her hands shake and her body tense. "What is going on?"

"Kyrie, I don't know the specifics of it. I know your parents went into hiding to avoid some trouble, but they never told me what that trouble was. Regardless, it's been sixteen years, and if they have both died of natural causes, it may be that whatever plagued them will be satisfied." She heard some papers move. "Until we know more, I want you to keep a low profile. Don't do anything that will draw any more attention to yourself."

"Like what?" she demanded. "I know I did wrong, but mother said if father had gotten to a hospital sooner, he might have lived. I wanted my mother to live."

"Kyrie, I'm not blaming you. Looking for help is not wrong. However, the police are going to ask questions and want to understand your past."

"Well, I hardly know what is going on, so good luck to them to get anything from me. Not even compulsion can make me tell them what I don't know."

He remained silent for a moment. "You sound just like your mother. Even have her sarcastic tone. I don't know much either. I spent the better part of my college years getting into trouble with your parents. While I never got to know you, I promised them I would look out for you as best I can. I won't leave you to fall into the system for long, but I'll have to file some legal documents in the morning to try and get custody of you. It may take time, but just pretend you don't know anything. Try to avoid lies if you can because they can come back to bite you later. However, please also don't mention anything about people being after your parents. That will likely get the police curious about what happened and that will cause more delays."

"They think my…" Kyrie turned to the sound of a door opening. Her mind reached out and felt Ms. Conner coming down the narrow hall.

"What are you doing?" The older woman demanded.

"Kyrie?" Lars' voice questioned through the phone.

Kyrie turned to the woman; the phone lowered from her face. "I wasn't sure how this thing worked and wanted to try it."

Ms. Conner huffed and came charging forward. "You can't just go calling people at random. In the middle of the night no less." The woman took the phone from Kyrie's hand. "Hello? Hello? Who is this?"

Kyrie strained to hear Lars' reply. "I might ask you the same. Your daughter woke me up."

"She's not my daughter," Ms. Conner said, more than a trace of irritation in her voice. "But I'm sorry she bothered you."

"It's quite all right," Came Lars' mellow response.

Ms. Conner pressed down on a button on the handset and the lights on the keypad went dark. "You can't be doing that. People don't like to be woken up and I'm likely to get a bill for that."

"I'm sorry," Kyrie said, keeping her head bowed. "I miss my mother," she added aloud. *You shouldn't have let yourself get distracted. You should have paid attention to Ms. Conner.*

The heavy sigh that came out of Ms. Conner's mouth carried no absolution. "Go back to sleep." Ms. Conner went to hang the phone on the wall hook, but then paused. She instead pressed on the cord and separated it from the handset. "Just so you don't get any other ideas."

Kyrie nodded her head and walked with slumped shoulders back to the sofa. She pulled the covers up under Ms. Conner's watchful eye. Once the old woman was satisfied, Ms. Conner returned to her own room.

Exhausted, and suffering a throbbing headache, Kyrie closed her eyes and drifted off to sleep.


Kyrie woke to Ms. Conner hovering over her. The older woman moved back with a startled expression, but quickly recovered herself.

Kyrie tried to determine the time, but her head felt muddled. The only thing she did know was that it was later than she normally slept.

"I'm sorry about the phone," Kyrie said to fill the silence.

"Dearie, never mind about the phone, you are in need of a shower. Your hair is a mess."

Kyrie let the woman's judgment pass without response. She felt the grime on her and would love to get clean.

"Well, get off the couch and come on. I know you need a good cry and some breakfast, but first, you need to look decent enough. Your parents might have been a little odd, but we don't want social services thinking them terrible." Kyrie found herself pulled from the sofa. "Or me, for that matter." Kyrie let the woman usher her into the bathroom. The movement started to clear her head.

Kyrie had used Ms. Conner's bathroom the day before, but she had paid almost no attention to the room with her mind as tired as it had become. Now she allowed her natural curiosity some freedom. The small space had brightly colored surfaces that looked to be made of yellow plastic. The toilet, the sink, the floor, the tub, and even the curtain hanging from a rod over the tub looked strange compared to the wooden bathroom in the cabin.

There were many objects scattered about the flat surfaces. Dust covered many of the items, most of which she had never seen the like of before. Tubes and containers of different colors filled baskets and cups. Brushes of various sizes and shapes exploded out of another basket. The things with wires coming out of them bemused her the most. A part of her wanted to pick through all the odd items next to the sink, but she knew if she disturbed anything, the covering of dust would reveal her examination.

Ms. Conner knocked on the closed door. "I'm on a septic tank and a well here, so don't run the shower too long."

Kyrie rolled her eyes and shook her head. *What do you think the cabin uses?* Ms. Conner had already walked away, so she did not bother to reply. Instead, she turned on the faucet and splashed water on her face and drank from her hands. After getting her fill of water, she examined the bathtub and found an array of bottles hanging from the shower head. The confined space smelled like a musty field of flowers molding from too much moisture.

This shower lacked a pair of knobs to turn it on, but she took a chance and push on a central lever halfway up the wall. It twisted under her hand and water flowed out of the lower spigot. Feeling some comfort at figuring out the shower, she pulled up the familiar diverter, and after several moments, water rained down from the shower head. *See, you can do this. These new things are not so hard.*

She opened her worn senses and only felt Ms. Conner. Her mother and father had always reminded her to be aware of her surroundings and watch for potential threats, which she had failed to do last night. However, this was the first time she could remember feeling truly exposed. *Miss you, Mom.*

She placed her hand into the stream of water; it felt cooler than the water that came from the shower at the cabin. Undeterred, she stripped out of her moderately clean clothing and stepped into the tub. The chilly water gave her goosebumps, but she endured the temperature by drawing in energy to compensate. She grabbed the bar of soap and started scrubbing her body and lathering the soap into her hair.

A sudden jolt ran through her as she sensed three people approaching Ms. Conner's home. She stopped the scrubbing and quickly started rinsing off the soap. Her hands trembled at the thought of being caught so vulnerable. Water splashed everywhere as she raced to clear her eyes and hair. The new people were too far away for her to get a good sense of them, but she thought one was the sheriff.

She did not hear a knocking on the front door, but she felt Ms. Conner letting people into her home. The first-person Kyrie sensed enter the building she now felt certain was the sheriff. The next two she thought might also be men, but she found it hard to tell.

Not bothering to clear all the soap from her body, she stepped out of the shower and dripped water on the pale-yellow plastic floor. She grabbed a towel from the wall and dried her face and long blonde hair. From the other side of the door she heard Ms. Conner speak.

"She's in the shower. We can talk now before she gets out if you don't want her involved. Anyone want coffee?"

Kyrie more felt than heard the sheriff reply. "There are some things we need to know. And yes, to the coffee."

Kyrie pulled the curtain back into place and left the shower running. She crept to the door and listened while she dried herself.

"What were their last names?" the sheriff asked.

"Smith," Ms. Conner replied. "Robert and Rachel Smith."

"Nope." The sheriff replied so low that Kyrie struggled to hear it. "Stan, you want to take a try?"

She heard a new voice through the door and recognized him as their landlord. "Oliver, did you call me out here to play twenty-questions? I've always known them as the Smiths. If that is not their name, then it is news to me."

"Did you do a background check?" The sheriff's hard voice challenged.

"Oliver, it was, what, sixteen years ago? Of course, I didn't do a background check. They paid their rent every month and never caused trouble. Heck, they took better care of the cabin than I would have."

"And they paid you in cash every month. Looks like you even cover their electric bills and everything else. They have no actual form of ID. No accounts in their name."

"What are you after? I report all my income, even what comes in cash. And so what if I still have the electricity in my name. Plenty of apartments in the cities cover utilities. They never used much. Early on they said they had credit problems and no checking account. Cash worked for me and they paid the rent on time, every month."

Kyrie heard something dragged across the floor, perhaps a chair. Then the sheriff spoke again. "I ain't looking into what you do Stan. The farms that potentially hired him under the table…those people I will look into. But right now, I'm just trying to figure out how these three people got through the last sixteen years without really showing up on anyone's radar. Social services seem to have lost track of the girl and no one has followed up on her schooling or anything. These two own nothing that needs to be licensed or registered, yet no one thinks it's strange."

"Sheriff Sawyer," said another male voice. "It is possible they were abusing the girl and trying to keep a low profile."

"Ya think?" A moment passed before the sheriff spoke again. "I'm as much to blame as anyone. I should have looked into things when the father died on that farm last summer. But, since the medical examiner declared it a heart attack, and because it happened in another jurisdiction, I didn't think to. And now we can't because the wife had him cremated a day after they returned his body. I now plan to ask how the death certificate managed to get filed without a better confirmation of identity, but that is neither here nor there."

"Oliver," Ms. Conner said, "would you please tell us their real names if they are not Smith."

Kyrie struggled to hear as the sheriff's voice dropped lower. "I've been up most of the night, but her name was Rachel Leighton before she married a Robert Landvik…assuming that was the man that died last year."

Kyrie felt her stomach tighten. *My name is not Kyrie Smith?* She grabbed her clothing and then returned to the door. She wanted to draw energy into herself and hold it in case she needed it. *Don't be stupid, you draw energy fast enough,* she reminded herself. *Just don't forget to regulate yourself, like you did yesterday.*

"So, how'd you find out their real names?" Ms. Conner asked.

"Ran the dead woman's prints. Seems she was a professor at MIT until almost seventeen years ago. She took time off, then didn't go back. The girl was born and several months later the whole family goes missing. They turned everything over to a lawyer. He sold all their things and put the money into some form of trust." Kyrie could feel the sheriff shifting in the seat at the small table. "The girl is worth a few mil."

"What?" Ms. Conner's voice filled the home.

The sheriff's voice deepened. "That shyster lawyer appeared to be a friend of theirs. He's been filing their taxes under a power of attorney. Not sure how they got so rich, haven't had the time to dig into that, but whenever I see a rich person, living in a shithole of a cabin, out in the middle of nowhere, under a false name, I have to wonder."

"You going to arrest the girl?" Ms. Conner asked.

Kyrie finished sliding her shirt over her head and then glanced around the room again for an exit. Her mother would be furious if the police arrested her, but she could not fit through the small window in the wall. Shifting focus, she wondered if there might be something she could use for a weapon in the drawers.

"No," the sheriff said. "I've not found anything they've done illegal yet…aside from working under the table and the death certificate being filed under a false name. But that could hardly be the girl's fault. However, I do want to question her."

"She's been in the shower long enough," Ms. Conner said. "Going to flood my septic tank."

Kyrie found no real weapons. *Bluff yourself out of this.* She moved back to the shower and reached in to turn the lever. It moved, but the water did not shut off, only grew warmer. *Figures.* She pushed it the other direction and the water stopped flowing.

"Kyrie," Ms. Conner yelled from the other side of the door. "Hurry up and get finished in there. The sheriff has some more questions."

"Yes, ma'am," Kyrie replied. *Lars said not to run. He said not to run. He'll come for us, perhaps this morning.* She glanced around the room again, doubting Lars' advice, but the door provided the only exit into the rest of the house. *And if you run, he said they would find you anyway.* She hesitated. *Your parents said to trust him.*

She turned back to the mirror. Her blonde hair remained tangled and disheveled. It poked out at odd angles where the towel had roughed it up. She picked up a brush and worked at the ends to buy herself time so that those on the other side of the door would not realize she had been out of the shower and listening to them.

After several painful knots, she gave up, used her hands to flatten the mess, and then left the bathroom. The sheriff, and another man, sat at the table while Ms. Conner and Stan Potter, her parents' landlord, stood off to one side. The landlord she had seen a few times from a distance and the balding man did not trigger any concern in her.

The man sitting next to the sheriff wore what she knew to be a suit based upon pictures she had seen in one of her early algebra books. Her four-year-old self had been amazed by the different clothing styles. Her mother had explained professionals and those looking to impress others wore suits. This was the first time she had ever seen one in real life.

She glanced around the room trying to place the source of a strange smell. She did not see anything cooking, nor did she see any new plants the people might have brought with them.

"Kyrie, what is your name?" the sheriff asked, a distinct challenge buried in his voice.

"My name is Kyrie," she replied, uncertain of why he would ask her to repeat her name. The scowl on his face told her that answer did not meet with his expectation.

"Last name," he replied curtly. "Don't lie to me."

Kyrie swallowed. The tone held a force of expected commandment and she felt the weight of his desire on her mind as a dull ache that would only get worse if she disobeyed the compulsion, but she had to at least try. She did not want to reveal she had been listening at the door. "I didn't know that is what you meant. The name I know is Kyrie Smith." She winced as the pain grew sharper.

The sheriff's eyes narrowed. "Wrong." He stood, the rolled-up plastic bag that had been in his lap, clasped in his hand. "What is your real name?"

Kyrie felt her knees weaken under the demand, but she remained standing despite the compulsion he used on her. A slight draw of energy countered some of the effects, but she knew she would not be able to hold out much longer before the pain would drop her to her knees. "Kyrie Smith is the only name I know." She put a hand to her head. "Please stop."

"Oliver," the second man said, rising to his feet and walking over to stand next to the sheriff. "I believe her. She just lost her mother yesterday. It is likely she never knew the truth." The man took the bag from the sheriff and carried it over to Kyrie. "Here. These valuables were on your mother."

The pain diminished immediately, and Kyrie's head started to clear. With the man close, the first thing she noticed was the strange smell emanated from him. It carried a pleasant muskiness. "Thank you, sir." She accepted the offered bag, but she did not open it.

"My name is Jim." He stepped back and held out an arm toward a chair at the table. "Please, sit. What we have to say may startle you a bit."

Kyrie walked past Jim and the sheriff to sit down. She felt a sense of distrust from the sheriff and an odd sensation from Ms. Conner. *You can't run, they will chase you,* she reminded herself as she looked up at the four people standing around her. She held her thumbs in her closed fists to keep from reacting to the closeness of the men.

"Kyrie," Jim said, moving a chair so he could sit facing her. "It turns out that your last name is actually Landvik and not Smith. Have you ever heard your parents use that name?"

"No, Sir," she replied, struggling to remember if that was true while keeping her expression natural.

"Well, that is your name. It appears your father was born Robert Landvik and not Robert Smith. Do you know why your parents decided to use the name Smith?"

Kyrie looked at Jim. She could tell the sheriff was older than this man, as was Ms. Conner, but she could not decide Jim's age. She wanted to trust him, but she could feel his desire to extract information from her. *Please don't use compulsion,* she pleaded silently. "I don't know. I've lived my whole life here. I never heard a different name."

Jim nodded his head. "I'm sorry to tell you this. However, your parents lied to you for some reason. You were born Kyrie Landvik in the state of Massachusetts sixteen—almost seventeen—years ago. We know your parents moved into the cabin just before your first birthday. Your father had a good job dealing with computers and your mother, a Rachel Leighton before she married your father, worked as a professor of physics at MIT. Something caused them to give up their lives, move out to nowhere, and sequester—which means lock away—you from everyone else, including your grandparents, an aunt, and an uncle."

"I don't understand," Kyrie said aloud. Her mind raced to put into context her parents' claim that they had no family. She knew her parents moved to the mountains to avoid people and a threat, but her parents would never tell her the full story and had compelled her not to ask. She never thought to question their honesty.

"Unfortunately, all of your grandparents, and your uncle, have passed away since your disappearance." Jim shifted in his seat at her expression. "It is another way to say died. However," he brightened, "we have located your Aunt Kimberly, who is still alive."

"Aunt Kimberly?" Kyrie questioned, as if the sounds had no meaning.

"She is your mother's younger sister," the sheriff said from behind her.

"Now," Jim said, drawing Kyrie's attention back to him. "Because of your unique circumstances, I have to ask a difficult question." He paused and waited until Kyrie nodded her head. "Did your parents abuse you? Did they touch you in places they should not have?"

Kyrie narrowed her eyes as the man looked at her chest and crotch. "No. I don't understand. Why you would ask me that?"

"Did they do sexual things to you?" The sheriff moved a step closer.

Kyrie shook her head and looked over her shoulder at the sheriff. "No. Why would they? I don't understand why you would think that."

The sheriff's voice hardened. "You're a girl, locked away in a mountain valley with a couple of parents that gave up their whole lives, and all their money, and live in poverty under a false identity. Home schooled you to avoid other students. Abuse is the first thing we assume."

"Oliver." The scowl on Jim's face spoke volumes. "Nothing young Kyrie has done has been her fault or is wrong." He turned his attention back to her. "The good news is that we contacted your aunt. She had looked for your mother for several years, but never discovered where she had gone with you. Kimberly's going to fly out here from Kansas City. She should be here tomorrow."

Kyrie felt her hands shake. The man sitting before her did not seem to be lying, but how could her parents have left out so many details. *How could they have concealed it?*

"You've overwhelmed her, Jim," the sheriff said from behind her. "The girl's not able to process this."

Kyrie wanted to frown, she could tell he thought her stupid, and that did not settle well with her. However, she did not want them to suspect her of something, and her parents always taught her that acting as expected made other people feel in control. "What happens now?" she whispered after a long enough pause.

The man sitting in front of her leaned forward. "Well, normally, we'd take you into protective custody, but we are a long way from any major city with those kinds of resources. We spoke with Ms. Conner earlier on the phone and you can stay here until your aunt arrives tomorrow. We understand your aunt plans to file paperwork to establish her guardianship of you. If her lawyer hasn't already. The courts will have the final say, but you look healthy and the state would rather not have to spend a lot of resources to house you if you have a relative who wants to care for you."

Kyrie nodded. *Which way is the dice rolling? Is it a failed save?* She looked over at Ms. Conner who continued to keep her distance. "Can I get my things from the cabin?"

The sheriff cleared his throat. "The Staters still have a couple guys looking through your parents' things. Once we are certain your parents were not breaking any other laws, you'll be able to get your things."

Kyrie nodded yet again, unwilling to speak. She doubted anyone would find the money her father had stashed high up the slope. The last five years it had been her job to retrieve some of the bills when they had a need. She knew she would need it if she tried to run, but she dared not risk retrieving the money before that time.

"Do you need to speak with someone about how you are feeling?" Jim asked, placing a hand on her leg and drawing her attention back to him. "There are people that can help you work through the pain of your loss. Perhaps a priest."

Kyrie's eyes narrowed for a moment in confusion, her mother and father had always told her game magic did not work in the world and that her powers were different. *You must not have understood the offer,* she thought, but her curiosity and hope overrode her desire for caution. "Do you mean if I had enough money, I could ask a priest to resurrect her?"

The sheriff snorted. "Her parents have filled her head with all that Dungeons & Dragons nonsense. There's a shelf full of those books. Right next to something about Darwin. The Staters found stacks of pages with that crap."

Kyrie held her tongue as she felt tears leak from her eyes. *You'll never get to play with your mother again. Her characters will die with her, as Father's did with him.*

"Oliver, leave it be," Jim said. "Just because you don't like those kind of games, doesn't mean they are—"

"The work of a deranged mind?" The sheriff shook his head. "If you've made your decision about leaving her here, then let's get going. The Landviks have dropped a mess on me to sort out, and if I have any say in the matter, their lawyer will wind up in trouble for it."

The man before her stood up. He pulled a small piece of thick paper from a pocket in his suit. "Kyrie, if you need me, this card has my number on it. Just call and I will try to help. Otherwise, I will see you tomorrow with your aunt." He moved around the table. "Ms. Conner, it was a pleasure to meet you as well."

"Do you think there is a reward for helping take care of her?" Ms. Conner asked. "I mean, if she's got money, I wouldn't mind a little compensation for everything I have done over the years."

"Megan," the sheriff said, "that's not for us to say, you'll need to talk to the aunt."

# Chapter 3

Michael Rodgers felt his second phone vibrate. He pulled it from his suit pocket and glanced at the screen. A contact he did not expect had texted a code that indicated a request for an urgent call back. He looked up at the four men and the woman in the small conference room and made careful note of each. All five of them had been part of the organization for more than ten years. Each of them had proven their loyalty. He decided to risk making the call.

"Just a moment," Michael said as he dialed the phone. His calloused fingers had lost much of the roughness, but not the scars. Just as he had allowed his sandy-blond hair to grow out from the buzz cut of his twenties, his exterior polish was simply a covering for what existed within. He spoke into the phone with a hard coldness. "You have something to report?"

"The computer flagged a name," came the female voice. "A sheriff out of Gould Colorado is looking into a Rachel and Robert Landvik. They both appear to be deceased based on the inquiries, but the reports are not consistent. Someone is trying to confirm their identities."

Michael felt his throat constrict and his voice weakened. "Are you certain? Any mention of a girl?" He did some quick mental math. "She'd be almost seventeen. Is the girl dead as well?"

"No mention of a girl. The identities appear to be unconfirmed, though my information is several hours old," came the response. "It does appear the sheriff attempted to contact a relative, so there may be a survivor, or perhaps a household of goods."

"Kimberly Leighton would be the only one left," Michael said as he regained control of his voice. "This is taking place where?"

"Northeast of Gould Colorado, but it appears the woman's body was taken to Walden. That is a small town. Six or seven hundred people. The report says the family was going by the name Smith."

*How original.* "Inform me if any additional details emerge. I will send someone to confirm the identity in person." He hung up the phone and set it on the table. The five people in the room showed obvious interest. *If only I could read minds,* he thought looking at them. He shook the idea away; that kind of power would make him a slave. *Or a hunted man.*

"Henry, get me the name of someone who can get to Walden Colorado tonight or tomorrow. They need to confirm some details of a death and report back."

"Yes, Boss," Henry said quickly. "Do you want me to do it now? I haven't given my report on the shipments."

Michael dismissed him with a wave of his hand. "Do it now. This is more important than the shipments." He took a deep breath and tried to remember the date the room was last searched for listening devices. No one could enter the lower levels of the facility without security clearance and the room's subterranean existence eliminated windows for someone to use a laser against to extract audio. Those in the room all had years of practice to never discuss illegal activities in plain words, but this effort needed even more security than normal.

Michael watched as Henry rose and left the conference room. He caught the eye of the guard stationed just outside the door. The large man glared with loathing that spoke of complete hatred until the man schooled his expression.

Michael ignored his guard. He would punish him later with a mental lashing when there would be no witnesses. Not even the people in this room knew that truth. *Of all the times to surface, it would have to be now.*


Kyrie found herself on the sofa after the sheriff and the two men left. Her head still hurt from the compulsion she resisted, and she did not want to move. The self-imposed confinement left her with little to do except run through the things they said about her parents. She tried to balance what she knew as truth with the intent her parents had. *They worked to protect us. Taught you to defend yourself. The idea they gave up everything, including family, feels possible.* Her eyes moistened. *Why couldn't you explain it? Why the secrets?*

"Dearie, let me take that bag," Ms. Conner said, offering her a bowl of chips in exchange for the plastic bag the man in the suit handed her. "They are your mother's personal belongings. I'll put them on the table."

Kyrie did not want another adult to use compulsion on her so soon, so she willingly handed over the bag and took the food.

"Eat and then rest. You have a lot to take in. It sounds like things might work out well for you in the long run. You might have a lot of money and no need to grow crops to eat."

Kyrie nodded her head. She sensed the old woman's greed.

"Let me microwave something hot for you as well." Ms. Conner pulled open a door on a small box, slid in a plate with something on it, and pressed a button to cause it to come to life. Her tone and attitude to Kyrie now as sugary sweet as the soda.

Kyrie stood up and moved closer, the device capturing her attention and took her mind from the pain of her loss. "So that is a microwave. My mother told me how people used the EM spectrum for lots of things. The osculating magnetic field will cause polar molecules like water to rotate, which converts the energy wave into kinetic energy and makes heat." Kyrie felt Ms. Conner blanch and lean away from her. Kyrie forced herself to not bite her lip. "Sorry, I'd just not seen one before, but my mother told me about them."

"I don't know anything about your EM whatever, but it heats food."

Kyrie kept her face contrite and looked down at the floor. Eventually the microwave dinged and went dark. Ms. Conner took out the plate of pasta and handed it to Kyrie. She thanked the older woman for the food and then moved to the table to eat.

Little else was said for the remainder of the day. Kyrie covertly observed the older woman's activities and even learned about television and movies, two things her parents did not have in the cabin. She wanted to behave as Ms. Conner expected, only she did not know what that was.

By the late afternoon, Kyrie found herself growing restless. She ached to go for a run and a chance to be active, but she resisted the urge to ask, and managed to endure the idle time by taking a nap. She awoke for dinner and then allowed herself to snooze again until Ms. Conner went to sleep for the night.

*Apparently, sleeping all day is expected,* Kyrie thought as she slipped from the sofa. She ached inside, missing her mother, but the practical part of her mind understood she had to move forward.

Kyrie glanced to the wall and noted the phone was still missing. *She doesn't trust you.* Kyrie's desire to challenge Lars about the truth would have to wait. *And having more facts will let us steer the conversation.*

She quietly made her way across the room to the front door. Her earlier covert examination of the lock revealed it was similar to the ones in the cabin. Careful to avoid any loud noises, she unlocked the door while keeping her senses on Ms. Conner. The old woman did not wake and so Kyrie pushed the door open and stepped outside into the cold night. She closed the door behind her, but she did not move away. Instead, she remained standing at the top of the steps as the wind whipped her hair around her face; her focus remained on Ms. Conner.

Once she was certain the woman remained asleep, Kyrie descended the steps and moved away from the trailer. She looked up into the clear sky and thanked the moon for being three quarters full. Even with her excellent night vision, the extra light would help her navigate the gravel road.

Without waiting to get any colder, Kyrie broke into a jog and started to run up the mountain toward the cabin. The air burned her lungs, but the more she moved, the warmer she became, and she soon settled into an easy pace. The effort relieved the excess energy of sitting idle, but the normal pleasure a run might bring remained elusive in the wake of her mother's death. *Perhaps something in the cabin will lead us to some answers.*

At the end of the road, she slowed to a walk as she crossed the broken ground to reach the cabin door. The building remained dark, and for the first time in her life, foreboding. *You can do this,* she reminded herself as she turned the knob and opened the door. Despite their avoidance of people, her parents never locked anything.

She stepped into the cabin, shut the door, and turned on the lights. What normally gave comfort by banishing away the darkness weighed heavily on her. The surrounding trees and protected valley hid the cabin, but if someone watched from within the valley, the shutters and curtains would not conceal the sudden illumination.

She stretched her mind again and confirmed no people were in the immediate area. "We are truly alone now." She closed her eyes a moment and fought back the tears. After a deep breath she opened them again and examined the mess that flowed through the cabin. Whatever the sheriff's 'Staters' were, they moved everything and put almost nothing back. Piles and piles of papers covered the table. Stacks of books covered the floor, the sofa, and lay flat on the nearly empty bookshelves. Every cabinet door in the kitchen hung open with the large items spilling out.

She entered her bedroom and found all her clothing tossed on the bed and her chest of drawers pulled away from the wall. The devastation in her parents' room was worse. The mattress leaned against a wall, removed from the bed in someone's search for whatever might have been under it.

Kyrie's hands clenched. After a moment she forced herself to relax. She lacked any position in which she could express her anger, so holding on to it would do nothing for her. She walked around a stack of books and passed her parents' clothing that now sat in a pile at the foot of the bed frame. Memories of many evenings spent in this room with her parents filled her mind. She longed for the sound of their voices reading books to her or arguing over losing hands at card games played on the bed.

Kyrie looked at the empty bookshelves in the bedroom and then returned to the main room. Most of the books and papers that had been in her parents' room sat on the table. She noticed a few handwritten notes on top of the piles that reflected neither her mother's, nor her father's, hand. The closest one had the label 'D&D.' She removed the note and lifted the top three inches off the two-foot high pile.

As she flipped through the loose paper, she grinned at the maps her mother and father had drawn. She remembered one from when one of her characters died spectacularly. The death had been her own fault, she allowed herself to be cocky and had assumed she could handle any of the monsters or traps that might be lurking. Her father always rewarded cocky with a harder challenge. "And I rolled a nat-one, while he rolled two nat-twenties. The dice did not like you that night." *And we would never cheat a roll.*

She set the maps aside and pulled out some of the sheets of NPCs, or non-player characters, her parents used frequently. Most of them she tossed aside, but she stopped on a Kim Lym. Her parents often giggled when they used her. Kim Lym would always get everything wrong and would annoy Kyrie. She had preferred it when they did not run that character. *Is there truth in that NPC?*

Kyrie put the pages back onto the stack and looked at a pile of notebooks and loose pages unevenly stacked in the middle of the table. *Perhaps slid there because they seemed uninteresting.* The note on the top of that pile held the words 'science things.' Kyrie knew they were her mother's personal journals. She had paged through them many times to look at drawings and some of the math, but most of the contents were more advanced than she could understand. Aside from taking care of her education, playing Dungeons & Dragons, and doing work in the gardens, those journals had consumed her mother's time.

Kyrie reached over and lifted the stack of notebooks. She moved to the floor to sit cross-legged as she set them down in front of her. She flipped through the books, looking for something that her mother might have hidden in the detailed theories.

Kyrie wiped her eyes as she read her mother's neat handwriting. There were numerous attempts to solve mathematical problems, each failing in some manner. Her mother always made notes after each attempt, trying to explain rationally where the math went wrong and how her logic failed to prove her theory.

As the night drew into early morning, Kyrie moved into the section of journals her mother had started to write after Kyrie was born. These were all in a different language. The first couple of them were full of crossed out words and roughly scribbled handwriting; the marks of a hesitant hand not yet familiar with the language.

Kyrie struggled to puzzle out the meaning of different sections in these books. She almost grabbed a piece of paper and a pencil to work out the translations. However, her mother had forbidden her to ever share the language with anyone else, and Kyrie knew writing down even a small translation provided the easiest way for someone else to learn how to read it.

Kyrie moved into later journals where the writing become more natural, but most of what her mother described were all mathematical theories. "Mother, what are you trying to say here?"

Kyrie paused in her reading and narrowed her eyes as she focused on a memory. "This was an adventure you ran last year." She turned the page. "Alternate universes with wormholes and quantum transference?" Kyrie shook her head. The things her mother wrote violated Newtonian physics and general relativity. *Why game a theory that has no place in reality?* "Neither you, nor father, would forget about the conservation of matter and energy." Quantum mechanics still remained mostly a mystery to Kyrie, but she had enough background to know that while many quantum mechanical theories violated the laws of the macro world, and seemed like magic, they were not magic.

Kyrie glanced down at a notation of the last line of the entry and translated the marks into an alphanumeric code. Recognizing the notation, she hopped to her feet and went to the stack of Dungeons & Dragons adventures. Everything was out of order, but after flipping through the bundles of pages bound by binder clips, she found the English code at the top of the adventure she had been thinking about.

She flipped through the pages. While she had experienced the adventure, neither Kyrie, nor her father, ever looked at the notes her mother made because they might reveal secrets that could come up in a later adventure.

"What are you doing, Mom? This role plays that journal theory without the math." The adventure had sent her and her father through a gateway into an alternate reality, but once they got there, they lost most of their magical abilities and her mage character barely survived.

The sound of wind buffeting the cabin drew her attention. She reached out instinctively to see if anyone was around and relaxed when she felt no one nearby. However, the clock on the wall indicated it was nearly sunrise. She needed to get back down to Ms. Conner's house before the older lady woke and found her missing.

Kyrie put back everything as she found it; a decision fixing itself in her mind. *You can't leave these things and you can't carry them if you run.* She chuckled. "Plus, you want to see if this Aunt Kimberly is anything like Kim Lym the Incompetent."

# Chapter 4

Kyrie ran to Ms. Conner's home as fast as she dared. The moon had set below the mountains and it was now darker than when she had gone to the cabin. The cold air left her shivering, but she did not take any clothing from the cabin for fear the older woman would notice. As it was, the fear that Ms. Conner had already found her gone raced through her mind. However, when she reached the mobile home, she sensed no activity, only Ms. Conner sleeping in her room. Exhausted and cold, Kyrie snuck back inside, curled up under the blankets, and immediately fell asleep.

She awoke late in the morning. Ms. Conner had not bothered to wake her, though the woman had obviously been about the room. *The phone is back on the wall.* Kyrie wondered how she managed to sleep through the other woman's activities.

She dragged herself from the sofa and took a much warmer shower. Ms. Conner had a small breakfast ready for her; Kyrie devoured the food and wished for more, but did not ask, instead she dropped her chin and looked up at Ms. Conner. "Do you think it would be all right if I go to the cabin and get some things?"

Ms. Conner hesitated for a moment. "I don't know. I'd have to call the sheriff and ask him."

"I was just thinking to get a few things. That way when my aunt arrives, I will be ready to go."

"I spoke to Sheriff Sawyer this morning. Your Aunt Kimberly should be here in just another hour. So, you should just sit and watch TV. Then we can see about getting your things."

"Yes, ma'am," Kyrie replied. The thought of just sitting and waiting irritated her. *Come on, an hour is not that bad,* she reminded herself. *The trouble is you never just sit.*

She looked around the room for something to do other than sitting in front of the 'box of noises' as she labeled the television. On the table sat a pad of paper and a pencil. Overcome with the urge to be active, at least mentally, she slid the paper and pencil in front of her and started to doodle. She let her mind wander as the pencil moved and before long a familiar image took shape: an image of humanoid hunters hiding in dense tropical vegetation with organic-looking city spires between them and the mountains in the far distance.

The faces of the people had sharp angular lines, flatter than human heads, and ears reminiscent of cats. However, their nimble and muscular bodies, covered in fine, yet durable, clothing, remained distinctly humanoid. She focused on the eyes, the orbs were larger than a human's, but still in a logical proportion to their heads.

"What are you drawing?" Ms. Conner asked, standing over Kyrie's shoulder.

"My father always called them Kattians," she responded without looking up. "They are a race I created for our games."

"They look…strange."

Kyrie allowed herself to frown since Ms. Conner would not see it. Her parents had treated the race like elves when they played, but Kyrie always envisioned them with more complexity. To Ms. Conner she said, "They evolved differently than humans, so they look different and have different traits, but the bipedal form has a lot of evolutionary advantages."

Ms. Conner huffed and walked away. Kyrie was not sure what she said that irritated the woman. However, her parents had included many NPCs in their games and some of those non-player characters took significant offense to science and reason. Ms. Conner's reaction to her explanation of how the microwave worked made Kyrie wonder if her parents had not exaggerated those NPCs as much as she thought they had.

She finished the last parts of the sketch just as she heard a car—*or cars*—coming up the gravel road. Instinct drove her senses outward and she felt two vehicles pull into Ms. Conner's front yard.

Ms. Conner went to the door and opened it so she could watch those approaching. Kyrie felt her own interest piqued as her senses continued to scan what her eyes could not see. She felt a woman shutting a vehicle's door, followed by the sheriff and Jim Mitchel exiting another vehicle.

Ms. Conner pushed open her screen door and stepped outside. "Hello Oliver. Mr. Mitchel. This must be Kimberly Leighton."

Kyrie heard the sheriff's strong voice, "Miss Leighton, this is Megan Conner, whom I've told you about."

"It is a pleasure to meet you," the woman replied.

Kyrie struggled to hear the unfamiliar voice from where she sat. However, she could tell the vowels were sharp and precise, just as her mother had used when teaching her Latin words.

"Where is my niece?" The woman asked.

"She is inside." Ms. Conner turned her head and leaned back into the house. "Kyrie, come on out here."

Kyrie rose from the chair and hurried to the door. When the older woman moved to the side, Kyrie exited onto the top of the metal steps. She could now see a short lady bundled in a heavy coat. The woman looked up at her with brown eyes and a sharp nose. A wool cap covered the top of her head with her long brown hair blowing loose across her coat. The woman stood in front of a large blue car; a thin pair of pants with pleats concealed her legs.

Her lips compressed into a smile. "My, you are big. The last I saw you, you were but a bundle wrapped in your mother's arms."

"It is a pleasure to meet you," Kyrie said ignoring the differences she felt from the woman's emotional energy and the artificial tone of her voice.

"Likewise," the woman said and then took several uneven steps forward. "Let's get out of this infernal wind and inside."

Kyrie, cool, but not cold, stepped to the side as she watched the woman cross the uneven ground in what she recognized her mother would call high-heeled shoes. The woman reached the metal stairs and Ms. Conner backed into her home, inviting everyone to follow her.

"I am your Aunt Kimberly," the shorter woman said as she reached the small platform at the top of the steps. "Your mother was my older sister."

Kyrie registered a floral scent coming from the woman as she looked for any resemblance to her mother, but like herself, her mother had blonde hair and blue eyes, not brown ones. Her mother was also taller, though admittedly, Kyrie had four inches of advantage over her mother and even more over this woman and her shoes. "I am Kyrie."

"I'm aware of that." Her aunt shooed her inside, and after Kyrie entered, the woman followed quickly behind her. "This is terrible weather. There is snow in Denver and the roads are just miserable." Her aunt narrowed her eyes. "Aren't you cold?"

Kyrie noticed her aunt's vowels had lost a little of their crispness as her speech had grown faster. "The weather here has actually been warmer than normal. We've been planting crops."

Her aunt unzipped her puffy coat as the sheriff and Mr. Mitchel came inside and closed the door. She looked Kyrie in the eyes. "You should know better than be out without proper clothing. You'll catch a cold."

"Yes, ma'am," Kyrie replied automatically.

"Don't get smart with me," her aunt snapped. After a moment, she shook her head and slipped off her coat. "Sorry, I was up before the crack of dawn to get to the airport. But, you should know better." She handed Ms. Conner her coat and then Kyrie watched as the woman looked her up and down several times. "You are rather thin. My sister not feed you well?"

"Mother took good care of me." Kyrie bit her lip, wishing she were less defensive.

"So, your parents were calling you Kyrie Smith. That is even worse than Kyrie Landvik, but then again, I never agreed with naming you after some stupid 80s song. You look like a Jennifer or an Abby. What is a Kyrie anyway?"

Kyrie held her tongue.

"An 80s song?" the sheriff asked as he moved around the two of them.

"Yes, some group…" Her aunt shook her head. "I can't remember their name. Never liked the song. But at least they didn't name her Flower or Moonbeam, I guess."

"Mr. Mister is the name of the group," Kyrie said. "I happen to like the song and my name." *And the group.* Her parents had a number of CDs they listened to again and again, and Mr. Mister's second album was one of them.

Mr. Mitchel smiled at her and moved around the sheriff. "That is good. One's personal sense of identity is important."

"Oh, yes, there is nothing wrong with her name," her aunt said quickly. "I had suggested Jennifer when she was born, but my sister was swooning and threw herself into Robert Landvik's charms and let herself be led astray." Her aunt moved to a chair, examined the seat for several moments, and with a slight frown, finally sat down at the table. "I never liked the man."

"What can you tell me about Robert Landvik?" the sheriff asked.

Kyrie opened her senses again and allowed herself to feel her aunt's response.

"The man was a bit odd. Always playing games and hanging out with strange people. My sister got caught up in all that and let herself be dragged to renaissance festivals and the like." She looked over at Kyrie. "They ended up waiting quite a while before they had her. My sister was in her mid-thirties." She turned to look at Sheriff Sawyer. "I was in my twenties when I had my son. I was not going to wait until I got too old. There are a lot of years between me and Rachel." Her aunt turned back to Kyrie. "You nearly killed Rachel when you were born, and it took months before you would even move." Kimberly turned her focus back to the others. "Everyone thought she was…" Her aunt shrugged. "Well, she hardly made a sound until right before they disappeared. Someone broke into their house. Rachel thought someone was after Kyrie, but they were living in a big city and break-ins happen. I told her to get a guard dog, but my sister said they couldn't risk something happening. She had the gall to tell me not to try and find her and that she was going away." Her aunt shrugged again and shook her head. "I blame that Robert. Him and his stupid associations must have led to my sister running off."

"Renaissance festivals you say?" The sheriff asked. "Was he into swords and knives?"

"Oh yes. Robert got my sister into them as well. I understand when they were in college, the two of them went all out and bought some Viking clothing and even booked a cruise—if you can call it that—on a Viking long ship. Slept out in the open on the deck of a ship dressed in raggedy clothing."

"Kyrie," Mr. Mitchel said, interrupting her aunt. "Have you heard any stories of your parents going on a long ship?"

Kyrie nodded her head. "My father was Norwegian. My mother was from England, but she had Norman heritage as well as Saxon."

"Like that means much," her aunt snapped. "It was our great-grandparents that emigrated to the States. It's not like we had any real ties to England and your father was just pretending at being some warrior. He was a computer programmer before he convinced my sister to give everything up and move out here. It broke my mother's heart when she left."

Kyrie bit her tongue and remained quiet. The woman had some facial similarities to her mother. *But if they kept you from her, was there a reason?* She would decide later what to do about the woman.

Kyrie turned her attention to Sheriff Sawyer. "May I go to the cabin and get my things?"

The sheriff pursed his lips and then nodded he head. "The state police have looked through what they wanted, and they found nothing they plan to pursue in the contents of the cabin. That does not mean I won't be talking to the district attorney about the false identification filed with the death certificate, and looking into your parent's taxes, but that should not affect you."

"I would like to get my things then," Kyrie said, certain the sheriff would prefer to find a way to punish her parents if possible.

The sheriff looked toward her aunt, "Assuming you permit it, I will return the weapons as well."

Kyrie saw her aunt hesitate and remembered her parents' portrayal of Kim Lym. "They are valuable. My mother always said they were crafted by a master bladesmith."

"Well, I suppose I can take them back with me. We'll have to drive back to Olathe anyway. Until we get you an ID, we can't fly. However, I don't plan to rent a truck, so you will only be able to take a few things that will fit into the car."

Kyrie kept her face neutral. *She is just as your parents made her to be.* "Thank you, ma'am."

"Call me Aunt Kim." Her aunt turned to the sheriff. "You said my sister's body is currently in Walden?"

"Yes. It is about forty minutes or so west of here." The sheriff glanced at Kyrie and then back to her aunt. "From my records, Kyrie's father's urn is at the Walden Cemetery."

"I won't have my sister burned to ash. I want her in a coffin with a proper burial."

The sheriff smiled at her. "Of course, ma'am. You can make any arrangements you want for your sister."

"Well, I checked, and it would cost a lot to have her transported back to Kansas City. There is no other family, and she's not been in touch for years, so, if I can have her buried at that cemetery, I will."

"Kyrie," Mr. Mitchel said softly, "you have been fairly quiet. How are you feeling about burying your mother in Walden Cemetery? You may not be able to visit the grave very often."

Kyrie tried to puzzle out what the man in the suit wanted her to say, but she could not get a good sense of him. "Why would I visit the grave? She is dead. Why would I visit the place where the body is buried?"

The sheriff chuckled softly. "Pragmatic."

"Well," Mr. Mitchel said with a sharp glance at the sheriff, "it can help in the healing process to get a sense of closure."

"I never visited my father's grave," Kyrie said. "That event is behind me."

"I think the funeral should bring enough closure." Her aunt crossed her legs. "When she is old enough, she can come back out here and visit when she wants to."

"Can I go up to the cabin and get my things?"

Her aunt sighed. "I guess we can drive up and see how my sister lived."

"You won't want to take the rental," Ms. Conner said. "The road is not fit for that. I can take you up in my truck or Oliver could manage in his four-by-four."

The sheriff agreed. "And, you will want to change out of your heels if you brought something else. There is a bit of a walk from where you can park before you get to the cabin."

"Was she really living that far out in the sticks?"

"From all appearances, your sister and her husband did not want visitors," the sheriff replied.

Her aunt turned to her, "Kyrie, would you be kind enough to get my flats out of the suitcase in the trunk?"

"Flats?" Kyrie asked.

"Flat shoes. If I have to walk over more of this gravel, I'll trip and fall." Her aunt reached into her purse, pulled out a small box, and pressed a button. She craned her neck and looked out through the window. "The trunk's open. They will be in the smaller bag."

Kyrie stood up and walked to the door.

"Where's your coat?" her aunt demanded.

"In the cabin. I'm fine. It is not that cold right now." Kyrie waited a moment to see if there would be a protest, but her aunt said nothing, and Kyrie opened the door and slipped outside. The back end of the blue car stood open and she wondered just how the little box in her aunt's hand had done that. *So much you don't know.* She assumed it was not like her ability to move things with her mind. *You're different,* she recalled her father saying many times.

Kyrie moved to the back of the car and looked inside the large opening. Two red suitcases sat next each other, one consumed half the space in the trunk, the other one about a third the size of the first one. Kyrie pulled the smaller one toward her, located the zipper, and opened the suitcase. Articles of clothing were packed tightly around even smaller cases. She pulled things out until she found a pair of shoes near the bottom. Kyrie removed the shoes, repacked the other items, and zippered the suitcase closed. She paused before she closed the trunk. Curious, she stuck her head into the back of the car to see if she could find any indication of how the small box had caused it to open on its own. When nothing obvious stood out, she frowned, closed the trunk, and returned to Ms. Conner's mobile home.

After her aunt changed her footwear, they went back outside; Kyrie climbed into Ms. Conner's truck and sat between her aunt and Ms. Conner. The sheriff and Mr. Mitchel climbed into the sheriff's four-by-four. The five of them drove as close to the cabin as they could and then walked over the broken ground to the place Kyrie had called home for her whole life. Her aunt complained the whole way and Kyrie had to close her mind slightly to keep out the strong sense of disgust coming from the short woman.

When they entered the cabin, her aunt gasped. "You will not live like this in my house."

"Ma'am," the sheriff stepped forward, "I will defend the girl in that regard, this place was spotless until the state troopers made a mess."

Kyrie wanted to protest about the mess the sheriff had made on his own, but she knew it would not benefit her. Instead, she headed into her parent's bedroom and picked up her father's old suitcase from where it had been tossed on the floor. She returned to the living area, set the case down, and started loading up her mother's journals and the Dungeons & Dragons papers.

"What are you taking?" her aunt demanded. "I thought you were we going to get your clothing."

Kyrie paused a moment. She looked for a way to prevent her aunt's objection and noticed Mr. Mitchel watching the exchange closely. "These are my mother's documents. They are all I have left of her and I want to take them." She sensed the argument had little impact on her aunt. *Direct, then.* "I thought I understood Mr. Mitchel would like me to remember her, yes?" she asked, hoping that her statement did not give away her ability to sense surface thoughts.

"It is healthy for her to have some mementos that remind her the most of her parents," the social worker offered as he moved slowly about the room.

Kyrie looked up with large eyes. They seldom worked on her mother, but they could sway her father.

"Well, you will have to carry that. It will weigh a ton."

Kyrie nodded her head and resumed loading up the suite case in an orderly fashion while the others continued to examine the various items strewn about the cabin. When the suitcase was full, she entered her parents' room again and found a couple of canvas duffel bags. The duffel bags would not hold things as neatly, but she hoped to be able to fit the rest of the most important documents and books in them.

In addition to the Dungeons & Dragons manuals, she grabbed her schoolwork and the advanced physics books she had been working through. Finding there was some room left, she went into her room, grabbed her sketchbooks, her coat, some extra underwear, socks, and her bag of dice. Finally, she went to the bookshelves closest to the table and grabbed the small box with the miniatures. She managed to squeeze the box into the full bags. When done, she stood above her things waiting.

"Is that all the clothing you plan to take?" her aunt asked.

"Everything else is torn, worn thin, or too small. Mother was going to order me some new things after we finished the planting."

Her aunt frowned. "We will have to do some shopping when we get back to Olathe. You look like a street urchin." She turned to the sheriff. "There was some money you found in a shoebox?"

The sheriff nodded his head. "Yes, you will have to sign for it."

"What made you take the physics books?" Mr. Mitchel asked.

Mr. Mitchel's desire to probe her pushed the thoughts of money from her. "I still have homework to finish," she responded, uncertain what he wanted to know. "The rest mean something to me."

Her aunt pursed her lips after having found nothing she found interesting in her own searching. "You should put your coat on. It is starting to get late. If we are to get to Walden and arrange for my sister's burial, we need to get going." She sighed. "Hopefully, my lawyer is making progress with the judge in Ft. Collins. I want to finalize the guardianship paperwork."

"Right," the sheriff said. "We can put the weapons in your trunk back at Megan's after you sign for them and the cash we found. Then I can follow you into Walden and have George with the coroner's office release the body to you. I gave Jose a heads up this morning about the burial, so they will be ready for you to fill out the proper paperwork and you can arrange the funeral."

"Good. I'm exhausted from all that driving and the flight. I will let you take care of the paperwork while I get a room for the night, then I can meet you at the funeral home to finalize the details. You said there are some hotels in Walden?"

The sheriff looked annoyed, but he did not challenge the shift of responsibilities. "Yes, ma'am. There is at least one motel. The other is getting renovated. It's not like Fort Collins or Denver."

Her aunt turned to her and motioned with her head toward the door. "If you've got your things, let's go."

"What do you plan to do with the rest of it?" Ms. Conner asked.

"Well, the books might have some value, but not enough to haul them out of here. You and that man who owns this place…"

"Stan," offered Ms. Conner.

"Yes, Stan. You and Stan can have what you want. It'd cost me more to ship it back than any of it is worth."

Kyrie bit her lip. She had no real idea of the value of the furnishings, but the books had cost her parents a lot of money. They had never hesitated on her education, even though she knew they worried over the costs. However, she had learned what she could from most of the books and practicality won out over sentiment. *And you will only stay with her until Lars finds you a safe place to hide.* She kept the frown from her face. *Where is he and why isn't he here yet?*

Kyrie shifted the suitcase on to its end, squatted down, and then lifted it onto her back. Holding the handle with one hand over her shoulder, she reached down to grab the straps of the closest duffle bag.

"Hey, let me help you with that," Jim Mitchel said, grabbing the heavy strap before she could.

The sheriff stepped up and grabbed the other duffle bag and gave her a weak smile. "You've got your hands full."

"Thank you," Kyrie said to both men. Her aunt frowned, but she said nothing as she walked to the door.

Kyrie easily traversed the uneven ground with the heavy suitcase on her back. *Weighs less than a deer.* Ms. Conner had her place the suitcase in the back of the truck and Mr. Mitchel and the sheriff set the duffle bags beside it.

The sheriff rubbed his hands together. "I'll give your aunt the weapons when we get back down to Megan's." He paused a moment, changed his mind about saying more, and then walked back to his vehicle.

"Well, I will give you credit for being hardy," her aunt said coming up behind her. "That place must have been horrid in the winter."

Kyrie shrugged. "I don't know. It was always warm enough with the wood pile and the snow never got too deep for snowshoes. Plus, it's easier to drag a deer back on a sled than to butcher it where it fell and have to lug the meat back piece by piece." Kyrie looked away, trying to hide the smile that wanted to make its way to her face at her aunt's dismay. *That was wrong, but…we don't care.*

The ride back down the road brought forth more complaints from her aunt. Kyrie refrained from saying anything and Ms. Conner kept her responses to a handful of words.

At Ms. Conner's house, they slipped out of the truck and her aunt pressed the button on the small object, causing the trunk to pop open again. "Get your things into the back of the car, but don't scuff my bags. Then we can head to Walden and see about arranging the funeral for your mother." Her aunt then turned to Ms. Conner. "I need to get my things from your home."

"Yes, ma'am," Kyrie said, though her aunt did not seem to hear. She moved around to the back of the truck and used the wheel to climb up high enough to reach the duffle bags and suitcase. She moved them one at a time to the trunk and when she finished, the sheriff brought over the swords, dagger, and longbow. The bow would not fit in the trunk, so he pulled a lever in the back and the rear seat fell forward to make room.

He chuckled at her expression. "You have a lot to learn about everyday things." He stood up and grew more serious. "You leave these weapons be, hear me? Your parents might have let you play with them out here where no one would ever notice, but you can't do that in civilized places. Even after you are no longer a minor."

"Yes, sir," Kyrie said. "What about the rifle?"

"Sorry, your aunt said no to that."

The sheriff's softened attitude toward her left her both relieved and unsettled. *Is he after something else now, or does he feel sorry for you?* She let him shut the trunk. *It doesn't really matter. As soon as you learn what you need to, we'll disappear.*

Her aunt came back down the stairs and motioned toward the car. "I'm ready to go," she said to Kyrie.

"Miss Leighton," Jim Mitchel said. "The final decision will be in the judge's hands, but I don't see anything that would prevent your guardianship. I'll file my report tonight, but I will call in a verbal approval."

"I should hope there would be no problems. My lawyer is taking care of all of it. He said it should be done in a few days."

Kyrie saw Mr. Mitchel's eyebrows rise. "I would expect things might take a little longer than that, but my guess is you will be able to take her with you to Kansas."

"I better be able to. I am not in a position to suddenly take an extended vacation." Her aunt turned to her. "You ready?"

"Yes, ma'am." Kyrie walked over to the passenger side of the car, opened the door, and quietly sat down. She watched her aunt for signs she had done anything wrong, but her aunt was talking quietly to the sheriff and Mr. Mitchel. After a moment, her aunt got into the car as well.

"Oh, wait a moment," Ms. Conner said. "Her mother's things." The older woman ran back into her house and then several moments later, came rushing back out with the rolled-up plastic shopping bag in her right hand. The older woman came over to the passenger door, and after her aunt pressed something, the window opened on its own. "You don't want to forget these."

"Thank you," Kyrie said as she accepted the bag.

Her aunt leaned over and spoke to Ms. Conner. "Thank you for taking care of my niece."

"Of course. It was my pleasure. I wrote my number down so you can let me know how things go. Please keep in touch." Kyrie accepted the paper from Ms. Conner.

"Okay. We are running late." Her aunt said, pushing a button on the dash, the vehicle sprung to life.

Ms. Conner stepped back and Kyrie watched as the window closed by itself.

"Put your seat belt on," her aunt said, drawing a belt over her own lap and pressing the metal end into a slot. "It would not do to drive off in front of the police and child services without doing that. They'd find me unfit."

Kyrie looked to her right, found a similar strap, and drew it over her body. It took her a moment to figure out how to properly insert the parts together, but she smiled when she heard the click.

Her aunt frowned. "Buckling your seat belt isn't something to be proud of. Everyone can do it." She leaned forward, pressed on the screen of a small box affixed to the windshield. After a moment, the box started talking about turning left. "What's in the bag?"

Kyrie felt the car lurch backwards as her aunt shifted it into gear and pressed the pedals on the floor. The sense of desire coming from her aunt grated on Kyrie's nerves and she closed off her mind.

"Well?"

"I've not looked yet." The expectation that she open the bag hung thick in the air. She had pushed things already and did not want her aunt to compel her. Kyrie unrolled the plastic bag and removed the items inside. She felt her eyes tear up as she placed her mother's mittens on her lap. Her mother had knitted and embroidered them herself. A ring on a leather cord slipped from between the mittens.

"What's that?"

"It's my mother's wedding ring. She always wore it on this cord because her fingers would swell from working in the fields." Kyrie looked at the gold band with a diamond mounted between the raised edges of gold. The gold protected the low set stone.

"Pretty small and plain," her aunt said as she changed the gear and drove the car forward.

Kyrie ignored her aunt, slipped the cord over her neck, and tucked the ring under her shirt, just like her mother used to wear it.

"What's that?" her aunt asked, pointing at something else sticking out from between the worn mittens.

Kyrie separated the mittens and revealed a worn and dirty brooch with a large green stone in the middle of a filigree oval. The gold color had long ago worn down to reveal the copper metal under the plating. The cloudy, dark green stone measured half an inch on the long side and a third of an inch on the shorter one.

"A bit of costume jewelry," her aunt said and then focused her attention back on the dirt road.

Kyrie swallowed her emotion, unzipped her coat, and pinned the brooch to her shirt. She had never seen her mother without the brooch, or the ring, and she did not realize what they meant until she had opened the bag. *Come on you, hold yourself together.*

To distract herself, she looked out the windows of the car as they drove down the mountain road. Most of what she saw resembled the road into her parent's valley. Trees and rocks blocked the view, but the road had a gentler slope and there were more houses and debris scattered about. Eventually, they came to a paved road and Kyrie felt a wave of excitement as the car sped up, causing everything outside to fly past her window. The speed thrilled and captivated her.

"What does the city of Gould look like?" she asked seeing a sign with the name. Her father had mentioned it before.

Her aunt scoffed. "City? Please, Gould is a collection of rundown buildings. Not even a town. It's nothing. I don't expect much better from Walden. What?"

Kyrie closed her mouth. "I thought it would be a city.

Her aunt laughed. "You've been locked away in a valley with no exposure to the outside world. You will need to be careful. These country hicks are simple and don't really understand the city either. Denver is a big city. Kansas City is reasonably sized. When we get back to Olathe, you will need to let me look out for you. Otherwise those in the city will eat you up. You can't be so trusting of people there." Her aunt took her eyes from the road and looked at her. "Don't worry, I'll take care of you. It may take a few years, but I'll help you adapt." She turned her attention back to the road and slowed as they went around a sharp curve. She checked the rear-view mirror and then sped up. "I will be your guide. Help you understand. My lawyers will make sure I'm able to protect you until you are able to function on your own."

Kyrie nodded her head and glanced out the window as another house nestled in the trees whizzed past the car. *We don't trust anyone, least of all her.*

# Chapter 5

The car ride with her aunt felt like hours, but Kyrie knew it had not been that long. Her aunt did not stop talking and all the conversation focused on how dull and limited her life must have been and how dirty and poor Ms. Conner was. The only fortunate aspect was that her aunt did not seem to require many responses and Kyrie could focus on the wide valley that stretched across the whole horizon. The flat land appeared in sharp contrast to the slopes she had grown up upon. Fields and farms spread as far as she could see and the realization of just how many people had to exist to consume all that food started to formulate in her mind.

When they reached the city of Walden, Kyrie stared in awe at all the buildings and the people. She knew fundamentally the city was not large, but it did contain more people and buildings than she had ever observed through the course of her life.

They took several turns, following the instructions from the small box attached to the windshield. As her aunt drove past a cemetery on the way to the motel, she slowed, but she did not stop. "That is where we will bury your mother. It is not much, but since your mother made this area her home, it seems fitting."

Kyrie nodded her head. She had not been allowed to come to her father's funeral and only knew that they had cremated him. *There are no such things as resurrection spells, so does this even matter?* She tilted her head to one side. *Coming back as a lich could be interesting, though.* She would not like her mother's body to suffer the indignity of being reanimated as a zombie or skeleton. *But a lich is a powerful, and intelligent, undead sorcerer. You could use the help.*

They drove on, taking several more turns before the box announced that they had arrived. Her aunt swung her critical gaze to the parking lot and the buildings advertising Oscar's Motor Lodge before she turned in and parked. "This will barely be tolerable, but we don't have many choices. Come on. I will get us a pair of rooms. Then I will take care of the funeral arrangements."

Kyrie exited the car and remained a step behind her aunt as she followed her into the motel's office. The small room held two chairs and a counter that blocked access to a door leading to another room.

"I need two rooms for tonight," her aunt said to the young woman who emerged from the other room. "Just for tonight. Unless we are forced to stay here longer for my niece to bury her mother."

Kyrie watched as the woman's jaw opened to say something, but she remained speechless. Kyrie had no reference for age, but the young woman did not appear much older than herself.

"I don't know the name of the guy who runs the funeral home," her aunt continued, "but my sister needs to be brought over to him from the morgue."

The young woman regained her composure. "Walden is not small enough that we all know everyone." Kyrie sensed the woman wanted her aunt to challenge that statement. However, her aunt just glared, and the woman continued. "Fine, you want two rooms for the night."

The woman pressed her fingers against a thin plastic box that stood on the counter between them. Kyrie wished she could see the other side and thought it might be like the box in her aunt's car, only larger.

"That will be one hundred twenty-two dollars and sixty-five cents." The woman said.

"I should have stayed at the other motel," her aunt sniped as she pulled out a small multi-colored plastic card and handed it to the woman.

"Well, they're doing upgrades. Oscar's is the only one open in town right now."

"And you're charging rates like you are."

The woman tilted her head to the side and smiled. "One key card for each room?"

"Two keys for her room and one for mine," her aunt replied.

Kyrie could not see what the woman did behind the counter, but the young woman handed back the small plastic card Kimberly had handed her and then handed over a pair of cards that looked identical in size, only they were white. "These are for room 105. She handed another card to her aunt. "This is for 106."

"Thanks," Kimberly said, taking the cards and turning to Kyrie. "Let's get settled while I make some calls and arrange for your dear mother's funeral. You'll stay here while I deal with the sheriff."

Kyrie tuned her aunt out. *Has money changed? What happened to paper?* She dared not ask and reveal details that might result in questions.

Her aunt marched outside and the woman behind the counter raised her eyebrows as Kyrie caught a burst of sympathetic emotions from her. Kyrie offered a forced smile and then followed her aunt. *These encounters were always easier with Mom and Dad. But life is not a D&D game, is it? If it was, you'd cast teleport and go back to the cabin.*

"Come," her aunt demanded, and Kyrie hurried to follow her across the parking lot to a series of doors in another building. Numbers on each door started at 101 and went to 107. Her aunt pulled out one card and pushed it into a slot above the latch. She pulled the card out and then turned the latch, but she did not push the door open. Instead, she handed Kyrie another card and made her repeat the process. "Good, now you know how to open the door. With any luck, you'll be tying your own shoes by morning."

Kyrie narrowed her eyes and knew the comment referred to the seat belt incident earlier.

Her aunt cleared her throat. "Anyway, if we're lucky, we will only have to stay here tonight and then head to Fort Collins tomorrow. My lawyers are good, so we might not even have to stop in Fort Collins. For now, just wait in the room and I'll be back."

Kyrie glanced at the card; the dark strip on the back was the only distinguishing feature. *Can any similarly shaped key open any door?* These were not like any of the keys she had seen others use in the past. Sensing her aunt's growing irritation, she used the card to open the door again and entered her room. Her aunt had already started to walk back toward her car before the door shut. "Figures."

Kyrie ignored her aunt and decided to explore the room. A massive bed occupied most of the room, with a television, a refrigerator, a desk, and a chair squeezed in around it. To her left was a small bathroom. The whole room smelled of disuse and dust. She walked over to the desk and picked up what she suspected was a phone. The base contained the buttons instead of the handle, but the moment she lifted the handle, she heard the tone that Ms. Conner's phone made.

She held the phone in her hand for a moment and mentally searched for her aunt. The woman had taken her bags to her own room. Kyrie pressed the numbers she had memorized for Lars and waited for the ringing to stop.

"Hello," came Lars' voice without delay. "Are you safe?"

Kyrie felt the words slip from her before she could moderate her tone. "The sheriff said my name is Kyrie Landvik, is that true?"

The pause on the other end extended for several seconds. "Yes, Kyrie, that is your name. I honestly don't know what name your parents were using. They kept that information from me so that no one could use me to find them."

"My aunt—a Kimberly Leighton—came for me this morning. You said you were going to come and get me."

"Unfortunately, the sheriff started asking too many questions and found your aunt before I could even start the process of filing the paperwork. Where are you?"

Kyrie bit her lip, testing the truth of what he said. *You made the decision to try and help your mother when we were supposed to run. You will see this to the end.* "I'm in a town called Walden," she finally replied. "Two blocks from a cemetery where my aunt is going to bury my mother. My aunt rented rooms in a place called Oscar's Motor Lodge." She paused a moment. "Is money not used anymore? She acquired the room with a piece of plastic. My father had me hide lots of paper money and said I needed to keep it safe, but if it is not worth anything, then how do I get this plastic?"

Lars chuckled. "Your parents taught you to be observant." He sighed. "Kim Leighton is your mother's sister. She's about twelve or fifteen years younger than your mother. Don't remember her birthday off the top of my head. But, to answer your question, money is still valuable. However, there are cards that can be used in place of paper money."

"What is going on Lars? Why didn't they tell me the truth about who I am and that I had an aunt?" Kyrie looked up and felt her aunt moving about the other room.

"Kyrie, I wish I could tell you. I don't know most of it. Your parents and I were good friends in college, and we kept that friendship after graduation. Everything was normal. They were doing well. Then you came along and I know things were hard on you and your mother. A difficult birth and you were not well. Your mother put her life on hold to try and make you better. A number of months after you were born, they took a trip and came back ecstatic. You were healthy. A month later, someone broke into their house. They told me someone wanted to take you. At first, I thought they overreacted. Homes get broken into; things stolen. But they insisted on giving me power of attorney over everything so they could disappear." Kyrie heard him pause a moment. "In general terms, it means I can legally act on their behalf without consulting them."

"Why? Why would they leave everything? The sheriff said they must have abused me because no one would give up all their things to live in a shithole of a cabin in the middle of nowhere under a false name."

Lars chuckled again. "You sound more like me than your parents there." His voice grew serious again. "Your parents were scared, and though I thought they were crazy at the time, I did as they asked. I put Robert's family home in Allston on the market and started to liquidate their assets. Then someone broke into my home, as well as my office. They stole all my files related to your parents. At the time, I kept recordings of all my conversations, even your parent's conversations, just in case there were ever questions later. I had no knowledge of where your parents went, and I assume whoever stole all of it believed the recordings and notes, because no one ever came after me again…at least not that I know of. But that did not stop us from taking more precautions."

"Someone is really after me," Kyrie mused. A part of her had hoped that perhaps her parents had also lied about that.

"It's been sixteen years now since it happened. I can't say for certain if there is anyone after you anymore, or if they were ever after you personally. Your parents would tell me nothing of what was wrong. For my protection they said. We can hope that with your parents having died of natural causes, and the amount of time that has passed, perhaps whatever trouble they were in has passed."

Kyrie closed her eyes. She wanted to go back to the cabin and work the fields. She wanted to play Dungeons & Dragons with her mother and father. She wanted to study math and physics. She wanted to draw.

"Kyrie, I had a call from your aunt's lawyer today. Unfortunately, Sheriff Sawyer is a bit more thorough than I prefer when he's investigating someone I'm trying to protect. He's got connections and managed to track your parents tax filings to me. Because of the tax filings, he also found out you are worth over ten million dollars."

"What does that mean?"

A somber chuckle came across the phone. "It means you have a lot of wealth and Kim is after it. Your parents didn't start that rich, but Robert inherited property that was worth a lot because of where it was. When I sold it, a combination of timing and luck had me investing all of your parents' assets when the market was down. I managed to pick some stocks that did really well. Eventually, I reinvested everything in index funds, you are in a good position and your money keeps growing." Lars shuffled something and cursed under his breath as the sound of something hitting the floor came through the phone. "Dropped my drink," he explained. "You following all of this?"

"You and my parents have been trying to hide things, but the sheriff is uncovering everything, and my aunt knows about the money my parents had and wants it."

"It is your money now. At least as long as I can keep it protected. Your Aunt's lawyer hoped no official wills existed, but I could thankfully tell him that the notarized wills do exist…meaning other people have attested to the authenticity of the document signatures. Rachel and Robert each left everything to each other, and if they should both die, everything goes to you. Of course, the trust also has restrictions, which will help protect it."

"I don't have context for how much ten million is. I'm assuming it is a lot based on the way you said it."

"It is a lot," Lars said. "If you are not reckless, you might never have to work a day in your life." He paused, then grew more serious. "I want to add for full disclosure, that if you are also dead, I do not get any of the money. Everything goes to a list of charities. They did that to protect me from suspicion of a conflict of interest. Besides, I'm a rather successful lawyer and have my own money."

Kyrie looked toward the wall separating her room from her aunt's and confirmed her aunt's position in the room. "So, based on how my parents always played their characters, I should not trust Kim."

"Kyrie, you pick things up very quickly. Her lawyer tried to warn me that I should stay out of this unless I wanted a lot of trouble. While your parents and I were careful not to break laws, we did push them. For example, your father sent me a detailed list of all his earnings every year to make sure no one would come back and accuse him of tax fraud. But, in hiding as they have done, we've lied about their location, state of residence, and other things. I had hoped we'd have a lazy county sheriff and I would quietly be able to file paperwork for your guardianship. I'd be able to protect you and your money until you were eighteen and then you would be completely free to do what you wanted. Unfortunately, despite the will, in which your parents named me as your guardian, Kim is seeking to get guardianship of you and she has some influential friends. I'm going to work to protect you and your money as much as possible, but I don't think I can protect all of it."

He cleared his throat. "Because, I am not a beneficiary in the will, it is likely a judge will suspect my motivation to gain guardianship is related to the money as well. They will assume the worse of me, especially with the legal games I've played to protect your parents."

Kyrie wiped her face with her hand. "So, what am I to do?"

"You may not like it, but I would say, go with your aunt for now. It is better than being locked up in the child services system, and in all likelihood, a judge won't give you a choice in the matter anyway."

"But my parents told me to run. They wanted me to hide."

Lars' voice hardened. "Kyrie, I don't want to speak poorly of your parents, but they told me they never wanted you to rejoin society. They purposely withheld things from you to keep you from wanting to be part of the world. They expected you would live your whole life in hiding."

Kyrie swallowed. She wanted to disagree and argue that Lars misunderstood them. She wanted to offer proof he was wrong, but tears welled up in her eyes because in that moment, she knew he was correct.

He continued without pause. "They wanted me to help you find a place to hide, but I don't think that is what is best for you. I'm very hopeful that any threat your parents were under is over. And even if it is not, whoever they are would know that your mother and aunt did not get along that well. They didn't fight, but they didn't share the same interests. Your mother enjoyed the outdoors and learning. Kim's is more about looking pretty, drinking, having status, and meeting men. The one thing that is certain, if you run, Kim will get your money and I won't be able to do much about it. They will use it to say you are not competent to take care of yourself and restrict your movements. They might even try to declare you incompetent."

Kyrie's voice barely exceeded a whisper. "Mother always said to listen to you, Lars."

"Thank you. You'll be seventeen in less than a month. We can always work to emancipate you from your aunt…that means allowing you the rights of an adult before you turn eighteen."

"I better go, my aunt is coming."

"Kyrie, quick, I have a new number for you, just like the coded one you used to call this number. It is 14431616034. Do you need me to repeat it? It is for a different phone. I will get rid of this one once you start using the new one."

"14431616034," she said quickly. "I'll memorize it."

"Be safe, Kyrie. Also, be careful of the phone you use to call me. Your aunt and others might be able to see the number you dial, which they would try to trace back to me."

"So, don't call unless I have no choice?"

"When you get to your aunt's house, find a phone not in her house and let me know how you are. Then we'll find a way to stay in touch."

"Okay," she said and quickly placed the phone back on the desk as she sighed. Visions of her parents came unbidden. *Why did you make us a prisoner? You compelled us to never leave.* Memories flooded her mind. *And then you told us to forget you told us to obey.*

Kyrie turned toward the door as her aunt opened it.

"You just standing there?" Kimberly asked.

Kyrie moved to the middle of the room in response. "May I go for a run?"

"A run? What on earth for?"

"I've been cooped up for the last two days and I need to do something."

Her aunt shook her head. "You'd get lost. Then I'd have to have someone find you. If you have to do something, run in place."

*Run in place? Really?* Kyrie had seen the size of Walden as they drove into the town. While it was larger than any other place she had been, she knew it was not so large that she would get lost. Not wanting to feel the effects of compulsion, she adjusted her approach. "May I at least sit outside?"

He aunt's jaw tightened and after a moment softened. "Fine. You must be going through a lot, having just lost your mother." She stepped aside. "Just don't lose your card, otherwise you won't get back into the room until I return."

Kyrie nodded her head.

"Come here, child. I'll give you a hug."

Kyrie would rather not have to touch her aunt, but she moved forward to get embraced by the shorter woman. "See. Things will be better." Released, Kyrie stepped back as her aunt continued to speak. "I'm just as unsettled as you are. I've wondered where my sister got to all those years ago and for me to learn about it only after she died is heartbreaking. Plus, I need to adjust my life to raise a young girl. That will upheave everything."

Kyrie felt no sympathy for her, despite her aunt's desire that she feel that emotion. However, she could pretend. "I don't mean to be a bother," Kyrie whispered, trying to project the expected response.

"I know, child. It is not your fault. Sit outside if you want."

Kyrie nodded her head and followed her aunt out of the room. Outside, she looked around the gravel parking lot and saw four cars, including her aunt's. The only seating appeared to be a bench near the office, and she started walking in that direction as her aunt got into the blue car.

The view across the street reminded her of Ms. Conner's trailer with several older vehicles parked in the yard. She recalled pictures from her textbooks of cities and towns with neatly cut grass and large, brightly painted buildings. The buildings here needed maintenance and care.

Kyrie looked at the cars in the parking lot as she approached the bench. There was a green one that had not been there when they had arrived. Like the one her aunt was backing out of the parking lot, this one appeared new, and in very good condition. *Are motels like inns in the campaigns? Only used by people traveling from place to place?* Kyrie suspected that to be the case.

As she walked by the other new car, she felt a person in room 101 and had to resist the urge to turn her head. Her instincts had already caused her to draw energy into herself for defense. The mind felt male and based on the location, he looked out the window at her. The intensity of his focus made her uncomfortable and she hurried toward the bench as her aunt drove away.

*Like gravity, your ability to sense his emotions will fall off at the square of distance to him.* She did not know this to be absolutely true, only that it had always seemed to play out in that fashion, and by the time she reached the bench, the man had either changed his focus, or she had gotten far enough away that she could not feel his desire.

*Mother, why?* She held back the tears that wanted to leak from her eyes. "What should I do?" She did not care about the money, when they had gamed, she often gave away a lot of the coin her characters would find. She knew she could hunt and forage for food in game, as in the real world. Her father had taught her that from an early age and the skills felt natural. "But I don't know the rules of this world. There is no campaign description for me to read."

"Hey, you okay?"

Kyrie looked up at the young woman who had been behind the counter in the office. She was standing in the office doorway with a bundle of towels in her arms.

"You aren't being trafficked or anything, are you? Do you need me to call the cops?"

Kyrie shook her head, sensing the woman's concern for her. "I don't know what that means, but the sheriff was the one who contacted my aunt."

"I'm Shelly," the woman said. "Is it true you just lost your mother?"

Kyrie nodded. Her parent's warnings not to trust anyone fought with her instincts about the girl's intentions. "Two days ago."

"I'm so sorry. Is there anything I can do?"

Kyrie shook her head, still uncertain of how much trust she wanted to extend to a stranger. "Wait, a pen and paper?"

"Inside on the counter. Help yourself." Shelly paused and then leaned closer. "There was a creepy man asking about someone who had died. A Rachel Landvik." She waited a moment for a response, but Kyrie offered none. "Said he was a reporter, but I don't know any reporters with tattoos on their necks. I didn't say anything, but he's in room 101." Shelly inclined her head backwards to indicate the row of rooms behind her.

"Thank you," Kyrie replied, her own discomfort with the man's focus on her from the window resurfacing. *Mom, what chases us?*

Shelly gave her a sad smile and then carried the towels to her aunt's room. Kyrie got up and walked into the office, found a pad of paper and a pen on the counter. She jotted Lars' number down, tore off the paper, and stuffed the number into her bra. No one watched her, so she then returned to the bench to sit. The idea of ignoring her aunt and exploring the town passed through her thoughts, but the memory of the compulsion the sheriff used on her remained too fresh in her memory. *Don't give Kim Lym an excuse to use it on you.* Her mother had rarely disciplined her in the last two years and the pain of the recent correction still lingered.

Shelly returned to the office without saying anything more and Kyrie remained content to sit on the bench and look at her surroundings. She slowly allowed her mind to adjust to a broader world view as she released the excess energy from her body.

Her mind calmed as she watched a car drive by and wondered where the people inside were headed. Down the street, and mostly hidden from her view, a woman hung clothing from a line stretched between two poles. The short fence that separated her yard from the rest of the town showed as much wood as it did flaking paint. The scene felt like the setting her mother might spin before the starting a new adventure.

Kyrie allowed herself to get lost in memories of Dungeons & Dragons sessions long past. She relived laughter and failures and successes. When her aunt drove up and parked, she realized how late it had become.

"Are you hungry, Dearie?"

Kyrie took a moment to process the statement because she disliked that form of address. "Yes, ma'am." Kyrie kept the grin from her face as she correctly deduced the fact that her aunt hated being called 'ma'am' as much as she disliked 'dearie.'

"Let's get something to eat."


They ate a meager meal at a local restaurant, and with the sun already dropping below the horizon, Kimberly drove them to the northern side of town where she parked in front of a building that appeared to be slightly larger than most of the houses Kyrie had seen. A sign in the front yard proclaimed the building to be Cedar Hill Funeral Home.

"We'll say our goodbyes to your mother. In the next day or two, they will bury her in the cemetery on the other side of town, assuming the ground thawed more than a few inches. I decided to skip the embalming," she added hastily. "Better for the environment."

Kyrie did not know the term, but she knew not doing it saved her aunt money.

"I spoke with Jim Mitchel and my lawyer a little while ago. The judge back in Fort Collins has given me permission to take you home tomorrow." Kimberly grinned. "It always pays to know people and have money."

Kyrie bit her lip. "I don't want to remember my mother like this. She's dead, there is no goodbye she will hear."

"This is for you, not her. I've paid extra to have a small service. You will appreciate it and you will be a proper daughter and say your goodbyes."

Kyrie nodded her head. The tone spoke of compulsion, but her aunt had not actually used it. "Yes, ma'am."

"Good, now get out of the car and let's go inside."

Kyrie unfastened her seat belt and got out of the car. She shut down all her senses. *You might see her body, but don't allow yourself to feel her,* she told to herself as she followed her aunt into the building.

The smell inside the building struck her as overly floral with an under tone of unpleasant chemicals. An uninspiring tune played from somewhere, though Kyrie could not see the speakers. The green carpet felt like hard tiles beneath her feet.

"Good afternoon," spoke a man with a voice so soft that Kyrie had trouble hearing him over the background music. "If you will follow me, we have the dearly departed resting peacefully in the viewing room."

Kyrie followed the man and her aunt into a room with several rows of benches. At the far end of the room sat a plain, dark wooden box about the length of a person. Half of the top stood open. Her aunt ushered her forward until Kyrie looked down at her mother.

Kyrie forced her mind to remain closed off from everything around her. She could still remember the empty feeling of her mother's body and did not want to reinforce that memory.

"Rachel, you should never have run off with that stupid Robert. I told you that you were being a fool. May god forgive you for whatever you have done." Her aunt nudged her. "Now you say your own goodbyes."

"Goodbye, Mother."

Kyrie did not so much sense, as notice out of the corner of her eye, the change in her aunt's position. "I should spank you for being disrespectful. If you don't care that I spent a lot of money to arrange this, then we can go back to the motel and wait for morning."

"I don't mean to be disrespectful," Kyrie said, her voice whinier than she wanted, "but I already saw my mother after she was dead. I don't need to keep seeing her body."

Kimberly sighed. "I keep forgetting, though your body may be grown, locked away as you were, you are still a child. One day you'll learn to thank me for what I've done for you." Her aunt turned and walked over to the man in the suit. "Thank you. You can bury her now."

*Think what you want, Kim Lym.* Anger and energy burned in her. *Mother never considered us a child.* Kyrie exhaled, managing to release the energy in her without knocking over anything in the room.

# Chapter 6

Michael Rodgers picked up his burner phone and checked the number. With a swipe of his thumb, he answered the call, "Yes?"

"I've got a report," a voice on the other end whispered. "I did some digging just as I was asked."

Michael glanced at his watch. He already knew it was near midnight from the screen of the phone when he answered it, but he could not resist the compulsive tic. "Is it her?"

"The old woman appears to be the lady I was told to look for. Died of a heart attack. Father died of the same last year. They cooked him, threw the ashes in an urn, and plopped him into the ground with a pathetic marker."

"And the girl?"

"She's in the town where I am. Tall little minx. Not had a chance to get a good look at her face, so she might be a dog. Don't know. Blonde. Ragged clothing that's a bit too small. I got the address of the cabin they lived at."

Michael leaned forward in his chair. "Okay, bring the information back. Don't interact with the girl or her aunt."

"You sure? I can snatch her pretty easy. Got some things that would knock her out. She'd be placid as a puppy."

*More like vicious as a cat,* Michael thought. "No, leave now. I have other things for you to do." Without waiting for confirmation, Michael hung up the phone, fearful that the patsy would dig too much. "Bastard better obey. Otherwise, Henry will need to end him."

Michael got up from his chair and went into the kitchen of his apartment. The granite counters were spotless and that reflected the rest of his home. He retrieved a bottle of whisky and a tumbler from a glass-doored cabinet next to the stainless-steel refrigerator. He poured a double shot. The aroma tickled his senses and without pause, he drained the contents. The burn of the alcohol woke him.

"After all this time." He shook his head. "I had hoped they were wrong." He contemplated another glass but knew that would be a mistake.

Michael woke the phone and dialed a different number. It rang several times before a groggy voice answered. "I have a job for you. I will send you an email with the details. Take two with you and head to Olathe Kansas."

The phone disconnected with no verbal acknowledgement of the instructions. However, Michael knew his man had received the message. He went to his computer, signed on, checked that the VPN was active, remotely logged into a server located in Venezuela, and started drafting the encrypted email to his hacker. The email would never leave the server and there was little chance the hacker, or the other two, would betray him. The hacker made too much money from the connection. "And the other two…" He rested a hand on his pelvis and felt the nineteen stones secured in the special belt under his clothes. Those stones ensured obedience and he never let them out of his possession. The fear he felt now was in having to report to his own boss.

Kyrie woke, papers and books surrounding her on the bed. Her heart raced in her chest and energy filled her body. Someone stood outside the window of her room. *The man from 101,* she acknowledged without moving. The blinds were closed and her room remained dark. The rational part of her mind said he could not possibly be looking at her, but instinct told her to hide.

Quiet as an owl, she shifted her body to the edge of the bed and away from the window. She slowly lowered herself to the floor, being careful not to send any of the materials on the bed tumbling. She kept her eyes closed, fearing that if she would turn her head toward the window, a glint of reflected light might give her away.

Her breath came in rapid gulps. The man's intense focus on her filled the room and her mind, feeding the fear within her.

She cast her senses wider and looked for other threats. Her aunt, sleeping in the next room, remained the only other person near. *What do you want?* As soon as she started to probe, she immediately blocked the man's thoughts from her mind. *You don't want to know.* The image of a terrified girl lingered in her thoughts.

Kyrie slept fully dressed, save for her shoes. Faced with the potential need to flee, she regretted placing her shoes on the other side of the bed. *Stupid, now you realize that one door is the only way in or out of the room. Where did you think an attack would come from?*

After what felt like eternity, but Kyrie rationally knew to be minutes, the man left her window and headed toward his own room. She kept her eyes closed, seeing better with her mind than any of her other senses. Stretching herself to the limits, she sensed the man go into what she expected to be his room. The walls and distance, coupled with his own diminished focus, turned him into a vague feeling and Kyrie lost any real sense of his movements.

"Come on, we should not be afraid of a man who walked past the room." Kyrie knew she had lied to herself. When her father ran their Dungeons & Dragons campaigns, someone who lurked outside a room was a thief or worse.

She considered climbing back into the bed, but the feeling of exposure kept her on the floor and the excess energy in her body. She reached up with one hand and pulled down a pillow before curling up so that no one coming in through the door or window could see her. Sleep took a long time to arrive, but eventually it returned, allowing the surplus energy to gradually leave her body.

Kyrie heard the knocking at her door and came awake. Her mind reached out and sensed her aunt. "Get up and get ready, I want to leave in thirty minutes."

Kyrie rose from the floor with the pillow and tossed it on the bed. "Yes, ma'am," she responded automatically. Her balance felt slow and she walked into the bathroom to clean her face. Her father had always risen before the sun because he had to walk several miles before someone would pick him up and take him to work the fields. His movements would wake her with him. Her mother had relaxed the early rising rule after he had died, but Kyrie still considered herself a morning person.

She finished in the bathroom quickly, her hair more tangle than order, but she had forgotten to grab her brush from the cabin and there was only so much her fingers could do. She pulled on her shoes, repacked her bags, and went outside. A hint of frost covered the ground as the orange glow of the sky faded. She inhaled the surrounding scent. Unlike on the mountain, where decaying leaf litter mingled with the odor of pine, here the air carried a faint trace of chemicals and livestock. Kyrie could not see the source of the smells, but she wrinkled her nose all the same.

A glance toward room 101 revealed an empty spot where the green car had last been. Her instincts pushed her awareness further and she found the room empty of the man. She turned, relying on her eyes to try to spot the car, or the man who had attempted to peer into her room, but she could not see either one.

"What are you doing?" Her aunt asked as she emerged from her own room. "And you look terrible. Didn't you clean yourself up?"

Kyrie did not bother meeting her aunt's gaze, the stark disapproval she felt left her in no mood to be polite. "I was told there was a reporter here and I was looking to see if he was still around."

"A reporter?" Her aunt scanned the area with her eyes as well. "Where'd you hear that? Damn nosy bastards."

The change in her aunt's emotions caused Kyrie to turn. The stern disapproval that she imagined on her aunt's face was actually one of concerned annoyance. *And not focused on you.* "The girl behind the counter told me yesterday when I sat outside."

Her aunt glared. "You should have told me then." She shook her head. "Get into the car so we can get on the road. I had to press hard to get a judge to approve things as fast as he did. Those rabid dogs in the news media would love to torment me some more." Her aunt shooed her toward the car with her hands. "We'll eat in a few hours when we reach a decent city. I just hope we don't have to wait until we are at Fort Collins."

Kyrie looked out the window as her aunt drove the twisting and turning road toward the east. She absorbed everything she saw as the hours passed, taking in the style of houses and the variety of vehicles on the road. The larger towns and cities raised her eyebrows, each of them presenting more lavishly styled buildings and yards. She saw many worn and dilapidated properties, but Kyrie wonder what sort of person lived in the fancy buildings she observed. *Are they rulers and powerful people with many followers? Or are they just rich merchants?* Without a way to know, she continued to adapt her view based on the campaigns her parents had run.

"What are you thinking about?" Her aunt asked.

"Just wondering about the people who live in those houses," she responded without turning her head.

"You would be living in something like those had your parents not run off." Her aunt shook her head. "Instead, you ended up like immigrants in a dirt hut."

Kyrie turned her head toward her aunt. She had imagined several angles she might use to get her aunt to talk about things she wanted to know, but she opted to start broad and narrow her questioning later. "What happened?"

"What do you mean?"

"What happened to my mother and father? Why'd they take me out here?"

"Your mother never told you?"

"No," Kyrie said, the word hard in her mouth.

"Your fool mother decided to have you when she was too old. I had Sam a year after you were born, but I'm twelve years younger than Rachel." Her aunt glanced in her direction. "Well, you came out all wrong. I wasn't there, but I know that for the first six months of your life, you hardly moved or made a sound. They knew something was wrong with you. Some trouble with your brain."

*Our brain is just fine.*

"My sister quit her job at MIT and started getting into all kinds of crazy things." Her aunt smashed a peddle to the floor and whipped around a silver car in front of them. "Leave it in God's hands I told her, but she never listened. Next thing I know, she and Robert go on some vacation and when they came back, they said you were all better. Less than a month later, they disappeared."

"Where'd they go?" Kyrie asked.

"I don't know. Somewhere in Arkansas. It was close enough they could have come visit me, but they didn't." She sighed. "Anyway, you have a cousin Sam. He's fifteen. From my first marriage. He's costing me. My last husband, Surge, just filed bankruptcy. He ruined his business. I think he did it to get out of the alimony. Fortunately, I know a lot of lawyers; Edward, Sam's father, is one. I used Edward's best friend to divorce him." Kimberly's snicker filled the car. "They never got over that, but Charles is still my lawyer. And a bit more," she added under her breath. "Anyway, the good thing is you seem to have some money coming to you, which will help a lot, otherwise, I'd never be able to afford having you move into my home. The state would have to take care of you." She frowned. "I've always heard girls are so expensive. I wasn't when I was young, but these days they are. And if some stupid reporter is going to come looking for a scoop just because I made use of my friends, well, I have to do what is right by my niece, I'll sue his ass into the ground."

Kyrie turned her attention back to what flew by the window. Her aunt had resumed the chatter that was more talking to herself than to anyone else and Kyrie allowed her thoughts to drift back to the campaign notes her mother had written. She had stayed up late finding even more references from her mother's journals to different campaigns. So far, each one spoke of worm holes and other theories for energy conveyance. *You will find out what happened.*


At their next stop, Kyrie gathered her textbook from the trunk and alternated between studying and looking out the windows. She dismissed her aunt's question of why she would bother, with the response of 'I don't need someone to grade it to learn.'

Eventually, they drove out of the mountains and turned toward the plains where rain poured from the sky. Kyrie grew bored with the flat landscape and followed her parents' advice to take full advantage of any situation. She closed her eyes and caught up on some needed sleep.

Her aunt continued to talk, sometimes to other people on her phone. Kyrie paid little attention to her. They finally stopped at a hotel late in the day and then continued driving the following morning. By the early afternoon of the second day, Kyrie suspected they were getting close to their destination. They had left the highway and were driving along city streets. The contrast to Walden was night and day. Cars and people were everywhere, the houses massively large, and the yards dedicated to grass and plants, even though it was still early in the year.

Eventually, they turned into a driveway that already had a large vehicle parked in front of the two-story house. "This is my home," her aunt said. "I'll have to have someone drive me to the rental place to drop this thing off. Sam's not old enough, and obviously, you don't have a license."

Kyrie felt a great deal of uncertain pride from her aunt and she offered a bit of confirmation. "It is a very pretty house."

"It is," her aunt agreed. "Over twenty-seven hundred feet finished. Two-story with a walk-out basement. Five bedrooms. Cost nearly four-hundred thousand."

Kyrie nodded her head; the figures meant nothing to her.

"Still have fifteen years left on the mortgage. I got the house in the divorce, but it wasn't paid for." She pressed the center of the steering wheel and Kyrie jumped at the loud noise she recognized as the horn.

Her aunt pressed the horn twice more before a young man came out through the front door. His brown hair jutted out at various angles and he wore only jeans and a t-shirt.

"It's Saturday afternoon, why do you look like you've just gotten out of bed?" her aunt shouted through the window she opened. "And where is your jacket?"

Kyrie watch the young man shrug. She was too far away to sense his emotions clearly, but he did not look happy.

"I've been up. I was just taking a break," he yelled from the porch.

Her aunt got out of the car and Kyrie did the same. The smell of fresh cut grass from the neighbor's lawn filled the air.

"Sam, put on shoes and a jacket, then get my bags and come down here to meet your cousin. She'll be in the front bedroom. I trust you've moved the boxes to the basement."

Kyrie could tell her aunt did not believe her last statement.

Sam brushed back his hair with his hands, ducked inside the house, and then came back out and down the front sidewalk to the car wearing sandals and a coat. He walked past his mother and came over to Kyrie with a hand extended. "Hi, I'm Sam. Don't call me Samuel." More softly he added, "You don't look like what I imagined. I was led to believe you were some unwashed urchin."

Kyrie took his hand and shook it. A confused wash of emotion emanated from the young man. She examined him, trying to adjust her sense of age to his appearance and the fact he was supposed to be a year younger than herself. She felt his curiosity and noted how he stood more upright, failing to compensate for the two-inch difference in height she had over him.

"I'm Kyrie."

"So, my mother said a few times on the phone." He glanced over his shoulder at the house and then lowered his voice. "Your room might not be completely ready. Mike's here and we've had a bit of a LAN party."

"Mike's here?" Kimberly had come up behind Sam without his noticing.

Kyrie made note of Sam's lack of mental awareness to those around him. *No one, but you, so far, seems to feel the presence of others.*

His shoulders dropped and he turned around to face his mother. "Yeah. Sorry, I forgot to mention it, but I thought he could help move the boxes."

"Which are still in the room. Where's your cousin going to sleep? I'd never ask her to sleep in your bed. It'll stink because you've not done the sheets I'm guessing."

Kyrie injected herself into the conversation. "I can help move boxes. I've been cooped up for too long as it is."

Sam's eyes brightened and he started walking toward the house. "Excellent. I'll show you where the room is."

His mother cleared her throat. "You'll get my bags." She pressed on what Kyrie now knew as the key fob and the trunk opened.

Kyrie walked to the back of the car and pulled out her two duffle bags and then her suitcase.

"Swords! And a bow." Sam reached in and pulled a sword out of the trunk and drew the weapon from the scabbard. "Are they for me?"

Kyrie tensed, ready to disarm Sam and protect herself.

Sam's mother ran toward the back of the car. "No. They belong to Kyrie, but neither of you are old enough to have them. I'll lock them up. They are too valuable to allow someone to break them."

Kyrie relaxed and took care to not roll her eyes. Her bouts with her father had left many scratches and marks on the blades; however, there were very few chips despite all the practice.

Sam frowned as his mother gathered all the weapons into her arms. "Get my bags," she repeated as she carried the weapons to the house.

"You must've had cool parents," he whispered to Kyrie. "I've been trying to get my mother to buy me a sword for years, but she won't." After a moment he suddenly panicked. "Sorry."

Kyrie nodded her head. She felt overwhelmed by the confused emotions coming from Sam and had to take a moment to clear her own thoughts. "They are dead. There is not anything that can change that." She strained her muscles and lifted the suitcase onto her back and kept it steady with one hand. She then squatted and lifted the two heavy duffle bags with her other hand.

Sam raised his eyebrows and she noticed him glancing at her arms. "Okay, let me show you your room," he said as he lifted his mother's cases higher.

Kyrie sighed. Her abs and back muscles strained to keep all the weight steady, but she felt no need to lift any of it higher than necessary. As she approached the front door, she felt another male presence inside and next to her aunt. The male mind held so many confused similarities to Sam's that she initially thought her aunt might have had two kids.

"We are glad you made it home, Miss Leighton," the young man said.

"Mike," her aunt replied with what was both a tentative greeting and an implied assumption of some guilt.

"Sam was out of control and I had to do everything in my power to keep him in line." Mike smiled at her and she felt Sam's brown-haired friend's interest and desire so strongly that she closed her mind.

"Mike, this is my niece, Kyrie," Kimberly said, shifting the weapons in her hands. "Sam, lock the front door. How many times do I have to tell you."

"Hey, nice to meet you. Sorry about your parents. Sam didn't say much about what happened."

"I don't know much about what happened," Sam replied as he locked the door.

Kyrie felt her irritation rising with the straining of her muscles. However, she refused to set the duffle bags down. *You won't lift them high, but you will still show off.* "My mother died while we were planting vegetables," Kyrie answered.

"Planting vegetables? Don't you just buy them at the store?" Mike asked, a crooked smile crossing his face.

Kyrie wished she could know his intention with the statement, but she did not want to deal with all the emotions in the air. *Mother and father must have learned to shield their minds around you, everyone else is giving us a headache.* "We had to have something to eat," she responded as she examined the interior of the house, wondering where her room would be.

The entry rose two-stories high with a large chandelier above their heads. To her right was a large open area with a wooden table and six heavy chairs. A floor to ceiling glass enclosed cabinet sat against the far wall. Light came in through the front windows, illuminating a railing and an open stairwell going down.

In front of her were a set of stairs going up to the second floor and they sat above the ones going into the basement. Beyond the stairs was another room with a glass enclosed fireplace in the far wall. "This is a massive house," she mumbled as she moved forward to adjust the weight on her body.

"Let me take those," Mike said as he stepped forward to grab the duffle bags.

Kyrie allowed him to take the handles from her and a smile crossed her lips when he nearly dropped them from the weight.

"What's in these?"

"Books," she said, lifting her left hand to help steady the suitcase on her back. She moved forward again to look into the room on the other side of the stairs. A large television sat fastened to the wall across from a sofa and several chairs. The room extended further to the right where a second table and chairs stood in front of a large kitchen with an island. Out the back windows she could see trees and more houses. "You must be very wealthy."

"We are well off," her aunt said. "Sam, bring my bags to my bedroom, then the two of you move the boxes to the basement like you were supposed to have done." Her aunt then walked up the stairs with the weapons.

Sam shook his head at Kyrie after his mother was near the top of the stairs. "Not really wealthy. This is average. Mother wouldn't be able to afford it if she had not remarried the Loser."

"My bags!" came her aunt's demand from upstairs.

Sam rolled his eyes and Kyrie wondered just how long it would be before her aunt used compulsion on her son and his friend. So far, she could not see any signs of them feeling the effects, though her aunt was definitely irritated.

"Coming, Miss Leighton," Mike said, his wide grin showing his teeth, but his eyes did not leave Kyrie. "After you." He stepped back so Kyrie could go up the stairs. "You got a boyfriend?"

Kyrie tilted her head. "I don't have any friends, boy or girl."

Mike chuckled. "Sam said you were slow, but he didn't say you were a looker."

Sam's face became pale and he stammered, "Your room will be on the right. Mine's on the left. Mother's is the large one at the end. Don't go in there unless she asks you to."

Kyrie looked at the two boys and knew something had passed between them, but she could not tell exactly what. Her parents had roleplayed many scenarios with her, but nothing that felt like this. She put the problem aside and easily walked up the steps with just her suitcase.

At the top of the stairs, she saw five doorways. The one at the end of the hall led to a large room with a massive bed. More doors inside that room lead to additional rooms. *The whole cabin would fit into that space.* To her right, one doorway led to a bathroom and the other to a bedroom. Boxes lined the bedroom walls with nearly as many things stacked on the bed. The first door on her left was closed, but a second door lead to another bedroom packed with scattered clothing, toys, a desk, a bed, and piles of other yet unidentified items.

"Sorry about the boxes," Sam said as he walked past her and into the room at the end of the landing, where her aunt had re-entered from the adjoining room.

"On the bed," Kimberly demanded, "then finish moving the boxes downstairs as you were supposed to do."

Kyrie walked into what was to be her bedroom with Mike right behind her. The room smelled of dust and old papers. Piles of clothing sat on the simple bed. The boxes against the walls allowed just enough space to walk around the bed.

"No boyfriend in Colorado," Mike stated with some satisfaction as he set the duffle bags on the floor.

"It was just me and my parents," she replied. The desire she was feeling from Mike leaked into her mind despite her attempts to block it out.

"Sorry about not getting the boxes moved." Mike looked away. "Sam said…" He shrugged. "Sam didn't think you'd…"

"Mike, quiet." Sam pushed his way into the crowded room. "Let me show you where we can put all this." He grabbed a box near the door and Mike followed his example.

Kyrie, still uncomfortable, shook herself before grabbing a box. The musty smell of the old cardboard bothered her nose, but the weight was minimal. The two boys waited for her in the hall. *Come on kid, you have to learn how to deal with the rest of the world at some point.*

The boxes went to the basement, which consisted of an entertainment room complete with a wall sized television, another bathroom with a shower, a fifth bedroom already filled with junk, and a large storage room.

Sam led the way to the storage room, which had winding pathways through a maze of items stacked on each other. The primary path offered just enough space to walk to the far side of the room where Sam stacked what he carried against the wall.

"We're supposed to fill this back corner. This area is for all the old things my mother is keeping from her former husbands because she thinks she'll be able to sell them and make some money." Sam offered the shrug Kyrie started to assume was his most used expression. "I doubt she'll make anything off of any of it."

"And she'll make you do all the work to sell it," Mike said as he set his own box down. He pulled the top open and rummaged around inside before he pulled out a desk lamp. "This will be your college fund."

"Shut up." Sam took the lamp from Mike and tossed it back into the box. "Here, let me take that," he said as he took the box from Kyrie's hands. "It's not really that bad. She just clings to things."

Kyrie stepped back. "All the boxes in the room need to come down here?" she confirmed.

Sam nodded his head. "Yup."

Kyrie turned without another word and headed back up to the room to finish the work the boys would take hours to do.

# Chapter 7

A fair amount of Kyrie's excess energy had burned off by the time she moved most of the boxes to the basement. Mike and Sam had initially been eager to show their virility in the effort, but they quickly tired, and the actual work fell to her while Sam and Mike played some form of combat game on the basement television.

Her aunt spent most of the time on the phone to various people and then disappeared for a while to return the car. Curiosity had slowed her movement through the entertainment room as the boys directed soldiers across the screen with handheld controllers. However, when they offered to let her play, she declined, wanting to finish the work set out for her before taking the time to relax.

Her aunt returned with food and called them all to dinner when there were just five boxes left to move. Kyrie obeyed the command and joined everyone at the kitchen table to eat something she heard them call pizza.

"Your cousin embarrasses you," her aunt said to Sam. "She's doing all the work that you, and Mike," she added, "should've done before we got home."

"It is okay, I have been looking to do something," Kyrie said. "Sitting for three days is not what I'm used to."

"It is still disgraceful," her aunt said. "Is that your third piece?" She asked, changing topics.

Kyrie looked down at the slice of pizza and nodded her head. "Am I not to eat that much?"

"You'll get fat if you eat like that. But then, you've been working all day." She looked at Kyrie from the corner of her eyes. "Just watch yourself. You're skinny now, but you eat too much, you'll gain weight, and that is not attractive, especially on someone as tall as you."

She kept her face neutral, but she found her aunt's advice insulting. *Eat based on what you do*, she said to herself. Her internal appraisal of her aunt continued to diminish. *Her veneer is showing*, Kyrie thought. *The more she barks, the less impressed you are. Just an NPC.*

Kyrie turned her attention to Sam and Mike. Their oscillating interest and distraction confused her. When they had helped move boxes, they both watched her, and she could feel them discussing her body. Then without warning, they would shift their conversation to sports and computer games. The randomness of their attention left her confused. Now they stared at her with an eager hunger.

"Did you have to grow all your own food?" Mike asked, drawing her out of her thoughts. "I mean, it sounded like you never had pizza before?"

Kyrie shook her head. "This is the first time I've had pizza." She considered her answer, hoping it would seem reasonable. "We planted plenty of vegetables and some fruit, but we didn't grow all of our food. My father brought us flour and some meat from the market." She glanced to the plate in front of her. The statement made her realize that her mother had remained as isolated in the valley as she. After her father died, her mother paid Ms. Conner to do extra shopping for them instead of going herself. She looked up. "I hunted when I could, though my father warned me to be discreet and not get caught because the police would get involved."

"Did you use the swords to hunt?" Mike asked.

"What'd you hunt?" Sam inquired at the same time.

Kyrie frowned. "Swords are not good for hunting. I used a bow or snares. Sometimes rabbits." She sighed. "Too many rabbits. I would occasionally bring down a deer." She continued eating her slice of pizza and eyed a fourth one. "That was always a lot of work to drag back though."

Her aunt placed her own half-eaten slice back on her plate. "Sounds terrible. Your mother should have done better." Kyrie watched as her aunt scrutinized her again. "Tomorrow we need to get you some new clothes. Charles, my lawyer, said it would be good to get you enrolled in school on Monday." She sighed. "I'll also need to buy you a dresser and a desk. I have to take care of you like I do for Sam. The judge will want to know that I'm meeting your basic needs."

Kyrie felt some of her aunt's surface thoughts leaking out of her head and knew she calculated every cost. *It is only what is in it for her.* Kyrie forced an expression of confusion to her face so she would not reveal her irritation.

Her aunt shook her head. "I'll need to take another vacation day to enroll you." She turned to Sam and Mike. "The two of you, having done so little while I brought Kyrie home, will be spending the day tomorrow helping me shop for Kyrie."

"Mom," Sam's distress filled the room and Kyrie's mind. "We just downloaded a new game and if we don't spend time on the beta, they'll drop us."

"Don't talk back to me. Kyrie says, 'yes ma'am' when I ask her to do something, perhaps you can learn from her."

Kyrie looked away, wondering where her aunt might keep important paperwork. Several of the boxes she had moved to the basement had folders in them. *Maybe you can find something on your parents.*

Kyrie woke well before dawn and slipped from the bed. She knew Mike had stayed the night and she could feel him and Sam in the basement. She assumed they were asleep, but she could not be certain at the distance. *And if you rummage around in the storage room it is likely you will wake them.*

She could feel her aunt asleep in her bedroom. *The office?* She expected her aunt would keep important things closer to her and not scattered in the chaos of the basement. However, Kyrie did not know how important her aunt considered her parents.

Still dressed in her clothing, Kyrie pulled on her shoes and carefully went into the hallway. She tried to quietly open the office door, but found it locked. She bit her lower lip. It would not be hard to open, but she did not want to risk waking her aunt from her light sleep. Frustrated at being blocked yet again, Kyrie descended the stairs to the first floor. Sam had told her the night before that the alarm was just for show and would not go off if the outside door opened. She winced at the memory of his complete disbelief that she did not understand how an alarm system worked. *It's not like you've had a chance to learn these things.* A bitter taste filled her mouth.

Resolved to put the thoughts from her, she unlocked the front door and stepped outside. *You need to burn off this energy.* The air was crisp, but not mountain cold. The lack of a jacket would resolve itself as soon as she started moving. Quietly closing the door behind her, she moved toward the street and started jogging. The streetlights, providing more light than she had most mornings, allowed her to easily navigate along the sidewalks.

She felt no one near her, and few, if any lights, were on in any of the homes. She turned down a side street, making note of the names on the street signs. Unlike a mountain trail where she needed to remember rocks and trees, here she had to remember names. *More differences.*

Kyrie picked up speed, moving from a jog into a full sprint. *Damn you both. This life is not like D&D. How dare you decide I should know nothing about it.* She felt guilt for showing anger at her parents, but the mixture of guilt and anger only pushed her harder. With the lower altitude, she knew the oxygen content would be richer and it would allow her to go further before exhaustion. *But is that something everyone knows, or is that something that will startle anyone you tell like microwaves did with Ms. Conner?*

Kyrie felt tears on her face and swung a fist at the air as she spun to a stop. Panting, she used her left hand to wipe her eyes. *We are alone. We are so alone.*

The acknowledgement hurt, but she could do nothing to change that. Instead, she concentrated on controlling her breathing and within moments her heart slowed to a normal pace. Still full of pent up energy, she turned right onto another side street and resumed a fast jog. She vowed to herself to memorize the neighborhood. "You always need to understand your surroundings," she heard herself say in her father's voice.

\*    \*    \*    \*    \*

Kyrie returned to her aunt's house just as the predawn light turned the sky red. She slipped back inside, confirmed everyone still slept, and then made her way to her bedroom. She pulled out a sketchbook and started working on another version of the images that had plagued her dreams for as long as she could remember.

This time, she focused in on a particular street with clay houses that had oval openings for doorways. The hot climate meant there were never any doors that would block the breeze or the small, winged lizards that ate all the bugs. The tall mountain remained a hazy form in the distance, just visible in the abstract behind the buildings.


"If you've never been to a city or a store, how'd you get your clothes?" Mike asked from the back seat of her aunt's vehicle, which Sam referred to as an SUV.

"My mother had a neighbor order my clothes for me. They would get delivered to Ms. Conner's house and we'd pay her back for them."

"So, you didn't have any computers. Did you even have electricity?" Sam asked.

"Do you know what electricity is?" Mike mumbled under his breath.

"Boys, leave Kyrie alone. She can't help what her parents did to her."

Kyrie turned her head to look at Sam. "Electricity is something we had, and I understand how electrons will oscillate at approximately sixty Hertz to generate the power you use when you plug something into an outlet. In most of the world, they work at fifty Hertz. Fifty Hertz is better for long distance transmissions and lowers the hum you might hear. However, Westinghouse wanted sixty Hertz because it reduced the flicker in their arc lamps, and so the U.S. is stuck with that standard."

"Okay." Sam slumped back in his seat.

Mike's lips turned up on one side. "Sounds like you memorized a science book."

Kyrie shook her head and turned back to face the front of the vehicle. "That's not science, that's history. Science is using the power of the universe to do something useful. History is knowing what other people did with science."

Her aunt cleared her throat. "Kids, settle down. We need to buy a lot of things for Kyrie today. Perhaps even get her a haircut."

"We'll be out all day," Sam complained again.

"I hope your battery brick is charged," Mike added.

Kyrie allowed the experience of shopping in department stores to wash over her. The masses of people forced her to keep her mind closed. While Sam, Mike, and her aunt had been a confusing mess, the mass of people at the stores gave her an instant headache.

She tried hard not to frustrate her aunt, but Kyrie found herself so far outside of her comfort zone that she continued to say and do the wrong things. She had assumed a single set of new clothing would be enough, but her aunt assured her that she needed at least a dozen shirts and nearly an equal number of pants. The requirement that they all be varied and yet match was never something she had discussed before with her mother. Something sturdy that would last rough treatment were the things her mother had bought for her. The items her aunt insisted she acquire were thin, often tight, and not very practical.

When it came to new shoes, her aunt said, "You're tall enough not to need heels, but a woman always needs some heels to make her ass look good at certain times." The choice of boots available to her were all made from thin leather and looked like they would not keep out water.

Underwear was different. Kyrie had no trouble understanding buying a dozen new pair of underwear and seven new bras.

She found Sam and Mike's obvious discomfort when she and her aunt looked for items in her size interesting. Up to that point, they had been quietly speculating about her, and other women in the store, now their cheeks were pink, and they could not make eye contact with anyone. Kyrie understood her ability to sense emotions was not something others could do, but the two of them seemed out of phase with even the obvious signs around them.

After the department stores, they made a trip across town to a monstrous building with nearly unlimited variation of furniture. They wandered along the twisting path that led through numerous sections until they arrived at a massive warehouse with shelves that towered over their heads. Kyrie knew Sam and Mike found the experience tiresome and she got the idea they had spent significant amounts of time in the store before.

Her aunt stopped at one last store for things she called 'essentials.' Kyrie found the idea that a person could need so many places to purchase things disturbing, but as she walked along, an alarm clock, soap, shampoo, brushes, and various health care items, some of which she had seen in Ms. Conner's bathroom, ended up in the basket. Her aunt, complaining about how much the day had cost her, decided Kyrie did not need any makeup, and Kyrie felt some relief that they had reached the end of the shopping experience. By the time they left, she had grown to feel sympathy for Sam and Mike, who had been dragged along through the whole day. *Today was a very long side quest with random loot to show for it.*

They took a slight detour on their way home and her aunt dropped Mike off at his parent's house. Kyrie noted that she had run past it early in the morning. Mentally, she retraced the route to her aunt's house. *We should probably call it our new house, at least for a while.* Happily, she remembered the route correctly and felt some measure of control returning to her life.

"Can I help?" Kyrie asked as Sam ripped open the boxes for her chest of drawers. Sam's bravado had diminished after they dropped Mike at his home. In fact, once they got home, Sam even helped show Kyrie how to use the washing machine and dryer.

"Sure. I still can't get over all the things you've never seen before."

Kyrie offered him a shrug. "I never thought about what I was missing until I saw all this."

"But you still had an awesome childhood. Swords, running around the mountains, not having to go to school. I would love that."

He set the screwdriver on the floor and then looked over at Kyrie. "I hate school. Such a waste of time."

Kyrie raised her eyebrows. "I loved learning from my mother. She taught me a lot."

Sam shrugged and returned to opening the boxes and stacking the various parts around him on the floor. "My mother is not capable of teaching." He sighed. "Sorry about Mike. We weren't that great to you so far. I've just never had a sister. Or even a brother."

"I've never had a brother or sister either. I've never even had a friend."

Sam reached out and place a hand on her arm. "I'm sorry about your mother. I'll try to look out for you." He sat back. "Don't date Mike. He's a good guy, but don't date him. He'd just try to get into your pants."

Kyrie tilted her head.

"Try to have sex with you."

"Oh." *That's what we were feeling from him.* She opened her mind a little more and searched Sam's emotions. The initial desire she had felt from him now felt more protective and less possessive. "My parents explained sex, but that is not something I think about."

Sam blushed. "Who's getting with who is a big topic at school. You're hot enough that you'll have a lot of guys after you." He sighed. "I'm not a jock and I'm just a freshman, so I can't really shield you from that."

Kyrie felt herself blushing as Sam stroked her ego. *You're pretty, despite what your aunt implies.* She returned her thoughts to what Sam had said and asked for clarification. "Freshman?"

"First year of high school. I'm guessing you'd be a sophomore or junior based on age. I was born in November, so I had to start later."

"My birthday is nineteen May," Kyrie offered.

"Stupid cut off is August thirty-first. I was mad because the kids my age are typically a year ahead. Lost a friend growing up because of it."

Kyrie nodded her head, though she did not fully understand the rules he referred to, she did not have the desire to press for more details. Instead, she shifted her focus to the parts on the floor. "How do these things go together?"

"Here's the instructions," Sam handed her the pamphlet. "No words, just pictures."


Kyrie woke early the next day and went for a run. She noted a change in the behavior of the rest of the neighborhood. While the numbers were not large, there was a percentage of homes with lights on and people awake. There were also more cars on the streets.

When she returned to her aunt's house, she showered and dressed in one of the new outfits. She managed to get her hair mostly tangle free and then pulled it back and tied it off with a piece of string as she often did at home. She returned to her room and pulled open the duffle bag with the Dungeons & Dragons books and campaign notes. Her desk had two small drawers and she carefully arranged the dice and miniatures in one drawer. She also removed her mother's mittens and set them beside the brooch that sat on her desk. Her earliest memories were of that green stone and she picked it up to look at it. It was not pretty. The irregular facets did not generate any internal glow and the stone more resembled a river rock, or a broken piece of tumbled glass, than jewelry. The metal showed wear and dirt. However, she still loved it.

She allowed a smile to come to her face and her happiness seemed to feed back into itself. For a moment she felt content. *Mother never left this out of her sight.*

She looked to the door when she felt her aunt approaching. A moment later, the door opened, and her aunt peeked her head through the opening. "You're up early. Perhaps you can get Sam out of bed and moving. I don't have time to deal with him this morning." She started to back out of the room and then pushed her head back in. "I've changed my mind; you do need some make up...and someone to style your hair. Nothing to do about it now, but...well, you could be passable with a little attention." Her aunt smiled and then shut the door.

Kyrie felt her irritation rise exponentially. No direct malice came from her aunt, the woman simply did not think her pretty. *Screw you!* The anger in Kyrie fed back on itself and she tossed her mother's brooch into her duffle bag with more force than she would otherwise have used.

A wave of despair passed through her and she slid from the chair to the floor. She fished the brooch out of the bag. "Damn it," she mumbled, noticing the bent filigree. She fought back the tears that wanted to burst free and she caressed the face of the stone while she examined the back. One side of the clasp broke and she could no longer lock the pin in place.

*Damn it.* She pushed her aunt's lingering thoughts from her head. *Mother always said we were pretty. Don't let that woman make you think differently.*

"Kyrie, you need to get Sam moving or he'll be late for school," her aunt called from the other room.

Kyrie breathed slowly and released the energy she had absorbed. She pointedly stood up and put the brooch in the drawer with the dice. She did not like her aunt, but refusing an order of an adult would make her day even worse.

Sam did not respond to her calling his name, so she entered his room and shook his shoulder. The obvious embarrassment of being mostly naked in her presence startled him awake. He gathered his blankets around himself and demanded she leave. Still reeling somewhat from her aunt's thoughts, she had kept her mind closed, but suspected Sam had been dreaming about something he did not want others to know about.

She went back to her room and shut the door so Sam could use the bathroom they now shared. She resumed her work with the duffle bag, pulling out papers and books, sorting and organizing the items she had hastily gathered before leaving the cabin. By the time Sam finished in the shower, she had several neat stacks on the top of her small desk.

She pulled a bundle of notes from the top of the stack of Dungeons & Dragons campaigns and started reading her mother's handwriting. She looked up as Sam knocked on her door. "Come in," she responded.

"Hey, sorry about yelling earlier."

She smiled at him. "I was in your room, but your mother insisted I wake you. I couldn't tell her no."

He chuckled. "Yeah, well, you'll find she can be a pain in the ass. But I just wanted to let you know that I've got your back."

She looked at him and tried to puzzle out the statement.

"I will protect you," he clarified.

"Sorry. Unless my parents used a phrase, I have trouble figuring out the meaning sometimes."

The two of them heard Sam's mother bellow for them from downstairs.

"Don't let school, or my mother, get to you. The school is big and if some people are rude, there will be others who will be nice."

Kyrie set aside her papers and got up from her desk to follow Sam downstairs. "Thanks."


Kyrie found the process of entering the school intimidating. Her aunt explained Olathe Central opened the year before with the idea of security first. Eight-foot-high fencing surrounded the facility. All vehicles and people entering had to check in at a guarded gate.

At the main building, Kyrie had to pass through a rectangular arch, which her aunt called a metal detector. Her clear plastic backpack went separately through a scanner, which Kyrie looked at closely to puzzle out how it functioned. She had some ideas, but she dared not linger long because of the large queue of students trying to enter the half dozen lanes.

The cacophony of noise, both mental and physical, left her jumping at various sounds and movements. Everyone, except for her, appeared to know where to go, what to do, and how to act. She now understood the fear of a deer when it realized someone stalked it with the intent to turn it into food.

Sam headed away from Kyrie and his mother. "Meet me here after classes," he called out as he merged into the mass of students. "I'll make sure you get home."

"This way," her aunt said, grabbing her arm to lead her into a glass enclosed room that contained several people on both sides of a counter.

Kyrie offered no resistance; she simply followed behind her aunt. She noted the rather heated conversation between two students and a lady behind the counter.

"I have warned you before, Liz." The woman's short brown hair bounced around her head as she waved a hand at the closer girl. "I'm tired of your protest stunts. This is not appropriate." The woman indicated a clear plastic backpack filled with small rectangular packages.

"It's not my fault you insist on having stupid clear backpacks." The girl flung her deep reddish-brown hair over her shoulder. "All the boys get to know when I'm on my period because they can see my tampons, I might as well advertise when I'm in the mood."

"It is disgraceful," said another girl, wearing a green sweater over a t-shirt and jeans; the acid in her tone matched the hate in her eyes. "She's advertising sex. The slut."

"Jessica, there will be none of that from you," the woman behind the counter said.

"You're just mad that there are no condoms left for you and now you can't do your boyfriend between classes," Liz said loud enough for everyone to hear.

Jessica swung a hand to slap the first girl but missed.

"Stop it now!" The woman behind the counter demanded. "You'll both end up suspended." The woman looked over at Kyrie and her aunt, then back to the girls. "You two stand here quietly while I take care of this." Over her shoulder, she added, "Liz, take the condoms out and put them on the counter. I'll give them back at the end of the day, if you behave yourself."

Kyrie's aunt cleared her throat. "I need to enroll my niece."

The woman behind the counter raised her eyebrows. "Mrs. Leighton, it is already April. Term is almost over. Far too late to do a transfer from another district."

Kimberly crossed her arms. "Her mother died last week. Her father last June. I had to fly out to Colorado and bring her home. I'm the last of her family and I'm her guardian. This is not some favor to a relative to move my niece to another district. She is now my responsibility and needs to be in school."

*You won't be our guardian for that long,* Kyrie thought, the smug tone of her aunt and the hostility of the two girls bleeding emotion into her mind despite her trying to keep it out. She took a moment to clear her thoughts. *You need to learn to filter out other people. They are making us testy.*

"I am sorry for your loss, my dear," the woman said to Kyrie.

"It is okay, ma'am. I'm adjusting as best as I can." Kyrie heard the second girl snicker softly, but everyone ignored the sound.

The woman behind the counter turned back to her aunt. "Mrs. Leighton, I—"

"Miss Leighton, please, Carol."

The woman behind the counter deflated. "Miss Leighton, do you have all of your niece's paperwork?"

Her aunt handed over a folder. "Those are copies of the documents the judge signed that make me her temporary guardian until they complete the final processing. I also have her birth certificate, which my mother had acquired when my sister ran off and disappeared." Her aunt paused, looked at Kyrie, and then back to the lady behind the counter. "She's sixteen with a May nineteen birthdate, which should make her a junior based on your website, but she was home schooled by her mother, so I'm not sure where she falls."

"No transcripts? Do you have any tests or results filed with the state of Colorado?"

"There were none. My sister…let's just say, she had her own issues. The doctors said Kyrie's birth left her special."

Kyrie narrowed her eyes, the tone around the word 'special' held no compliment. She also noted the two other girls in the office paying close attention to the conversation. Despite the fact that she stood several inches taller than both girls, she straightened anyway.

"Miss Leighton, this makes it very hard for me to enroll her."

"Well, I sure can't home school her. She needs real lessons and the longer she waits, the further behind she'll be. Can't you enroll her in the basic classes and allow her to take finals and see where she lands? If she fails all of them, we can put her in summer school, or even make her take the year over again next year. If she's held back, I will just have to extend my guardianship until she is able to catch up."

Kyrie's eyes widened. Her resolve to play stupid fought every instinct in her body. *You do not fail things!* She told herself. *But that is exactly what Kim Lym wants.* "I—"

"Miss Leighton, I cannot—"

"My lawyer was adamant that I get her enrolled. I can have him contact the superintendent," her aunt tilted her head, "if you think that is necessary."

The woman behind the counter shrunk in size. "I can put her in basic algebra and some of the other junior classes. Phys-ed is easy, since we changed the curriculum to make it mandatory for every year. Basic English and government."

Kyrie's initial response was one of loathing. Her mother would have NPCs behave rudely, but her facial expressions and voice never took Kimberly's tone, even when the NPC was at its worst. *Learn from this.* "Ma'am, I've done advanced math," Kyrie interjected, not wanting to be thought of as needing a basic algebra class.

Her aunt leaned further over the counter. "Her mother did know physics, but…" she shrugged.

The woman behind the counter paused, looked at Kyrie, then her aunt, before she deflated again and typed some more into her computer. "Has she been immunized?"

"I do not want to be enrolled in basic algebra," Kyrie said, taking a small step closer.

"You don't want to be overwhelmed," her aunt told her. To the woman behind the counter, Kimberly said, "I will need one of the forms for religious exemptions."

"Miss Leighton…"

Kyrie watch the woman behind the counter slowly cross her arms. "Ma'am, I'm not religious," Kyrie said, hoping someone would listen to her.

Her aunt turned on her and hardened the tone of her voice. "My sister ran off to live on a mountain in Colorado with no computers, no Internet, no phone, and no contact with the outside world. If she didn't do that for religious reasons, then you tell me why."

Kyrie wanted to explain that people had chased her, but she held her tongue.

Her aunt took a deep breath and turned back to the lady behind the counter. "I will get her added to my insurance once I get back to work, then I'll find her a doctor and get her shots. But until then, I can't have a teenage girl, who doesn't know anything about the world, running around unsupervised." Her aunt looked at the backpack that still had most of the condoms in it. "She'd be pregnant within the month."

"I would—" Kyrie started to challenge that accusation.

"Silence," her aunt demanded.

Kyrie stepped back, expecting pain from compulsion. Her brows narrowed when the pressure on her mind and body never materialized.

Her aunt turned back to the counter. "See? You know my son and his friends. I know how boys think and I won't allow my niece to be unsupervised. So, please give me the form and I will sign it."

Kyrie met the eyes of the woman behind the counter and felt the stares of the two girls who stood off to the side. Their earlier argument apparently forgotten.

"Kyrie? Kyrie Landvik, that is your name?" The woman behind the counter asked.

"Answer her," her aunt said after a moment.

"Yes, ma'am."

"Okay, your ID will be LandvikK. I'll get you a tablet in a moment. We don't issue textbooks anymore. Everything will be on the tablet with perhaps the exceptions of some workbooks. You'll need to set it up, but we have instructions for that, and I can assign someone to help you if you have trouble." The woman looked over at the two girls. "Liz, finish getting those condoms out of the bag. Jessica, you are late for first period. Get to class."

The woman moved to the opposite end of the counter. "Kyrie, stand over on the green square and we'll get a picture for your ID and accounts. Miss Leighton, how will you be paying the fees?"

"Credit card," her aunt replied, pulling out the small piece of plastic from her purse. As she handed over the credit card, Kimberly turned to Kyrie. "Make sure to go home with Sam. I don't want you to get lost. I have things to do and won't be home until later."

"Yes, ma'am."

The woman behind the counter looked at the other student. "Liz, you get to class as well."

# Chapter 8

Carol from the office escorted Kyrie to her second period class. The paperwork took enough time that the first period had passed, and they were already twenty minutes into the second period. "It may take a little getting used to, but I'm sure you'll adjust in no time. I'm sorry again about the loss of your mother."

Kyrie nodded her head, unwilling to speak about her mother yet again. All the people offering her condolences or sympathy annoyed her instead of giving her comfort. *Why can't they just leave it alone?*

She push the thoughts away and examined the building as they walked through another corridor. The school seemed huge and the number of rooms astounded her. *This could be a dungeon to explore. A different trap and test behind each door.* Kyrie smiled at the memories of random dungeon crawls her parents would occasionally throw into a campaign. Those few times provided pure entertainment of exploration instead of a means to teach her how to interact with others.

"We have over two thousand students between ninth and twelve grades," the woman said to Kyrie's apparent wondering gaze, but Kyrie barely heard. "Everything is state-of-the-art. Your ID will get you in and out of the school, check you in and out of classrooms, sports games, and even pay for lunch. Your tablet will show your schedule and even has maps of the school to show you which building, and which wing you need to be in for each class."

Kyrie looked down at the piece of electronics in her hand. The instruction she received for setting up the device did not go into how to use it. She just knew her face unlocked the thin screen. She expected she could find the application with her class schedule again. The rest would require help or take time to work out.

The woman continued talking. "We even have reinforced doors and windows that will stop a bullet, so you don't have to worry about an assault on the school."

Kyrie nodded her head, unsure of what the woman wanted her to say. *Is everyone running from someone? If we are in danger, why consolidate us in one place?*

The woman stopped in front of a door and drew Kyrie's attention to a small plastic box on the wall. "You need to badge into and out of every room. Just flash your ID against the reader and that way if something happens, we know exactly where everyone is."

Kyrie pressed the ID to the box as instructed. A small green light illuminated at the top of the reader and something clicked in the door. The woman reached down to the handle, turned it, and pushed the door open.

Her senses told her the room contained twenty-one people. A African American woman stood next to a white wall with a red marker in her hand. Kyrie thought the other twenty people sitting in rows of desks, looked to be around her age. She straightened and swallowed, intimately aware everyone stared at her. She shut everything out of her mind; the jumbled thoughts hitting her made her wobble in place.

"Miss Pelni," the woman from the office said. "This is Kyrie Landvik. She is a new student."

Miss Pelni raised her eyebrows and examined Kyrie. Kyrie held herself to the inspection and then Miss Pelni turned her attention to the woman behind Kyrie. "There is not much time left in the term."

"I know. But there are extenuating circumstances. Do you have a moment to talk in the hall?"

Miss Pelni put the cap on the pen and set it on her desk. "Please take a seat," she said to Kyrie as she walked past and went into the hallway, the door closed behind her.

Kyrie looked around at the classroom. Four large televisions hung from the left-hand wall. Mathematical formulas scrolled across the screens. The right-wall's white surface mirrored that of the front of the classroom. Handwritten quadratic equations covered that wall, several included the answers, a few remained unsolved. She glanced at the front wall and noted the first half of a proof for the Pythagorean Theorem written in red.

Aware of the attention on her, she looked at the two empty seats in the front row. Both seats put her in proximity to boys who grinned at her not unlike the way Mike had. The only other seat not taken put her in the back of the room two rows away from the girl she saw in the office. *Jessica,* Kyrie recalled.

She headed toward the back to avoid the desires of the boys in the front row. Along the way, a girl with long curly hair offered a small smile that she returned.

"She was home schooled," whispered Jessica to a boy next to her.

Kyrie looked in Jessica's direction and the girl smiled broadly. The glint in her eyes shone of pure pleasure. *Not your prey, Jessica.*

Miss Pelni returned to the room, stood in front of her teacher's desk, and then leaned against it. "Kyrie, I don't mean to put you on the spot, but I need to understand your math skills before I waste both of our time."

"Yes, ma'am," Kyrie replied.

"Do you understand the calculation on the whiteboard next to you?"

Kyrie did not bother looking at the equations; she had seen them when she entered. "Yes, ma'am," she said formally. Kyrie heard a snicker from one of the other students, but she did not know who it came from. *What's funny?*

"Can you describe them? Can you solve for x?"

Kyrie glanced at the board and then back to the teacher. "Quadratic equations tell you where a curve will cross the x-axis. The value of x in the first equation will be either -2 or 5. The second one 0.125 or 0.675."

"You certain?" the teacher asked with a slight tilt of her head and challenge in her voice.

"Yes, ma'am. I've been solving quadratic equations since I was five."

A murmur went through the class and the word 'autistic' bounced between the students. Kyrie could not help but feel the disbelief coming from those around her. *Play stupid,* she reminded herself.

"Got a tongue on you." Miss Pelni folded her arms across her chest. "Think you're better than public school because you had a dedicated home school environment?"

Kyrie's eyes widened. "No, ma'am. I am sorry. It wasn't my intention to be rude. I…I just have…I understand algebra is all."

"What's on the board behind me?"

"Ma'am, you've started Bhaskar's first proof of the Pythagorean Theorem."

Miss Pelni's eyes widened, this time in honest surprise. "So, what has your mother been teaching you?"

"Ma'am, I finished her course on linear algebra two years ago. She set me to work on trying to solve the Toeplitz conjecture when I'm not studying physics." Kyrie clarified when she saw Miss Pelni's expression. "The inscribed square problem."

"Why are you in my basic algebra class?"

Kyrie shrugged. "I was told to be silent when my aunt enrolled me." Kyrie heard more snickers and this time Miss Pelni glanced at the class.

"Well, for today, just sit there. We'll have to have a conversation with the office later."


After the basic algebra class, Kyrie managed to make her way to her third period by asking a couple of students for directions. She lacked the required workout clothing to participate, so she watched other students run around the indoor track. She understood the next day they would discuss nutrition and she tried unsuccessfully to pull up the textbook on her tablet.

After physical education, she made her way to government, where Professor Earl Donigan put her in the front of the class while he discussed civil liberties. Kyrie fished her sketchbook from her backpack and started taking notes on a blank page. She knew the names and dates Mr. Donigan rattled off would likely appear on a test, but she doubted she would remember them without significant study.

The class ran longer than the prior two because the students rotated through the large open area in the main building to eat lunch. When her class was released as the third, and final, group for food, she followed the other students, stood in queue, paid for her lunch with her ID, and then sat down at a table to eat. Many people looked in her direction, but few people spoke to her, even the other students at her table.

*Sam may be right, this could become a very tiresome consumption of our time.* Learning had always been pleasurable on the mountain, but the mechanical nature of the government class gave her almost physical pain. *These classes don't seem to be of much use. You need to figure out what your aunt might know before Lars gets his papers filed.*

She exhaled and stopped eating the pasta on her tray. The taste and consistency were wrong. She missed the food from the mountain.

"Hey, Kyrie," Jessica said as she sat down at the table across from her. A moment later, two boys sat down, one on her right, and the other next to Jessica. "My name's Jessica. We met in the office this morning and had algebra together. I could not help but hear your aunt. I'm sorry that your mother died."

*Again?* "Thank you." Kyrie keep her arms in close to her body. The boy next to her sat only a few inches away and the proximity made it harder to keep his thoughts and emotions at bay.

"That's Steve," she said, pointing to the blond boy that sat too close. "This is John," Jessica indicated the olive toned boy next to her.

"Hey," both boys said in turn.

"How is your first day going," Jessica asked. "I imagine the transition to public school is rough."

Kyrie narrowed her eyes. Her few attempts to allow in the surrounding emotions had left her overwhelmed. *You don't need to read thoughts. Whenever mother got sugary sweet in game, the NPC wanted something. Just figure out what Jessica wants?* "It has been different," Kyrie admitted aloud.

"So, your parents home schooled you?" Steve asked. "What was that like? Lots of praying?"

Kyrie turned her head so she could see Steve's face. The width of his grin irritated her. "I'm not sure what you mean. Why would I be praying?"

"Your aunt said your parents were part of a cult. But we know that home schooled kids might find life in a large school difficult," Jessica said, leaning over the table to get closer as she lowered her voice. "A much larger body of students. Not a small network of like-minded, religious people. There is sex here. The scandalous behavior of Liz with all the condoms this morning." Jessica tilted her head as her eyes widened.

"Well, until last week, I never heard the word home schooled. I just learned what my mother and father taught me. No praying involved. No cult."

"Really?" John's arm moved around Jessica's shoulders.

"What was growing up like?" Jessica leaned into John to prevent him from saying anything more.

*You might as well admit what they already know or will hear. Stupid Kim Lym. Plus, more will leak out from Sam.* "I had a quiet childhood. I learned a lot. We played games. I helped farm and hunt."

Steve leaned forward to get into her line of sight. "You're saying your parents didn't make you do rituals and things? I don't believe it. You had to do some. Jessica heard what your aunt said."

John spoke up. "Jessica also said you were like some god with math, but then I heard you almost cried in gov."

John's comment passed over her; the closeness of Steve pressed on her mind. *Don't give in to them!* She pushed down the urge to move seats and straightened her back as she drew energy into her body.

The power warmed her flesh as it coursed through her mind and body. It cleared her head of their emotional pressure. Her voice hardened. "I'm not sure what your intent is, but I'm not your prey."

"What?" Jessica said, sitting back, a frown forming on her face. "We were just trying to be friendly."

Kyrie shook her head. "No. You failed to intimidate me. You came over and sat down with your NPC thugs to make me uncomfortable. I've looked into the deep brown eyes of a mother bear with a cub. That is a predator worthy of respect. I don't know what you want, but this doesn't come close to raising the hairs on my arms."

"Bitch. I will ruin you." Jessica leaned over the table and lowered her voice. "I make and break people in this school. Your life will be nothing. You'll wish you had died with your parents."

Kyrie shook her head. "Is this school that central to your existence? Is your very identity tied to your position here? That seems sad."

"I will end you," Jessica growled.

Kyrie leaned forward. The security staff around the edge of the lunch area appeared bored and uninterested, but that would not last if she attacked the three students. *A shot to Steve's throat or nose should give you time to deal with John. Just need to move fast enough to avoid the wardens.*

She pushed the thoughts of a fight from her mind. It would only take one adult to compel them to stop. There would be nothing they could do to avoid that. *Besides, these three are puffed cats trying to look big.* "I'm not afraid of you. And if you had not noticed, Liz does not fear you either. Which means your rule of this school is on shaky ground."

Steve chuckled and shook his head. After a withering look from Jessica, he added, "That wasn't at you. I was thinking what you'll do to this ugly, gangly, twig on poles."

Kyrie forced herself to keep from tensing in case she needed to react quickly from wherever the threat might come. The insult meant nothing to her.

Jessica stood up. "You'll regret this, Bitch." The angry girl stormed away with John and Steve stumbling out of their chairs to catch up to her.

The energy in her burned and Kyrie smiled as she released it as a gravitational force that stuck Jessica's feet to the floor. Her use of power had no visible effect beyond the blonde girl falling and landing on her tray of food.

Jessica cried out in surprise, then fear, and then embarrassed anger. Several students in the area laughed and giggled as she stood up, her clothing stained with the remnants of her lunch. Kyrie's smile grew, but then she frowned. *Probably shouldn't have done that. But it was fun.*

Kyrie looked down at the tray in front of her as Steve and John helped Jessica to her feet. She ignored the unfolding scene and picked up a cookie. It was hard, but it tasted better than the pasta.

Kyrie sighed as she entered her fifth period art class several minutes after the bell rang. She felt the two dozen students looking at her from behind their easels as the door shut. *Center of attention, yet again.* A young woman, barely older than anyone else in the class, moved out from behind an easel. The short woman wiped her hands on her paint-covered apron as she crossed the room.

"You must be Kyrie," the woman said. "I'm Mrs. Stine."

"I'm sorry I'm late," Kyrie said. "I had trouble finding the classroom."

"Don't make a habit of that and you'll be fine." Mrs. Stine smiled. "How is your day going? A bit hectic I'm guessing."

Kyrie nodded her head.

The teacher put her hand on Kyrie's shoulder. "First day at a new school is always challenging. I was home schooled as well. That adjustment takes a bit longer to get used to. Too many people will make assumptions about you and home schooling. Don't let them bother you. Home schooling can provide lots of advantages, such as no overly large class sizes. Most people would be jealous if they truly understood."

The teacher turned back toward the circle of easels that surrounded a collection of potted plants. Most of the plants were shades of green with some yellow tones. The only real variation came from the shape and texture of the leaves and the brightly colored pots. "I took the liberty of setting up an easel for you, but the class has been working on this still life since last week and the time is almost up on it. Instead, I will have you practice with a value study. It involves a series of boxes all shaded between the lightest and darkest values."

Kyrie followed Mrs. Stine across the room. She stopped in front of the easel Mrs. Stine had been standing behind. A large sheet of white paper greeted her.

"Is that a sketch book I see in your bag?" the teacher asked.

"Yes, ma'am," Kyrie replied. "I thought I might have some spare time in the classes. I often draw when I don't have anything else to do."

"I don't imagine you've had a lot of free time today."

"No, ma'am."

"Kyrie, I'm definitely not old enough to be a ma'am. I'm just twenty-six. Call me Sara. Everyone in my classes do."

"Yes, Sara."

"May I look at your sketches?"

Kyrie set down her clear backpack, pulled out the sketchbook, and handed it to Mrs. Stine. She noticed the girls at the easels on either side of her peeked around the edge of their work to watch.

Mrs. Stine opened the book to the first page. "Dice. Lots of dice. Good shading and shadows." She continued to turn pages and make small comments. "That is a very nice rendering of a dragon."

The brunette on the left moved closer to look at the next drawing. "Wow, that is some library."

Kyrie looked at the page. She drew the living area in the cabin during a winter snowstorm. The table, covered with Dungeons & Dragons books, maps, dice, and miniatures, had inspired her. However, the background, with all the shelves of books drawn in precise detail, simply consumed idle time.

The blonde girl to her right peeked over Mrs. Stine's other side. "You play D&D?"

"Girls, I put Kyrie between you because you wouldn't stop talking. It wasn't an invitation for you to bother her."

"But look at the detail," the blonde said. "You can make out the titles of the books and even the character sheets on the table. Are those old DM screens?"

"Tina, you should be finishing your drawing," Mrs. Stine said, though her tone lacked any real demand, or even request. "Kyrie, do you mind if they look through your book?"

Kyrie shook her head. "No. They're just things I've drawn."

"I want to see them," said a boy from across the room and then several others added their demands to his.

Mrs. Stine raised an eyebrow to Kyrie.

"I don't mind," Kyrie replied. She did not need to open her mind to sense the awe and excitement her work had evoked from the girls on either side of her. *Don't get too proud of yourself.*

"Okay everyone, please come around. Be polite and introduce yourselves to Kyrie and we can take time to look through her sketchbook. But this doesn't mean you will get extra time on the still life. If you don't finish, you'll need to stay after school tonight to complete your work."

The twenty students left their work and gathered in an open area around four tall tables. Each one offered their names as they passed by Kyrie. Once everyone settled in a place they could see from, Mrs. Stine held up the drawings. As she flipped the pages, she offered more detailed critiques of each one. Most comments remained complimentary, though several times she offered suggestions around line quality. A few centered around balancing the compositions, but everyone agreed Kyrie had a great talent.

"I'll find something other than a values study for you to work on," Mrs. Stine said as she closed the book and handed it back to Kyrie.

Kyrie smiled and felt herself standing taller. The worry about the government class and the people at lunch now forgotten. She always felt her drawings superior but hearing confirmation from so many others energized her.

"Okay, everyone back to work. You need to finish today. I will set something new up tomorrow."

Kyrie disbanded with everyone else and walked to the easel assigned to her. She put her sketchbook away and waited for Mrs. Stine, who rummaged through objects against the far wall.

"I'm Michelle, in case you forgot with all the other names," said the brunette on her left.

"And I'm Tina," the blonde said. "You play D&D?"

"I did," Kyrie said. "I played with my parents almost every day."

Tina's eyes got big. "Every day. That's a lot of play time. But with your parental units? That's a bit weird."

"I didn't have anyone else to play with."

"Tina, don't judge," Michelle said. "Where'd you move from?"

"Colorado," Kyrie replied. "My mother died last week. I'm living with my aunt now."

"Oh my god, I'm so sorry," Michelle came around the easel and wrapping her arms around Kyrie.

Kyrie stood fixed in place, uncertain what she should do. Instinct wanted her to break away, but she felt no malice or threat from the girl that held her.

"Are you okay?" Michelle ask, taking a step back, but keeping her hands on Kyrie's arms.

"I'm so sorry as well," Tina said. "Why are you even here? I don't like my mother, but I'd be devastated if she died. Where's your father if you're living with your aunt?"

"He died last June," Kyrie said, then quickly added, "There isn't anything to be done about it."

Michelle grabbed her and wrapped her arms around her again, clenching her.

"Girls," Mrs. Stine said, a trace of disapproval in her voice.

"Sara, did you know Kyrie lost her mother last week," Tina said loud enough that the others in the room started to murmur comments. "And her father last June."

"Kyrie, is that true?" the teacher asked.

*Kim Lym already told everyone, so it is not a secret.* "It is true, but I'm okay."

Mrs. Stine set down the white ball and the white plate she held. "Are you sure you're okay? The office didn't fill me in on the details, they just told me you'd be starting today and that you'd been home schooled."

"Please," Kyrie said, breaking contact from Michelle, "I'm fine. I'm strong. My parents taught me to be."

Mrs. Stine looked uncomfortable and Kyrie wondered if her youth factored into that response. The other adults had limited their reaction to pity. "Well the class is half over, so I'll let you just draw what you like today, or just rest, then you can start with everyone else tomorrow."

"Thank you, Sara," Kyrie said, finding the teacher's age made it easier to not say 'ma'am.'

"Let me give you my number," Michelle said and Kyrie could not school away her questioning expression fast enough. "My phone number," she clarified. "We can text and meet up later. I want to see some of your other drawings. Plus, Tina and I are part of a D&D group. I think we can make room to add another player, if you are interested."

"Text?" Kyrie asked.

"You're joking?" Skepticism dripped from Tina's mouth.

"I don't know what you mean."

"You have a phone, right?" Michelle probed and Kyrie shook her head. "OMG, your parents didn't allow you to have a phone."

"My parents treated me just fine. They didn't abuse me." Kyrie looked down at the hand Michelle put on her arm.

"Oh, no, I wasn't saying they did. Let's talk. You need to tell me everything."

Kyrie would have forced Michelle to let go, but the physical contact allowed Michelle's thoughts to leak into her mind and she felt the other girl's desperate desire to help. After a moment more of consideration, Kyrie nodded her head. "Okay."

"Girls," Mrs. Stine said, "you really need to finish your drawings. Talk after class."

Both Tina and Michelle gave her an understanding smile and went back to their drawings. Kyrie turned to her own blank piece of paper. *Can they lie with their thoughts or is what you felt the truth?* She did not know; she did not have enough experience reading other people to feel confident one way or the other. *Mother told you to trust no one. But we really need someone to explain things to us.* She bit her lip and decided to make these two her friends.


Her sixth period physics class did not go as well as the algebra class or art class. Mr. Ulnrich told her if she already knew the material that she would likely pass the tests, but he would not customize his class to accommodate one student over the other pupils. As a result, she sat quietly and endured a lecture on acceleration, a subject she mastered a decade prior. The class ended with a homework assignment that she expected would take her no more than five minutes to complete.

History rounded out the day and she now understood Sam's aversion to school. *You will never learn all that in time,* she admitted to herself as she followed the other students to the school exit. The concept of failure had remained foreign to her until her fourth period government class. Now seventh period history felt even worse.

"Hey, Kyrie," a skinny boy her own height called at her from down the crowded hall. His brown hair a bit rough and disordered, but almost in an intentional fashion. He pushed through the crowd to get to her. "I'm Jake, Michelle's friend. She asked me to catch you as you came out of history." He held up his phone to show her a bit of text on the screen, but he turned it away before she had a chance to read anything except for her name. "She wanted to meet up after classes and didn't want you to sneak out the front door."

Kyrie looked into the boy's brown eyes and searched for anything that might give him away as being false.

"You're Kyrie, right?" He asked.

"I am. I just don't know you."

He chuckled. "You wouldn't, 'cause we haven't met yet." He extended his hand. "Jake. It is a pleasure to make your acquaintance. Oh," he added quickly, "my condolences about your mother and father."

Kyrie sensed his genuineness through the physical contact. "Thank you. I'm supposed to meet my cousin, though."

"Well, let's get Michelle…and I'm sure Tina will be there too… and then we can find your cousin." Jake offered his bent arm to Kyrie. She looked at his elbow and she turned her head slightly. After a few moments of her silent gaze he retracted his arm. "Sorry, I was just trying to be a gentleman. Didn't mean to insult you."

She shook her head. "I don't understand. Why did you show me your elbow?"

Jake chuckled. "Sorry, Michelle said you were home schooled. No boy-girl dances I'm guessing?" He started walking. "Let's talk on the way."

Kyrie moved to stay at Jake's side as he led them through the thinning students. "I really didn't know anyone else. My parents didn't dance. Though I liked to on my own."

"Kyrie," Michelle called as they entered the main hall. The brunette rushed over with Tina and another girl right behind her. The third girl had long black hair that hung straight down. She stood about Tina's height and had a definite Asian heritage. "This is Aki. She's part of our group."

"Hey," Aki said as she shifted her book-bag on her shoulder. "Michelle says you play D&D."

"I did," Kyrie said. She glanced over toward the exit and saw Sam and Mike standing next to each other. Both stared at their phones. She turned back to the people surrounding her. "I was told to meet my cousin so he could make sure I got home."

Michelle smiled. "I've got my full license last month. I can drive us all home. Save you from having to walk."

"I can't," Jake said. "I've got practice, which if I don't get going, I'll be late for."

"Oh, great First Murderer," Aki said, "break a leg."

Jake bowed to Aki. "Oh, Sarcastic One, I will get you interested in Macbeth if it is my final act." He turned to Kyrie. "Please don't tell them all the good things about yourself without me. I want to hear something fantastic about you firsthand."

Kyrie looked around at the group that had formed around her. With the bulk of the students having exited the building, she opened herself slightly and felt no hostilities from those near her. "I guess I can, but I didn't know I was going to be telling anyone anything."

Michelle stepped closer and put a hand on her arm. "You don't have to tell us anything you don't want to, but honestly, we really want to get to know you. Your artwork is amazing. And we could use a sixth person in the D&D group."

"Hey, Kyrie," Sam called as he walked over to the group. "We waited for you. What's the hold up?"

"Sam? Mike?" Michelle asked and then crossed her arms and turned to Kyrie. "Sam is your cousin?"

"Yes, why?" Kyrie turned her attention between the two.

Mike laughed at Michelle. "Had you come home at a reasonable time last night, I would have told you. But no, you were out until Mom and Dad were just about to ground you."

"Well," Michelle said to Kyrie, ignoring Mike, "you've met my younger brother. I apologize."

# Chapter 9

"You can only take Kyrie to your house if you give me and Mike a ride as well," Sam demanded.

"My car does not fit six people," Michelle countered. "The two of you can walk."

"Tina is seventeen," Mike challenged.

"So?" Tina glared at Mike. "I haven't bothered to get my unrestricted license yet. I can't drive any of you anywhere and I'm not supposed to drive to people's houses." She crossed her arms. "Plus, I don't have my car here."

"That's not fair," Mike said. "I don't want to walk. It's nearly a mile."

"I run at least nine miles every morning," Kyrie said, not wanting to miss a chance to put Mike on the spot for his attempts to show off his physical prowess on Saturday and Sunday.

"Really?" Tina asked. "Before school?"

"No, you don't," Sam challenged.

"I do. I've gotten up early yesterday and today and went for a run. I used to run up and down the mountain road at home. That was four and a half miles each way. This area is flat, which means there's not much of a challenge, so I press for speed."

"At what time?" Sam demanded.

"I get up around oh-four hundred. Do my run, then come back and read until everyone else starts getting up."

Mike shook his head. "Freak."

"For that, you walk. Come on, Kyrie, I'll show you where we do our homework and then we can play." Michelle took Kyrie's hand and started leading her toward the exit.

"Becca going to be coming as well?" Aki asked. "I didn't see her in class today."

"She's sick," Tina answered without looking up from her phone.

Kyrie could not place the odor coming from inside Michelle's car. There was only a hint of the pungent smell, but it was still discernible. She considered asking if it was intentional, but she did not want to insult her new friends.

"Sorry about that," Michelle said when she noticed Kyrie's nose wrinkle. "My older brother had the car before he went to college. One of his friends, or so he claims, puked in the back. We've tried everything except ripping out the carpet to get rid of the smell, but it keeps coming back."

"It's not the carpet," Aki said, "you need to rip out the seats. He let it soak in for at least a week."

"It's not that bad," Kyrie said. Michelle had insisted she sit in the front seat while Aki and Tina sat in the back.

"We've gotten used to it," Tina said. "Plus, Michelle is the only one who really drives us anywhere, so we take what we can get."

"How were your classes?" Michelle asked.

Kyrie opened her mind a little more and felt the genuine interest from the others. Her instinct to conceal everything melted away and she found it a relief to have people to talk to. "I didn't make it to first period. I'm worried about that English class in case it is like government and history. I don't think I'll catch up in those two. I shouldn't be in algebra, and Miss Pelni agrees, though I don't know that they will move me. Phys-ed isn't a concern. Art was good, but physics boring. The only plus is that it won't take any time."

"Physics boring?" Aki asked. "You mad? That stuff is terrible. I've made it a point to avoid that—and math—as much as I can."

"My mother was a physics professor at MIT," Kyrie said. "I've been doing advanced math and physics my whole life."

Aki leaned forward. "You go girl, take over the world. Kick the male dominated assholes in the balls and show them who's the boss." She shrugged. "One of us has to do it and I know it won't be me. I suck at those things. None of it makes any sense."

Kyrie opened herself further and sensed a bit of jealousy from the darkly toned girl. "I don't understand."

"Kyrie was home schooled," Tina said to Aki. "She's not had to deal with the creeps and assholes."

"I've not had to deal with anyone." *You told Sam. You can tell them; these four seem to actually like you.* "It was only me and my parents. I would occasionally talk with a neighbor, but I never talked at length to anyone else before my mother died."

"Oh my god! Is that true?" Aki said. "How could your parents do that to you? I'd have run away."

Kyrie shook her head quickly. "No, they were good to me. They just tried to protect me. They never abused me or hurt me. At least not intentionally. My father once caught me unaware when we practiced with daggers, but the cut wasn't that deep."

"Daggers?" Michelle swore under her breath as she corrected the car's direction. "They cut you with a dagger?"

*You should be more careful.* She moderated her tone. "I was learning to defend myself. Anyway, my mother taught me math and physics. But she never taught me about history and government. At least not that I know of. Though I'm finding some campaigns we played might have been based on those things."

"I can help with history," Tina said. "I've always been interested in the past."

"Jake and Aki can help with English," Michelle offered as she turned down the street that Kyrie knew led to Mike's house. "Jake wants to be an actor and so he really gets into all the old English plays."

"And I'm just useless," Aki said with a laugh. "Don't know what I want to be, just know it won't involve science. I guess my Japanese genes failed me."

"Don't let her talk herself down too much," Tina said, "her French is excellent and she's studying German on her own."

Aki waved the compliment away. "Whatever. My parents are pissed that I can barely speak any Japanese."

"You're an activist and will end up a lawyer helping people who need saving," Michelle said as she turned the car into the driveway and then turned it off. "We all work on our homework and help each other get it done, then normally we play for a couple of hours before my parents kick everyone out. Some nights it is over at Aki's house. Just depends on who is available to play. With Jake stuck working on the play and Becca working a job, we have three different campaigns running."

Kyrie wondered at Michelle's energy. Her positive attitude appeared infectious. "Okay."

"Come on." Michelle got out of the car, grabbed her backpack, and headed up to her house. "Plus, since you are a math whiz, you can help me with my calc, and we'll help you with the other items."

Kyrie followed Michelle into the house, aware that Aki and Tina watched her from behind. The entryway reminded her of her aunt's house, but with the rooms set in the opposite direction and without stairs going to the basement. She appreciated the decor's muted tones with darker wall colors and a more lived-in appearance. The smell of roasting meat permeated the air and made Kyrie's stomach growl.

Just as Tina shut the door, an older woman came from the kitchen and stood with her arm's crossed. Aside from the grey in her hair, and a full frame that came from age, she held a striking resemblance to Michelle. "What do you think you were doing leaving your brother to walk home? He called and said you had been very rude to him."

Michelle crossed her arms to match her mother's. "That lying bastard. I was not rude. He was. Besides, I only have five seats in the car, how am I supposed to get six people in there. It would be illegal."

Kyrie cringed. She knew the disrespectful tone in Michelle's voice would result in a compulsive punishment.

"Don't speak to me like that. You came home late last night and now act like you can do anything you want. I'll take your car away from you."

"Why would you take the lying bastard's word over mine? You know he makes shit up."

"Language! You are not too old I can't bend you over my knee and spank you."

Michelle turned away from her mother and headed up the stairs. "Come on, we're going to my room."

"Don't you walk away from me, little girl!"

Kyrie remained frozen in place, worried she might get reprimanded through association with Michelle.

"Sorry, Mrs. Windall," Tina said. "Sam was with Mike and you know how they can be when the two of them are together."

"Sorry for yelling, but Michelle is on my last nerve. She's not done any of her chores and is staying out past curfew."

"She's not with any boys. Beyond Jake that is," Tina said. "We were at Aki's house last night and lost track of time." Tina glanced at Kyrie. "We made a new friend today and wanted to help her with her homework. This is Kyrie. She's Sam's cousin."

The older lady noticed Kyrie for the first time. "Oh, my. I am sorry. Mike mentioned that your mother recently passed away." The older woman brushed back her hair. "I'm Peggy, Michelle's mother. Are you doing all right?"

Kyrie still fearing the possibility of a reprimand, replied softly. "Yes, ma'am. I'm adjusting to the change."

"You coming up here?" Michelle called from the top of the stairs. "I won't be accused of being a bitch to my brother when he was being an asshole to Kyrie."

Michelle's mother frowned. "You girls behave. I'll deal with my daughter after you leave."

Kyrie followed Aki up the worn stairs and down the hall to the second bedroom on the left. "Don't worry about Mrs. W. She's not as bad as she sounds."

Kyrie looked around the room. The walls jumped out with bright colors and scenes. A castle and a lake, not expertly drawn, but painted with flare, covered the far wall. A more realistic image on the right hand wall depicted a forest with a flock of birds flying in front of a series of clouds.

Clothing lay scattered around the room, including the unmade bed, the desk, and the floor. A computer, with a rotating set of images sat among the pants piled on the desk. Aki cleared a spot on the floor and sat down with her back to the bed. Tina closed the door and flopped onto the bed with her head hanging off the side next to Aki.

Kyrie remained standing and watching.

"You look panicked," Michelle said as she cleared the desk chair, tossing shirts into the corner. "What is it?"

Kyrie exhaled. "Aren't you worried about your mother? She seemed furious."

Michelle shrugged. "I didn't come home on time last night because I'm pissed at her. She's being unfair and I don't want to deal with her."

"But what about her compelling you? Don't you worry about that?" Kyrie watched as the others looked at her with confusion. *What don't you know?*

"She can try to ground me, but I'll just go out anyway. The deal was I keep my grades up and I can stay out. My brother is fifteen and I'm not his keeper. There's no reason I should get in trouble for not being home to watch him when he's that old."

"And jacking off to porn in his room," Tina added.

Aki offered a deeper explanation. "Last weekend, he and Sam set the bush on fire all on their own and Michelle would never have known even if she had been here."

"Why I should have been in trouble for leaving a fifteen-year-old on his own is beyond me," Michelle sat on the bed with Aki between her and Tina. "So, don't worry. My father agreed I wasn't to blame. My mother can suck it."

Kyrie took a deep breath and let it out. "If you are sure."

"Don't let her bother you," Michelle said. "Let's get started on the homework."

Kyrie nodded her head. "I could use help with this tablet. I don't know anything about computers."

"Nothing?" Tina said as she propped herself up on her elbows. "You've never played computer games? Well, we can show you what you are missing. Then we can do some homework."


Kyrie allowed Tina to show her Michelle's computer and several games, but they resembled the game she observed Mike and Sam playing. Her interest waned a bit after Tina rattled off a long list of key combinations she would need to learn. However, when Tina and Michelle showed her how to navigate through several applications on the tablet, her excitement grew. "This is fantastic. There's a whole library in here. I could only take some of the books from the cabin with me. I would never have thought you could get all that information into such a small device."

"Nerd," Aki said with a smile.

Tina looked up. "You've not seen Michelle's video collection on her phone. But, important, don't do anything on the tablet that you don't want the school to know about. They have spyware on this thing that reports back everywhere you go on the Internet."

"Stupid overprotective parents," Aki said from the floor. "Can't trust us to do anything on our own."

Tina's eyes grew huge. "Shit, you don't know what the Internet is."

Michelle stood up. "That will take a long time."

Kyrie looked toward the door. She could feel Sam, Mike, and Michelle's mother approaching. A moment later the door opened abruptly.

"Michelle, a word with you," her mother demanded. Mike stood in the background smiling.

Kyrie noticed Tina glaring at Michelle's younger brother, which only made his smile grow wider. The confused emotions around her spoke of a passionate anger and frustration. *Do they all hate each other?* She watched as Michelle got up and left the room, shutting the door behind her. A moment later, the door opened, and Michelle came back in, but her mother, her brother, and Sam remained in the hall.

"Sorry, have to cut tonight short," Michelle said.

Kyrie could feel Michelle's frustrated deflation. *Was compulsion used?* She could not tell, but both Tina and Aki quietly gathered their things.

"I'm walking Kyrie home," Michelle said over her shoulder, a trace of the defiance she had used earlier back in her voice.

"And you will come right back home. You've lost your car for the rest of the month." Her mother turned away and headed back downstairs.

"Asshole," Michelle said at her brother in a low voice.

He shrugged. "You shouldn't have gotten that speeding ticket."

Kyrie followed Aki and Tina out of the room with Michelle trailing up the rear. Sam looked away as Kyrie passed him in the hall.

"You'll live to regret this," Michelle said as she shut her door.

"Threats. What would mother say?" Mike shook his head and went into his room.

Kyrie found herself growing angry at Mike's smug reply and quickly closed her mind. *You're picking up emotions from the others.* She followed Tina and Aki outside. "What's a speeding ticket?" she asked.

Aki continued walking off the porch. "She got pulled over a week ago doing thirty in a twenty. The cop wouldn't let her off. He should have. Michelle has a killer cute face."

Michelle's jaw remained clenched. "Sorry, guys, I'm in some hot water."

Tina hugged Michelle. "Don't worry about it. The part that really sucks is the two of us have to walk home. And we don't live just down the street."

Aki turned around to face everyone. "It was great meeting you, Kyrie. If Michelle is out of the doghouse tomorrow, we can hang out then."

"Yeah." Tina raised an eyebrow. "Tomorrow?" she asked, looking at Michelle.

Michelle frowned. "I'll try. Going to have a long night." She turned to Kyrie. "I'll walk you home, they have to go in the other direction."

"I know the way, you don't have to walk me home," Kyrie said, certain that Michelle felt guilty for the scene that had unfolded.

"I need to be out of the house for a while."

Kyrie nodded her head. "Okay."

"Tomorrow," Aki and Tina yelled from down the sidewalk. Michelle acknowledged the statement with 'tomorrow.'

Kyrie slowed her pace to match Michelle's, which was a fraction of Kyrie's normal walking speed. Michelle had her head down and her eyes did not leave her feet. *She needs me to say something.* "I still don't know what a speeding ticket is, but you got in trouble with the police and managed to get out of it?" Kyrie wondered the effort needed to break out of police custody. *Mother's campaigns made it nearly impossible.*

Michelle looked up. "I didn't get out of it. I got the ticket. Which means I was going too fast. But, in my defense, there was no one else around and I was late." She shook her head. "The part that sucks is the ticket will go on my record and I have to blow all my money to pay the fine. The worst part is now that my parents know, I will have to deal with them being angry and they'll likely make me pay for my own insurance, which I don't have money to do. I'll have to get a job, which like Becca, will kill game time."

Kyrie considered asking about compulsion again, but held back, not wanting to reveal things about herself if the others had no way of knowing. "You don't get along with your family?"

Michelle shrugged. "My brother is a jerk most of the time. Always wanting to get all the attention and praise. He's better at sports. He wrote a phone app. He's getting better grades in math than I got. And on and on. I'm tired of how my parents just think of him as the golden boy and give me crap." She looked up. "How were your parents?"

Kyrie glanced at the car driving past. She had no idea of the brand, but the four-door vehicle was painted an attractive blue. She turned her attention back to Michelle. "I loved my parents. They gave up a life like your family has. They moved out to a mountain to raise me. They never showed me that they ever regretted doing that."

"Sounds wonderful. My parents always seem to be pointing out things I'm doing wrong and complaining about my lack of focus. I didn't get my homework done. I didn't clean my room. I was out too late. I'm spending too much money. Playing too much D&D." Michelle sighed.

Kyrie felt the conflict in the girl beside her. The mix of guilt, anger, frustration, lack of confidence, and overall confusion. The emotions fed into her own sense of abandonment and betrayal. "My parents were good to me, but I'm learning they lied about a lot of things. They didn't tell me things they should have."

"Amen, sister," Michelle said, the smile back on her face. "That is what parents do."

They reached Kyrie's aunt's house and approached the door. She tried the handle and found the door locked. When Michelle gave her a questioning glance, Kyrie frowned. "I don't have a key."

"Really?"

"My aunt never gave me one. Her car's gone, so I'm guessing she's not home. She did say she'd be home late."

Michelle pulled out her phone, looked at the surface, and then swiped it open. She pressed a couple icons on the screen and then put it to her head. "Yeah, Shithead, Sam and his aunt never gave Kyrie a key, so you need to send Sam here to let her inside. Don't give me any crap. You spent your wad ratting me out. You'd have been better off saving that little detail for when it really mattered." She rolled her eyes. "Screw you. Get your ass here." She pulled the phone away from her face and pressed the icon to hang up the phone.

"Thanks," Kyrie said. She hesitated and then asked, "Can I use your phone?"

Michelle raised an eyebrow. "Going to rat out Sam?"

"I need to make a call, but I can't use my Aunt's phone."

Michelle smiled and handed her the unlocked phone. "Help yourself."

Kyrie quickly looked at the screen and pressed the numbers she had memorized as Lars' new number. When nothing happened, Michelle reached over and pressed the green icon that looked somewhat like a phone. "Thanks." She put the phone to her ear and then walked a short distance away from Michelle.

"Yes," came Lars' voice through the phone.

"It's me."

"How are you doing, Kyrie?"

"I don't know. They sent me to school today and there are so many things I don't know. Some people think I'm special, which I think is just saying I'm stupid. When are you going to get me?"

She heard Lars take a deep breath. "It's gotten a bit worse. Your aunt's lawyer friend is good, and I don't have a license to practice in Kansas. So, I'm trying to get someone to pick up the case and argue it for me. This is not going to end quickly. It may take months."

"What?" Kyrie felt her knees wobble as she paced in the yard. "Months? I don't want to be here months. Let her have the money."

"Kyrie. You can't run away. You need to be patient. Even if you throw away the money, they will come after you. And even if they didn't find you, you don't want to become homeless. Bad things happen to young ladies living on the streets. I don't want those kinds of things to happen to you."

Kyrie looked down the sidewalk and noticed Sam and Mike coming her direction. "I have to go." She lowered the phone and pressed the red button as she saw Michelle do. She then concealed the phone against her body and walked back to the porch.

"That didn't sound good," Michelle said.

Kyrie wiped the moisture from her eyes. "Someone was supposed to help me, but they said it might be months."

"Are you in trouble?" Michelle asked. "I can try to help."

"You're a bitch," Mike yelled from the front of the driveway.

"Just let us in," Michelle demanded.

Kyrie swallowed and took a deep breath. She knew she had revealed more than she should have to Michelle, but she needed someone she could talk to. Opening herself more, she took Michelle's hand as she had seen Aki and Tina do. She allowed the physical contact to give her better access to Michelle's surface thoughts and picked up the other girl's fear for Kyrie's safety.

"You need your own key," Sam said as he pushed his way through them to the door.

"And you need to go back home," Mike said to Michelle.

"Do you want to see my room?" Kyrie asked, not wanting Michelle to leave just yet.

"Of course, I do," she replied, full of bubbly energy that figuratively spat in Mike's face.

Kyrie and Michelle went upstairs, while Mike and Sam went to the basement. When Kyrie knew the others were too far away to hear here, she spoke softly to Michelle. "My parents had a friend who is supposed to look after me, but my aunt is fighting him. I'm not supposed to let anyone know I'm talking with him."

"Something wrong with your aunt?" Michelle asked as they came into Kyrie's room.

"My parents' friend thinks she's after the money I'm supposed to inherit. But I don't care about that." Kyrie sat down the on the bed. "I feel out of place here. Nothing is what I know."

"Hey," Michelle said, sitting on the bed beside her. "You're part of our group now. We're an odd collection, but we've all been friends for several years and there is room for one more."

Kyrie took a deep breath and closed her mind again. *Feedback from the others. It's impacting your emotions.* She slowed her heart rate and turned her head to Michelle. *You can do this.* "Thank you. I'm just feeling overwhelmed," she admitted.

Michelle smiled at her. "I'm here for you." She shifted her focus. "I like your desk. Oh wow," she stood up and grabbed a Dungeons & Dragons manual from the pile. "Advanced D&D!" She looked at the books below it. "Second edition as well. That's awesome. These are old and in great shape."

"Those were my parents. I took them when I left." Kyrie moved over to the desk and pulled open the drawer where she had put the dice and miniatures. She lifted out two painted figures and handed Michelle a female elven wizard in green robes. The second miniature resembled a slim human thief with leather armor and a broken sword in his hand. The colors had dulled over the years and the high points worn down to reveal the lead beneath.

"These are heavy," Michelle said. "The new ones are just made of plastic."

"Those were my parents minis. They had others, but those were their favorites."

"What about you?"

Kyrie pulled the drawer out further and found another figure of a wizard. The golden hair came down the back of the mini's blue robes. "I usually play a mage. Sometimes a druid."

Michelle looked at the mini closely. "We play fifth edition. I understand there are lots of differences from what you played." Michelle reached into the drawer and pulled out her mother's brooch. "What's this?"

Kyrie frowned. "It was my mother's. She never took it off. My aunt says it is worthless. I guess she's right because I broke the clasp throwing it into my bag this morning."

Michelle flipped over the worn jewelry and examined the back. "Aki's father is a jeweler. I'd think he could fix the bend and the clasp. Perhaps even put a new coat of plating on it." She looked up at Kyrie. "May I get it fixed for you?"

Kyrie hesitated, but then nodded her head, having already sensed she could trust Michelle. However, she added, "Please don't lose it. I shouldn't care, but…"

Michelle cradled the brooch in the palm of her hand. "It reminds you of your mother. It might take a few days, but I promise I will take excellent care of it. And Aki owes me a few favors, so I'm sure she can butter up her father to do it for free. He never tells her no."

Kyrie smiled, feeling better.

"I should probably go before I get into too much more trouble."

"Okay. Thank you for being nice to me," Kyrie said.

Kyrie let Michelle wrap her arms around her and give her a hug. "You can repay me by drawing something for me."

"I will."

# Chapter 10

Kyrie woke early and went for a run. The argument that Michelle had with her mother kept playing through her mind. *Why wasn't Michelle forced to comply?* Kyrie knew her own mother had allowed her some flexibility in their arguments, but when her mother grew mad, Kyrie felt the impact. *And Sheriff Sawyer had compelled you to answer him. Why are others not doing the same to their kids?*

She sped up, pushing herself up a gentle hill. "Is it something that just impacts me?" she mumbled with shortened breath. Her parents told her she was different, but she did not know the full scope of those differences. *You avoided talking about the compulsion and being able to sense emotions with them.* Some things just felt too intimate to talk about. *Thought they knew about both. They knew they could control us with their desire alone. And now that I think about it, they made sure we wouldn't read their minds.*

She pushed the regret from her mind. *So, what is the truth? Are you the only one impacted by compulsion? No one else seems to fear it.*

She crested the hill and kept going, turning down a road she had not yet explored. Another jogger mumbled 'morning' to her as they passed in the opposite directions. The knowledge that others took to a morning run brought a smile to her face. *You're not completely abnormal. But who can compel us?*

The turn she made opened onto a more heavily traveled street and she kept going. The brightening sky illuminated a clump of trees on her right. She slowed as she realized she had underestimated the size and wild feel of the wooded area. The idea of the natural space caught in the middle of all the houses and businesses seemed alien to what she knew of the people she had met. She stopped so she could examine the spot in more detail.

The area appeared to be a swath of trees along a ravine. *Perhaps a stream.* The streetlights illuminated the grass leading up to the boundary just enough for her to know it had recently started growing for the season.

The sound of a car accelerating quickly drew her attention and she turned her head. A moment later she felt the intense concentration of the driver.

Instinct drew energy into her body. She leaped upwards and back as the car jumped the curb and raced toward her. A wave of gravitational force flew from her and slammed into the front of the car, crumpling the hood and smashing the windshield.

The energy that emanated from her encountered the far greater mass of the old car and transferred the momentum into her body. She flailed her arms and legs, twisting in the air as she flew twenty feet into the edge of the woods. Instinct helped to cushion the impact, but the collision with a tree sent pain through her body. Secondary impacts with several branches and the ground left her gasping for breath.

Kyrie struggled to orient herself, but nothing felt like it worked correctly. She tried to see, but her face pressed against young spring grasses and moist soil. The musky scent of earth fill her nose. Unable to lift her head, she reached out with her mind and sensed the man— *it is a man*—getting out of the car. His intense focus on her forced her legs and arms to move. She pushed herself across the ground and into the tree line hoping the darkness of the morning would conceal her.

As her breathing slowed and normalized, her limbs started to respond, and she shifted to a crouched position. Her chest and shoulder throbbed. Her hip ached. She pushed through the pain and moved through fallen branches to hide behind a tree.

The distance to the man muted her ability to know his emotions, but his intense focus on her allowed Kyrie to keep track of his movement. After a brief run around the car, he got back into the vehicle, drove off the curb, and sped away.

Kyrie leaned her head against the tree. Her father had knocked her down in their training multiple times. She knew the effects of getting the wind knocked from her, but never had she felt such a strong force. Only the compressible nature of the gravitational energy had protected her from the full impact of the car.

She closed her eyes and allowed more energy into her body. The flow of power burned sharply through her mind because of how much had poured through her already. *You have to control it. You can't let panic burn you out.*

She allowed the energy to seep into the parts of her body that hurt the most. The sharp pain in her side began to fade and her breathing eased, but a dull ache in her shoulder and hip remained. Exhausted, she stopped the healing process before the energy did more damage than good.

"I may not be able to wait for Lars."

She pushed herself to her feet and tested her movement. Her left hip prevented her leg from having a full range of motion. The stiffness of her shoulder and chest kept her from twisting her upper body. She knew the injuries would slow her. The reduced speed also meant she would have to press hard to get back to her aunt's house before the others woke.

"Ignore the pain," she mumbled as she exited the woods and climbed the slight slope to the sidewalk. The grass and ground were disturbed where the car had left the street and almost hit her. However, the marks on the ground did not tell her much.

She looked up and down the street for new threats. The traffic had increased slightly, but still remained sparse.

Kyrie forced herself into a slow jog, hoping to work through the pain and discomfort. By the time she arrived at her own street, she found herself more limping than running. She glanced down at her clothing and saw the dirt and damage. Twigs and branches still clung to her hair. She reached up to pull them free as she noticed a blue car parked across the street from her aunt's house. She thought back to when she left the house that morning and chastised herself for not paying attention to her surroundings. "It's the same one that drove past me and Michelle yesterday," she mumbled. *Twice.*

Exhaustion plagued her mind, but she reached out looking for threats. A moment of concentration told her the car was empty. She tossed the twigs as she continued walking to her aunt's house. Inside, her aunt had awakened, but remained in her room. *At least Sam still sleeps.* Keeping to the side of the stairs, she quietly slipped into her room, grabbed clean clothing, and went to the shared bathroom to shower, and get ready for school.

Michael hung up the phone and then immediately dialed a different number. "Good morning, Sir," he said, feigning a confidence he did not feel.

"I am about to do an interview," a silky voice replied. "Do you not have things in hand?"

Michael swallowed. "The team is in place. We have been waiting for an opening to take action. But my spies have seen some of Hurlington's followers. I think they tried to harm her this morning. She went out for a run before dawn and I was told she didn't come back for a long time, and when she did, she was limping. She had obviously been knocked to the ground."

"I hired you all those years ago to handle things that I am not in a position to handle."

Michael bit his lip. "It would be easier to eliminate her."

"Have you determined if the binding took?"

Michael shook his head and then spoke. "No. We cannot be certain."

"You know how hard it is to kill a Bound."

"Sir, I do." Michael pressed his view, knowing it might get him an angry retort. "But assuming it took, we don't even know if the stone exists. Her parents could have buried it anywhere. If we wait, Hurlington's people could blow everything wide open. They could try to do something in public where others can see. Your Bound would not react, but there is nothing to stop her from doing something to show her powers."

"Hurlington started a cult. He's been preaching his religion for years and everyone with any sense knows he is crazy. He never managed to get any mainstream attention. He's an Internet kook."

"That we have not been able to find," Michael challenged. "We can find his people, but not him."

"And whose fault is that?"

Michael bit his tongue. He had been ordered to not kill indiscriminately. His activities might be illegal, but they were based on profit and risk. Killing dozens of men to go after someone who generally was not a threat provided none of the first, and lots of the latter. "And if she uses her powers on film?"

"A deep fake. A hoax. Who is going to believe any of it is real?" The voice on the other end became hard. "Confirm if the stone exists. If it does, bring it to me. If not, kill her. But if she is bound, I want her alive."

Michael looked down at the phone is his hand; the connection broken. "Don't piss off the boss." He used that line on his henchmen. "I need to remember I have a boss as well."

He returned his focus to the computer screen and the flight lists to Kansas City. The layers of the organization were intended to isolate crime from the top. He did not want to get personally involved, but it had been his mistake sixteen years ago that threatened his boss' current plans.

# Chapter 11

Kyrie found her English class as bad as government. When she admitted to not knowing Shakespeare, Jane Austin, or any of a dozen other literary figures, the teacher told her she would make no exceptions for quality or material covered, and due to the lateness of the term, Kyrie would have little chance to catch up to the rest of the class.

Miss Pelni suggested Kyrie use the algebra class to study for other classes and Kyrie would only take the tests. She accepted the offer graciously and used the class time to read the history textbook on her tablet.

Gym and government passed quietly enough, but her body hardly wanted to move by the time lunch arrived. She knew Michelle and Tina had first lunch, but she hoped to find Aki somewhere in the crowd of seven hundred students. After spending half the lunch break looking for her, she found the Japanese girl at a table with several other people.

"Hi," Kyrie said, standing next to the table that would have room for her if some of the people slid to the side.

"Hey, Kyrie," Aki said. "This is my other family." She rattled off a series of names that Kyrie tried to remember. "Make room for her to sit down," Aki said to the redheaded girl beside her.

"Thank you." Kyrie sat down after the girl moved.

"Can you believe that no one is doing a damn thing in congress?" A blond boy named Nick said; his long hair pulled back and braided. "Those assholes just ignore climate change and get rich. They are leaving us a shithole of a planet and then call us lazy and ignorant. Someone needs to teach them a lesson." The venom in the boy's voice spoke of violence. "What's your thoughts?"

Kyrie shrugged. "I don't know the issues."

"Bullshit," another boy said. "Conservative moron is what you are if you insist on ignoring climate change."

"Hey," Aki said, leaning forward. "Kyrie's being honest. Her parents had her isolated on a mountain in Colorado. She's been home schooled her whole life."

"Sorry," said the blond boy. "We didn't know."

"That's some heavy shit," a dark-haired girl with an olive complexion said. "We can teach you the truth of things. Time's running out and we can't sit back and do nothing while we wait for the world's wildlife to die off—"

"Or someone to break in and shoot us dead," another girl near the end of the table added.

"Let her eat," Aki said. "I'll make sure she knows the truth."

"Did you see the no bid contract Nalitran Industries got this week?" asked a boy wearing a t-shirt with the word 'Resist' printed across his chest. "They're going to develop on protected parkland."

"The CEO's talking about running for congress," said the redhead. "Just trying to get into power to make more money."

Aki smiled at Kyrie and whispered. "Don't worry. The 'Crew' is agitated. The news report came out today. We don't always yell, but it's a big deal."

The redhead spoke up. "We're passionate about making the world a better place and trying to find ways to stop companies like Nalitran from destroying everything in their quest for money and power."

Aki looked at her. "You okay?"

"Yeah," Kyrie said. "I just feel so far out of touch. There is so much I never learned."

Aki smiled. "As long as Michelle doesn't get too mad, I'll tell you about it tonight. Unless she's still in trouble."

Kyrie wished her trouble was just an angry parent. *You need to talk with Lars. Getting run over is not part of the deal.*

\* \* \* \* \*

Kyrie hurried to her art class after scarfing down her food. Michelle and Tina immediately greeted her. "What happened?" Michelle asked as she released Kyrie from a hug. "Aki said you were looking strange."

"I'm okay. But can I borrow your phone again?"

"No time now. Less than a minute before class starts. Sara would take it away if it's out when the bell rings."

Kyrie nodded her head. "After school?" She forced herself to walk to the easel without a limp.

"Sure," Michelle's voice climbed along with an eyebrow.

Kyrie could tell her new friend did not believe her denial. "How much trouble are you in?" she asked to change the subject.

"Well, I tried to be good, but I ended up telling my mom off, so I can't have anyone over after school this week."

"And you have to walk home," Tina said. "You should have kept your mouth shut. We were supposed to work on the campaign maps together."

"Sorry," Michelle offered as the bell rang.

Kyrie allowed the conversation between the two friends to wash over her. Despite the warm friendliness Michelle offered the night before, she knew she remained an outsider. *Like adding a new character to an established party.* Instead of worrying about being accepted, she went to work blocking in the subject Mrs. Stine had set up for them to draw.


Kyrie made sure she found Michelle and Tina when her last class finished. Aki, Jake, and an African American girl, almost her own height, waited for her. "Kyrie, this is Becca," Michelle said as she approached.

Becca watched her. "Got the text stream from Tina and Aki last night. So, you're an honest to goodness troglodyte, living in the backwoods without a phone or a computer."

Kyrie narrowed her eyes. "I don't know what that means, but yes, my parents raised me without electronics. However, I'm pretty sure I know more math and physics than anyone else in this school, even the teachers."

"Ouch," Becca said. "No insult intended, just curious as to how anyone could function beyond grunts and gestures without a phone. Guessing you've never seen a meme. If I Google you, do you even exist?"

"Becca," Michelle said, "take it easy on her." She turned to Kyrie. "I can walk you as far as my house. Please, tell me what happened since last night."

Kyrie looked at Michelle and the group of people that surrounded her. She did not feel any malice from anyone, though Becca carried a little annoyance. *So many of them,* she thought. *You only wanted two friends.* She suppressed the anxiety building in her, stepped closer to Michelle, and lowered her voice. "I really need to use your phone."

Michelle nodded her head, pulled her phone from her back pocket, and unlocked it. "Okay, but please, tell me what is going on."

"Thank you. I will." Kyrie turned away from the others and started walking toward the exit. She dialed Lars' number and waited for him to answer.

"This is becoming a habit," she heard Lars say. "I have nothing new."

"A car almost hit me when I went for a run this morning."

"What?"

Kyrie could not bring herself to tell Lars about her powers. "I jumped out of the way just in time, but still got knocked several feet into a tree."

"Start from the beginning," Lars said slowly. "And then tell me what the car looked like and who drove it."

"I was running before dawn. Kim Lym doesn't know I leave the house to get a run in. She keeps thinking I'll get lost, but I have a very good sense of direction."

"Okay," Lars said. "Tell me what happened."

Kyrie breathed deeply. "Several miles from the house, I turned onto a street called Mur-Len. I slowed down when I saw a forested area. Next thing I know, a car is racing toward me. It left the road and almost ran me over. The vehicle had four doors. Painted tan. I didn't see it that well. A man drove it. He got out, looked around, but I crawled into the trees and hid. Then he drove off. I'm not safe."

She heard Lars take a deep breath. "I might be tempted to write this off as a drunk, but your parents said time and again they were in danger. I can't do anything officially. Asking to put you into protective custody would raise too many questions and I'd have to fight your aunt's lawyers. That would take too long." He sighed. "I don't know what I can arrange that is off the books, but I will start working on it as soon as I hang up."

"Thanks."

"Whose phone are you using?"

"A friend I met in art class yesterday." Kyrie felt the group of people behind her. She could feel the curiosity coming from them. "Lars, I'm scared."

"Stay with others. If someone is after you, they will hesitate to do something when you are in a group. You also need to get a phone your aunt doesn't know about. Do you have any money? If so, you can get a prepaid one from a store. That's what I'm using."

Kyrie looked around the parking lot. Students were leaving as fast as water runs down the mountain in spring. "I have a little. Unfortunately, my aunt took the eight hundred in cash the police found in the cabin. The rest is hidden, but I don't think I can get to it. It's hundreds of miles away and I don't have a car." With enough desperation, she thought she could get to the buried money, but it would not be easy. "I'll see if my new friends can help me get a phone."

"Good. I would like to be able to call you without others knowing. Be safe. I'll get to working on something right now."

Kyrie hung up the phone and then slowed so that the others could catch up to her. "Thank you," she said to Michelle and handed the phone back.

"So, the girl from the mountain knows how to use a phone," Becca said.

"How can I get a prepaid phone?" she asked Michelle, ignoring the others.

"Oh, a burner," Becca came closer. "You'll want more than one and you'll want to use a VPN if you are going on-line."

Kyrie looked at Becca and her black curly hair. She probed the other girl's emotion, looking for her intent but found very little.

"Hey, I don't have a problem with you," Becca said. "So, get the stick out of your ass. I give everyone a hard time."

"Becca's a good person," Michelle said.

Kyrie relaxed her body. "I don't know much about computers, but I know I need to learn this stuff."

"And history, gov, and English," Tina added. "You're screwed for this year."

"Did I hear you telling your friend on the phone someone tried to run you over this morning?" Jake asked. "Sorry, I've got good hearing."

"Is that true?" Michelle and Aki demanded almost in unison.

Kyrie sighed. She saw Sam and Mike coming out of the school. "Can I tell you on the way home? I don't want other people knowing." When the others all agreed, she started walking toward the parking lot gates. "On my morning run, someone drove their car at me."

"Did they hit you?" Michelle asked. "Is that why you're limping? You seem so stiff."

"You need to go to the police." Jake remained at her side. "It was likely a drunk. Did they even stop?"

Kyrie nodded her head. The memory of the man's intensity caused her to draw energy into herself. "He did get out and look for me."

Aki shook her head. "Drunks should be shot. Get a damn ride share or call a friend."

"A drunk scared he killed you." Jake leaned closer. "If you got a good look at the car, or person, the police might be able to find him."

"No police," Kyrie demanded. "I can't trust the police." She searched for a plausible reason that would not reveal the truth. "They think my parents were bad. They wanted me to say my parents abused me. They tried several times to make me say it. Even tried to trick me. My parents did nothing wrong and I won't say otherwise."

"Kyrie,—" Michelle started.

Kyrie shook her head. "My parents' friend is going to find someone to help me."

"The deep state," Aki said.

"I will walk you home," Michelle said. "No one tries to run over my friend."

*    *    *    *    *

Michelle's entire group of friends decided to walk Kyrie home, even though it took them out of their way to their own homes. Sam and Mike trailed behind them a few hundred feet and out of ear shot. Kyrie answered questions about her life on the mountain and talked about her studies, planting, hunting, and gaming.

"Jake wants to be an actor," Michelle said. "And Aki will become president."

"Only if she doesn't get arrested for sedition first," Becca added. "I'm working on half a dozen open source code projects. I'll hack the election and make sure Aki wins."

"Thanks," Aki said, her phone, for the first time since Kyrie met her, fully tucked into her back pocket. "I'll have to first become a lawyer before I can get elected."

"And I have no idea what I want to do," Tina said. "Nothing makes me really excited."

"Be an artist like me," Michelle pushed. Tina shrugged. "What about you, Kyrie, any plans for when you graduate?"

Kyrie shook her head. "Disappear. I grew up without others. The school feels so crowded."

"Hey, is your front door open?" Jake asked.

Kyrie followed Jake's gaze and noticed the slight gap in the door. Her aunt obsessed about making sure everyone kept the doors locked at all times. The rigor went against Kyrie's upbringing, but outside her morning run, she had honored the request. She turned her head; the blue car remained parked in the same location. Sam and Mike approached slowly. *You need a weapon,* she thought. She stood too far away to sense if anyone waited in the house. "My aunt makes a big deal about making sure we lock everything."

"Do you even have a key yet?" Michelle asked.

"I'm supposed to get one tonight." Kyrie moved up the driveway and opened her senses.

"If someone almost ran you over this morning, you don't want to go into that house," Becca said. "You'd be like any black woman in a horror movie...dead."

Kyrie did not know what Becca meant, but she moved closer and closed her eyes so she could extend her concentration. She found no one inside the house.

"What's going on?" Sam asked when he reached the group standing in the middle of the driveway.

"I don't think anyone is in there," Kyrie said to Michelle and Jake, who had followed closely behind her.

"What makes you say that?" Michelle asked.

Kyrie felt Michelle's curiosity and regretted saying anything.

"Hey, what's the big deal?" Sam asked, coming up beside her.

"Sis," Mike said as a greeting. "Now I can tell mom you didn't go straight home."

"Asshole," Tina mumbled and Mike flipped her off.

Jake brought the conversation back to point. "The door's ajar. You sneak home for lunch and forget to shut it?"

Sam frowned. "Me, yeah, right? Well, perhaps mom didn't get it closed." He headed up the sidewalk and approached the front door. Kyrie followed a couple steps behind him. Sam pushed open the door and swore. "Someone robbed us. Shit's everywhere."

Kyrie looked inside and saw things scattered all over the floor. *Lars, this isn't good.*

"This kind of thing happens," Aki said from where she stood in the driveway.

Michelle pulled Sam away from the door. Her phone out and she had started to dial a number. "Don't touch anything. I'm calling the police."

"I've got to call Mom." Sam stepped off the porch.

Kyrie watched the others. Tina seemed the most unnerved. Michelle and Jake had taken charge. Aki and Becca spoke of various injustices and tried to keep Tina calm. *If it was up to us, we'd grab our things and run.* She knew the impulse turned her into a prey animal, but part of her honestly wanted nothing more than to hide where no one would see her. *You can't do that, though,* she told herself. *You have to figure out what is going on. You're done hiding. Start the campaign and see it to the end.* She straightened and allowed more energy to course through her body, burning her mind, while taking away some of the pain and stiffness in her shoulder, hip, and side. *Father's*

*campaign to dragon mountain was about laying a trap and tricking the*
*people that pursued you. Perhaps that is what we need here.*

"Yeah, Mom. Michelle is on the phone wit—of course I haven't gone into the house, you think I'm a fool?" Sam rolled his eyes and turned in circles. "I think I hear the sirens. I should go. Yeah, I will wait for the cops."

Kyrie did not hear the sirens that Sam spoke of. As he hung up the phone, she used her chin to indicate the blue car across the street. "Your mom complained that car made it hard for her to back out this morning. You ever see it before?"

Sam shook his head. "No."

"When something changes, understand why," she said aloud and started to move toward the car.

"What?" Sam asked.

"Something my father always said to me."

Becca and Jake followed her over to the car. "What is it, Kyrie?"

"Sam's not seen the car before, but I saw it drive past me and Michelle twice yesterday when we walked home. It was here when I went for a run and still here now."

"Someone watching you?" Becca asked.

"No one was in it this morning," Kyrie responded.

Becca and Jake looked into the tinted side windows. "Shit," Becca said turning her head away. "There is a web cam pointed at your house. It must have got a good image of my face."

Kyrie reached down to try the door, but Becca grabbed her wrist. "Don't touch it. You could ruin any fingerprints that might be on the door."

"What are fingerprints?" Kyrie asked.

"Oils on your skin. They get left behind when you touch things and the police can use them to identify you. Each person's is different. At least that is what they claim, but I've read that it really hasn't been proven."

Kyrie's eyes widened. *Tracked by what you touch.* She could now hear the sirens and watched as several police cars raced up to the house. "Please don't mention the call I made to my friend."

"I've got your back," Becca said as they crossed the street to the driveway.

# Chapter 12

Kyrie's aunt arrived after the police cleared the house to confirm no suspects remained inside. They had taken statements from Kyrie, Sam, and their friends as they wrapped the blue car with police tape.

"I need to see what they stole," her aunt demanded. "My cheap ex didn't give me enough alimony to cover the alarm system. Damn him."

"Ma'am, we are still taking pictures and looking for prints. Though, if what they have in the car is any indication of their professionalism, there is a strong likelihood we won't find prints outside of the expected ones, meaning, you and your family."

Becca stepped closer to Kyrie. "If they were professionals, why'd they leave the car?"

"But I have a lot of valuables in the house!" her aunt whined from across the driveway. "I have to find out what they took."

Kyrie, with Michelle in tow, followed Becca back over to the car. They all stood far enough away that the officers would not object to their presence, but close enough to listen to what the police said.

"Stolen car," Becca whispered. "The cops ran the plates. Went missing yesterday. I saw the video camera, cheap thing you can pick up anywhere. They had a microcomputer, perhaps a Pi, or something similar, which they powered from a battery pack. I also saw a cell phone connected as well as a motion detector."

Michelle pulled Kyrie and Becca to the side. "You need to tell them about the guy who tried to kill you this morning."

"That will lead to questions I don't want to answer." The hardness of Kyrie's voice silenced the others. She softened her expression, knowing they needed more. "I had a cop compel me to talk after my mother died, I don't need these cops doing the same."

"What do you mean?" Michelle asked, pulling Kyrie further away. "Did they torture you?"

*You need to find the limits.* "I…" Kyrie pulled Michelle further away from Becca, who drifted back toward the car. "Do you never feel the pressure to obey your mother or other adults?"

"Perhaps as a kid, I felt obligated. Or now if I know I will get in a lot of trouble, but I would let no one physically abuse me." She frowned. "Kyrie, did the police in Colorado do something to you?"

"Not a feeling of obligation, but a pressure in your chest and mind. Pain that will drop you to your knees. Nothing like that?"

Michelle shook her head. "I've never heard of anything like that."

*As suspected, it is just us they can control. Why isn't magic like D&D?* "My parents tried to protect me from something, but I have no idea what. They said I couldn't trust the police. The person I called is trying to get me to safety, when he can, but my aunt has lawyers and that is causing trouble."

"Oh my god." Michelle pulled Kyrie further away from everyone else. "You need police protection. You can trust them. There might be some crooked cops, but not all of them."

*You can't tell the truth.* "Before my parents died, they left standing orders for me to run and get to safety if anything happened. But I thought I could save my mother. I didn't follow their instructions. I asked for help from a neighbor and now everything is falling apart." Her lip trembled and she looked away. "This is all my fault."

Michelle stepped closer and Kyrie allowed her friend to wrap her arms around her. "It is not your fault. Don't think that. I won't tell anyone. Your secret is safe with me, but we need to—"

"Kyrie, come here," her aunt demanded. "The police need us to check for what the thieves stole. Not that you have anything of value, but you still need to look through things as they tore up your room."

Kyrie looked at Michelle. "I'll be back." She walked to the porch, where three officers with clipboards waited with her aunt and Sam.

A female officer looked at the three of them. "One of us will go with each of you. We'll record descriptions of what might have been taken and where it was taken from."

Her aunt huffed. "Finally." Without waiting for direction, she entered the house and headed up the stairs. Sam followed his mother with another officer in tow.

Kyrie remained hesitant. She wanted to offer no reason for the officer to compel her to speak. "I don't have much and it is all in my room."

The officer offered a smile. "I'll follow you."

Kyrie led the way upstairs and into her bedroom. The mattress leaned against the far wall. Her clothing lay scattered on the upturned end of the bed. Kyrie turned her attention to her desk. The drawers' contents covered the floor. Her organized piles of papers and books were now a jumbled heap on top of her dice and miniatures.

"Most of the searching took place in your aunt's bedroom, your room, and in the basement," the officer said.

Kyrie squatted down and quickly gathered the dice and miniatures. It took time for her to confirm the rough treatment had not broken or lost anything. *At least the minis are not bent.* "It looks like these are all here," she finally declared.

"Any other valuables?" The officer asked.

"It will take a while to go through all the papers and books to put them back in order," Kyrie said. "I won't know if anything is missing until then."

The officer smiled. "Well, I doubt they would have stolen schoolbooks and notes. Though if they are college books, my son might disagree. Those cost a fortune each semester and the school gives peanuts on buy-back."

Kyrie frowned at the expression, but she said nothing. Instead, she started gathering her mother's journals into a pile and confirmed nothing had been removed. She then moved to the campaign notes.

The officer capped her pen. "I'm going to go back downstairs. If you do find something missing, come find one of us."

The rumble of her aunt's bellow reverberated through the walls. "All my jewelry is gone! All of it. Even my pearls!"

Kyrie ignored her aunt's distress, instead, she kept working on organizing the papers and books in her bedroom. She did not think anything went missing until she found one of her sketchbooks. *Why did they take those pages?* She put the book on her desk and picked at the scraps of the paper left in the spiral rings. The missing drawings completed a series of images she had made from her reoccurring dreams.

"You okay," Michelle asked as she arrived at the door. "My mom's on her way. She's worried because of the robbery."

Kyrie nodded her head. "Only a few drawings stolen. Nothing else."

"Anything important?" Michelle offered a reassuring smile. "Drawings that would be worth millions in the future after someone recovers them in a rich guy's mansion, perhaps?"

Kyrie remembered the images clearly; she drew them over the prior winter. Ten pages of a Kattian family and the tree-filled town they lived in. She flipped a few pages further into the sketchbook and found four images that remained from the series. "They were pictures of this family. This sketch is a street in their town."

"These are really good," Michelle said. "I'm sorry they took the others."

Kyrie shrugged. "I've been drawing these all my life."

From the other room, they heard her aunt complain, "All my clothing is scattered about. How do you expect me to know if they took anything else?"

"Ma'am, I would guess they were looking for jewelry that you might have hidden in your clothing," the officer replied.

Her aunt did not appear to notice the policeman's attempt to calm her. "I don't hide things of value with my underwear. What they took from my closet was worth well over twenty thousand dollars."

Michelle patted Kyrie's shoulder. "Sorry you have to deal with that. I've rarely spoken with Sam's mother over the years, though they had come over for parties and dinners every once in a while. I never knew that she sounded like that."

"Until last week, I didn't know I had any relatives," Kyrie said and then fell silent as she felt her aunt approach her bedroom door.

"What'd they take from you?" her aunt demanded.

"A couple of drawings is all," Kyrie replied. She could feel the metal of her mother's simple wedding ring between her breasts. *Were they after that?*

Her aunt frowned. "I'm surprised they found anything of yours to take." She left the doorway and headed toward Sam's room. "What did they take of yours?" she called, her voice booming down the hallway.

"I had a hundred dollars hidden in a drawer, but that appears to be it," came Sam's response.

"Well, go down to the basement and see if you can determine if they took anything from there."

"Mom, you've got to be kidding. There is no way to know what was there in the first place. I already checked the game room and they left all the electronics."

Kyrie could not hear her aunt's reply, but her aunt stormed off and thundered down the stairs. Kyrie turned to Michelle and felt the girl's sympathy. "Thank you."

"Becca's obsessed with the camera in the car. And the fact that they got an image of her face. She thinks the cops will screw it up." Michelle smiled. "I think she wants to try and hack it herself. My guess is she'll order parts off the Internet to set up something similar just to see what it takes. Her father is into all of that stuff as well."

Kyrie looked around her room. "Luckily, I have little to clean up. I'll have my room back together before bed."

"If you need anything, call...crap, we still need to get you a phone." Michelle looked at her phone that had vibrated in her hand. "My mom's looking for me." Michelle reached out and hugged her before leaving. "I'll find a way to get out of being in trouble and help you get a phone."

Kyrie did not follow Michelle out of the room. Instead, she pulled her mother's ring out from under her shirt and stared at the small stones. "Why the jewelry and those sketches?"

Kyrie sat with her aunt and Sam at a restaurant that served fancy hamburgers. Her aunt had hardly taken a pause to breathe. She simply continued to complain about the break-in and robbery.

"Things like that should not happen in our neighborhood. Perhaps in Overland Park, but not where we live."

"Mom, the police said, based on what they stole, the thieves wanted jewelry. And that we should be thankful that is all they wanted. If the cops find any similar robberies, they'll let us know."

Her aunt seemed to ignore Sam's statement. "Tomorrow, I'm calling to get the alarm activated, don't care what the cost is. And we need new locks on the doors." Her aunt turned to Kyrie. "Sorry about not getting your key made, but I think at this point, it won't matter, since we all need new keys and you can have one after that." Her aunt looked at her phone. "Have to find a locksmith that won't charge a fortune. This is a total waste of my time and money."

Kyrie started to tune out the conversation and focused on eating the burger on her plate. The idea that people had been through her things bothered her, but not as much as it appeared to bother her aunt and cousin. In the cabin, her parents had respected the privacy of her room for the most part, but she knew her parents would enter her bedroom if they wanted. Most of the family time they spent in main room. Everything there had been fair game for any of them. *Except the campaign details,* she admitted. *None of us violated that rule.*

*But they looked through your art and stole some of that.* That invasion of her privacy churned some anger in her. *Was the robbery about you or about something else?* Kyrie had listened to the police explain that the camera and the stolen car provided a likely way for the thieves to monitor the house. A motion detector they claimed triggered the camera.

*What about the car that tried to hit you in the morning? Related?* She found it hard to connect the two events. The man in the car had focused on her, but Lars and her friends had suggested it might have been a drunk who panicked after thinking he had killed her. She discarded the idea. *Your parents were hiding for a reason.*

She looked across the restaurant and noticed two large men take seats at another table. A tattoo of a Celtic knot on one man's face made him distinctive in his appearance. Both men had looked in her direction as they sat, but now they focused on each other, engrossed in a conversation that she could not hear. She felt little of anything from them.

She picked at the fries on her plate. *Tomorrow is your third day at school. It feels longer.*

"Hello. Who is this?" Michelle asked quietly. She did not want her mother to take away her cell phone as well as her car and her freedom.

"I think you have the wrong number," came the reply of a man on the other end.

"No. Don't hang up. My friend, Kyrie, called you earlier today and the day before."

After a pause, the man spoke again. "Do you have a message from her?"

Michelle considered lying, but she decided against it. "She's in trouble. She needs to go to the police and get help, but she refuses to do so. I'm scared for her. You need to convince her otherwise. We found her house robbed when we got home after she called you."

"Robbed. What was taken?"

"Jewelry, mostly," Michelle said. "Someone parked a car outside the house with a video camera and a phone. I think someone's tracking her."

Michelle heard a deep breath over the phone. "I do not know what trouble her parents found themselves in. They never told me. I didn't even know where they had gone." A bit of anger hung in his voice. "I'm tired of saying it. We were best friends in college. However, they would not tell me what happened. I'm doing what I can for her based on the situation. There is only so much I can do.

"She could get police protection," Michelle pleaded. "Even if some bad cops caused trouble before, they can't all be bad."

The man cleared his throat. "I do not think you, nor I, will convince her to do that." Michelle heard some movement over the phone. "Long ago, her mother told me police were involved, so I would guess she has made Kyrie very suspicious. But again, I don't know who was after her. Or if anyone was after her."

Michelle swallowed. "Then what can we do?"

"She needs friends. She needs friends who understand social media and computers and how the world outside a mountain valley works. She needs a phone of her own." The sound of something being set down came through the phone. "I have to go. I've got another call coming in. I'm pressing as hard as I can to legally help her, but I'm starting fifty-meters behind in a hundred-meter race and I can only do so much."

Michelle heard the line go silent and she looked down at the phone; the call had ended. Her hands clenched. "Okay, boomer." The call had not gone the way she had expected. "She needs help. Help from someone without a stick up their ass." Michelle looked at the phone and considered calling the police herself. She frowned and then set the phone down. "She'd never trust you again. She has absolutely no one. No one but you and the group."


The next morning, Kyrie woke up later than normal. The unregulated energy that had coursed through her body the prior morning still left its mark. Her father and mother had pushed her hard to learn her limits as soon as the nature of her powers started to manifest. She knew very well that an unregulated pull of power did significant damage to her internally. *You have to do better next time. Pay attention and don't get caught by surprise.*

Her late rising was still earlier than Sam and her aunt. After she stretched, she showered, dressed, and then returned to her room. She sat down at the desk and looked at the stack of campaign notes and her mother's journals. She picked up the notebook she had been reading the prior night and continued her study. The math and physics interested her, but she skimmed over the attempts to prove the ideas and focused more on the hypothesis her mother proposed. *Again, energy transference between universes in a multiverse. And not just energy, but complex patterns. An intelligent force?* The ideas violated so many understandings and theorems. *But who else violates those rules?* The snark in her mental voice brought a frown to her face. She knew her own powers did not conform to expected rules of the physical world, though many of her mother's journals tried to explain her abilities with math.

She picked up a stack of related campaign notes and looked at the drawings her mother created. "I remember that adventure. We brought a ghost to life. It possessed an NPC. It took days to show itself." Kyrie pursed her lips. "It merged it's mind with the NPC and they became one. The memories and powers combined." She put the campaign notes down and refused to think about the implications.

Kyrie used her mind to look through the wall, she could feel both Sam and her aunt moving about. She put the notes and journal back in the stack where they belonged based on numerical order. She knew where she left off, but anyone else who might think to look through them would only see ordered stacks.

Her aunt filled the morning drive to school with mumbling and repeating the list of calls she had to make. Sam had tried unsuccessfully to comfort his mother, but the older woman's preoccupation had her driving off to work without even telling him goodbye. Kyrie noticed her aunt's disconnected state had left Sam quiet and uncertain.

*Are you any better at adjusting to these changes?* she asked herself as she walked with Sam into the school. No one else seemed to be aware of what had happened to them the night before. "It will be okay," she offered her cousin. He agreed silently and then went his way toward his first period as she went to hers.

The first four periods went as expected, with little to no conversation with anyone else. She pushed herself into her schoolwork during the classes and tried to bridge the gaps of what she knew and what people expected her to know.

During lunch she shifted focus to planning how she would determine who might be pursuing her. *Capture someone and make them talk?* The idea seemed risky. *How is a girl going to capture someone and hold them? You'd reveal yourself.* She suspected computers and the Internet might be critical concepts for her to learn. How she would learn sixteen years' worth of skills and culture before her enemies got what they wanted; she did not know.

"Failure is not an option," she mumbled as she entered art class.

"Hey, Kyrie," Tina said, uncertainty in her voice. "How you doing? Could you even sleep last night? I know I would be a wreck."

"I'm doing okay. I slept later than normal, but otherwise, no problems."

Tina nodded her head, glanced away, obviously uncomfortable.

"How are you doing?" Kyrie asked, hoping to put Tina at ease.

Tina's eyes kept glancing about and then she calmed and spoke about something that seemed unrelated. "Prom is coming up in just a couple of weeks. Aki is boycotting it," she added, not really looking at Kyrie as she spoke. "Michelle and I were going to go stag, but she's getting a lot of guys asking her to go."

Kyrie felt Tina's insecurities. "What is prom?" Kyrie asked, not content to wait to see if the context would emerge, but willing to allow Tina to drive the conversation.

Tina looked up to meet Kyrie's eyes. "A dance for the senior and junior years. Everyone gets dressed up. This year they have a nautical theme." Tina pulled out some charcoal sticks and moved to her easel. "I doubted anyone has told you about it. The trouble is, there are not likely to be many good dresses left. Perhaps you and Aki could hang out that night and boycott it together."

Kyrie bit her lip. Tina definitely felt apprehension for this dance and that underlying fear leaked from her mind. *She's uncomfortable around boys,* Kyrie realized. *Why? She also doesn't want you around for some reason. Jealousy?*

"Hey," Michelle said as she came into the classroom and joined them at their easels. "You good?"

Kyrie kept herself from rolling her eyes. "I'm not that fragile. My parents made sure I could take care of myself." She shifted her mental attention from Tina's sudden anger.

"Good. My mother relented because of the robbery. She said I could have people come over. She didn't think it was a good idea for anyone to be alone." Michelle frowned. "I still don't get my car back until May, but at least I'm not in solitary confinement anymore."

"I told Kyrie about prom," Tina said. "We still going together, or will I need to find a boy of my own?"

Michelle's voice took on a hard tone. "I did not tell Kerny yes." She started getting her own art supplies ready. "He's got some nice abs and is witty, but he thinks D&D is stupid. I just don't think we would be compatible."

"So, game tonight then?" Tina asked, her voice a bit too high.

"Definitely!" Michelle looked at Kyrie. "You'll play with us, yes?"

Kyrie felt a grin rise to her face. "Yes. That is one of the things I have been missing the most." She took a breath, "But I need to go by my aunt's house first and get my things. I'll come back after."

"Okay, but I can lend you anything you might need," Michelle said.

Kyrie felt Tina's discomfort and avoided looking in her direction. The other girl no longer felt affection for her. *Trouble does follow you.* "Still need to go home. I won't take too much time."

# Chapter 13

Kyrie managed to get Michelle to let her go home on her own by saying she felt the need to run. She promised to watch for threats and when she added that not everyone else would want to go the extra distance, just to turn around and come back to Michelle's house, Michelle relented her protests. Neither statement was false, but the manipulation left a bad taste in her mouth. Her parents had encouraged deception in many of the campaigns but doing it for real felt like a betrayal.

The run gave her a chance to loosen up the muscles that had grown stiff from sitting all day, and an opportunity to burn off some nervous energy. With Sam and Mike going over to another friend's house, Kyrie hoped she might get some time to herself.

She reached her aunt's house in only a few minutes, opting to run at full speed instead of a simple jog. Her senses remained open as she pushed her body, watching for anyone following her and for cars parked along the street that did not look like they belonged. She sensed nothing that caused her concern, and when she reached the house, Kyrie ran across the empty driveway and up to the front door. She still lacked any keys, but without her friends to see her, she put her hand on the door handle and closed her eyes. More energy flowed into her and she focused her senses inside the house. The locks stood out easily to her mind and she carefully crafted a gravitational field around the latch that controlled the deadbolt. With a little tug, her mind rotated the lock and she heard the satisfying click of the bolt sliding free of the jamb. She did the same with the lock in the handle, and then opened the door and walked inside. The time it took her to unlock the door barely exceeded the time to use a key.

She closed and locked the door before jogging up the stairs. The office door stood ajar. Just like the backdoor, the robbers had used a solid kick to bypass the lock. Her aunt found nothing missing from her office, but the damage meant the door no longer remained closed.

Kyrie noted the desk, computer, and chair set in the middle of the room. A file cabinet and some bookshelves sat against the far wall. To her right, she saw several display cabinets filled with ceramic figures untouched by the robbers.

Several piles of loose papers lay scattered across the desk. Most had names and notes of discussions. Not comfortable with computers, she ignored the electronics and pulled open the desk drawers. Pens, a stapler, and other office supplies filled the bulk of the space.

With nothing of interest in the desk, she moved to the damaged file cabinets. The thieves had pried open the drawers, bending the metal. Kyrie pulled opened the drawers and started reading the tabs on the files. Most documents pertained to taxes, bills, and product manuals. A section of one drawer contained color pamphlets and advertisements. The folders listed names of cities and states with a subheading of 'vacation.'

While the images of other places looked interesting, Kyrie did not have the time to examine them. The bottom drawer had some boxes that were hastily piled back into the space, which in turn had pushed a series of folders to the back. The first four folders had the title 'Samuel's grades.' The three folders after those had her mother's name on them.

Kyrie's heart beat faster and she pulled the folders from the drawer and went to the desk. Careful not to disturb anything, she set the folders down and opened the first one. She looked closely at the handwriting and then glanced to one of her aunt's notes on the desk. "Someone else wrote this."

Kyrie leaned over and started to read the top page. It listed names, addresses, numbers, dates, and notes. Not every entry contained all the details, but after a couple of pages, Kyrie could tell this folder represented a log of conversations someone had with people when looking for her mother. "They called everyone my parents knew. My father's boss. His coworkers. My mother's neighbors. The police," she mumbled aloud.

Kyrie continued to turn the pages as she mentally calculated the time she had before she needed to return to Michelle's house. "Would Kim Lym know if I took them?" she wondered aloud as she skimmed the pages. She considered the risk of taking them for herself without a good place to hide them. *Probably not a wise plan.*

The idea of transcribing the contents into a journal of her own seemed inefficient and when she flipped over to a series of photos, she knew she needed a better way to get her own copies of the files.

She paused as she looked at the photos. The images showed her mother and father at a much younger age than she remembered them. She examined another image with a person's name written in marker at the bottom. "So that is Lars Solberg," Kyrie said aloud. She had not known his last name. The picture showed a man with his arm around her father's shoulder, the two of them with their long blond hair pulled back. They smiled as they hung over the edge of a ship's wooden railing. Rolling waves filled the background of the image. "Thirty years ago, based on the date."

She flipped through more than two dozen other photos of her parents with various people. Lars featuring in more than half of them. She wanted to study them all in detail, but she did not have the time.

She opened the second folder and found it full of pages with itemized lists and dollar amounts. The handwriting of this folder matched that of her aunt and Kyrie frowned. "The money she wants." She continued to flip through the pages, many had printed pictures with notes that indicated when something sold and for how much.

The third folder caused Kyrie to sit in her aunt's chair. These documents described her parents' movements for the six months prior to their disappearance. "Tuesday, March 11th, received email that Rachel and Robert had willingly turned everything over to Lars and that I should not search for my own daughter and granddaughter." Kyrie paused and realized she read her grandmother's handwriting. She blinked away the moisture in her eyes. "My grandmother spent a lot of effort to find my mother."

Kyrie looked up at the clock on the wall and realized she had spent too much time already. She closed the folders and returned them to the file cabinet just as she had found them. She put the chair back in place, left the office, pulling the door closed as far as it naturally wanted to rest, and then went to her room to gather her dice and minis.

By the time Kyrie returned to Michelle's house, the others—Tina, Becca, Aki, Jake, and Michelle—had setup in the basement around a long table. They had already started on their homework. Kyrie joined them and Michelle helped show her the best way to use her tablet to speed up the assignments.

Kyrie helped the others with any math or science questions, demonstrating that in addition to physics, she had also learned a bit of chemistry from her mother. The others in turn helped her with her classes, allowing her to catch up on the English and government homework due the next day.

Kyrie sighed as she hunted the screen for the letters to finish the questions for history. "I just need to find the time to read these books from cover to cover. I don't see any other way to catch up."

Tina shook her head. "If it was me, I'd just give up. Reading the whole textbook is cruel and inhumane punishment."

"Gov is the worst to read," Jake said. "I hate it. So dry."

"Hear anything more on that camera that watched your house?" Becca asked. "Or did the cops screw it up?"

Jake piled on his own question. "Do the police have any leads on the robbers?"

"Nothing that I've heard on either question," Kyrie said, again conscious of her mother's ring under her shirt. "Though my aunt doesn't tell me much."

"I wonder if the people covered their tracks." Becca started to doodle on the paper in front of her. "I'd have entered the target server address in memory of the Pi, not saved it to the storage, then used a VPN to mask the IP where I sent the images. And I would only send the images to a compromised box, which would then have uploaded them to a TOR server, where I could use another compromised box to pull them from the dark web so that no one would find me."

Kyrie understood almost nothing that Becca said. She appreciated the time and energy Becca put into unwinding the puzzle, but the gap between their understandings pulled the life from her. "I doubt my aunt knows enough about computers to tell me anything the police would tell her. And even if she did, I wouldn't understand it."

The others laughed and agreed.

Tina changed the subject. "I told Kyrie about prom today. I doubt she would be able to find anything to wear this late."

Kyrie did not need to read the emotions of the room to know that Tina's statement held a bit too much pleasure. "Am I required to go?"

"Definitely not," Aki said. "It's a hold back to traditional male and female norms. It's outdated and wrong."

"You're just mad that the guy you like doesn't know you exist," Becca said. "I'm more than happy to get a little loving from Mit." Becca smiled and leaned into Jake. "That guy has dreamy eyes. Can you get him to come around?"

Jake shook his head. "He's already got two dates. I don't think he needs a third. And his balls are probably shrunk with all the roids."

Michelle broke into the conversation. "Hey, Kyrie, what character race do you want to be?" She shifted her schoolwork to the floor and brought the Dungeons & Dragons books onto the table. "Fifth editions' a bit different from what you've been playing based on what I've read on all the forums. I'll add you into the party at fourth level."

"Yeah, Jake got us all TPK'd three weeks ago, so we had to start over," Aki said, pulling out a dice bag and some papers.

"Human," Kyrie said. "My parents let me create some other races for our games, but if the rules are different with fifth edition, then I'd just play a human."

"When did they start playing D&D with you," Jake asked.

"I think I was three or four," Kyrie said. "I know we played just before my mother started teaching me physics. I remember the chair being too short for me to see the table and I had to sit on my schoolbooks. They made me read all the rulebooks before they…" Kyrie looked around at the others and opened herself to their emotions. "What?"

"When you were three?" several of them asked.

"Yes," Kyrie answered tentatively.

"You read all the rule books?" Aki asked, skepticism filling her voice. "At three years of age?"

Kyrie felt all the stares on her. *What don't you know?* "Yes."

"I can't remember what I did at five," Jake said, "let alone reading anything like a rule book."

"I might have read a picture book at five, and I'm smart," Becca challenged. "No way you read the D&D player's handbook."

"I can barely remember anything before I was ten," Tina offered, a bit of accusation in her voice.

Kyrie felt the urge to leave. She remembered doing what she said. *But apparently, that is something else that is odd about you. Mother, why didn't you say anything? That's right, you didn't want us to ever have any friends or to trust anyone.* The others continued to watch her. She could see the doubt growing in their eyes and feel it in their thoughts. "Maybe I was ten?"

"It don't matter," Michelle said, "we are playing tonight. Human you are. Fourth level. What character class do you want to be? And do you want to roll stats or do point buy?"

"Mage," Kyrie said. She could feel the others still staring at her. *Some of them think you were intentionally lying; others are not sure.* "And roll, I guess. But, if you would rather not have to teach me the new rules, I can learn them and play some other time."

"You're playing tonight." Michelle's statement offered no room for discussion as she made some notes on a preprinted character sheet. "I'll make you a wizard and not a warlock. I think that will be closer to what you are used to."

Kyrie nodded her head, accepting what Michelle said, along with the emotional support she broadcast, and made the decision to stay. The choice banished some of the isolation that had been building in her. "Thank you." She glanced at the others. *You are making Tina jealous. Aki and Becca don't trust you, and Jake is uncertain.*

She let Michelle walk her through all the rules quickly, and with a handful of dice rolls, she had a new character created. She played an older human wizard named Elia that had lived as a hermit on a mountain side. Michelle told her the party would encounter her shortly. They were still running away from a horde of bandits from the last session. Her character would know the way through woods to get them to safety, should they live.

Kyrie watched and listened as Michelle reminded the others of where they had all left off and who had injuries as she unrolled a big mat on the table. Trees and other obstacles covered the grid in marker. Kyrie took a moment to examine the mat's material and texture as Michelle finished setting the scene.

"The four of you, two elves, a dragonborn, and a dwarf, are still on the ridge and in the small clearing. The six humans wearing tabards with a skull on them are coming into the clearing from the south. At least a dozen more are visible in the valley and heading in your direction."

The others immediately fell into action, rolling initiative, and reacting with their strengths. Tina was a gender bent—and confidant—barbarian, charging forth to smash the enemies. Jake also played the opposite gender, a female dwarven cleric at the rear, healing and buffing as if he already knew what the others would do.

Kyrie observed the differences in the rules as Aki's mixed class caster threw spells. Becca's elven thief she understood well enough. Becca kept her character out of close-range combat so that she could leverage her bow.

Kyrie found herself envious of the others. The efficiency of their play indicated that they had functioned as a group for a long time. With the five of them, the combat and interactions held a depth that had not existed with just her and her parents. The laughter and joking really only came from having enough people.

Kyrie also admired Michelle's DM'ing. Michelle continued to press the players, but as long as they made decent choices, she seemed to hold back from actually killing them. Her mother had not always been that kind and her father had been brutal when it came to honoring the dice rolls. He always said that real life did not fudge the chaos that one faced.

"And Elia," Michelle said, drawing Kyrie's attention, "you finally see the commotion that had caused you to investigate. There are two elves, a dragonborn, and a dwarf desperately fighting against four humans with skulls on their tabards. Two humans are dead on the ground, but more are coming." Michelle leaned to the side of her screens. "You know the humans are mercenaries from the neighboring province. Your turn."

Kyrie felt everyone's eyes on her again. She wanted to do something heroic and clever, but her character had little dexterity, basic armor, and limited magical weapons. With only second level spells, she would not be that deadly of a force. *If father ran the campaign, you would be rewarded by watching and observing before acting. Mother might have tried to trick you with the party being the bad people and the mercenaries being the ones to save.* In this case, she knew that she had to save the players, to do otherwise would make them like her even less. Kyrie had obeyed her strict rule of not reading their minds or emotions during the game, but she had observed Michelle silently counting squares without moving any of the minis.

Kyrie jotted 'cast see invisibility' on a piece of paper and handed it to Michelle. When her father had lived, things that one player did, and the other could not know through observation, where handed to the DM on paper.

"Hmm," Michelle said. She scribbled something on the note and handed it to Kyrie. It read: there is one man moving behind the cleric, attack imminent, but after your next turn.

Michelle continued through everyone's turn until Kyrie came back to the top of the initiative. Kyrie had already written a note explaining she would use magic missiles on the invisible person. She then rolled three of her four-sided dice and added up the damage.

"Jake—sorry, Gwen, you hear a cry of pain behind you and everyone can now see another mercenary who had just been about to execute a wonderful backstab." Michelle smiled at Kyrie. "But his concentration and surprise is lost. You also see an older woman hiding in the trees to the north. She appears to have just cast a spell and might have injured the bandit, since he is grasping at his back, which is turned toward her."

Kyrie felt herself smile. She scooted forward in her chair and looked down at the map, finding joy in the simplicity of playing the game. Even the others were grinning.

*     *     *     *     *

They had finished the battle, introduced Kyrie, and had started moving along the paths that Kyrie's character 'knew' when Michelle's mother interrupted. "Kyrie, you aunt called to see if you were here. She wants you to come home."

"Yes, ma'am," Kyrie said as she gathered her things. Michelle's mother turned and headed back up the stairs.

"Really?" Becca asked. "Just like that you're leaving. Right in the middle of the game. We normally play for at least another hour."

"We can continue after Kyrie leaves," Tina offered.

Michelle shook her head. "It's not her fault her aunt wants her home. We got through the combat and moved the plot along."

"I'm sorry," Kyrie said. "I don't know my aunt very well, but she is very demanding and easy to anger."

"I'm good with breaking early," Jake started to gather his dice. "I've been meaning to catch up on some TV watching."

"Let me walk you to the door," Michelle said as Kyrie finished gathering her things into her clear backpack.

Kyrie smiled and walked upstairs with Michelle. "Thank you. I would rather stay, but my aunt is…"

"I've heard her," Michelle agreed. "You still doing okay?"

Kyrie pursed her lips. "I'm starting to feel more and more out of place, but I kind of expect it. Though I do have a question. My mother and father talked of copy machines where you could reproduce a piece of paper. They had wished time and time again for them when it came to maps and character sheets. Do you know a place I can copy some papers?"

Michelle contemplated the question for a moment. "There are some stores you can take papers to and copy them. I'd drive you to one if I still had my car. Otherwise, we can scan them and put them on the computer. Would that work?"

Kyrie nodded her head. "I just want to have a copy that I can keep and read. I don't want my aunt to know I have them. She might hide the papers."

"If you have a phone, I'd say take a picture of them and upload them to the cloud. You can get free storage and email."

Kyrie sighed. "I still need to get a phone."

"I know. I wanted to talk about that with the group tonight before you left. We just need to get to the store. I think I can ask the others and we can probably get enough money to buy you one."

Kyrie reached into her jeans pocket and pulled out the bills she had taken from the cabin. "It's eighty dollars. Is that enough?" She handed the folded money to Michelle.

"Becca said the burner phone in the car cost thirty bucks or so. I'll see if she can get to the store and get you a phone. Then we can set up some accounts and show you how to take pictures and upload them. You'll be able to read your aunt's documents whenever you want."

Kyrie felt the smile rise to her face. "That would be great."

Michelle gave her a hug. "You are not alone. If you are ever in danger, come here, I'll make sure you are safe."


Kyrie's smile remained on her face as she approached her aunt's house. She slowed when she saw the van parked in front, but when she got closer, she noticed the advertisement for John's Locksmith Service on the back and sides. With the assumption the van belonged to someone her aunt summoned, she continued to the front door. There, she found a brand-new door handle and deadbolt.

She tried the handle and found the door secured. *Still treated like a child; summoned and then left outside.* She rang the doorbell and waited. Her aunt, Sam, and some other man moved about inside the house. A moment later her aunt opened the door.

"How nice of you to join us. You should have been home hours ago. It is almost eight."

Kyrie bit her lip. *There is only one way to know for certain.* She entered the house without saying anything and headed toward the kitchen. She had snacked at Michelle's, but she still felt hungry enough to eat more.

"Not even a hello, Aunt Kimberly? Not even a by your leave? You don't come home. You don't say where you are. I have to hunt you down and you don't even have the decency to offer a greeting."

Kyrie turned around to face her aunt. She drew energy into herself to buffer the impact if she had come to the wrong conclusion. "You've not given me a key. Why should I come here to just stand outside until either you or Sam decide to come home? You've not given me a phone to be able to call you and let you know where I'm."

"Don't take that tone with me." Her aunt stormed toward her, but then stopped when Kyrie stood up straight.

"Treat me with respect and I'll do the same." Kyrie sensed the man by the garage door. He was not in their direct line of sight, but he was definitely within hearing distance of the argument. *Not even a tingle of compulsion.* She considered releasing the power she held, but she knew she had not pushed her aunt that hard. "Give me a key. Give me a phone. Give me an allowance." She had heard Tina speaking of the money her parents gave her and thought that might be a way to antagonize her aunt.

"I've spent a fortune on you already. All the cloths, the desk, flying out to Colorado, and taking the time to drive back." Her aunt shook her head. "Now you want a phone and money. Ungrateful is what you are. Just like your mother and father."

Kyrie felt Sam on the basement stairs, but she sensed no compulsion. *Don't push too much.* She did not want her aunt to throw her out until she had a chance to learn everything she could about her parents. *Don't be a fool, she wants your money, she won't throw us out no matter what you do.* "My mother far exceeded you. She was smart and knew how things worked. You complain about everything and do nothing. You even kept the money the sheriff gave you."

Her aunt moved forward again; her arm raised. "Go to your room!"

Kyrie stood her ground, prepared to block the strike, but she doubted it would come. *She can't compel you. But what are the rules for who can? The sheriff did.*

Her aunt hesitated and then her phone rang. Kyrie observed her using the sound as an excuse for not following through with the slap. She also met Sam's gaze from where he stood at the top of the basement stairs. Her cousin looked at her with trepidation as though he saw some truth of her hardened nature that her aunt missed.

Kyrie turned back to the kitchen, ignoring her aunt's call and her cousin in her hunt for food. *You have to figure out who can control you and who can't.*

"What do you mean someone broke into the funeral home and my sister's coffin? I get that the ground is still frozen. But I don't get..."

Kyrie turned around and narrowed her eyes. Her aunt paced around the sofa and chair in the living room as she alternated between listening and yelling into the phone.

"They cut her open. What the hell is going on out there! I will sue them." Kimberly stopped and met Kyrie's gaze. "No, I understand, you have actual video of the people who broke into the funeral home. Well, how the hell do I know what they were looking for. Someone broke into my house yesterday and stole all my jewelry. I've got someone replacing locks right now." Her aunt covered the bottom of the phone with her other hand. "Your mother's wedding ring, it is not worth anything, is it?"

Kyrie felt a wave of panic wash over her. "I'm not giving it to anyone. It's mine now."

"I'm not going to take it away from you, I just wanted to make sure it wasn't stolen with all my other—yes, Sheriff, I'm still here. No, none of the things Kyrie took from the cabin were taken in the robbery. Just my jewelry and some cash." Her aunt looked at her. "Well, do you still have it?"

Kyrie nodded her head and put her hand to her chest to cover the ring. *You have more than the ring. But why would anyone want either of them?* "I have it," she said aloud. "I keep it on the cord my mother kept it on."

"Well, Sheriff, the only thing I can think is they were after the ring, but why they would be after a wedding ring is beyond me. It was just a small diamond set in a rather plan gold band. My first and second husbands did a lot better in picking rings." She crossed one arm under the other holding the phone to her ear. "Well, I'm not paying for any damages and they better burry her as soon as the ground thaws." Her aunt turned away. "Yes, I will call you if I hear anything." Her aunt hung up the phone and turned to face Kyrie.

"I'm not giving up the ring," Kyrie said before her aunt could speak. "I don't care how much it is worth."

"I'm not suggesting that you do. However, I want to know what your parents were up to. It is obvious to me that this robbery is related to that ring. Someone ransacked the immigrant shed you were living in as well as broke into the funeral home. They broke open the coffin, dumped your mother on the floor, removed all her clothing, then cut open her gut and pulled everything out looking for something. What do they want?"

"What?" Kyrie stammered, angry that her aunt would ask her when she had asked her aunt the same question previously. "You…" She caught herself before she admitted to seeing the files. "How am I to know anything? I was a baby. You tell me what you know about what my parents were up to. Where did they go?"

"Miss Leighton," the man who had been replacing the lock on the garage door said after coming into the kitchen. "If you have someone looking for something like a ring, you might want to consider adding security cameras, motion sensors, and reinforced plates over the locks and door frames."

Her aunt rolled her eyes. "Like I can afford all that."

"Well, I was just making a suggestion," the man said.

Kyrie narrowed her focus on the man, probing deeper into his thoughts and emotions. Money stood out as a significant motivation. His desire to see the ring they had been talking about filled her head. *Too much desire.* She pulled back her awareness of the emotion in the room and kept her back turned to him. She did not feel comfortable showing him her face.

"I will take it under advisement," her aunt said. "Did you finish the last of the doors?"

"I did." He moved closer. "Four exterior door locks replaced. Deadbolts upgraded and steel plates installed with reinforced anchors. I can repair the office door as well, if you want. But the damage there was worse than the back door."

"No, I will do that one later."

Kyrie felt a moment of pity for her aunt. The woman appeared exhausted and out of her element. *But she still only brought me here to get money.*

"Well, here are eight keys," the man said, coming up to stand beside Kyrie as he extended his hand to her aunt. "All the locks are keyed the same."

"Thank you, please send me the bill." Her aunt took the keys and immediately handed one to Kyrie. "Here, you can take that complaint off your list."

Kyrie took the key and looked down, partially to avoid the locksmith being able to get a good look at her face, but also to avoid her aunt's gaze. Twinges of guilt for testing the compulsion entered her thoughts. "Thank you."

Sam emerged from the stairs and came over to his aunt. "They went after Kyrie's mom? Did you say they cut her open?"

She handed Sam a key. "Don't lose it." She turned to the locksmith, "Let me show you out."

Kyrie felt Sam's gaze as her aunt led the locksmith to the front door. She looked at him. An expression of fear on his face kept her from snapping at him. "I don't know what is going on either," she said softly. *But you do know they are after you, or something your mom had and they now think you have.* She adjusted her thoughts around the car that tried to hit her. *It would not appear they need you alive. Or did they test you? Did you reveal yourself to them?* Her heart raced and she felt her chest tighten.

Her aunt returned to the living room after locking the front door. "I don't know what your parents were up to, Kyrie. If I did know, I would have told you already. They told no one and my mother died of a broken heart because her favorite daughter abandoned her."

"I thought grandma died of cancer," Sam said.

"She didn't fight the cancer because her heart broke," her aunt snapped. "If my mother couldn't find her, or figure out what happened, then no one can." She sighed. "May I at least see the ring so I can tell if there is anything obvious as to why someone might want to steal it?"

Kyrie forced herself to calm down. She pulled the ring out from under her shirt, slipped the cord over her head, and handed it to her aunt. Her aunt looked at it for a long time, turning it over and looking at the bottom as well as the top. She rubbed the stone and scratched a fingernail on the gold.

"It is just plain fourteen karat gold. A small stone. No other markings I can see." Her aunt shook her head. "Why would anyone want to steel this? It can't be worth more than a couple hundred.

Rings have a terrible resale value." She turned her head to her son. "Remember that if you ever give one to a girl. It is not worth fighting the girl to get it back, she won't make any money trying to sell it anyway." She looked at Kyrie. "I learned that in the first divorce. I let the bastard claim it as being worth the replacement value in the settlement. Sold it for less than a fourth of the value."

"Yah, Mom, I know Dad was an ass," Sam shook his head.

Kyrie sensed Sam's conflicted emotions, but she could offer no verbal statement without revealing herself. "I'm not selling the ring," she told her aunt. "It reminds me of my mother and father."

Her aunt handed it back. "It doesn't mean someone else doesn't think it is valuable. They apparently wanted to make sure your mother had not swallowed something, because the Sheriff said they... they looked through her insides."

"Can I go to my room?" Kyrie asked. She had butchered enough animals to have a solid visual of what they had done to her mother.

"Eat some dinner if you want. But I can understand if you don't want anything." Her aunt placed a hand on her shoulder. "I'll get you a phone. If someone is after the ring, they might try to hurt you. It would be good if you could call the police."

Kyrie nodded her head. *Don't trust the police. Mother and Father said never trust the police. But you could call someone else.* "Thank you." *Read through more of the notes tonight,* she told herself.

# Chapter 14

Kyrie entered the main hall of the school and waited as more students filed past her. She hoped to see Michelle come into the building, but she could not be certain if her friend had already arrived or if she would be late. The clocks on the wall indicated just ten minutes left before the bell rang.

Kyrie's focus shifted toward a group of students walking past her. A murmur of conversation included her name. After they passed, Jessica, John, and Steve approached her.

Jessica raised her eyebrows and tilted her head down so she could look up out of the corner of her eyes. "I am so sorry to tell you this, but I heard some terrible rumors about you going through the school."

"Yeah," Steve said. "I know it wasn't your fault that your parents did those things."

"Did you enjoy it?" John asked. "Some people said you must have."

Kyrie glared at the three of them. She could tell they were enjoying themselves. "What are you talking about?"

Jessica shrugged and took a sip from the cup in her hand. "Well, someone found out that your parents were being investigated for child abuse. Seems a county sheriff in Colorado is certain your father had sex with you. Repeatedly."

John grinned. "Now word through the school is that he took turns doing you and your mother in the same bed."

Kyrie stepped forward and John stepped back. "My parents never did anything to me. If you think you can take me, go ahead and try. I'll break your arms and castrate you."

John stepped back again and raised his hands. "I'd never lay a hand on a girl. But obviously, we've hit a nerve."

"And when that happens," Jessica exclaimed, "it means we have uncovered a truth." She laughed. "Told you that you'd regret being rude to me."

Kyrie took a deep breath. She looked around her. Several people had watched the confrontation and she knew Jessica had set a trap for her. *Don't do it.* Kyrie looked at the clocks and turned in the direction of her English class; Michelle was either going to be late, or she was already in the school.

"Running away?" Jessica teased.

Kyrie concentrated on Jessica's hand and formed a small gravity well just inside the cup's wall closest to the blonde. The field sucked her hand closed and drew it toward her chest. Jessica shrieked as the coffee splashed all down her front; others giggled as the crumpled cup fell to the floor.

*It was worth it,* she told herself.


Kyrie felt eyes upon her through her first four periods. She did not bother to interact with anyone and simply waited until fifth period arrived.

She entered the art room and knew immediately that some people had heard the rumors. When she saw Tina and Michelle, she knew they discussed her in their quiet conversation.

"Hi." Kyrie hardly expected them to respond. She felt the coldness of Tina's emotions and saw the distance on her face. Michelle, however, exuded sympathy.

"Don't listen to the rumors," Michelle said. "We know better."

Kyrie more felt than heard Tina mumble "do we?"

"I never did what Jessica is claiming." Kyrie took a deep breath and leaned in closer to Michelle so she could whisper. "I need help. I need the brooch back."

"I can check with Aki to see if her father finished it," Michelle replied in her ear. "What's the rush?"

"Someone broke into the funeral home where they have my mother. They stripped her and then dissected her looking for something."

"Oh my god," Michelle exclaimed. "When did that happen?"

"Sheriff Sawyer called my aunt last night. I don't know when it happened." Kyrie felt Tina's irritation that Michelle was giving her so much attention. She lowered her voice again. "I just need my things back and I need copies of those papers."

"You think it's tied to the robbery?" Michelle asked as the bell rang.

Kyrie bit her lip. "My mother had two pieces of jewelry. I can't think of anything else."

"All right class," Mrs. Stine said, "we need to start working on your final projects for the year. There are only a few weeks left of school, so it needs to be big."

Kyrie turned her attention to the teacher so that Tina's anger and frustration would not fill her mind.


When the bell rang to dismiss school, Kyrie bolted toward the exit and waited outside for the others to join her. Michelle, Jake, and Becca came out of the school in a group and walked over to her. She looked for Tina and Aki, but she did not see them.

Michelle clarified the situation. "Aki's getting a ride to her father's shop and then she'll bring it over to my house. She said her dad had not started on it yet, but he would at least fix the clasp before she gets there."

"Then we get these papers of yours," Becca said, "and I can help you get them securely uploaded. If they are important, you don't want others having access to them."

Kyrie nodded her head to both Michelle and Becca. None of them mentioned Tina's absence. "Thank you. I appreciate it."

"No one should defile your mother like that," Jake offered. "We'll help you find out what is going on. And more importantly, we won't leave you alone."

Kyrie smiled at the group around her and then they hurried through the gate to leave the school property. The near mile trip to Michelle's house felt long only because Kyrie allowed the others to set a pace comfortable for them.

Kyrie walked next to Michelle as they turned off the main street and into the housing development. A few cars, driven by parents, or students on their way home, passed them, but as usual, the neighborhood remained quiet.

"I don't think I will be able to stay here very long," Kyrie said quietly to Michelle. "I've enjoyed meeting all of you, but things are happening."

Michelle leaned closer. "You're not talking about running away are you? Let us help you. You need a support group to help watch out for you. You don't want to live on the streets with no money and resources."

Thoughts of the journals and the implications of her mother's work slipped through her mind. *Power from another universe? Mother couldn't prove the math, but she was getting close.* She wanted to explain to Michelle, but she doubted her friend would grasp the theories. *We barely grasp them.*

Kyrie's attention shifted to a white SUV that slowly passed them. The man behind the wheel examining her in his mirrors. Kyrie slowed and the man kept driving. *You are jumping at everything. Just get back to the mountains. We can disappear there.*

"What is it?" Michelle asked. "Was there something with that car?"

Kyrie thought about it, trying to remember if she felt any particular emotion from the driver. *It's too hard to know if they are just watching you because you are walking or if it's because they know who we are.* "I don't know. I've never seen it before."

"But you noticed the blue car that ended up outside your house when it drove by a couple of times," Michelle said to complete her thought.

*There is still so much for us to do and learn.*

They turned down the tree-lined street Michelle lived on and Kyrie voiced a concern that had bothered her the whole afternoon. "I'm sorry for causing a fight between you and Tina."

Michelle shrugged. "It is not our first fight. Not even that bad of one." She turned her head to the side and gazed into a memory. "She gets possessive. She wants me to herself all the time. The prom issue's been bubbling up for a few weeks. Her plans just didn't excite me as much as they excited her. Then you came along and she's feeling abandoned."

Kyrie opened her mouth to comment, but a vehicle raced up the street behind them and she pushed Michelle to the side in case it tried to run them over.

She turned her head to see a white panel van. The driver's attention focused on her. Energy flooded into her as she prepared to use her powers to push the rest of her friends out of the way. However, instead of jumping the curb and running them over, the van screeched to a stop beside them as the side door slid open. Kyrie already sensed the two men in the back of the van, and she put herself between them and Michelle.

"Stay back," she demanded of her friends. The two men jumped out of the van, swords brandished and held over their heads. *Control,* she reminded herself.

"Die, Demon!" The man in a green t-shirt shouted. A cross tattooed on each of his forearms stood out with the bright pigments. The revolutionary era saber in his hand swung toward her head.

Kyrie dodged easily to the side, using a gravitational field to compensate for the sharp angle of her movement. She came in close, under the man's swing, and landed a punch. Her fist, augmented by another gravity field, crushed his right side. The impact of the blow hurt her hand, but she felt at least one of the man's ribs crack.

The second man, wielding a katana, thrust his sword at her, forcing her to dodge again, leveraging more energy to nearly float horizontally under the attack. She feared demonstrating her abilities, but the men gave her little choice.

She rotated away from the men and manipulated gravity to bring her feet back under herself.

"God will smite you, Demon!" The second man demanded as he pressed his attack, jabbing and slashing at her as she fell back in retreat.

*They know I have powers!* She had no time to contemplate how they knew as she ducked under a swing and moved in close to deliver a punch to the man's gut. Kyrie recognized the blade's oriental nature, but she remained thankful that the man did not have any real martial training, or he would have blocked her punch.

She moved back from the second man and away from his sword.

"Take her head!" Shouted the driver, still in the van and watching through the open door.

The first man, in the t-shirt, ran toward Michelle. "Surrender or they die!"

Kyrie heard Becca and Jake yelling behind her, but with her friends split into two groups, she could not physically position herself in front of both attackers. *Don't reveal yourself,* she heard her father swearing and she wondered if she could explain her movements as simply being nimble. *You don't abandon friends,* came her own reply as she allowed energy to flood into herself, burning and causing pain.

Kyrie divided her attention. She slammed energy into the man with the katana, who charged at her again. The gravity wave hit him squarely in the face and upper body, sending him flying backward. The blade fell from his hand as he smashed into the side of the van with enough force to crumple most of the sliding door.

A half-second later, she turned her full attention on the man in the t-shirt. A gravity wall pushed him backwards and away from Michelle, but then she crafted a more complex field around his body, holding him firmly in place. Michelle's panicked cry died in her throat when her assailant froze in place.

"The witch has me!" The man cried.

The driver cursed and struggled to get out of his seat and to come to the aid of companions. Kyrie saw a revolver in his hand. *How about a singularity?* She thought with a grin. Energy left her mind as she created a sharp point of gravitational force where his hand gripped the weapon. *Control, Stupid!*

He screamed as muscle, bone, and tendons collapsed upon themselves and were crushed against the pistol handle. When she released the power, the bent weapon fell from his mangled hand.

Becca cursed from behind her.

"Lord, free me," cried the man in the t-shirt. "We do your work. Don't let this demon take me!"

"Kyrie, what is happening?" Michelle stood fully upright and no longer cowered under the blow she thought would end her life.

"Who are you?" Kyrie demanded of the frozen man. "I've done nothing to anyone." She wanted to say she was no demon. To profess innocence. *But are you innocent? You don't even know what you are.*

"What is going on?" demanded Becca. "What are you?"

"She's a wizard," Jake said. "Or a monk."

Kyrie ignored her friends. Her mind throbbed as energy still coursed through her into the gravity field around the man in the t-shirt. She recognized his mind as the man who tried to run her over. His upper body and head moved as he struggled with the field holding his arms and legs in place. His movements kept causing her to adjust and adapt the pressure so that he would remain held. Tired from the effort, she enlarged the field to cover his whole body and strengthened it to limit her concentration. The man now struggled to breathe.

"Kyrie, talk to me," Michelle said, coming closer.

"I have to know who these people are and why they are trying to kill me," she responded, the emotion in her voice not only from the frustration of being in the dark, but also from the pain of the energy coursing through her. She put her right hand on his back, instinctively opening part of her field to avoid hurting her own hand.

"Look, a hold spell," Jake said to Becca.

"Jake, please, we need to get out of here," Becca pleaded, pulling at his arm.

Kyrie shut out her surroundings and focused on the man's mind. The fear of suffocating filled his thoughts, blocking her attempts to probe deeper.

"Kyrie, the other guy with the sword is waking up," Michelle cried, placing a hand on her left arm.

"Church of the Revenge," Kyrie mumbled. She stepped back, overwhelmed with the man's fear, she barely kept her feet under her. Her awareness picked up movement from the driver, as he dealt with the pain of his crushed hand.

"I'm not whatever you think I am," Kyrie told the man she held. She could hear another car coming. "We need to go," she said to her friends.

"That's what I've been saying," Becca demanded, trying to pull Jake with her.

"You're a bloody wizard," Jake declared, allowing Becca to pull him down the sidewalk with his head turned back to look at Kyrie. "A real-life mage."

Kyrie took Michelle's hand and ran with her. She released the field around the man in the t-shirt after only a couple of steps. The energy draw had brought blood to her nose, and as the distance to him increased, so did the amount of power and control it took to maintain the field. One thing she knew from his mind, the man would not pursue her immediately. *It is a good thing they fear you, because you're spent,* she admitted to herself. *You didn't regulate the flow well enough.* She grew somber. *They called us a demon. Mother's campaigns were around possession. What are we?*


Kyrie felt out of breath as they neared Michelle's house. The four friends had continued to look over their shoulders, but the van had not pursued them. In fact, they had all heard it do a rough u-turn and speed away.

"What are you?" Becca demanded again.

Kyrie blinked back tears. "I don't know. I really don't know."

"You're bleeding," Michelle said. "Did they hurt you?"

Kyrie shook her head and wiped the blood from her nose. "I overspent myself. Drew too much power through me."

Jake moved into her line of sight. "I didn't hear any verbal components. How'd you cast those spells? Hold person. Was the other fly? They are both concentration."

Jake's excitement made Kyrie feel even more tired. "This is not the same as D&D." She looked at Michelle. "It is not safe to be around me. Can you have Aki go to my aunt's house to drop it off?"

Michelle started to stay something and then changed her mind. "Kyrie, you need to call the police and let them know what just happened."

Kyrie shook her head. "I can't risk it."

"Well, I'm not going to leave you alone to deal with sword wielding mad men." Michelle crossed her arms. "I'm not."

"I could not live with myself if any of you got hurt." Kyrie felt herself trembling. "I can't go to the police." *Because you are a demon.*

Becca stepped closer. "Well, you can't just let people break into your house, run you over, and now try to cut you up. We have to find a way to stop them. What did you say when you touched the man?"

"Church of the Revenge," Kyrie said. "It is like an identity. A group of some kind." She bit her lip and held back the tears that wanted to come. She could not push the idea that she was possessed from her thoughts, but more of the man's memories percolated in her mind. "He's the one that tried to run me over. These three parked the car in front of the house to monitor me."

Becca pulled out her phone and started typing on it.

"I hate to bring it up, but we should probably not stand out here a hundred yards from Michelle's house." Jake looked around at the others. "The papers Kyrie wanted to get copies of are at her house. Go there?"

Kyrie nodded her head. "Those men won't be back any time soon. We have some time. I shattered the driver's hand. The one in the t-shirt has a fractured rib and is filled with terror. I may have broken a bone or two in the other man."

"Okay," Michelle said. "I'll text Aki to meet us at your house." Michelle started typing on her phone as well. "But, Kyrie, you are not running away. We'll find a place to keep you safe."

Kyrie felt Michelle's protective determination. *She doesn't fear us.* The realization calmed her. "Thank you."

# Chapter 15

Kyrie wheezed as heavily as the others by the time they reached her aunt's house. She spared enough energy to confirm no one hid in the house and then went to the door, unlocked it with her key, and entered. The alarm company had not activated the alarm yet, so she did not have to enter a pass code.

"You still need to go to the police," Jake said, picking up Michelle's argument. "Sword wielding men trying to kill you is not something you can handle on your own."

Kyrie held back the angry retort she initially wanted to give him. "Things outside the valley are not as I understood. However, my parents always said that if the police knew what I could do, they would lock me in a cage and experiment on me."

Michelle's eyes widened and then she nodded her head. "She's right. I was wrong. We can't go to the cops. The government would make her disappear."

Becca held up her phone. "You said the Church of the Revenge. I found a site. Not super popular, and there is the word 'Righteous' in the middle of the name." She showed the others as they came closer. "I've not read a lot, but their landing page is some serious nut job... well, I would normally say it is crazy, but..." She looked at Kyrie and shrugged.

Michelle read from Becca's screen. "Their aim is to slay the demons walking among us."

"I'm not a demon," Kyrie pleaded. "I'm just a confused girl who lived her whole life away from everyone else."

"I believe you," Michelle said, then looked pointedly at the other two.

"I seriously need to understand what the hell is going on." Becca turned her phone back to herself and started scrolling again. "But anyone who puts out crap like this and tries to kill someone on the street with a sword is not the good guy."

"I'm with you as well." Jake glanced out the window next to the front door. "They can't track you, can they?" He asked Becca.

"Please," the disdain in her voice withered Jake. "I'm black, not stupid. I use a VPN to access everything." Becca turned her attention back to Kyrie and Michelle. "You might not be alone in this, Kyrie. There has to be others like you out there. They are talking about politicians and others being taken over by demons. God fearing citizens who had normal lives, then changed and turned into slaves. They claim the demons want to infiltrate our world to take over."

"Not alone?" Kyrie asked.

Becca softened her expression. "Hey, don't worry. I'll figure this site out."

Kyrie nodded her head as she realized just how thankful she felt that they had not abandoned her. *We need them to help us understand computers and how to move about with other people. And you like them.* "Let me show you the papers my aunt has. I hoped to use them to find out what might have happened when I was a baby. Something caused these people to come after me." She started for the stairs.

"We know the name of the group," Michelle said. "What if I went to the police and say they attacked me? Leave you out of it?"

"That only works if Kyrie disappears," Jake countered, following behind Michelle and Kyrie as they went upstairs. "Otherwise, they'll ask questions and find her. I've seen enough movies to know what they would do to her."

Becca hurried after the others. "I'll keep digging on this site. I might be able to find who registered it or tie some blog rants to real people. Extremists often don't know anything about computer security and that reveals their true identities."

Kyrie took the others to her bedroom and then quickly retrieved the files from her aunt's office. She had not realized the level of anxiety that had built within her. The relief of finding the files where she had left them made her shake. She calmed herself before she returned to her bedroom where the others had already started looking through her things. "My aunt says she doesn't know much, but these documents, most of which my grandmother wrote, have some details. I've not had a chance to read them all yet."

"These are some excellent D&D books." Jake picked up the second edition player's handbook. "Sweet artwork. Sorry." He set the book down. "Your powers. You read that man's mind, moved things, flew…those are things you can do in D&D."

Kyrie rubbed at her nose, dislodging some dried blood. She wiped the flakes on her jeans. "It's different. There is energy all around us. In us—"

"Star Wars," Jake mumbled.

"I don't know what that means. The world is made up of matter and energy. There is gravity, strong nuclear forces, weak nuc—"

"That is physics," Becca interrupted.

Kyrie nodded her head, wondering if she would ever get to finish her explanation. "Yes. Physics. My mother spent years trying to explain it with math." She looked at each of the others as they watched her. "I can sense the energy. I can feel gravity. And if I concentrate, I can adjust the energy fields. I can cause energy to move from one location to another. A lot like fluid mechanics, but I'm controlling it with my mind. However, most of what I do well is just a manipulation of gravity in a very localized area. Make it stronger or weaker."

"Holy shit," Jake said. "You could be the key to antigravity and FTL travel."

Michelle stepped between her and Jake. "Kyrie needs our support, not someone to turn her into some spaceship."

"Sorry." He paused, but his excitement still flowed. "What else can you do? Can you turn invisible? Cast fireball? Lightning?"

She felt as if she had already explained most of it, but then accepted they had less formal training with physics and might not be able to infer the depth of her abilities. "If I concentrate energy in one place, things will get hot. If it gets hot enough, things will spontaneously combust, assuming there is enough oxygen." Kyrie sat down in her chair, feeling worn out by the efforts to fight off the men. "I've never thrown lightning, though I've created sparks. Invisible?" She shook her head. "Perhaps if I created a strong enough gravitational field, I could bend light around me, but I imagine that would be like creating a black hole and the gravity from that would kill me."

"What about the nosebleed?" Michelle asked. "You looked pale by the end of the fight."

"When energy flows through something with resistance, it generates heat. Human bodies have a lot of resistance. I don't channel everything through me, but enough energy moves through my body that it starts to burn me internally. The bleeding is because I used too much power too quickly without regulating myself."

"Like mana." Becca looked up from her phone. "You ran out of mana and started burning health."

Michelle knelt next to her. "You need to be careful. There's no heads-up display showing us what you have left. Do you need us to get you anything to eat or drink?"

"A health pack," Jake added.

Kyrie smiled at her friend. "That would be good. I can go for a large glass of water and maybe some cookies." She looked toward the window, mental movement outside drawing her attention. She pulled a very limited amount of energy through herself to confirm her suspicions. "Aki is outside."

Jake moved to the window and looked out. "Amazing." He headed to the door. "I'll get Aki. And some water and cookies for you."

"These are some messed up people." Becca stopped scrolling and looked up. "Let me see those folders. We'll setup some secure cloud storage and upload pictures of them there."

Kyrie got up from the chair and spread them out on the bed. "The first and last ones appear to be notes from when my grandmother tried to find my parents."

"Your parents never told you anything about yourself and why you have these powers?" Michelle asked. "Nothing?"

"I think my mother and father ran some of their campaigns to simulate things that might have happened to me. That, and to show me how to function in this world without them." She took a deep breath. "They never had any powers, except for the ability to compel me to do what they wanted."

"You've asked about that before," Michelle said.

Becca looked up from the folders, having just taken another picture of a page, and grunted a desire to know more.

"My mother could make me do what she wanted. Sometimes my father would compel me. They could exert an enormous force on my mind to make me behave if I acted out. It didn't happen very often. Normally, I would just feel the tingles of the force if I goofed off too much instead of doing what they wanted. Mostly a threat of what they could do kept me in line." She rubbed her nose. The taste of iron still overwhelmed all other smells.

"The sheriff in Colorado exerted the same force on me." Kyrie shook her head. "My parents never explained it and I just assumed all adults could do it to me. They had me afraid to speak with any adult for fear I would be compelled to obey them and reveal things we didn't want anyone to know."

Becca crossed her arms. "That does not sound like loving parents. That sounds like controlling and manipulative bastards."

"Be nice, Becca," Michelle said, moving closer to Kyrie.

"My parents loved me. I know that. They wanted to keep me safe, but I'm frustrated with them." Kyrie picked up three journals off the top of the stack. "My mother created a secret language to record her theories. They were afraid and I think for a good reason. Ever since I screwed up, people have been circling around me like a flock of vultures."

"How'd you screw up?" Michelle asked. "This isn't your fault."

"I went for help instead of running away. Had I done as they told me, I would not be here. Their friend would have helped get me someplace safe." Kyrie set the journals down. "Becca, can we upload all these as well? They will weigh too much for me to carry away."

"You're not running away," Michelle repeated. "We'll find another way. Besides, are you sure you can trust this friend of theirs? I mean, do you know anything about him?"

*You really don't,* she admitted and then pursed her lips. "He has not done as he promised. He's not come for me yet and keeps telling me it will take a long time." She looked at Michelle, hoping to gain an answer to the question that nagged her. "I've never met him. I know my parents trusted him, but he claims they didn't tell him anything about what chases me in order to protect him. The trouble is, who else can I trust?"

"Me. I want to help."

Kyrie wondered at the devotion of this girl she had known less than a week. She felt it strongly from Michelle. *Perhaps normal people can trust that quickly.* "I just don't want any of you to come to harm."

"Kyrie," Becca said, interrupting the conversation. "It appears your grandmother spent a lot of time trying to find out about this trip to Arkansas your parents took the month before they disappeared."

"My aunt said when I was a baby something was wrong with me. I didn't move or make sounds. Then right after the trip, I appeared normal." Kyrie knelt beside the bed to look at the papers. "I could not get my aunt to tell me where they had gone. I don't think she actually knows."

"Well, your grandmother tracked them to a hotel in Fayetteville." Becca flipped a couple of pages. "Interviews your grandmother did with the hotel staff said they stayed the night, left in the morning, then didn't come back until very early the next morning. They stayed until the next day and then left." She frowned. "The staff said their car came back covered in mud. Someone had to clean up the parking lot because a rain shower washed a bunch of mud off their car."

Michelle knelt beside Kyrie and started looking through the first folder while Becca continued looking at the third one. "So, you're thinking this trip to Arkansas gave you superpowers and you want to understand where and how that is possible."

Kyrie smiled and looked at Michelle. "That is exactly what I have been thinking. My mother was obsessed with the multiverse and energy transference. Many of the journals are about those theories and several of the campaigns had me traveling between worlds." She took a breath. *You can't tell them about the possession themes. No, that would make them think we are a demon.* She swallowed the fear building in her. *What if we are?*

She turned to Becca. "I noticed a man that appeared to reach out to my grandmother on his own and then continued to call her."

Aki's voice came from down the hall. "Jake, what do you mean Kyrie is a witch? Quit being a jerk. I'm not in the mood." When Aki came into the bedroom, she looked around. "What the hell?"

"Tell her," Jake demanded as he handed Kyrie the glass of water and a bag of cookies. "Aki doesn't believe me that we were attacked on the way home by sword wielding nut jobs and that you can cast spells."

Becca looked up from the page she was reading. "Jake, don't be an ass. Aki doesn't need your crap."

Aki punched Jake in the shoulder. "I told you I wasn't in the mood."

Becca smiled and stood up. "Actually, Jake is telling the truth. Kyrie has some weird powers and two men wielding swords, calling Kyrie a demon, attacked us on the way home. They wanted to cut her head off. The driver pulled a gun, but she used her mind to crush his hand."

"I'm not a demon," Kyrie clarified.

"Screw you, Becca," Aki said. "I'm not in the mood."

"Kyrie, do you want to start from the beginning?" Michelle asked.

Kyrie nodded her head and then drank nearly the whole glass in one gulp. "I will, but do you have the brooch?"

Aki put her hands on her hips. "I'll punch all of you if you don't knock it off." After a moment of silence, she pulled a small box out of her purse and handed it to Kyrie.

Kyrie opened the box and removed the worn jewelry. A sense of dread washed from her and she took a seat on the bed. She cleared her throat and retold her tale to the four of them. She kept to the facts that other people already knew, explaining in more detail how the sheriff had compelled her and her fears that the others might get compelled for how they acted before she learned no one knew of this punishment.

When she finished, Aki glared at her. "This is a fancy story, but I find it hard to believe. You already pissed off Tina, you trying to do the same to me?"

Kyrie glanced to the stack of books on the desk, pulled in a small amount of energy, and lifted the top two into the air, floating them right past Aki, and into her hand.

"Shit!" Aki looked around the room at the others. "You saw that? Kyrie levitated a book!" Aki stopped dancing around. "And you have some religious bastards trying to kill you. We'll nail their balls to an ant hill and let them get bit by a million fire ants."

"Aki, settle down," Michelle said. Then she smiled. "I like it though."

"What about Tina?" Jake asked. "Do we tell her?"

Michelle shook her head. "Tina's crush on me is getting out of hand. I keep reminding her we are just friends, but her emotions get the better of her sometimes and she's likely to tell someone if she gets angry."

Becca raised a thumb. "Agreed. There are four of us who know beside Kyrie. Her parents never even told their friend Lars."

Kyrie frowned at the others. "Had we not been attacked together I wouldn't have ever told any of you. I don't know who these people are and what they'll do. My father had several campaigns where he would use NPCs I liked as hostages to make me do what the bad guys wanted." *His lesson was always to sacrifice the NPC, you can't tell them that. And you still won't do it.*

"What happened to the NPCs?" Jake asked.

"If they died, he would never bring them back." Kyrie picked up the glass and finished off the last of the water.

"I still want to know how this is possible," Aki demanded.

"Based on my mother's journals, she believes it was an energy transference from another universe." Kyrie glanced at the stack of papers from her mother. "She never finished the math for the theory, but she was close."

"Sign me up," Jake said. "I want to be a mage."

*He might not want it if he knew the truth.* Kyrie picked up the brooch. The green stone seemed to have an internal energy that she never paid attention to before, but now that she felt it, she realized it had always been there. "Somehow I think this is a key to part of it. My mother always had this on her, and my father always stood near her when he compelled me. I remember now that the sheriff held the bag that contained it when he demanded I tell the truth." She handed the brooch to Michelle. "I'm going to trust you. I want you to demand I do something."

"I am not comfortable with that." Michelle handed the brooch back. "I don't want to cause you pain."

Kyrie nodded her head and looked at the others.

"I'll do it," Jake said. He stepped closer. "How do you think it works?"

She held out the brooch. "Try thinking of something you want me to do. I don't think the sheriff knew he could control me, yet he did. If that doesn't work, say it aloud."

Jake took the brooch, stepped back against the wall, and then looked at her. She felt the tingling sensation of compulsion building in her. Jake's desire did not come clearly to her at first, but she found herself unable to look away from his lips. She tried to remain standing where she was, but pain built in the back of her mind when she resisted the desire to move toward him.

Kyrie moved forward and the pressure lessened, but the moment she slowed, the pain grew crippling. She lunged forward.

"Wait," Jake said, putting a hand out to stop her. He immediately handed the brooch to her. "I'm sorry. I couldn't think of anything and that just came to mind."

Kyrie felt the pain clear as soon as she had possession of the brooch again. As her mind cleared, she felt anger build in her.

"What did you do, Jake," Michelle demanded, coming to stand beside Kyrie.

"I wanted to make sure she did not fake it." His eyes darted to each of them and then back to Kyrie. "I wouldn't have let you do it."

Kyrie felt the others looking at her and her rage started to fade. "Don't ever do that again." She took a deep breath, let the anger leave her, and wondered why her emotions were so confused.

"Jake, tell us, or get out." Michelle stood five inches shorter than Jake, but he appeared smaller than her.

"I simply thought she should try to kiss me." He shook his head. "I swear I would not have let her do it. I just wanted to make sure."

Becca cleared her throat. "Well, we know that the brooch controls her. Or can at least causes her a lot of pain if she refuses. Obviously, someone knew about it and hoped to find it. Hence the robbery." She then frowned at Jake. "That was an asshole move, dude."

"I'm sorry," he said to Becca and then turned to Kyrie. "Please believe me, I'm so sorry."

"Count me out of being a mage if someone can control you like that," Aki said.

Kyrie shook her head. "I'm not angry at Jake. I needed confirmation of what it could do, and he provided it." She put the brooch into her pants' pocket. *It's the stone that is important.* "I need to understand how this happened." *That was one thing neither of you gamed. Mother, Father, you knew. You used that on us and you knew what it could do.* Her anger built again, but she knew it had nowhere to go.

Becca held up another sheet of paper. "Michael Rodgers is the man you mentioned. Your grandmother spoke to him a lot. Based on the notes, he played her for information instead of providing it." She put the paper down and picked up another one. "She asked him to look for anything dealing with 'revitalization' and 'rebirth' and a number of other spiritual health terms. But I can't see that he ever found anything for her. He just kept asking her if she heard anything and making promises." Becca looked up. "I want to say your grandmother eventually figured him out."

Kyrie smiled. "I hope so. My grandmother wrote that he heard about my mother's and father's disappearance and wanted to help. He had contacted her first."

Becca crossed her arms and shook her head. "This guy is a hacker. He'd feed her something, perhaps truthful, perhaps a lie, and get her to tell him everything she knew." Becca looked at the others. "My dad's a computer security expert. You think he doesn't tell me how hackers think?"

Michelle looked at the notes. "So, is he one of those Church of the Righteous Revenge freaks or someone else?"

Becca shrugged. "No idea from this. I have his phone number. I'll do some cyber stalking and see what I can find." She sighed. "I really need my laptop. It would go faster."

Michelle flipped through the photos. "So, we have a name of someone who looks like he wanted to find your parents as much as your grandmother and a place in Arkansas sixteen years ago that no one knows about."

"Could Kyrie be a stolen baby?" Aki asked. "Perhaps they swapped their own child for another one. Could explain why you have powers and your parents didn't. Also, why people are after you."

Michelle shook her head. "I'd say no." She held up a photo of her parents in college. "Your mother was very pretty and your father very handsome."

"Thank you," Kyrie said.

"And you look just like your mother," Michelle added.

Becca grinned. "Yeah, a hot girl who can literally set things on fire."

"Not a stolen baby," Aki admitted.

"I wish someone would steal my brother," Michelle said.

"He's okay sometimes," Jake countered. "You have not always hated him."

Michelle nodded her head. "Maybe, but he's been stealing my underwear and gave some to Sam. So, I'm not going to give him that much credit."

"When was that?" Becca asked.

"Three weeks ago. They were new and I yelled at my mother for losing them, but then I caught him sneaking another pair out of the dryer. I beat his ass, but then I got in trouble for that." Michelle sighed. "Sorry, not really important, compared to what you have going on."

Kyrie laughed. "I've never had a brother or sister or even a friend. I enjoy hearing about things other people have to deal with."

"Well," Aki said, "some time I can tell you all about how Japanese parents can screw up their kids if you want. But, Kyrie, did you really read all these D&D books at three?"

Kyrie nodded her head. "Why?"

"Sorry for doubting you last night. But I have a thought, what is the earliest memory you do have?" Aki dropped to the floor and sat cross-legged. "Perhaps you can remember what happened in Arkansas. Maybe whatever they did to you made you have super memory as well as these powers."

"You think like a concoction of serums that turns someone into a mutant?" Jake asked.

Michelle frowned. "How about a superhero instead of a mutant?"

"Girl power!" Aki raised her hand and gave Michelle a high-five.

Kyrie raised a hand to silence them. "I have clear memories of being two years old in the mountains. My legs were too short, and things were always out of my reach. I have some vague memories from before that, but nothing concrete." She chuckled. "I remember not understanding why I did not have the strength or balance to move about as I thought I should be able to." *Or even had done previously.*

Kyrie watched Michelle, Aki, and Jake exchanging looks. Becca was still into her phone. "You think I'm possessed."

Michelle frowned. "I don't know what to think. Reading at that early of an age. Understanding things like D&D manuals and physics…"

Kyrie nodded her head. *Said too much.* "I understand."

Michelle put her hand on Kyrie's arm. "We're still here. No one is abandoning you."

"You could be a good demon," Aki said. "I don't know my own history, but there are good demons in Japanese religion." She frowned. "Or at least I think so. My parents are Catholic." She brightened. "Maybe an angel?"

Becca interrupted. "If you're done being touchy-feely, how about I tell you a little of what I'm finding."

Kyrie and the others turned to face Becca.

"So, looking around Fayetteville to see what her parents might have gotten into sent me down a few options." She tossed one page over her shoulder. "The hotel is a dead end. The people there didn't know anything sixteen years ago, so they would know less now. However, what is obvious is that Kyrie's mother spent months looking for alternative healing before they found something in Arkansas." She held up her phone. "So, with the power of the Internet, I figured I might do some of the same searching."

Kyrie felt herself leaning forward. "You found something?"

Becca smiled. "In due time."

Kyrie's eyes narrowed.

"Okay. Okay." Becca handed her the phone. "I did a little crawling in the Internet Archive and the Wayback Machine to look for dead websites and found one. Not exactly in Fayetteville, but still in Arkansas. It went by the name Healing Spring Arkansas. It looks like a combination of Native American shaman healing, with some hillbilly, and a bit of spiritual consumerism. Buy yourself magic healing. Let the ancient spirits heal you. All for a reasonable low price of 'call for a quote.'"

Kyrie started to scroll up and down and page.

"Terrible design," Becca said as she looked at the screen over Kyrie's shoulder, "even for sixteen years ago. But there is an address and a phone number. They promise to revitalize the sick and heal the injured using the power of nature. And I quote, 'Where the fabric of the universe is thin, energy flows, and lives are restored.'"

Michelle looked at the screen and copied the address into her phone. After a moment of navigating she frowned. "I don't want to get all creeped out, but there still appears to be a business associated with the address. Awan Brown Pottery."

"The location is really backwoods," Becca said. "It could explain the mud on the car." She took Michelle's phone and followed several links before she added, "Awan Brown Pottery, no phone, no website, no business hours. Seems like a front." She changed applications and entered a few more items on the screen. "I'll show you. It's a handful of miles south of some town called Japton. It's in Arkansas, off state Highway 295. Estimates four and a half hours to drive there."

Kyrie stood up. "That is not that far." She bit her lip. "If this is what gave me powers, I need to know. Perhaps there are others there like me that could tell me what is going on."

"Not far says the girl without a car." Aki shook her head. "That's a long drive when parents are wondering where you are. It's a full day there and back."

"How hard is it to dive?" Kyrie asked. "I could learn and then go there myself."

Jake and Aki frowned, but Michelle spoke up. "Driving is not that hard, but it can be unnerving to deal with traffic. I don't like getting on the freeways. Always afraid I will get hit."

Jake got to his feet. "Are we really considering driving to Arkansas to investigate some hillbilly website that dropped off the Internet sixteen years ago? We almost got killed today." He looked down at

Kyrie. "I'm on your side, but this is risky. We should find a better way."

Kyrie shook her head. "I don't want any of you to go. I don't want anyone to get hurt. But I have to go." She looked at each of them. "I heard people talking about getting a ride through some app in the lunchroom. I can do that."

Michelle stood as well. "You won't find anyone to drive you that far. At least not unless you have a lot of money."

"They'd be pedos and pervs if they agreed to it," Becca said. "They might take you, but then you'd have to fight off a rapist."

"I'm serious," Jake said. "Sword wielding freaks jumped from a van in this neighborhood today. You might find more there."

Kyrie moved to her desk. "I know. But if I don't figure this out, I will be dealing with them again. Perhaps even breaking into this house to kill me at night. Eventually, they will get me. I have to go on the offensive."

"I wonder why the swords," Aki said. "Don't tell me they absorb your powers by cutting off your head." She looked at Michelle. "What? I watch retro movies."

Kyrie frowned at Aki, not following the conversation. "I've not been killed yet, so I really can't say." She looked at Jake. "I'm not asking anyone to come with me. I just need your help figuring out a way I can get there."

Michelle cleared her throat. "I will drive you. We can leave Friday after school. I just need to think of a way to convince my parents to let me have the car back." She raised a hand to stop the others from interrupting. "I'll tell my parents we are spending the weekend at Aki's. That we'll be studying and playing. It would not be the first time we've had a big weekend like that." She turned back to Kyrie. "That would give us all day Saturday to find something, then we drive back Sunday."

"You're crazy," Jake said. "Your parents would never let you have the car back."

"If I apologize to Mike this evening in front of them and promise to go to KU like they want, I think I can get them to give it to me."

"Michelle," Aki's voice carried her dismay, "you can't do that. You don't want to go into medicine. You want to be an artist."

Michelle frowned at Aki. "I can always change my mind later. We still have another year of high school before we graduate. It won't be like I'm signing a blood pact. They can't curse me if I break the deal."

"I'll go with you," Becca said. "You'll need someone who is smart."

"Thanks," Michelle said, "I think."

"Well, count me in too then." Aki shook her head. "I'll tell my parents I'm staying at your house. It is a good thing they don't know each other."

Kyrie looked at the three girls in her room. *You better keep them safe.* "Thank you. I have spent my whole life not knowing about myself. The chance I might find out the truth means so much."

"Damn it." Jake shook his head. "I can't let the four of you go to Arkansas on your own. I have a tent and some sleeping bags I can sneak out of my parent's garage. We'll need them, because none of us are old enough to rent a hotel room."

Michelle crossed her arms. "You're just trying to go camping with a bunch of girls."

Jake frowned. "Yeah, right. I'm so harmless that even your parents stopped objecting to me staying over when we are all playing. The chance of any of you giving me the time of day is nonexistent."

Kyrie looked back at the documents on the bed. "What do I need to do to get copies of these?"

Becca raised an eyebrow. "We need to get you a phone so you can access them. I've already uploaded the folders to a secure site, but that won't do you any good until you have a device and learn how to use it." She glanced at the journals. "Those will take a lot more work to get uploaded."

"And what about tonight?" Jake asked. "I'm man enough to admit I'm a bit scared to walk home alone. But we can't just leave Kyrie by herself either, can we?"

Michelle, Aki, and Becca looked at each other. "No way our parents will let us have a sleep over during the week," they all spoke at the same time.

Kyrie started to gather all the papers and put them back in the folders. "I'm not back to normal, but I have recovered a bit. I will be careful and won't go out of the house. Plus, I'm pretty certain the men who attacked me today won't be in a position to do it again for a while."

Aki added, "And if we all call each other, and stay on the phone until we get home, then we'll at least know if anyone else is in danger."

Michelle paced to the door and back. "I don't like leaving you alone, but I don't think we have a choice. Plus, I need to set the groundwork for our trip tomorrow."

"And make sure your parents don't object to our spending the weekend gaming," Jake said.

Kyrie spoke before Michelle. "And I need to convince my aunt I will be spending the weekend with my new friends. I don't know her that well, so I will have to manipulate her."

"Like the suggestion spell?" Jake asked.

Kyrie shook her head. "Big eyes." She dropped her chin and looked up at Jake.

Michelle laughed at Jake's startled expression and red cheeks. "Mountain girl learns fast."

# Chapter 16

"What do you mean you want to spend the weekend at this girl's house?"

Kyrie adjusted her strategy and kept her posture slouched so she did not seem so tall. Her aunt's strong reaction informed her that getting permission would require more effort. She reached out mentally to skim surface thoughts. *You didn't tell the others about reading minds. What would they say?* "I want to fit in. I think Mr. Mitchel, the one that Sheriff Sawyer had talk with me, thought it would be good if I spent time with people my own age. I learned in phys-ed about healthy socialization." The statement was mostly a lie, but she had seen the chapter title on her tablet.

"But you've just got here," her aunt demanded. "How am I going to get to know you? We need to spend time together."

Kyrie knew her aunt really did not want to spend time with her. "We will have a lot of time. I will be here for a long time." *She just wants control.* The knowledge that the absolute means to control her rested in her pocket made Kyrie uneasy. "The group said there are few weekends left this year they would be able to get together like this." She looked to the floor. *Money…make this about money.* "If I don't make friends with this group, I guess I could try with the other girls at school. They want me to go to prom with them. They said I needed to get a prom dress." Kyrie frowned. "I just wasn't sure I was ready for that much exposure. The girls that invited me over this weekend don't really care about prom. But if you think it would be better for me to hang out with the prom girls, I could."

Her aunt shook her head and walked into the kitchen. "Prom dresses are expensive. I've already spent a lot on you last weekend."

Kyrie followed her aunt and nodded her head knowingly. "I know, which is the other reason I thought it might be better to spend time with the girls that are into less expensive activities. I already have all the dice and minis. I wouldn't need to spend anything on gaming. The other girls put a lot of pressure on me about prom. They said I needed to press you to get a fancy dress."

Her aunt turned back to face her and crossed her arms. "You are wanting to stay over Friday night and Saturday night. When are you planning to do your homework? I imagine you are behind."

Kyrie agreed. "Michelle, Mike's sister, has helped me with things I didn't understand. This weekend, they said they could help me catch up." Kyrie made her eyes large. She sensed her aunt's mixed feelings about catching up. Instinct made her aunt press for schoolwork, but greed made her want failure. "Please. It would mean a lot to me. I've never had a chance to do things with people my age."

"But you won't be at Michelle's. You'll be at this girl Aki's?"

"Yes, ma'am. Aki is a good friend of Michelle." Kyrie wanted to say her father owned a jewelry store, but she decided not to remind her aunt about the robbery. *But still appeal to her greed.* "Her family is very wealthy from what Michelle said." *Which is a lie, you got that from Jake and Becca's thoughts.*

"I don't know what I am going to do with you." Her aunt turned back to the refrigerator. "I want you to at least stop at home sometime on Saturday."

Kyrie felt her frustration rise. *Distract.* "One of the girls at school said that since I'm almost seventeen, I needed to get a car and a driver's license."

"What? Which girls are these?"

Kyrie kept the smile from her face. "This girl Jessica said it. I had lunch with her the other day. She's got a boyfriend named John. She's the one that wants me to go to prom with her other friend Steve." She barely listened to her aunt's reply knowing that she had already won. She would just need to get through the evening and school the next day. *But then, hopefully, we will be on the way to learn what is going on.*

*    *    *    *    *

Kyrie struggled to make it through her Friday classes. The art class turned out to be worse than any of the others because Tina's anger at her remained palpable and hung in the air like a bad smell. Kyrie could even feel Michelle's distress and wished she could do something to put the friendship back together.

She struggled through physics and history; her thoughts were only about the drive south. After the bell rang to close out the last period, Kyrie gathered with the others in the parking lot. Michelle led them toward the gates. "My mother wouldn't let me drive to school, but she did say I could drive to Aki's because of the distance and the fact I would need to bring all the books and maps."

Kyrie smiled. "My aunt wanted me to stop at home on Saturday, but I know she'll be gone for the better part of the day. On Sunday, I'll claim I came home when she wasn't there."

"You are becoming one hell of a liar," Becca said. "Let's get to Michelle's, get our things, and then get on the road. I want to do some more digging into your grandma's hacker."


Kyrie sat in the front of Michelle's small hatchback with Aki crammed between Becca and Jake in the back seat. Michelle drove them to each of their houses to get their overnight bags and gaming gear. Kyrie hid most of her Dungeons & Dragons books under her bed and opted to take the journals, campaign notes, and the files from her aunt. By the time they finished, their personal bags and camping gear filled the back of the hatchback to the window.

"Your aunt still not gotten you a phone?" Becca asked.

Kyrie smiled. "This morning she said she would have taken me to get one this weekend, but that will now have to wait because I decided to spend the weekend playing around." Kyrie flipped the page of a journal as she spoke. "She claimed she wanted me there to pick out a phone. Though, she insisted on her way for all my clothes, so not sure what choice I would get."

"Well, here's your eighty dollars back," Becca said passing the cash to the front. "I didn't get a chance to run to the store, but we can pick something up this weekend. You'll want something with a decent sized screen." She looked at the others. "Everyone give me your phones. I know a few bypasses and I want to make sure none of the parental tracking shit is enabled. Last thing we need is for them to look for us and find us in Arkansas." She reached forward and tapped Michelle's shoulder. "Plus, let's stop for cash. I'd rather not leave a credit card trail."

Jake unlocked his phone and handed it to Becca. "So, Kyrie, what do you plan to do with the stone?"

"I don't know yet," Kyrie admitted. "I don't feel comfortable leaving it, but what if someone grabs me and takes it..." She shook her head and resisted the impulse to check her pocket. "It makes me uncomfortable."

"You could always break it," Aki said and then elbowed Jake in the side. "Just because I'm the shortest here, doesn't mean I should have to sit in the middle. Keep on your side."

"I could let Jake sit up front," Kyrie offered.

"I'd just elbow you." Aki looked at Becca, then Jake, and then Kyrie. "Tall freaks. All three of you." Aki's smile took any sting out of the insult. "Plus, you're like our new god or something, right? That means you get the front."

Kyrie shook her head. "Not a god." She looked over her shoulder at Aki. "My parents told me all about religions, but we never worshiped anything. A part of me has always feared the idea of gods. The idea of a powerful man with his own narcissistic desires ruining his subject's lives. Killing indiscriminatingly." She pushed the dream image of a cat-like face from her memories. "History has been filled with people who claimed divinity to enslave others."

Aki leaned forward. "Yeah, but so far, I've never seen any of them personally. Lots of legends, but you're the first to show me actual powers."

Becca looked up from her phone. "Jake, where are we staying tonight?"

"I booked a campsite about thirty minutes south of Awan Brown's Pottery shop. That was the closest." He pulled out his own phone. "Something in the Ozark Forest. Not a lot of fancy things there, but cheap. And most importantly, we don't have an age limit to book the damn place."

Becca glared at him. "It's after five now. We are just leaving Olathe and you are telling me that we have a five-hour drive without stopping for gas, to pee, or to eat."

"Yeah?"

"It will be dark when we get there." Becca shook her head. "Camping is not my favorite thing, but even I know many places won't let you in after a certain time. Certainly, not after ten."

"Crap," Michelle said. "I'd speed, but I really don't like driving the freeways as it is."

"And if you get another ticket out of state," Aki said, "that would be hard to explain to your parents. 'Yeah, Mom, I got pulled over doing eighty while parked at Aki's.'"

Becca looked around Aki at Jake. "Plus, do we really want to be on some country road when it is that dark. The locals would likely shoot us."

"What do you want me to do?" He demanded. "There aren't a lot of options."

Kyrie did not fear exploring at night, but she could understand the others' hesitation. "Is there someplace else to stay on the way? We could stop sooner, before it gets too late, and then go to the address tomorrow morning after the sun comes up." She felt the immediate relief of everyone else in the car.

Jake woke his phone. "I'll look for something. Thankfully, campsites are not that expensive, so wasting one booking won't be that big a deal."

Becca tapped Kyrie on the shoulder. "I've been doing some digging. That Michael Rodgers that owned your grandmother; the phone number in your grandmother's notes seems to still be registered to him."

"You called it?" Aki asked.

"Hell no. I don't want him knowing something is up." Becca pulled up a profile picture to show Kyrie a Caucasian man with cropped sandy blond hair. "I think this is him. There are a lot of Mike Rodgers out there. When we stop, I'll get my laptop out and try to do more cross references."

Kyrie nodded her head and turned back to her mother's journal in her lap. The notes her mother wrote in the margin bemoaned her inability to find the proof of energy transference between closed systems. *Even your mother wondered if you're something else.* She could interpret the drawing on the page as focusing energy through a stone. *Not simple energy, but complex energy patterns. She thought a spirit came through the stone.*

"Back to Jake's question, what do you plan to do with the stone," Michelle asked. "Destroy it? Hide it?"

Kyrie looked up. "I don't know."

"It is your Achilles heel. Your kryptonite." Michelle sped up as she merged onto another highway, her eyes darting around at the traffic. "You could bury it somewhere."

Kyrie closed the journal in her lap. "My mother ran a campaign. My father and I had to rescue a girl stolen from a noble. Her kidnappers cursed her. They drove a narrow wire of gold into her side. It caused her great pain, but it allowed her to heal quickly." Kyrie glanced to those in the back seat and then to Michelle. "We rescued her and were taking her back to the nobleman. I remember this, because my father left the decision to me. Almost as if he wanted me to do it so I could see what would happen. He must have known."

"What happened?" Michelle asked.

"I pulled the wire from her side. She started to bleed and passed out. I was split class and cast cure serious wounds twice, but none of the healing spells worked. I tried to put the wire back in, but it no longer possessed its power. She died."

"Seems like a twisted campaign." Michelle glanced in her mirror as a sports car sped past them. "Did your parents explain why?"

Kyrie shook her head. "They usually never explained anything. 'That's how life works' they would always say." She looked out the window. "I think the message they wanted me to learn was that some curses can't be lifted. The stone binds me somehow and if I try to destroy it, I will die."

"You sure that campaign referenced the stone? I thought they had never told you what it could do?" Michelle asked.

"They never said anything, but they always tried to teach me something." Kyrie tried to think back to a time when they were not trying to teach her a lesson and realized even the random dungeon crawls she had enjoyed as pure fun often carried at least a small message.

"Messed up," Becca said after a bit. "I've got to pee when you see someplace where we can eat."

When Michelle pulled up to the campsite, everyone gratefully spilled out of the car. Darkness had fallen, so Michelle left her car running and used the headlights to provide light. Kyrie watched as Jake and Michelle worked to get the tent set up. Her father had relied on tarps and lean-tos when they camped outside, so she had little to offer with regard to poles and zippers.

"Kyrie, can you get a fire going?" Michelle asked, a bit of shiver in her voice as the cool April night settled in.

"Sure," she replied, taking the bundle of firewood they had bought at the campsite entrance to the fire pit. She pulled at the plastic film wrapping the wood with her fingers and then used her powers to enable her to rip it open. She stacked the wood and looked around for kindling. Small branches and leaves littered the ground and she quickly gathered handfuls to bring over to the fire pit.

Becca and Aki observed the work involved, and instead of helping, they grabbed their bags and headed to the showers. Soon, Kyrie gave up on gathering the proper kindling and simply piled everything into the pit. She pulled in some energy and concentrated on pushing it into the pile of wood. After a short time, smoke appeared and then a minute later, flames erupted from the kindling. She continued to push energy into the wood and soon a roaring fire blazed in the pit.

"That was fast," Michelle said as Jake started to pound stakes into the ground to tie down the tent.

"Lots of practice." Kyrie looked at the size of the tent and frowned. "Will the five of us fit in there?"

Michelle chuckled and then lowered her voice. "I plan to make Jake very uncomfortable. Had I known the size, I would have tried to sneak my parents tent out of the basement so we would have a second one." She put an arm around Kyrie's shoulder and led her back to the car. "Flash him a bit of bra and he'll be red as a tomato. If we tease him with the idea of an all-girl orgy, he'll pass out."

Kyrie smiled at Michelle's mischievous streak. She had never considered tormenting another party member before, but after Jake's attempt to make her kiss him, she felt he might deserve it. "I'm in. And since I didn't think to bring a change of clothes, I don't know what I will wear to bed."

"Nothing at all," Michelle suggested.


The five of them did not fall asleep quickly. Once Michelle started teasing Jake, everyone else added to his misery until he was so embarrassed that he turned away from them and buried his face into the tent wall. He did not roll back over to look at them until the conversation changed to something with less sexual innuendo.

Kyrie made sure she stayed awake while the others continued to talk. The topics of conversation ranged from boys in the school, goals for life, back to movies and computer games, and finally to Dungeons & Dragons. Just the sound of their voices calmed her. She joined in when she had something to offer, but she found herself more content to learn what other people her age were supposed to think about.

When morning came, Kyrie crawled out of the cramped tent, still dressed in her clothes, and took some time to explore the campground. She jogged to the large lake north of the tent site and looked across the foggy surface as the sun started to illuminate the sky. After she absorbed the peaceful beauty, she continued jogging until she made her way back to the tent.

Jake stood outside trying to coax the coals back to life. "Morning," he said when he saw her watching him. "You really do enjoy running in the morning."

"I've done it all my life. I find sitting in one place makes me crazy."

He cleared his throat. "I'm really sorry about the other day. I should never have tried to make you kiss me." He looked away. "I don't know why I did it. It was stupid. I'm not one of those guys who take advantage of women. I'm not."

She smiled at him. The guilt he felt was evident in both his face and mind. "Just don't do it again."

"Have I ruined any chance I might have had with you?"

She frowned. "Jake, I…"

"I know, you just want to be friends." He sighed. "Story of my life."

She came over to the fire pit and looked at the last piece of firewood that he had placed on the expired coals. She looked at the wood and pushed energy into it with more force than she had used the night before. The chuck of wood suddenly burst into flames and Jake jumped back.

Kyrie turned to him. "I'm not normal, Jake. I have powers that others don't, and I don't know what that means. Plus, because of how my parents raised me, everything is a D&D adventure in my mind. I've lived my whole life not thinking about 'being' with someone. I don't even know what the expectations of that are."

He smiled at her. "I guess I wasn't being fair. And being friends with a bunch of very cool girls is better than hanging out with a bunch of jerk guys. You always have much better conversations."

Kyrie shrugged. "I'm learning that myself." She grew more serious and stepped closer. The others still slept, but lightly. "You and Aki would make a good pair."

He frowned. "She's not interested in me. I tried to date her two years ago. She told me no."

"She picked the spot next to you in the tent and went the easiest on you last night." Kyrie did not admit that she had sensed their mutual interest when they sat in the back of the car. *The longer you wait to admit you can sense their emotions and thoughts, the worse it will be when they figure it out. Shut up.*

Jake pursed his lips. "Perhaps. But she's always punching me."

Kyrie shook her head. "Talk to her and find out. What I know is from the novels my parents had in the cabin. Dating was not something they put into our D&D sessions. I think it would have made things uncomfortable if they had."

"Yeah, that would have been a bit weird."


Arkansas 295 looked like any normal state highway until they reached the southern side of Japton. At that point, the state maintenance ended, and the paved road became gravel.

The views out of the windows of Michelle's small hatchback provided a dichotomy of perspectives. The tree lined road had a natural beauty that filled Kyrie with a sense of wanderlust. Dirt driveways went directly through running creeks; homes were concealed behind groves of trees, offering just a hint of the lives of their inhabitants. Ravines and valleys suggested paths waiting to be explored. Birds and other animals watched from safety, but their presence gave the land a sense of life. It reminded her of the quiet isolation of the mountains.

However, just below the beauty of spring, human debris and detritus poked out. Abandoned cars, appliances, and furniture lay scattered through the forested landscape. The refuse spoke of a world alien to those accustomed to manicured lawns and organized rules. Kyrie had seen evidence of that same behavior around the edge of her valley, and in Ms. Conner's front yard. She knew it had saddened her parents, who talked of the toxins and poisons that leaked from the rusting objects.

"These are the people who will kill you for stopping to ask for help," Becca said. She shook her head.

"Becca," Michelle said, her disapproval audible.

"You're a white girl. Don't Becca me."

"Let's hope we don't have to call for help." Jake held up his phone. "No coverage."

Kyrie listened to their banter as Michelle drove slowly along the rough road. She found it interesting how their playful sniping at each other allowed the four of them to deal with uncertainty and stress. *And how are you dealing with the stress?* She asked herself. She forced her hands to relax and did not answer the question.

"That's the turn we want to take," Jake said, leaning forward to put his hands on the back of Michelle's seat.

"Are you sure?" Michelle asked, bringing the car to a stop in the middle of the road. They had seen no other cars or people to that point, so she provided no impediment to traffic. "There have been no signs that even indicate what road we are on. I'm not even sure we are still on 295. Just small signs with those four-digit numbers. I can't tell what's a driveway and what's not."

"This place has me creeped out." Aki's eyes darted from window to window. "I'm not sure I should have come anymore."

Becca remained calm. "Jake's right. That is the road number. I screen captured the map when we had coverage, and this is the turn." She looked out her side window and down at the ground. "Just don't get stuck in the ditch."

Kyrie noticed Michelle's white knuckles and she reached over to pat her friend's leg. "These slopes are nothing compared to the road that led to the cabin where I lived. The car should be fine."

Michelle grinned at her and gave the car more gas. The hatchback kicked out some gravel and then started to climb up the slope. After a short distance, the rutted road leveled off and continued along what appeared to be a single lane. Trees extended far enough into the path that they brushed the side windows.

Kyrie could not see through the dense trees, but a tingling in her mind grew quickly. *The energy here has ripples and currents. And there is so much of it.* She glanced around the car, but the others had grown quiet as Michelle concentrated on navigating the twisting road. They bounced through a gully as they passed a large boulder at a bend. When Kyrie saw an archway made from entwined vines and plants, a memory rose up in her mind. "That's it."

Michelle allowed the car to slow to a stop. She remained a hundred feet from the driveway with the archway. "Do we drive in?"

"My mother ran a campaign where she had drawings that looked like that. Only my mother made it a cart path instead of a road." Kyrie pointed over her shoulder. "In the game, we even came around a boulder in the path before we could see the entrance."

"This ain't a road," Becca said. "I'd barely call it a cart path. I really want a bunch of NPCs to send ahead and scout for me."

"Invisibility spell," Jake offered. "You need to learn how to do that, Kyrie."

"Okay, not helping," Michelle said softly. "Do we drive in or leave the car here and walk?"

Kyrie looked around, but the trees blocked most of her view. She felt only small animals in the area, but that meant little. "The road goes beyond the driveway. I don't think we can leave your car here."

Michelle nodded her head and lightly pressed on the accelerator. Her hatchback inched forward and she eventually turned under the living entrance.

The driveway twisted down a path through a clump of trees to an open area with several buildings in a general state of disrepair. The house with its blue painted siding stood out from a barn and three sheds clad in weathered wood. The tree cover had long ago killed any grass. The gravel that once defined the driveway was now pressed deep into the dirt. Two cars sat in the front yard. The cleanliness and newness of one of the vehicles stood in vast contrast to everything else.

Michelle brought her car to a stop and put it into park. "I'm guessing someone is home. There is smoke coming from the chimney."

Kyrie sensed multiple people in the home, but had trouble getting a good read on them from their distance. "At least three in there," she said as she unfastened her seat belt, opened the door, and stepped out.

"Are you sure it is safe," Jake asked, followed immediately by a similar question from Aki.

Kyrie ignored her friends and started walking toward the house. *You've been here. You've seen this before.* She heard Michelle turn off the engine and the other car door open just as a man stepped out of the front door of the house. The man slowed at twenty yards, but Kyrie did not miss the shotgun in his hands. A second man followed the first, this one carrying a rifle.

Kyrie stopped as the men continued to approach. Her mental sense of the men remained limited, as though they suppressed their emotions. "Hello," she called, uncertain of their intentions with the weapons. "I'm hoping I might be able to ask some questions."

Michelle and Jake, both of whom now stood in front of Michelle's car, froze in place. A soft murmur of frightened conversation filled the air.

"Get out of here," demanded the first man. His curly red hair needing a trim. "This is private property."

"I'm looking for someone," Kyrie said, hoping she would be able to calm their hostilities.

The second man raised his rifle and pointed it at her. "Leave."

The first man narrowed his eyes as he looked at Michelle and Jake. "They know this place. They know the truth." He raised his shotgun to his shoulder.

Kyrie released the energy built up in her and pushed the shotgun's barrel into the air just before the man fired the weapon. The explosion of BB shot tore through the leaves above their head. She felt the second man fire just as she used her mind to push his weapon down and to the side.

Both men cried out in alarm and tried to swing their weapons back in her direction. Kyrie felt a hot wetness running down her side as well as a numbness that made her feel unbalanced. *You're shot!* Energy poured into her. *Control!*

Her friends screamed, but she lost track of their movements. Anger raced through her and she unleashed the energy in her. The redhead with the shotgun flew backwards. He slammed into the house; the weapon knocked from his hands.

The second, larger man shifted left as his weapon came back to his shoulder.

Kyrie felt the gravity wave hit her. The force had nearly the same impact as being hit by the car and she found herself thrown backwards just as the crack of gun fire filled the air again. The awareness of the second bullet tearing through her body registered much quicker than the first one had. Burning pain raced up her left leg as she hit the ground.

Kyrie staggered onto her injured leg, but gravitational energy kept her upright. *Fight!* The man with the rifle stood eighty feet away, much further than she could normally reach with her powers, but she had no other weapon.

Energy burned her mind as she generated an intense gravity well under the man. She did not bother demanding control as the power seared her nerves with more intensity than the bullet that ripped through her thigh. The man crumpled to the ground in a heap. His screams cut short by his breaking bones.

The redhead picked himself up from the ground and looked around for his weapon. He remained more than a hundred feet away and Kyrie knew the effort to do anything to him at that distance would knock her unconscious. She pushed herself forward, hobbling on her damaged leg, but then picking up speed as the shotgun flew through the air and to the man's hands.

Kyrie sprinted forward; energy poured into her, burning every nerve in her body. Gravel from the remains of the driveway leapt into the air and flew past her as she ran. The cloud of nut sized stones, directed by her will, slammed into the redhead and peppered the wall of the house, breaking windows and embedding themselves into the manufactured wood. The man used his own powers to deflect many of the rocks, but at least eight struck his torso and legs, dropping him back to the ground.

Kyrie came upon him, the shotgun flying to her hands. She expended more energy, pining his body in place with a gravitational field that sat on his chest. She pointed the weapon at the man's head. "Who are you? What are you?"

The man looked at her, fear leaking from his mind. "I will tell you nothing."

"I will rip the truth from you. You know I can."

The man started to tremble as blood oozed from his wounds.

"Tell me," Kyrie demanded. She used a small amount of energy to try to read his emotions. Panic filled her through the link to his mind. A moment later his eyes rolled back into his head and foam started to form on his lips. She could feel his heart racing and the blood seeped faster from his wounds. His mind became a torrent of pain and anguish as energy poured into him, burning him from the inside out. The emotional cyclone spilling out of him forced her to close her mind.

Kyrie turned the shotgun toward the door as the third man emerged. This man looked nothing like the first two. His wrinkled face showed signs of age and sun. His dark leathery skin stood in contrast to the straight grey hair that hung down below his shoulders. Kyrie suspected his hair once hung thick and black from his head. However, the man's deformities stood out to her the most. A long-healed scar ran in a jagged line from his brow, over a fused left eyelid, and across the side of his face. The mangled end of his forearm spoke to a traumatic event that took his right hand.

The man raised his arms. "I won't harm you."

Kyrie released the gravitational field holding the redhead. The bleeding man's heart still raced, but he had lost consciousness and she needed to conserve her strength.

Jake and Michelle sprinted to her side. "You've been shot! Oh my god. We need to get you to a hospital." Michelle shifted uncomfortably from side to side, not wanting to touch Kyrie, which left her distressed.

"Who are you?" Kyrie demanded, ignoring the blood running from her nose and into her mouth. The pain in her side and leg had grown until it rivaled that of her mind.

"I am Awan. This is my home and my land." He kept his arms raised. "I remember your mother and father. Though you look very different." He chuckled. "But then so do I."

Jake held out a hand to Kyrie. "Let me take the gun. You need someone to bind your wounds."

"You need a healing spell," Michelle pleaded. "Becca, bring my bag. Hurry. Kyrie needs help!"

Kyrie handed the shotgun to Jake and wiped the blood from her face. "Who are you Awan?"

"And why shouldn't I shoot you?" Jake asked, the weapon unsteady in his hands.

"Shit. Shit. Shit." Aki took a wide path around the man crumpled into a mass on the ground. "Is he dead?"

Kyrie slowed her breathing. *Control the pain.* "Awan?"

"It will take some time to tell, but I imagine you have a lot of questions." He looked at the redhead. "He will probably die on his own, but if not, we will need to end him. He would tell others you were here."

"He blocked most of the stones," Kyrie said. "Nothing hit his head or chest."

Awan nodded. "His binding is strong. He is forbidden from being questioned. Forbidden to the point that if there is a chance he will reveal anything, his mind will burn itself out. But if it does not, you don't want him to recover."

Kyrie looked down at the man as Becca arrived with Michelle's bag in hand. The man still bled from the wounds she had inflicted on him. "I am not a murderer."

"Kyrie, stand still." Michelle lifted the back of her shirt. "Aki, get the water bottle from the car."

"Anyone else in there?" Jake asked, the shotgun lifted to point at Awan's face.

"No," Kyrie and Awan said in unison.

"We're in a lot of trouble," Becca said. "I think that other man is dead. Bodies don't bend that way." She shuddered. "Necks don't bend like that."

"They shot Kyrie twice and tried to kill Jake and me," Michelle replied. "They deserve to die. Kyrie, how are you still standing?"

Kyrie looked down at Michelle who squatted beside her. Her friend had lifted the front of her shirt to examine the entry wound. "It hurts, but not that bad."

"It went right through her. Both bullets," Becca said as she looked at the blood stains on the back of Kyrie's clothing. "But I don't see a lot of blood." She inclined her head to the redhead. "He's got more blood on him."

"We have to get her to a hospital," Jake said.

Becca shook her head. "GSWs get reported to the police. As soon as we take Kyrie to the hospital, we're screwed."

Aki ran up carrying a bottle of water. "What are we going to do? We're all going to jail. My parents will kill me."

"Stop," Kyrie demanded of everyone as she wiped more blood from her face. "Once Awan tells me what he knows, we'll leave. No hospital. No police."

Michelle ignored Kyrie, took the water from Aki, a shirt from her bag, and started dabbing at the wound. Kyrie winced, but did not move.

"She's healed the wounds," Awan said to the others. "She is one of them." He stared into her eyes. "Though I think your young age at the time of the binding may have made you as powerful as whatever took over my cousin. These men did not have the power to do what you just did."

Becca reached around Kyrie's waist and started to unbuckle her belt. "You need to get out of these pants so we can see how bad your leg is." At Kyrie's expression, Becca blanched and then recovered. "Or you rather we cut them off?"

"Can we leave?" Aki's voice trembled. "I don't want to go to jail. I don't want to die."

Awan looked at the body of the man Kyrie crumbled into a heap. "Bruce was a rapist before they forced me to bind him." Awan turned to the redhead. "Nick was a grocer, but he had no family. Who they were died three years ago. What they are now would prefer to die than to continue in slavery." Awan looked at Jake. "If you help, we can drag them around back. The gun fire won't draw any attention. People around here shoot things all the time." He gave Kyrie a small smile. "Once we're done, I can tell you what you want to know."

Kyrie saw the others look at her for direction. Jake appeared very uneasy. She brushed away Becca's hands from the zipper of her pants and held out her hand for the shotgun. "Move the bodies, then you can look at my wounds."

Kyrie staggered away from the redhead as Awan led Jake over to the crumpled man. She followed closely behind the old man so that if she had to fire the weapon, she would not hit Jake as well. *Good thing father taught us about weapons.*

The man's body lay twisted and broken, as though someone had put him into a trash compactor. The rifle's stock and barrel were now cracked and bent. Even the ground had ripped away and been drawn toward the center of the force.

Jake stepped over the circular gap and down onto a highly compressed bit of ground. "This is like a black hole. Sticks and everything broken and compressed."

Kyrie shook her head. "A true singularity would have a lot more pull. We'd all be dead." She bit her lip and forced herself to breathe. "I didn't want to kill him. But he was going to shoot again."

"They would have killed all of you and thrown your bodies in the pit," Awan said. "Then your car would have been dumped somewhere. They have done it before."

"Other people have come here looking for whatever is here?" Jake asked.

Awan grabbed the dead man's left leg with his only hand and started to pull. "Not for a long time. But bindings are monitored more closely now and those that fail are eliminated swiftly." Awan looked up at Jake. "I'm not as young as I once was. I will need help."

"I need some gloves. I don't want to leave fingerprints." He looked up at the shotgun. "Shit, I need to wipe that down."

"Don't touch anything, Jake," Aki said. "We need to leave it all for the police. We have to tell them what is happening. We have to turn ourselves in."

Awan shook his head. "Whatever took over my cousin's body will not let that happen. The local sheriff is in his pay. The police will not help you, or me." He turned back to Jake. "The gunshots will not summon the locals, but if someone drives by and sees bodies and a strange car here, they will call the sheriff."

"Jake, please help him," Kyrie said. "I would, but I don't know that I can lift that much weight right now. Michelle, can you move your car?"

Jake nodded his head. "This must be what happens in real life when you roll a nat-one."

"Not a nat-one," Michelle said. "We're all alive. This is what happens when you are first level and are playing a campaign for level twenties." Michelle smiled at Kyrie as she moved toward her car. "The good thing is we have a very powerful friend to help level us up, right?"

Kyrie gave Michelle a smile, glad for her ability to ease the mood.

# Chapter 17

Kyrie sat uncomfortably in a dirty recliner. The living room of the house showed its age with floral print furniture and yellow wallpaper. Becca and Michelle had removed all of her clothing—aside from her underwear and bra—in their effort to clean away all the blood from her wounds. Her body had healed itself, closing the bullet holes with fresh skin, leaving deep purple bruises surrounding the injuries. *Damn kinetic energy.*

Kyrie moved her leg. That bullet missed her thigh bone and cut a straight path out the back of her leg. The bullet that ripped through her side took a longer route, tearing through her intestines to graze a rib next to her spine.

Aki calmed after Michelle and Becca agreed they would not need to go to the hospital. However, her nervous fear still had her jumping at any sound.

Jake continued to stand watch, the shotgun in his hands, but not leveled at anyone. Kyrie's state of undress left him both interested and uncomfortable. The only positive effect was it appeared to take his mind off loading the bodies of the dead men onto Awan's four-wheeler. The clinical and deliberate act of moving the dead men, along with Michelle's car, to the back of the house, had chilled everyone's mood.

"I've got a second pair of pants." Becca said, breaking the silence that had fallen in the room as she used a paper towel to wipe blood from her hands. "You're not that much taller than me, but I've got a bigger ass than you do. They'll be loose, but better than running around with blood-stained clothing or in your underwear."

Kyrie smiled at her. "Thank you. I appreciate it." She turned her attention back to Awan. "You said you remember me and my parents." She could not remove the skepticism from her voice.

The old man grinned. "It would be hard to forget the girl who caused me to lose my hand and eye."

Jake adjusted his grip on the shotgun, but he did not aim it at the man sitting across from Kyrie. "What's that supposed to mean? You threatening her?"

Kyrie raised a hand to silence Jake. The effort felt like lifting a boulder. "Start from the beginning. What did you do to me? Why are these people after me?"

The old man chuckled. "I would imagine there are two groups after you." He exhaled and grew serious. "These lands have been in my family since before they made Arkansas a state. The Caddo lived in these parts and protected the land."

"Caddo?" Becca asked.

"Caddo Indians," the man replied. "My ancestors were part of that group of tribes." He sighed. "They knew the sacred places in the world. Including this place on these lands. They felt the thinning of the veil, as I can. A place where the spirit world and our world merge."

Michelle looked up from where she knelt next to Kyrie. "How did your family retain their lands? I thought the government drove the Indians onto reservations."

"My ancestors married into white families until they repurchased the land. Then they continued to pass it down. I am actually two-thirds white, though I look more native than others in my family."

Kyrie took the water bottle from Michelle and emptied it. "There are snacks in the car," she mumbled.

"I'll get them," Becca said. "And my clothes." She grinned at Jake. "Don't want your face to get stuck that shade of pink."

"Hey," Jake shook his head as she went out the front door.

"Don't continue until I get back," she added to Awan as the door slammed shut.

"There is food here," Awan said. "It is safe. It is what we eat."

Aki raised an eyebrow and Kyrie nodded her head. *You are so drained,* she realized as she found herself fantasizing about drinking some of Michelle's soda. Kyrie watched the Asian girl slowly enter the kitchen and knew fear made her friend hesitant.

Becca raced back into the house. She brought the snacks, another half empty bottle of water, and her bag of clothing. Kyrie accepted the water and drained the contents in a single pour. She set the bottle aside and took the jeans Becca offered her.

"You need help?" Michelle asked as Kyrie struggled to stand.

Kyrie accepted the assistance, and once she was dressed, she again dropped down in the chair. Aki brought a box of cupcakes over and Kyrie tore open a wrapper and consumed the very sweet food.

Awan watched her. "You're not used to using your powers, are you?" When Kyrie did not respond, he continued. "My family has helped the ill for generations. We took those infirm and suffering from a lack of health to the sacred grove. We coaxed energy from the spirit world into them, giving them the strength they lacked. Never in my family's long history of guarding the veil, had anything passed from the beyond before my watch."

Kyrie forced herself to sit straight. The idea a demon possessed her chilled her blood. *You know the sessions your parents ran. Something came through.* "You're saying a spirit came through this veil when my parents brought me here? That I'm the first one to have something strange happen?"

Awan shook his head. "Something came through when you came here, but no, you are not the first. Let me continue." He turned in his chair so he could see the others more clearly. "More than thirty years ago, my cousin and I went to the grove. We had felt something strange in the air. Something drawing us there." He looked at the others. "I was much younger thirty years ago, but not as young as my cousin. He had not yet turned twenty."

Kyrie took another cupcake and devoured the cream filled chocolate.

Awan continued. "Something came through the veil on its own. It waited there in the grove. Frightened, I think. Barely existing. Dying. Neither of us could see it, but I could feel it in my bones. My cousin lacked the true sight that I have. He felt invincible and moved to the center before I could stop him." Awan sighed. "That youthful vigor sealed his fate. The spirit that passed into this world took hold in him. I knew something had happened, but I had no idea what. It took several days before my cousin truly started to show changes. But when he did, the man who I called cousin no longer existed. Something else looked back at me through his brown eyes. It took longer for his power to manifest. Or at least for him to show me his powers."

Kyrie kept herself from looking at any of the others. The old man had just confirmed her greatest fear.

Awan cleared his throat. "Whatever controlled my cousin had all of his memories and knowledge as well as the knowledge of the spirit world. Combined with powers like your own, he went to casinos and cheated his way into a sizable fortune. He then used the money to start buying businesses. However, there can be more money to be had in crime than honest work. For a while, he continued to come back here. Things would slip from his mouth, as though he needed someone to brag to. I grew to believe that in the spirit world, he wielded a great power, and that his enemies expelled him to this world as punishment."

"A fallen god?" Jake asked.

Awan shrugged. "I feared him. He placed in me a terror that eats at my soul. I did nothing to anger him. I had seen the evil he inflicted on others. He brought people—prisoners really—to the grove in an attempt to draw more spirits into this world. Many of those initial attempts failed and the people died. But over time, he developed the means to force spirits through the veil and bind them to a host. To a person."

Kyrie felt the others staring at her. She held back the tears that wanted to leak from her eyes. *You've known the truth all along. You just never wanted to admit it.*

"The spirit's binding happens with a stone, trapping part of the soul in the gem, while the rest of the spirit inhabits the person." Awan looked around the room. "Even after my cousin improved the process, many bindings failed for various reasons. Sometimes the person's mind held the strength to drive out the invading spirit and the host lived on. Sometimes the person died because the spirit had no desire to possess a host, but the host's mind no longer functioned."

"So, the spirit doesn't always win?" Kyrie asked, clinging to a desperate hope.

Awan's expression was grim. "Perhaps half the time the spirit does not survive the effort. Most of the time it takes a couple of days before the internal battles play out. I think it is because both the spirt and the person are very uncertain as to what has happened."

Awan looked to the floor. "In the early days, my cousin brought people here and he bound them while conscious and aware. They would fight and struggle. Watching those events took a toll on me." He shook his head. "My life had been one of peace and healing, not harming others. But I'm also a coward and I could not stop it."

Michelle's voice cracked as she spoke. "Did the spirit that you bound to Kyrie survive or did she survive?"

"You get ahead of the story," Awan said. He looked down at the end of his right arm. "This is slavery for both the human and the spirit. Neither wants the binding. The spirits often fight and scream. I think many recognized the being that possessed my cousin's body and see him as an old enemy. However, with the stones that bound them, he could control them. He bends them to his will."

Awan's face grew long. "The creature in my cousin soon had little time to spend in these back woods. He recognized a limited power in me. Something passed down through the generations. It meant that I could do the bindings for him. My power for healing turned to a means of pain."

"Why didn't you just leave?" Kyrie asked.

Awan shook his head. "He has me watched. He wants an army of slaves, but he also employs those whose loyalty comes from greed. Fortunately, only a handful of those know the truth, but those that do, they fear him as much as I."

Awan exhaled. "The spirits that come forth are intelligent. They bring their own memories and those aspects are combined with the host. However, my cousin uses his Bound primarily as muscle. He uses the stones, not only to exert pain, but to change the way they think. He can manipulate their thoughts and memories. I have seen him force one to constantly relive a single event, real or imagined, until the Bound man died screaming."

Awan shifted in his chair. "The manipulations prevent them from betraying him. However, a few who he feels have a natural loyalty, he gives more freedom. Those are the most dangerous, since they have powers and some free will to decide how to use their powers. One of those normally is present during a binding to ensure I follow the procedures correctly."

He turned to Kyrie. "Back to your story. Although my cousin forced me to perform bindings for him, when you arrived, I still practiced healing. My cousin did not seem to care that I did those things. It provided an excuse and cover for people to come out here. And because of that healing, your parents found me. However, I knew from the moment I saw you, that infusing you with energy would not cure your ailments. I told them as much. Your mother pleaded with me to try anyway." He looked away. "A moment of weakness on my part. I suggested binding power to you." He lifted his gaze. "I dared not fully explain things to your mother, but I told her some. She said to proceed, and so I did." He swallowed. "During a binding, I can feel something of the nature of the spirits that I pull through the veil. I found a soft one, kind and young. One full of life." His voice broke slightly. "Just as people have different temperaments, so do the spirits. I wanted your life full of happiness and joy. I did not want to create an angry monster." He looked away again. "For many years, I always searched for kind souls to bring across, hoping they could temper the evil of my cousin's possessor. I realized after I brought you across that I caused those spirits more pain and anguish than I did any good." A tear slid down his cheek. "I think the being in my cousin preferred my choices, as I turned his enemies into his slaves. These last few years, I have only brought across those already filled with anger and hate. It has made the Bound so much worse, but I…"

Kyrie leaned forward. "So, you can feel those on the other side." She voiced no question.

He raised his eyes to hers again. "Yes. After the spirit in my cousin came through, I have been able to do so. Never before. I believe when my cousin's possessor broke through the veil, the divide between our worlds tore."

"What of Kyrie's spirit?" Michelle asked again. "Did the binding take?"

Awan turned to Michelle. "I had never bound someone as young as her before, or since. With an adult, the change becomes obvious. Sometimes, both the person and spirit share the same body and live together. For an infant, how would anyone know? Her personality was not fixed. Though, the previously silent infant moved and made noises the next morning before her parents left."

Kyrie felt Michelle's hand on her arm, offering comfort. But Kyrie felt her strength returning and could sense the question in her friend through the physical contact. "I do not know," she admitted aloud. "I don't know what I am. Human or spirit."

"Perhaps both," Becca offered.

"Yeah," Michelle said. "Your human mind and body needed help. Perhaps the spirit gave you that so you could grow and be whole."

Kyrie searched within herself. She examined her thoughts. *What are we?* No solid answer returned.

"Whatever you are, you are a good person," Michelle said. "You are who you are since you were an infant."

Kyrie let out the breath she had been holding and nodded her head. *You are you, no one else.* "Can I be unbound? What if I break the stone that controls me?"

Awan looked up again. "I do not know for certain, but you would likely die. Part of your soul exists in the stone. The piece of soul is how someone can impose their will upon you. If the stone is broken, then your soul would be injured, and your human host could drive you out."

"What about the people who are after her?" Aki asked. "After us. They're going to be pissed. We..." She looked toward the back of the house and the direction toward where the bodies sat on the four-wheeler.

Awan did not follow her gaze. "As I said, two groups likely want to harm you. There is a man who works for my cousin. A man who had the responsibility to monitor me and keep me in line. I did not realize he had installed game cameras in the woods. A couple weeks after I performed your binding, he checked the cameras and found the video of your parents leaving with a stone." Awan raised his right arm. "As punishment, he slashed out my eye and chopped off my hand. He took me to the hospital and told them I had a farming injury." Awan shrugged. "It was not an impossible story, so the doctors believed him."

"Shit," Jake said. "We have to find those cameras and remove the footage. They will have video of us killing those men."

Awan shook his head. "No cameras monitor this location. Not since her binding. The being in my cousin does not want video evidence of what happens here. This man nearly lost his own life over the video of your binding. Capturing you and turning you over to my cousin would redeem him. He now controls my obedience with the pair of Bound that remain with me always." He smiled. "Until today. Hopefully their spirits return to the spirit world."

"Who is this person?" Kyrie asked, already suspecting the answer.

"A Michael Rodgers," Awan replied. "He uses a land-line to communicate with his Bound and they report on my activities. He also uses it to inform us of new arrivals that I am expected to bind."

"That's the man who phoned your grandmother," Becca said. "I knew he was playing her."

Awan continued. "Mr. Rodgers holds several binding stones. He is never without them. My cousin's wealth and importance means he can no longer perform the dirty work himself. He does not want his past revealed until he cements his control and power. Mr. Rodgers is now in charge of all bindings."

Kyrie considered her question and watched Awan closely. "How are you certain Rodgers is never without the stones?"

Awan smiled. "They allow him to control the Bound, even at great distances. If someone held your stone, and you knew they did not have it with them, what would you do?"

Kyrie nodded her head. The unease building in her had turned the cupcakes into a lump in her stomach. *You wanted to know the truth. Mother always said to be careful what you ask for.* "And he controls these people just by holding the stones and thinking."

Awan confirmed with a nod. "The stone holds a part of your soul and that makes you vulnerable. Even a weak-minded person could exert control over you. A strong-willed person could crush your mind." He cleared his throat. "Mr. Rodgers is very strong-willed."

"And someone stronger commands him through greed," Kyrie said. "Who is your cousin?"

"Steven Bishop," Awan replied.

"Shit." Aki shook her head and started pacing. "That bastard owns Nalitran Enterprises. He's lobbied congress for all kinds of terrible policies that will undermine our civil rights. His policies would lead to a totalitarian state. It could lead to war, and definitely will lead to unrest. And he's running for congress."

Awan nodded his head. "The same."

"You said two groups," Becca pushed. "Who are the others?"

Awan turned to her. "In the early days, the bindings were done on conscious people. They did not know the location of the grove, but they knew what happened to them. Now, drugs make the people unconscious during the binding. They do not know anything even took place until the spirit exerts control."

Awan shifted again. "My cousin did not monitor the early bindings closely. Some of the victims survived and escaped the failed binding. Those people have memories of the events and recalled the spirit they drove from themselves. One of these people believes Satan has come to the earth and is implanting demons in people. He believes God has charged him to eliminate the demons."

"The Church of the Righteous Revenge," Becca said.

Awan nodded his confirmation. "The man's name is Dennis Hurlington. I remember him well." He sighed. "I remember all of them." Awan swallowed. "In life, he practiced petty theft. Now he has a following of people who see it as their holy war. Dennis is not a stupid man. He assembled his followers into cells, and they operate independently and do not know anything about the other cells. Dennis directs them from deep underground. I know from things Mr. Rodgers has said to me that they cannot find Dennis, though they have tried many times."

"How did they learn about me?" Kyrie asked. "The church members tried to kill me."

Awan tilted his head and raised a questioning eyebrow. "Spies is my guess. Not at the highest levels, my cousin would know. But at lower levels."

"How far up in the organization is Mr. Rodgers?" Kyrie asked. "Are there a dozen of him?"

Awan shook his head. "My cousin spent ten years learning how to perform bindings and building his small force of slaves. He spent the next twenty separating his past from who he is today. He has not once come here since. Mr. Rodgers is the one man that controls this aspect of my cousin's empire, though I believe that is very much from a distance as well. Much of the other criminal parts of the organization I believe were shut down because he made enough money to pursue legitimate businesses."

"Legitimate?" Aki shook her head. "Criminal, just not illegal. Big difference. The rich bastard commits crimes against the planet and humanity every day. But because he makes rich people richer, they won't do anything to stop him." She wiped tears from her eyes. "We need to get out of here."

Becca nodded her head. "Gather all of Kyrie's cloths and anything with her blood on it. Get anything we brought with us. Jake, as you said earlier, wipe down anything any of us touched."

Awan shook his head. "It is not necessary. My cousin wants this place protected and Mr. Rodgers will send people to ensure that happens. He will not allow word to get out."

Becca flipped him off. "Screw you. I'm not leaving things to track back to me. I don't care what you think your cousin, or Mr. Rodgers, will do."

Kyrie stood up. She wobbled, but she remained standing. "I want to see the grove. Also, do you have other stones you use for the bindings, or are they created as part of the process?"

"What?" Aki said. "We should be going."

Kyrie continue to stare at Awan.

Awan rose to his feet. "The stones are really glass. The ritual hardens them. I think they change internally when the spirit is held in place. But you cannot tell just by looking." He moved to go into another room and Jake raised the shotgun. "I only want to get some stones for Kyrie. Then I will show you the grove and we can dispose of the Bound at the same time."

Kyrie nodded her head. "Follow him. I want them."

# Chapter 18

Michael Rodgers looked up from his laptop at the three people standing in his hotel room. He controlled the two with hate in their eyes. *If only I could command that away.* He had tried more than once, but he knew they would always despise him. Not only did they remember their lives as people, and the fact that he chose them for binding, but he also held their stones.

The third man, a good foot shorter than the Bound, brushed his dyed black hair from his face. Money bought Chuck's loyalty. Six years of cost, but Michael found the hacker provided more than enough reward because the man always managed to learn far more than he should know.

"Boss, I've checked social media." The short man shook his head. "The whole group, save for the girl Tina, went dark. Nothing with a public post since Thursday."

"What about private posts," Michael asked. "Any DMs?"

"Hacking isn't like you see it on TV. I can't just guess a password in three attempts. And with two-factor—"

"I know how security works," Michael interrupted. "No luck with any of the fishing campaigns?"

"I need time to build profiles. Heck, one girl's dad is a white-hat hacker. His business is pen-testing systems. I've had less than a week to work on this."

Michael waved away the complaint and changed topics. "The police report filed on Thursday evening near that girl Michelle's house, what do you know about it? I heard about a strange van and people shouting. The report didn't have many details. Could this have been one of Hurlington's groups?"

Chuck nodded his head. "I have confirmation of it. Hurlington sent cells out here. At least two, maybe three. I caught some chatter on one of their boards. Kyrie's location and details pop up all over the COTRR feeds. Looking back, it first showed up on the sixth."

"So The Church is talking about it a day after I asked someone to go to Walden," Michael reflected. He pursed his lips. "That gives me an idea of a couple of people that might be spies. I'll send you a list to research and then I'll test them out."

The short man glanced nervously over his shoulder at the two Bound behind him. "I'm down for just about anything, but going after teenage girls will get a lot of police attention."

"Your point?"

"None. But everything indicates that Kyrie and her group have gone underground. The only one still around is Tina, and from what my watcher is seeing, she's pretty upset. She walked to Michelle's house, then got a ride to Aki's. The parents went active as well, right after her trips."

"Where's she now?"

"Alone in her house."

Michael nodded. "We can't wait any longer." He looked behind the short man at the larger of the two Bound. This one had a tattoo of a Celtic knot of his face. *I really should have that removed.* "Pick up Tina. Do a snatch and grab and take her to the safe house off 69. Make sure to put her phone in the wire cage. I don't want anyone tracking it. I'll come once I'm certain no one followed you."

The two men turned around and left without a word. Michael knew they would do as commanded. They would take all necessary steps to avoid getting caught. They had no choice. *Besides, getting caught would mean death and they wanted revenge against me and Bishop first.*

"I want you to call off the watcher. No eyes on what those two are doing."

Chuck nodded his head. "I'll make the call now."

Michael's phone buzzed and he unlocked it to check the message. He frowned. *So, you don't trust I can do this?* He locked his phone and then looked up at his hacker. "There is some extra muscle downstairs. Please find him and send him up here."

Becca went through the house quickly before any of them left, wiping down everything they may have touched with a towel. She gathered towels, food wrappers, Kyrie's clothes, and anything else portable into a trash bag. Kyrie watched with fascination at her friend's diligence.

Once Becca declared the house clear, they went outside and around the back to where Michelle had parked her car.

Aki kept her face turned away from the four-wheeler with the pair of bodies strapped to the back. "This is going to make me sick."

"It will be okay," Jake offered. "We'll get out of here shortly."

Kyrie felt her hands shake as a force tugged at her mind from deeper in the woods. She forced herself to calm down and took the shotgun from Jake so he could drive the four-wheeler. She took measured breathes as he started the vehicle. *So much power. We need to see it.* She ushered Awan forward with the weapon as the group followed her onto a path leading into the dense woods.

The path grew narrower and narrower the further they went. The four-wheeler soon struggled to navigate the route as the trees grew closer together, making movement difficult. The canopy above their heads blocked out the sun, with the branches entwining to form a solid mass. The ground vegetation, which would normally have died from a lack of light, grew dense and green.

Kyrie felt her senses sharpening. Even in her exhausted state, she could not block out the mental mass of rodents and bugs that intruded upon her awareness. *So much power.*

Awan kept his attention on her. "We have to mow the path twice a week, even in the winter. Always cutting down trees to keep the path open." The old man stopped. A side path cut through the forest. "There is a pit just down there. We need to dump the bodies here."

Kyrie glanced down the very dark path. The trees almost formed solid walls. She breathed in, smelling the soil and the moisture of the forest. "Something changed the trees. They are all now a single organism."

"The veil is torn," Awan repeated. "The trees have grown faster and faster over the last few years. I wonder if the hole between the spirit world and this one grows larger." He walked to the back of the four-wheeler and started removing the straps. "The energy of this place drives the bugs to consume the bodies. Nothing will remain in a matter of days."

"Bones will be left. And metal from cloths," Becca said. "What did I tell you all about a black-girl going into the woods? This is when some shit comes out and kills me."

"The place is not evil," Awan challenged.

Becca wrapped her arms around herself. "Still creeps me out."

Kyrie allowed the energy of the place to fill her. She could feel its pulsing as it moved through her body. It reminded her of a memory long forgotten.

She watched without seeing as Jake got off the four-wheeler and helped Awan drag the two bodies down the path and into the pit. When they returned, Kyrie forced herself to focus. She handed Jake the shotgun and moved forward at her normal walking pace, making the others rush to keep up.

After another fifty feet, the dense forest opened into a large circle. The trees stopped with a ragged edge. Their branches and leaves stunted with just a short overhang into the clearing. The leaf color so green and vibrant that it did not look real.

"Too much of anything is not healthy," Awan said. "Grass, and even trees, filled the clearing when I bound you. Today, so much power is present, nothing can grow in the glade. I wonder if the forest grows to contain an infection."

Kyrie looked at the rocky ground. No plants had grown in the forty-foot wide circle for many years. A few large rocks stood out of the dirt, but there were no significant formations that would mark the place as anything more than just a random section of rocky ground.

The energy pulsed in her head like the beating of a heart, or of waves lapping at the edge of a mountain lake. She moved further into the clearing and closed her eyes to let the power flow through her.

"I can feel my skin tingling," Michelle said.

"That is common sense telling you we are about to die," Becca pleaded.

"I want to go," Aki demanded.

"I can feel it too," Jake said. "Like I could run a hundred miles."

Kyrie inhaled deeply. Her abdomen and leg still ached, but strength built in her. *We smell the other world,* she told herself and then she nodded her head and turned around. "This is not a veil to a spirit world. My mother's theories are right, she just didn't have the math yet. This is a link to another universe."

"What do you mean?" Michelle asked.

Kyrie opened her mind. She could feel distant beings that were not human. *Could they hear us if we called to them?* She resisted the urge fearing that the very act could bring one through the veil.

She turned her attention back to her friends. "So many of my mother's theories involved trying to move energy and substance between closed systems. The veil, if you want to call it that, is like a wall, but here it acts more like a filter. Semipermeable." She walked around the edge of the circle. "The drawings I created my whole life. They come from my dreams. Dreams so real I always felt like I had been there." She looked Michelle in the eyes. "At least part of me had been. Those beings in my drawings. They're not fantasy, they were, or are, real."

"Can we go now? Please!" Aki moved closer to Jake.

Kyrie exhaled and turned to Awan. "How do I get them to stop chasing me?"

Awan's face aged. "I wish I knew. My cousin wants an army so he can use them when he is ready to reveal himself as what he truly is. He will not want anyone that could challenge him. For Hurlington's men, they believe with every fiber of their being that you are the work of the devil and that God commands them. They seek the Bound, but they are usually ineffective at finding and killing them. I have been fortunate that they do not know where this place is."

"I can see that," Michelle said, remaining close to Kyrie. "Your grandmother's years of digging, plus your parents' trail is what led us here."

*I am, Kyrie.* "I am no demon." Kyrie glanced at the others, but none of them said anything. She moved to stand before Awan. "Breaking a binding stone kills the bound spirit."

"And the human, if the human's mind has been consumed," Awan added.

"But it could free the human if not?" Michelle half asked.

"It is possible." Awan raised his left hand. "But I would caution against it in her case. Even if Kyrie is the child I bound, and not the spirit, the dependencies between the two have formed over the last sixteen years." He looked at her. "I am so sorry for what I did. I can't say for certain, but I would say that whatever you are, you are at least a merging of the two."

"How many Bound exist?" Kyrie asked.

"At least five hundred." Awan stood his ground. "I don't know how many have died since the bindings have taken place. My cousin holds most of the stones. Michael Rodgers holds a handful. Perhaps twenty, maybe less."

"And if I give the stones back to the Bound. Then they would no longer be controlled?"

Awan considered the question and then spoke. "Depends on the damage to their minds. However, most of those subjected to binding came from the dregs of society. They were murderers, thieves, and rapists. Men that offended my cousin or Michael Rodgers when they failed at some criminal enterprise."

Kyrie frowned. *But what of the beings pulled from the other world?*

"What are you thinking, Kyrie?" Michelle asked.

"I have to stop Bishop. I have to find a way to stop all of it." Her eyes narrowed and her voice hardened as she looked Awan in the eyes. "What are you going to do?"

Awan's face told her he knew her thoughts. "I will leave this place and do no more bindings. I would rather die than subject another person to this." He glanced at his right arm. "I have a hook I can wear. The Bound have some cash stashed in the house. I have not driven in years, but I think I can manage. I will disappear. If they find me, then they will have to kill me."

Kyrie allowed a little energy to flow through her as she skimmed Awan's thoughts. Satisfied he likely spoke the truth, she turned her attention to Michelle. "Aki is right. We need to go. I need to think. To find a way to bring down this empire."

Aki bit her lip, her desire to leave fighting her activism. "Bishop is a very corrupt man. He makes people rich, which means they protect him. How do you think you are going to bring him down?"

Kyrie walked over to Aki. "With help. I don't know what I am. I don't know the world outside the valley I grew up in. But I know I want to be free of people hunting me, and as long as he's controlling things, I can't be."

Aki trembled visibly. "If we leave now. I swear I will help."

Jake put an arm around her shoulder. "I agree with Aki, let's leave." He pulled her closer. "I will help as well. The last thing I want is to become a slave to some demigod from another universe."

Kyrie breathed deeply, drawing more energy into her to compensate for the damage still done to her body. The power burned, but it flowed so easily that she hardly noticed. She wondered what would happen if she remained in the clearing. *Could you even return home? Some reactions are reversible. Others are not,* she reminded herself sternly as she continued to bathe in the rich energy. *It feels so refreshing.* She could feel Michelle watching her and knew Michelle understood her better than the others. "Thank you," she told everyone as she exited the glade.

# Chapter 19

Nalitran adjusted his suit and straightened his tie. The years since the crossing had allowed him to acclimate to the body he possessed, but he missed his natural form. The diminished sense of smell and weaker eyesight of humans left him feeling as if he interacted with the world through a veil. The frail nature of the skin, bones, and muscles left him feeling old, despite the fact for a human, the body represented a prime specimen.

Thoughts of inhabiting a younger body returned periodically, but the risk of failure kept him from attempting a transference. However, he knew one day the body would age beyond its usefulness and he would have no choice in that. *I just need to experiment a few times first.*

He put the thoughts from his mind. The need remained several years away, and before that, he needed to grow his position in human society. A new body, while it would feel nice, would come with a new face and that would reset too much of the work he had done.

"Mr. Bishop, do you want me to do anything about the situation with the girl?"

Nalitran smiled at Yrginda. The woman who owned the body before Awan replaced the human mind with one of the dolunar no longer existed. However, Yrginda had adjusted to the change of gender better than Nalitran expected his own reaction would have been. In fact, Yrginda used that change to his advantage whenever he could, and while Nalitran did not find the body attractive, others did.

"Yes, Elsa, I need you to make sure there is a team in place to clean things up in case Rodgers messes up again. Please be subtle about it. The press is watching me closely with my congressional move. I cannot afford to be tied to criminal activity." He fastened the top button of his suit. "A scandal might not prevent me from winning, but I really don't want to have to put forth the extra effort. I expect the attention will die off after I am elected."

"Of course. Unfortunately, things are happening quickly."

Nalitran trusted no one, but Yrginda had shown an incredible amount of loyalty over the last ten years. "Make sure to adjust corporate records. Rodgers should already be minimized, but I want plausible deniability."

"And the girl?"

Nalitran looked into Yrginda's brown eyes, but he put no pressure on the binding stone. He had rewarded the man's loyalty with freedom and did not want to diminish that with compulsion. "I need her alive. I need to examine the impact of a binding on a child." He regretted not pursuing the research sooner, but what becomes clear in hindsight is often murky in the moment. *What can be more poetic than bouncing through generations by possessing child after child, always leaving my empire to myself?* The irony that his people potentially gave him the gift of immortality instead of punishing him as they intended brought a smile to his face. "Alive please. This has become a sixteen-year experiment I didn't know I wanted."

"We'll need to burn and destroy all of this," Becca said as she got into the back of Michelle's car with the trash bag. "We don't want to leave any evidence."

"I can burn it when we get back to the campsite," Kyrie offered. "I can make it burn hotter than a normal wood fire."

Aki and Jake got in on Michelle's side of the car, and Jake immediately put his arm around Aki. She leaned her head against his shoulder and snuggled closer. Kyrie wanted to smile, but she knew terror and panic created that closeness. She wanted their relationship to have a foundation of happiness, not trauma.

*The death of two men hardly phased you. What does that say about you?* She had no answer as she stood outside the car. She killed in defense of herself and her friends. Her parents might admonish her for risking herself for others, but they would not baulk at the result. *What emotion are we supposed to feel?*

"It's midafternoon, do we head home or go to the campsite?" Michelle asked as she stood next to the driver's door.

"Home," Aki said from inside the car. "I just want to go home."

Becca nodded her head. Jake said nothing and Kyrie watched as Michelle looked at her over the top of the car roof. *Your decision then.* She glanced at Awan who stood a dozen feet away with the shotgun she bent in his hand. She turned back to Michelle and got into the car. "Let's go home. We can burn the bag on the way, after I recover a bit more."

Michelle jumped in the driver's seat, started the engine, and put the car into reverse. "I hate to say it, but it feels like we just found the hook for a campaign. The question is, did we level up?" She sped backwards, turned around, headed out the driveway, and drove under the living arch.

Kyrie chuckled. She knew Michelle did not feel that confident, but she loved the fact that her friend tried to lighten the mood. "I feel like I'm the next level. That grove helped me a lot. And you're now driving like a pro."

Michelle smiled and pressed harder on the gas.

"So, no internal damage?" Becca asked as she leaned forward.

Kyrie shrugged. "I feel bruised and tender, but I don't feel the sharp burning pain I did earlier."

"That's good." Becca leaned forward enough to put her head between the front seats. "I'm going to go on the record here that we must make a pact to never talk about having killed two people today. I'm too young to go to jail."

Aki jumped and shook her head. "Please. I don't want to go to jail either!"

"I had no plans to tell anyone," Kyrie said.

Michelle accelerated as they turned onto the dirt road that they thought was Highway 295. "Who is going to believe in magic anyway? Hard to prove how they died."

Becca shook her head. "Dead bodies are dead bodies. The cops will still think murder and just think they died by some normal means they understand. We have to swear to tell no one." She looked at Kyrie. "And we have to not start killing a bunch of other people. That won't end well."

Kyrie turned to face Becca. "I won't tell anyone about this. I didn't want to get the rest of you involved."

Michelle reached over to put a hand on Kyrie's arm. "We weren't going to let you face this on your own." She looked back at Becca. "And yes, I swear I will tell no one. I'm freaked out enough as it is."

"But," Kyrie said sharply, "I will do whatever is necessary to protect all of you and myself. I'm not going to let someone else kill me, or any of you, if I can stop it."

Becca leaned back. "Fair enough."


Kyrie sat and looked out the window, but she saw little. They passed through Japton and sped up now that they were on the blacktop. Her mind remained focused on finding a way to protect herself and the others. *And that is why you do not feel remorse. You protected the party.* She swallowed the discomfort building in her. *Even in game, you never had the stomach to simply kill people. You ran and hid.* She bit her lip. *But we can't run forever. That's where mother and father were wrong. But if Steven Bishop does take over the country and becomes unstoppable?* She had no answer for that.

Kyrie looked up as Becca's phone started to buzz. A moment later, Aki's chirped and Michelle's played a short song several times in a row.

"Shit," Aki said. "Tina's been texting all morning."

"Yeah," Becca said. "Crap. She said she's going to your house Michelle, since none of us cared to answer her."

Michelle unlocked her phone with a look and handed it to Kyrie. "Tell me what she's saying."

Kyrie took a moment to find the text app and then opened it. She started to skim through the messages and then felt uncomfortable. "She initially apologized for what she said. Asked you to forgive her for getting angry. Then she appears to have gotten angry that you would not return her messages." Kyrie skipped down a few more. "She cursed you out because your mother said you had gone to Aki's without inviting her." Kyrie looked up. "I'm sorry. We should have told her."

Michelle hit the steering wheel with her hand. "Tina overreacted. She's been jealous of the time I'm spending with you, but she didn't have to involve my mother." She looked at Kyrie. "She would not have done well with what happened at Awan's."

"No, she wouldn't," Becca agreed.

Aki cursed. "She went to my house and got my parents angry because she told them we were not at your place. Damn her, my parents have left a dozen voicemails."

Kyrie noticed a text message from Lars to Michelle's phone. It asked where she had gone and for her to call him back immediately because people inquired if he was responsible for her disappearance. She bit her lip and then looked at Michelle. "Lars reached out to me through you."

Jake removed his arm from around Aki as he kept reading through his own message. "My parents are livid."

"I don't trust Lars," Michelle replied. "He's not done anything to help you. What if he's feeding information to Bishop?"

Becca put a hand on Aki's phone. "No one reply to anyone. Including Lars, Kyrie. We have to get our stories straight." She looked at her own phone again. "At least Tina doesn't like going to my house. Nothing from my parents, but I doubt that will last."

Kyrie returned Michelle's gaze and then nodded her head.

Michelle smiled and then looked in her mirror at Becca. "Good thing you disabled the parental tracking. I wouldn't want to explain the road trip."

"Credit card receipts." Becca banged her hand against the side of the car. "Jake had to reserve the tent sites with his card. Both will show up when the bills arrive."

"If they look at them," Jake challenged.

"Wait," Kyrie said. "This doesn't look like Tina's normal message. 'Call me now. One of Kyrie's friends is demanding to speak with her.' There is a number that follows."

Michelle's phone started to ring. "Your mother," Kyrie said.

"Don't answer," Becca repeated. "We have to have our story straight and we need to know what is up with Tina"

"What if someone grabbed her?" Aki demanded. "We've got two groups after us."

Kyrie set the phone down and it rang twice more before becoming silent. "But which one?"

"Either one might kill her," Becca said. "Let me look at the message."

Kyrie held up the phone so Michelle's could unlock it and then handed it to Becca. "My father would use hostages in game to try and get me to do things. He'd never kill them until the people taking the hostage knew they could not force my hand."

"Your father role played hostage scenarios with you?" Jake asked.

Kyrie nodded her head. "I will need to call that number back and find out who has her and what they want."

"If it is that church, they want to kill you," Michelle said as she continued to drive faster and faster. "If it is Bishop's people, they want the stone so they can control you." She took a deep breath. "Either group will kill all of us, perhaps making you do it if they control you. We know too much. You can't turn yourself over to them."

"Damn it," Aki swore. "I don't want to be part of this anymore."

Jake put his arm around her again and pulled her close to him. "We'll figure it out."

"I still have to find out who has her." Kyrie reached her hand back to get the phone from Becca.

"Not from this phone," Becca said. "We'll finally stop at a store and get a burner. Michelle, do you have any ideas of what we can tell our parents we were doing?"

Michelle glanced in her mirror again. "Movies? We had our phones off because we were at the movies."

"Yeah, that might work," Becca agreed, "except that we have at least four-hours of driving to get home. If not more. We can't call now without them demanding we get home immediately."

Jake clenched his fist. "And if Tina is in trouble, we might not be able to go home."

"What about telling part of the truth?" Kyrie asked. "What would they say if we told them we all decided to go camping and have been gaming at the campsite and your phones were dead?"

Becca frowned. "All dead is unlikely. They know us well enough to know we'd charge them with the car or a brick. But," she added, "that we found ourselves in a cell dead spot is not out of the question. We just came from one."

"But driving to Arkansas?" Michelle questioned. "We might get away with it if we stayed close to home. Perhaps in Missouri, but this is a little too far."

"Blame me," Kyrie said. "Tell them I wanted to go to Arkansas because that is the last place my parents went before they disappeared. You did it to humor me. My aunt can yell at me, but it would match up with other things. We just leave out the trip down 295."

"The camp site did have spotty cell service," Jake admitted. "Not dead, but I only had one bar."

"Still plausible," Michelle said. "I've camped in places with no service. But, we'd still all be in a hell of a lot of trouble. My parents will ground me for a year."

"Yours?" Aki demanded. "I have Japanese parents. They will go ballistic."

Becca continued to search on her phone. "Kyrie's story has the best chance of success. Plus, if Jake's parents do look at the statement, they will see we went to Arkansas. If we said we went to Missouri and that comes, then they will know we lied."

"They'll be mad you turned off the phone tracking," Michelle said.

Kyrie shook her head. "Even more important, we still need to find out what happened to Tina."

"Yeah," Becca agreed. "I've got directions to a store. We'll get a burner and call the number. Then I will try to find out as much as I can about Dennis Hurlington. I've got a Chicago address for Michael Rodgers plus a second phone number. Once we know who has her, we can plan better."

Kyrie noticed Michelle glance over at her. "How long do you need to recover?"

"I've never been shot before. Normally, I need a couple of days to feel back to normal after using that much power, but the grove's energy helped."

"Take a short rest then. If we need a mage, I want her at full strength."

Kyrie smiled at Michelle's attempt to reassure her, but guilt over Tina and the others getting in trouble weighed on her. *Killing more people is a definite possibility.*

"Yes, Mom, I am so sorry for not telling you," Michelle said. "I know." Michelle turned around in a circle, obviously distressed by what her mother said. "I wasn't thinking."

Kyrie looked across the parking lot at Aki and Jake, similar conversation with their parents distressed them as well. Becca's talk with her father went quickly, leaving her pale and shaky. However, Becca recovered her composure within a minute when she focused on the phone they had purchased for Kyrie.

"The phone's plan doesn't have a lot of data, but there is a fair amount of talk." She glanced over her shoulder at the store's main entrance. "Stupid people have terrible selection." She handed the phone to Kyrie. "We can download some apps when we get to a Wi-Fi spot. But for now, we need to call whoever took Tina." She sighed. "I will need to show you how to get on-line and get your files before we get home. Otherwise, I might never get the chance. My ass is going to be a lot skinnier based on my father's tone." She chuckled. "I think he expects I've been out with some guy. The ironic thing is, we did spend last night sleeping with a guy."

Kyrie put a hand on her arm. "Thank you. I appreciate everything. If I can find a way to get you out of trouble, I will."

"Don't worry about it. I agreed to go." Becca laughed again. "Besides, you're my first friend with superpowers. If I can't get in a little trouble for superpowers, then am I really living?"

Kyrie smiled and then waited for the others to end their calls. They all wanted to hear what Tina said at the same time.

Aki's and Jake's calls finished well before Michelle's call. But eventually, even Michelle hung up her phone and joined them. "I'm in so much trouble," Michelle said.

"Just under ten months, then you'll be eighteen and free," Becca told her. "I've got a year and two months. My father reminded me of that. He said I will be out the door at midnight the morning of my birthday."

Kyrie did not fully relate to their distress, but she remembered some of the worst compulsion her mother had given her when she was twelve. The pain of that experience had faded, but the fear of disappointing them still lingered.

She considered calling Lars, wanting to get his advice, but the doubt the others had placed in her mind as to his loyalty changed her mind. "Let's call the number Tina left." Kyrie dialed the number from memory, put the phone on speaker, and listened as the phone rang. Becca held her own phone near Kyrie's new one, an app running to record the conversation.

"Hello," a male voice answered; confident and strong.

"I want to speak with Tina," Kyrie said, wishing she could see the person and read his emotions.

"Tina is occupied at the moment. She would love to speak with you of course. How about you come over?"

"You've kidnapped Tina," Kyrie demanded. "Tell me where you are holding her."

"I really don't know what you are talking about," said the voice. "But we can meet and discuss it in person."

"What is your name?" Kyrie demanded.

"I don't recall," the man said. "Nor am I in the mood for games. If you aren't interested in meeting for a simple discussion, then we're done."

"Wait," Kyrie said, trying to find a way to confirm who spoke to her without giving too much information away. "Are you the one after jewelry or…are you the one who likes to swing swords."

Kyrie heard a slight chuckle come from the phone. "Where are you? I will give you directions, but only when I confirm your location. You near Highway 69?"

Kyrie looked at the others and Michelle mouthed 'sixty-nine highway.' Followed by 'I know where it is.'

"No," Kyrie replied.

"Well, I would suggest driving to the Blue Valley Sports Complex at 135th and 69. Then call me back and I'll tell you where to go from there. Time is running out."

Kyrie looked down as the call terminated. "We are hours from home still."

"And my parents want me to go directly home," Michelle said. "Apparently, they have gotten your aunt involved as well. They were planning on calling the police. I'm not sure if she has or not." She looked at her phone for the time. "They had not seen Tina since the morning. No one apparently knows she is missing."

"If you get me somewhere, I can get a ride share to where they want me to go."

Michelle glared at her. "Forget it, Kyrie. Never split the party. Didn't your parents teach you that?"

Kyrie laughed. "In game and in life don't seem quite the same."

Michelle looked at the others. "Jake, Aki, Becca, I can drop you at your houses if you want."

"We are rescuing a friend, I'm in all the way," Jake said.

"Yeah," Becca agreed.

Aki shook her head and then looked at Jake and changed her mind. "Okay, I'll go."

"You sure?" Michelle asked. "No shame in going home."

Aki frowned. "I said I will go."

Kyrie nodded her head and then got back to the issue of Tina. "I think Michael Rodger's people have her. The man sounded composed. My parents played religious zealots as quite chaotic. Am I off?"

"No, that sounds reasonable to me," Michelle said.

Becca pursed her lips. "They won't tell us the destination until the last minute. They will want to make sure we aren't followed and don't have time to call the police with the real address."

Kyrie pursed her lips. "That Dennis Hurlington wants to destroy Steven Bishop and his empire. We should try to get them fighting each other. If they want to kill Bound, perhaps we can get them to fight Michael Rodger's Bound. That might give us a chance to rescue Tina."

Becca raised her eyebrows. "That's a tall order. I doubt they want to partner with a demon—no offense."

Michelle spoke up. "I ran a campaign where you all bribed a pack of demons to attack a royal family that had invaded a city."

"In game," Becca challenged. "But I didn't say I wouldn't try." She looked back at the car. "We'll need to get rid of the things with

Kyrie's blood on them. We are far enough away from the cabin that we might be able to just throw the bag in a dumpster."

Kyrie shrugged. "I will defer to you."

Becca considered it for a bit and then nodded her head. "I think it unlikely that someone will find it. Plus burning it out here would only draw attention." She opened the back of the car, grabbed the bag, and walked over to the dumpster near the edge of the parking lot. She hurried back. "Let's get on the road."

# Chapter 20

Kyrie continued to meditate as Michelle drove north. She wanted to recover as much strength as she could before whatever happened. *Father, what kind of trap would you set?*

Becca remained on her phone, searching leads on the Church of the Righteous Revenge. Her grumbling and complaining provided a background to the music Michelle played through her phone.

Despite Kyrie's focus, she could feel the resignation to the trouble everyone found themselves in. *Lars said not to run away. Would they see this trip as running away?* The idea of Lars still felt uncertain in her mind. She wanted to trust him, but at the moment, he remained nothing more than photos in a folder and a voice on the phone.

Kyrie opened her eyes and then pulled the brooch from her pocket. She examined it and then bent the filigree until the glass stone fell out. She hefted it testing its weight and feel. The connection to her wrapped itself around her mind now that she knew what it felt like.

She reached into her other pocket and pulled out the three glass rocks that Awan had given her. They looked similar to hers, *but they have no energy thread.* The idea she could give control of herself to someone else shortened her breath. *You trusted the others before you knew the full impact. And before they knew what it could do to us.* She bit her lip and then made her decision. The four stones shuffled together in her hands. She then took one of the unbound stones and put it on the brooch. With some gravitational energy, she bent the prongs back in place to secure it. She finally pinned the brooch to her shirt and shook it to make sure the stone would not fall out.

Kyrie reached over and placed her green stone on Michelle's lap. The other two unbound stones, she handed back to Jake and Becca. "Hold on to these for me, but don't let anyone know you have them."

"Who has the real one?" Jake asked.

She shook her head. "All of us do. None of us."

Becca nodded her head, leaving the stone in her hand as she continued to type on her phone. "Good news. I've got one of these freaks in a private chat. I had found a message board on the dark web and he's been trying to recruit me to their cause."

Jake leaned over Aki to look. "Really? Do you think it is one of the men from the van who attacked us?"

Becca shrugged. "Absolutely no idea who I'm talking to. Could be Michelle's brother for all I know. I'm just trying to play it cool and see where it goes." She typed some more and then looked up. "I'm hinting that I've seen things, but I'm not sharing too many details in case he thinks I'm playing him. Anything you want me to say?"

Kyrie turned around and kneeled in her seat so she faced Becca directly. "They were bold enough to attack us in public. Tell him you have seen some of his fellow holy warriors and heard them call out the church's name when they tried to kill a demon, which is how you found their site. Tell him you have seen Satan at work and that you've seen a demon floating through the air."

"You sure?" Becca asked. "Might scare him off."

Kyrie nodded yes. "We don't have time. If this works, great, if not, I still have another plan." She smiled. "Let me know what he says."

Becca frowned, but continued to type. "He's getting cold feet. His responses have slowed. Hope your other plan is a good one."

Kyrie wiped her mouth with her hand. "Tell him a demon girl has tormented you at school. Tell her she cast a curse on you and made you trip and then another curse that crushed a full cup of coffee into your face. This girl is the same one his warriors tried to vanquish with swords."

Becca grinned as she typed. "You've been messing with Jessica. Bitch deserves it."

Kyrie smiled. "I told myself not to do it, but I did it anyway."

"He wants confirmation. Asked what the men looked like and he wants the name of the girl doing the tormenting." Becca looked up at Kyrie. "You read this guy."

"Tell him you saw the white van from your house. One of the men had crosses on his forearms. Then give him my name." Kyrie looked at Michelle. Her hands had turned white on the wheel again.

"He is telling me to stay away from you." Becca grinned. "If only he knew the truth of what you are capable of."

"If only." Kyrie quickly played a couple scenarios out in her head. "Tell him you are following me in a car and that you think I'm going to join other demons. You saw me cast a curse on some other girls from school and that I laughed at how I made them my slaves and I planned to bind demons to them."

Kyrie noted Aki's eyes grew wide, but she kept herself focused on Becca, whose grin kept showing more teeth. *You have not bound your friends against their will,* she told herself and hoped it was true.

"Texting and driving. I should add some typos." Becca glanced at Kyrie. "He asked where you are going."

Kyrie looked over to Michelle. "How far away are we?"

"We're almost back on 435," Michelle said, checking her mirrors. "Perhaps twenty minutes."

"Tell him our location," Kyrie said. Still kneeling in the seat, she turned to face Michelle. "When you get to the park, do you think there will be a large parking lot?"

Michelle nodded. "I had to watch my brother play baseball there more than once. The lots are pretty large."

"Okay. When you get there drive around the lots, but don't stop. I'll make the call once we've had a chance to check it out."

"What spell you going to cast?" Jake asked.

"No spell," Kyrie said. "I imagine someone will be watching for us because my father's campaigns always had someone trying to trail me. If they concentrate on looking for me, I will hopefully be able to feel their focus." She bobbed her head. "At least if they are not Bound. But, if Rodgers has Bound watching, then I think I will be able to tell based on how muted their minds are."

"You're going to read their minds from the car?" Becca asked. "You able to read our minds?"

Kyrie had expected the question. "I don't really read minds. Not unless I'm touching someone. Then I can try, if they don't block me. What I feel is emotions. If someone is happy or scared or angry." *You lie. No, exaggerate,* she corrected. *No, you lie.* "When I'm around a lot of people, I have to block all the emotions. It gives me a headache and it can make me sick." She frowned. "Plus, if I let in too much emotion, then I start feeling what the people around me are feeling and I lose myself." Kyrie could tell Becca did not appear completely convinced.

"What am I feeling now?" Becca demanded.

Kyrie concentrated, separating Becca's thoughts from the others. "A bit of anger, mistrust, excitement, pleasure, and a fair amount of exhaustion. You're tired of being in the back of the car."

Becca frowned. "Like you had to read my mind to know any of that."

Kyrie agreed. "I don't pick up that much more than what someone would observe by watching someone and paying attention to how they talk and move and the expressions on their face."

"But you can feel someone in a car and know if they are paying attention to you?" Jake asked.

"Sort of. I'm looking for intense emotions. Someone looking for me is likely to be concentrating a lot."

"Well," Michelle added, "any adult sitting in a car at the sports center will be a bit strange anyway. Most people are there to watch their kids."

Becca turned her attention back to her phone. "And anyone our age in the car is going to be pissed because we got stuck watching a brother play ball." She continued typing on the phone. "Go back to what you do. I'll keep this guy on the chat. Though, what do you want me to have him do?"

Kyrie turned her attention back to the road. "Once we find out where we are going, we might use them for reinforcements. We just have to be careful to avoid them killing us in the process."

"Sure, I'll keep the crazy guy in check and convince him to only do what we want him to."

"Thanks," Kyrie said, getting the expected grunt of annoyance from Becca for taking her sarcasm literally. "This might also get all of you out of some of the trouble you are in."

"Really?" Jake asked. "How's that going to work?"

"Tell the truth." She took a drink from the water bottle near her. Kyrie felt Michelle's skepticism. "Well, leave out the details of my powers."

"All of the truth beside that?" Aki asked.

"We tell them about the men with swords attacking us on Thursday, but we change it to be that we managed to run away. We say—"

Becca interrupted. "No one rehearse our statements. If we are all using the same words, the police will get suspicious. The general statements need to match, but definitely don't use the same words."

"No rehearsing," Michelle agreed. "But let's make sure we only cover the same things. How do we explain going to Arkansas?"

"The timeline is this," Kyrie said. "The robbery of my aunt's house, then on Thursday, we get attacked by crazy people with swords screaming about demons. I tell you that I knew people were after my parents and I wanted to go find what might have started this. I knew a trip to Arkansas started it, so I needed to go."

"The camping trip was my idea," Michelle said. "You were planning to run away, and I didn't want you to go alone because I was scared for you. So, I said we all go camping to keep you safe."

"I planned to run away because I didn't want any of you to get hurt if I stayed in Olathe," Kyrie agreed.

"And to keep you from going on your own, I suggested we go camping and I take you down there." Michelle glanced in her mirror at the others and saw their faces, so she clarified. "Who is going to believe that Kyrie managed to convince us on her own? I'll own that. They will believe that I'm stupid enough to suggest it and that I convinced all of you."

Jake picked up the tale. "We stayed at the campsite, playing D&D, talking, trying to figure out what might have got these crazies fixated on Kyrie." He leaned forward. "No cell coverage. Then we drove around to get food and all the texts from everyone came through, including the ones from Tina. We call the number and the guy said we had to meet him and not to tell anyone, or Tina would be harmed."

"Right," Becca said. "We were just trying to keep a scared friend from running away. Then another friend got into trouble. I can work with that."

"Hopefully, that will get you out of trouble with your parents," Kyrie said. *Now we have to save Tina.*


Kyrie calmed herself and controlled her breathing as Michelle turned into the sports complex parking lot. Several evening games had just started, and the lots were filled with cars. A handful of people moved between the cars and down the aisles, but most of the activity centered around the numerous baseball fields.

Michelle turned down the first aisle. "We'll just pretend I need to find a spot all the way near the front because we don't like to walk."

Kyrie reached out and looked for people in vehicles, trying very hard not to get distracted by her friends. *Control. You must maintain control.* She frowned, not needing the reminder. She only used a trickle of energy as Michelle slowly drove down the second and third aisles. Kyrie felt people, but nothing that spoke to her as someone watching for them. *It's been hours, are they still here? Shut up,* she told herself.

"Call?" Michelle asked. "Perhaps they are watching from the stands.

Kyrie felt her stomach drop at the thought of having to scan that many minds. She picked up the phone and dialed the number, placing the call on speaker again. The same man answered after the third ring.

"I had a mind not to pick up." The man's anger coming through the phone clearly.

"I told you," Kyrie decided to echo his anger back, "we were not close to the area. It took time to get here. We are where you asked us to be. Now, where is Tina?"

"You in Michelle's car or a different one? I presume you are all listening?"

"I'm in Michelle's car," Kyrie said. "Where is Tina?"

"Drive around the lot once more, then leave. Get back onto sixty-nine south and call me again." The man on the other end hung up.

"A watcher," Becca said. "Someone to follow us."

Kyrie took a deep breath and forced herself to regulate the flow of energy into her body. "Drive slowly."

The others continued to look out the windows, searching for anyone suspicious. They pointed out people and wondered aloud about cars. However, Kyrie ignored them and focused on the thoughts and emotions of those she could feel.

*Got you!* She released the seat belt, pulled open the car door, and jumped out of the moving car. Michelle hit the brakes as Kyrie ran around the back of the vehicle. A short man with dark black hair saw her and immediately went for his phone. She sprinted between a pair of parked vehicles as she snapped a gravitational field around the phone. The small object flew from his hand to hers. The man shrieked in surprise and Kyrie surrounded him with a field that held him in place.

"Where do they have her?" she demanded as she stepped close enough to touch him. The man tried to shake his head, but he found himself immobilized. Kyrie opened a small area in the field and put her hand on his arm. She controlled her breathing, allowing the maintenance of the force to slip into the background of her mind while she searched for his thoughts.

*You can't resist us,* she thought at him. *Trying to block us will burn a hole in your mind.*

The man tried to speak, but her field kept him from opening his mouth. Kyrie could feel his panic, and then with a rush of chaotic imagery, felt him mentally replay the route he knew to a barn where they held Tina.

*Slower,* she commanded. The man's mind responded almost instantly. *How do we get there from here?* This time the man's memories came at a measured pace and Kyrie took the time to absorb the content. She exhaled when she felt confident of the memories.

Kyrie stepped back and almost released him when she realized the man would steal the first phone he could find and call Michael Rodgers to warn him. She shook her head at him. "That would not be nice of you."

With her mind, she sensed the electrical energy of the key fob in his pocket. She carefully adjusted her gravitational field and pulled the man's keys from his pocket. They floated through the air to her hand. *This might work.*

Kyrie stepped further away. She considered restricting the gravity field in such a manner that he could not breathe and would pass out, but another idea came to her. "Chuck, you are not a good man." She spun him, turning his face away from her. With his body ridged, he looked like a mini being pushed across a map. However, the surrounding vehicles concealed the unnatural movements from anyone else.

She drew in more energy and narrowed her concentration to adjust the fields. With a grin on her face, she forced his hands outward, smashing the side windows of the cars on either side of him, breaking both the windows and his hands at the same time. She let go of the control of his head and he screamed in agony.

Kyrie moved further away from him. The effort to control the gravity field grew exponentially, but she needed him out of the way without killing him. She slid him forward with stiff legs and forced his hands to smash another set of car windows, this time in full view of a police officer drawn in the direction by his screaming.

His howls of pain and anguish brought other people running. The officer, initially curious, started running in his direction with a hand on a weapon. Kyrie felt the strain of controlling him burn her mind, but she held out and forced his hands into the rear windows of the second set of cars. The officer shouted for him to drop as a weapon was drawn. Kyrie released him to crumple to the ground.

"Let's go," Michelle growled through the driver's window.

Kyrie raced around the other side of the car, jumped in, and shut the door. Michelle put her foot on the accelerator and took off quickly.

"What did you do?" Becca asked.

"He had already called his Mr. Rodgers to confirm we were in the parking lot." Kyrie said. "I know where they have Tina."

"Breaking windows with his hands." Jake raised his eyebrows. "That's got to hurt."

"He won't be using computers for a while," Kyrie responded. "He knew about my powers. He also knows three Bound men are with Mr. Rodgers at a barn. They're holding Tina tied up in the back."

"What's the address?" Becca asked. "I can try to get the nut jobs to go there as well."

"I don't know the address," Kyrie admitted. "I just have a mental image. Head south down 69. When I see the road, I'll tell you to get off. There is a farm a few miles off the highway." She looked over at Michelle. "I'll have you park in a field. The guy had thought it would be a good place to hide a car. Then I will head to the barn and rescue Tina."

"You are not splitting the party," Michelle said. "What if you need help?"

"I won't have any of you get hurt on my account."

"Hate to break it to you, but we're already neck deep in this," Becca said from the back. "And Tina needs our help."

"Becca, I need you to get the sword wielders to go to the barn. Then I also want you to call the police after they come. Give them the explanation we came up with and tell them we think Tina's being held there."

Michelle's voice hardened as she pulled onto the highway and accelerated. "Police? You don't want to get locked in a government facility."

"I don't plan for that to happen." Kyrie looked around the car. "All of you thought the Church of the Righteous Revenge were nut jobs who want to kill imaginary demons. I'm just taking a calculated risk that the police will believe the same thing. And if they are fighting Bishop's men when the cops arrive, there would be even less focus on me. And we know Bishop's men won't say anything about me, he wants things kept quiet."

"What if the nut jobs don't show?" Michelle asked.

"Then I defended myself against four men. I know what that hacker in the parking lot knew." Kyrie put a hand on her arm. "I'm the best shot at protecting Tina from injury. If the cops show up, Rodgers will likely kill her and then just come after another one of you. He's got a back way out of the barn. I have to stop him."

"How?"

"I think I can get control of his Bound. Awan said he carries the stones on him. I just need to get them, then he's mine. And a couple of Bound could easily handle Hurlington's sword carrying crazies."

"I still don't like this."

Kyrie frowned at her friend's lack of support. "Simple game mechanics. When fighting a group of opponents, first take out the casters. They do too much damage from afar. I can't get to Bishop yet, but if I get the Bound, I have his magic muscle."

Becca continued from the back. "Then take out the weakest fighters."

Kyrie agreed. "An orc might not do a ton of damage, but if you face a hundred of them, you'll die from all the small cuts while you try to take down the level twenty fighter. Kill the easy targets, then concentrate all attacks on the harder ones. In this case, Hurlington's men are the orcs and Bishop is the boss."

She saw Michelle's doubt. "It is a calculated risk. I know the police can't compel me without the stone. I won't have my stone, so they can't take it from me. And, I'll just be defending myself and helping a friend. That makes Rodgers the bad guy."

Becca nodded her head. "I wish I had a better idea."

Kyrie forced a smile for everyone. "This will work. I know it." *You're more confident than you should be.*

"Just make sure you come back to us," Michelle said. "We can't fight Bishop without you. And if you are gone, he'll eliminate us for knowing too much."

# Chapter 21

"Turn here," Kyrie instructed as she ignored the phone in her hand. It was the third time the watcher's phone had rung. Her burner phone had also rung once from the same number.

Michelle signaled her turn down a dirt road. "They must know something's wrong by now. We've blown the advantage of surprise." She looked down at the dashboard. "We're more than two miles off 69, how much further?"

Kyrie looked at the time on her phone. "We're here." She pointed to a gate leading into a field surrounded by trees.

"What about surprise?" Becca asked. "They will be ready for you."

"I'm hoping they are overconfident," Kyrie responded over her shoulder. "Let me get the gate for you." She barely waited for Michelle to stop the car before she jumped out. *You're already exhausted. Your father would object to you rescuing hostages.* She pushed the thoughts from her head as she snapped the lock with a bit of gravitational help. "Father also said to protect the party."

She pulled open the gate and Michelle drove into the field. "Behind that clump of trees," Kyrie indicated a drop in the ground where the water drained toward a stream. She closed the gate so their entrance into the field would not be obvious to casual inspection and then followed the car.

Once Michelle parked the car, the others started filing out. Aki, clearly disturbed, stood next to Jake. Kyrie knew she could not risk their safety. "Becca. I'm going to head to the barn. Go ahead and get the church coming since we don't know how long it will take." She looked at her friends. "The four of you stay here and hide so you can watch the road. When you think Hurlington's men have driven past, call the cops."

Michelle stepped closer. "We don't know when, or even if, Hurlington's men will show. We don't know how long the cops will take to arrive. You could be dead or a prisoner well before they ever show up."

"I'd rather the cops don't show up before the guys with swords do," Kyrie said. "My goal is to get Hurlington's men arrested to slow them down. For Mr. Rodgers' Bound..." She swallowed the uncertainty in her mind. "The humans, from what Awan said, deserve prison or worse. I will have to see what remains of them. But my plan is to use the Bound to subdue Hurlington's men. If I can slip out with Tina in the commotion I will, but I could also wait for the cops to clean up the mess. I just need to make sure no one harms her."

"You expect us to just sit here not knowing?" Michelle demanded.

"If something does happen, then get in the car and drive through the gate and run to the cops." Kyrie did not wait for any more debate. She checked the brooch to make sure it remained fastened to her borrowed shirt, turned toward the farm a half-mile away, and took off at a fast jog. She could feel the protests coming from Michelle, but she kept going until she moved out of range.

The exercise loosened muscles that had grown tight from sitting for hours in the car. However, the effort left her breathing hard because she refused to compensate with any energy. At the edge of the field, she moved into the tree line and stopped to catch her breath while she looked for watchers. She knew almost nothing about the farm's security from the hacker's mind. *You should have probed more.* The admonishment served no value and she pushed it from her thoughts.

A quick opening of her senses told her no one hid within a hundred feet. She studied the situation with her eyes. To her far left, a two-story farmhouse sat near the front edge of the property. A line of trees along the road shielded all the buildings from casual observation. More pine trees surrounded most of the house, providing additional cover for anyone that might be in the building and looking out the windows.

Directly across from her, an old pickup sat outside a large six-car garage west of the farmhouse. A door along the narrow side of the garage faced her. Kyrie knew from the hacker's memories that the garage had a lot of tools, a couple tractors, room for other vehicles, and most importantly to the hacker, a sports car.

She frowned. She knew from her limited experiences reading minds, memories did not always present themselves in a clear and concise manner. *But still, you learned about a damn car, and not if anyone is in the house.*

Between her and the garage, a pile of lumber sat in a heap with weeds and grasses growing up around the discarded boards. The pile stood nearly three-foot-high and offered some coverage, assuming she made it across the eighty-foot gap unseen.

On the other side of the garage, another tree line demarcated another field boundary. That line of trees mirrored the one she currently hid within, forming a long corridor around the buildings.

She turned her attention to her right and west of the garage. The steel barn stood tall on the property. The hacker knew the barn normally held countless bales of hay stacked more than a dozen feet high to keep them dry. With the lateness of the year, the barn sat only a quarter full. Assuming Rodgers had not moved her, they held Tina near the back wall of the building in an open area created by removing a section of bales. *If you go in through the front, to get to Tina, you have a twenty-foot aisle through the bales before you reach the back wall. Then you have to make it down the narrow passage between the bales and the back wall. If you go in through the back door, you just have to deal with the narrow gap.* She bit her lip and considered where Mr. Rodgers would position himself. *He is the first target. Get the stones, then you control the Bound. But, would he hide in the back or stand at the front?* She shook her head. *You don't know the man; can't predict his actions.*

With her breathing once again normal, she looked around again for observers. She saw none and immediately sprinted the eighty feet to the lumber pile. She dropped down and kept herself hidden from all three buildings. Her mind searched for people, but she hid a hundred feet from the garage and three hundred feet from the house and the barn, which meant the buildings were out of her range.

She knew Tina had last been in the barn, which would mean a higher likelihood for watchers compared to the house. She calculated the angles, moved to the east side of the pile, and sprinted to the north side of the garage, where she pressed herself against the white painted building. She would be visible from the house, but the garage shielded her from the barn. *You need a weapon.*

Kyrie spread her awareness again and the garage lacked any people. The side door was locked so she used a trickle of energy to unlatch it before she slipped inside. The dirty glass windows over the six garage doors allowed enough light for her to see. A van and another car joined the sports car and tractors. Tools hung from the walls and sat in piles on the workbenches against the back wall. She walked to a toolbox and removed a long-handled bar with a rotating end. She swung the break-over bar to test the weight and tucked it under her arm as she continued to look for other potential weapons.

A rusty machete hanging from a nail caught her attention and she pulled it from the wall. She hefted it and swung it a couple of times, testing the feel against the swords she had trained with. The weight felt off, but she had few other options and Kyrie headed to the south end of the garage. She exited through another side door and hoped anyone watching would expect someone to come onto the property along the driveway that ran north of the buildings.

"Cover." She smiled and moved into the tree line along the south side of all three buildings. She crossed over to the field on the other side and carefully approached the barn at a slow walk. Her mind remained open as she continued to search for the three Bound, Mr. Rodgers, and Tina. However, to keep Mr. Rodgers' Bound from feeling her as well, she remained a good distance from the building. *Hopefully, Awan spoke truth and you're more powerful than most.*

She got the first indication of a person standing near the front door of the barn at fifty feet. The mental activity remained muted and barely discernible. She paused, waiting to see if the person reacted. After a count of twenty, Kyrie continued moving slowly. She angled herself away from the barn to make sure she did not get any closer to the person.

As she walked along the other side of the tree line, she breathed slowly and deliberately, suppressing her emotions as best she could.

She moved out of range of the person at the front of the barn and started to sense someone at the back of the barn. This mind stood out as being very frightened, but the distance prevented her from being certain it was Tina. Because of the strength of the fear in the air, she almost did not feel the second person. *Is it just two?* She paused and concentrated, but she could only feel one muted person and presumably Tina.

*Damn it. Where is Michael Rodgers?* Kyrie kept her breathing calm and continued west past the end of the barn. She circled north to the trees and then approached the barn from the west side. *One Bound at the front, one in the back, and probably Tina.* The time before Hurlington's men arrived, if they even arrived, remained a significant variable in her plan.

"Mr. Rodgers might be gone. Perhaps the others were right." She frowned. She faced two on one before. If she could not get control of the Bound, she could take them out and rescue Tina.

Kyrie examined the west side of the barn and saw the door placed off center, and toward the northern corner. Based on the hacker's memories, she knew they held Tina in the southwest corner. "Waiting is done." She readied the weapons in her hands and crept forward. The moment someone inside the barn reacted in a way that showed they felt her, she would rush the door.

At thirty feet from the door, she knew the panicked mind was Tina. At twenty feet, she felt the muted person move. Kyrie sprinted forward as she generated a gravity well just on the outside the door. The wood rattled for a moment, then the door burst open, swinging around to slam into the side of the barn.

Kyrie raced through the opening and into the dark interior of the barn. She ducked low as she sensed something swing for her head. The muted man loomed over her. Kyrie swung the break-over bar, aiming for his right knee. The man shifted backwards and away from her swing.

Kyrie sensed more people at the front of the barn running toward her. She counted four minds, two muted, one a male, and one Michelle.

"STOP!" Came a loud male voice from down the aisle between the hay bales.

The man who had engaged her by the door moved back and she rose to a crouched position. Her eyes quickly adapting to the darker interior revealed a sandy haired man pushing Michelle ahead of him. The other two men, each over six feet in height, following behind them. *Damn it, Michelle.*

Kyrie stood up straighter, but she kept her feet at a wider stance. She saw Tina gaged and tied to a support post thirty feet beyond the man who attacked her. Tina's fear radiated like a streetlight in the blackest of night.

Kyrie slid her foot over the dirt floor, shifting a layer of loose hay in the process. *Bad footing.*

The man stopped fifteen feet from her. "Nice attempt to use distraction to pull us away, but you failed. Now we can finally meet in person."

Kyrie took in the man's details. His dress shirt and sport's jacket were clean and neatly pressed. Even his jeans and loafers lacked any signs of wear. *Someone who thinks himself a nobleman.* She looked closely at his face and allowed herself a small amount of relief. His face was a solid match for Michael Rodger's profile picture. *Now, where are the stones?* Panic filled her mind. *Does he have my stone since he has Michelle?*

Mr. Rodgers, observing her scrutiny, stepped behind Michelle.

Kyrie force herself to remain calm. She had felt no sense of compulsion yet. *Perhaps he doesn't know she has it.* She exhaled and decided to play dumb. "Who are you and why have you taken my friends?" She spread her senses wider to see if she could feel Jake, Aki, or Becca. She felt only those she could see and pushed her concern for her friends away. *The stones.*

Mr. Rodgers chuckled. "Really?"

She narrowed her focus back to Mr. Rodgers and continued to search for points of energy that might reveal the stones Awan said he always carried.

Mr. Rodgers hardened his tone. "You wonder why we are here?" He shook his head and then raised the pistol in his hand so she could see what he pointed at Michelle's back.

"Sorry," Michelle said. "I just wanted to make sure you were safe. They must have seen me."

Kyrie shifted her focus off Mr. Rodgers to the men behind him. She recognized the distinctive Celtic knot tattoo on one of the men from the restaurant. The other man was bald with a broad chest too wide for his shirt; she could not recall seeing him before. She glanced to the man on her right and nodded her head to the second man at the restaurant. "Those two were watching me."

"Indeed." Mr. Rodgers inclined his head toward her chest. "That is a lovely brooch."

Kyrie drew in more energy and resumed her mental search for the stones. She could not feel her own stone on Michelle, nor could she feel it on Mr. Rodgers. *If he has it, this campaign has ended quickly.* She looked past Michelle and tried to find the small points of energy that she hoped showed up in every Bound's stone.

"Well?"

Kyrie breathed. "It belonged to my mother." She continued to search while she spoke. "Are you the ones that broke into my aunt's house and stole all the jewelry?" Kyrie forced herself to control her energy usage. *You don't want to burn yourself out.*

"That brooch was stolen from me." The man pushed Michelle forward. "You will bring it to me."

"No," Kyrie said. "Let them go." She indicated Michelle and Tina with a nod of her head. "If you want the brooch, I'll give it to you, but not before they are safe." She felt her heart race when she sensed his waist. *Below his belt.*

"You are not in a position to demand anything. Your parents might have taught you math and science, but in business, the person with the money and power gets what he wants." Mr. Rodgers squared his stance, lifted the pistol, held it with two hands, and pointed it at Michelle's back. "You ever see what a bullet can do to a pretty girl?"

Kyrie felt Tina's panic grow even hotter. The girl could not see anything more than Kyrie and the large man between them, but she could hear the conversation. Kyrie also sensed Michelle's heart racing as her friend took a step toward her and then another until Michelle stood directly in front of her. Kyrie looked Michelle in the eyes and knew the subdued terror in her friend.

"Remember, I will put a bullet through your friend if you try anything."

Kyrie sensed Mr. Rodgers' desire to torment her and she expected he sent Michelle over to her so she would feel hope before he ultimately harmed her friends.

Still holding the break-over bar in her right hand, Kyrie reached up and ripped the brooch from her shirt. She stepped forward out of Tina's sight and put herself between Michelle and the pistol. "Come get it yourself." With Michelle behind her, she pushed his thoughts from her and considered how Mr. Rodgers might have concealed the stones under his clothing.

The man shook his head, shifted his weapon to her, and then motioned one of the men behind him to move forward. Kyrie tossed the brooch to the floor halfway between them and then stepped back, pushing Michelle one step closer to the open back door.

Mr. Rodgers' tongue moved over his lips, but he kept the pistol pointed at Kyrie's chest. "Difficult girl."

"Be ready to run," Kyrie whispered to Michelle. She continued to puzzle out the question of the stones under Mr. Rodgers clothing.

The Bound man stayed to the side and out of the direct line of fire. The tattooed man retrieved the brooch and returned it to Mr. Rodgers, who then lowered the weapon to take the worn bit of jewelry. "See, that wasn't so hard."

"Let them go," Kyrie demanded.

The man slid his weapon into the holster under his arm and then started to examine the brooch. "You have caused me no end of trouble. For sixteen years I truly hoped you had simply died. But no, you had to show up and remind people you exist. You had to remind certain people of my prior failure. I won't let that go unanswered." He shook his head as he bent the copper filigree and pulled the stone free, much the same way Kyrie had. He looked up at her as he tossed the copper away. "I think it is fitting that I make you suffer a bit before I turn you over to the man who will soon be your master."

Kyrie gave up on mentally separating the different layers of cloth and material. She felt more than a dozen stones above his pelvis. *So much for the sword men.* She cleared her mind and slowly crafted a series of gravity fields, one in front of each stone.

Mr. Rodgers held the stone from her brooch in his hand and stood very straight. "I think you should first break the foot of your friend Michelle."

Kyrie raised her left hand to her head, as though she resisted compulsion. She dropped both weapons to the floor and leaned forward into a crouch. Energy poured from her and strengthened the gravity fields she had crafted. The man stumbled forward as her energy pulled at the stones in front of his pelvis. His jeans exploded outwards. Nineteen stones flew at Kyrie as she pulled her fields toward her to guide the stones to her hands. The glass rocks pelted her stomach. She shifted her fields to gain control of the stones.

The man at her right lunged forward as did the two men near Mr. Rodgers.

"STOP!" Kyrie demanded, concentrating on the stones that threatened to spill from her hands.

The man on her right froze, as did the tattooed man, but the third one slammed a wall of energy into her, throwing her and Michelle backwards against the barn's outer wall.

Kyrie struggled to hold the stones in her hands. Mr. Rodgers had recovered his composure and went for his gun. "Kill Rodgers," she cried as a gravity well crushed her into the floor.

The two men from the restaurant rushed at the sandy haired man while the bald man continued to come at her. Kyrie heard the pistol discharge three times before she managed to compensate for the gravity that had pinned her to the ground.

*Bastard,* she swore. She held tight onto the stones, while another field tried to rip them from her hands. Kyrie gorged on the energy around her, dropping the temperature in the immediate area. The machete next to her rocketed from the ground and struck the third Bound in the gut. The man smiled as the weapon bounced off, now bent and twisted.

She increased her energy and thrust herself into the air to get her feet back under her. A narrow beam of force slashed her right arm, cutting through to the bone before her instincts countered the invisible field. Five stones fell from her hands.

Four more shots erupted from the pistol in quick succession. Mr. Rodgers' scream filled the barn. Then he fell silent.

Behind her, Kyrie felt a spike of pain from Michelle. She wanted to help, but the third man moved at her. She slammed a wall of energy into the man, driving him backwards. The man's focus remained on the stones in her hands. *Help me,* she directed into the stones. A moment later, the two men from the restaurant grabbed the third Bound from behind. They grappled with the bald man's arms, but he broke free of their grasp and knocked them back with his mind. The shorter man from the restaurant picked up the bent machete and started hacking the bald man. The majority of the blows bounce away, but a few of the stronger strikes broke through the gravitational shield the man had created.

Kyrie saw how limited the powers were of the two men working for her. She grabbed the stones and bundled them in her shirt, holding them with one hand. She reached out with her mind and the break-over bar flew to her hand. Two steps forward put her into range, and she swung the bar against the bald man's back. The swing, augmented with the energy that burned her mind, slammed into the man's body with an audible crunch that spoke of a broken shoulder blade.

The bald man continued to fight. An energy wave flung the man with the machete back. Another hit her, but she countered the gravity field with a field of her own as she swung again and again. Finally, the third man dropped to his knees. One of the Bound she controlled, picked up Mr. Rodgers' pistol from the ground and fired once into the man's face. The bullet ricocheted away. The pistol discharged twice more in rapid succession. Those next two bullets ripped through his head, spraying blood and gore everywhere. The bald man's brain ceased to function, and he collapsed.

Kyrie dropped the break-over bar and swung around to see Michelle on the ground, her face twisted in pain as she held a hand against her shoulder.

"Damn it!" Kyrie ran to her, blood running from her own nose and arm.

"I'm cold." Michelle's voice trembled as she shook.

Kyrie thought to the stones that she wanted Tina freed and then drew more power into herself. She pushed the energy into Michelle as she connected her mind to Michelle's subconscious. Instinct commanded Michelle's body to begin the healing process. "Stay with me," Kyrie mumbled as her hands shook from the pain of energy usage. She mended broken bones and torn flesh, working from the inside out so that she could push the bullet from Michelle's body.

"Stop," Michelle mumbled. Her blood covered hand moved to Kyrie's face. "You heal me, the doctors will suspect something."

Kyrie allowed a little more energy to flow into Michelle and then stopped. *She's right. But she needs help.*

Tina screamed and ran over to Michelle. "What is going on!" She turned to face the man who had freed her and scooted back. "Stay away!"

Kyrie looked at the two Bound. Blood surrounded the area around the bullet wounds in their chests, but the red stains did not seem to be growing.

"What is your demand?" the tattooed man asked.

Kyrie ignored Tina's hysterical sobbing. "I could give you your own stone. If I freed you, what would happen?" She looked between them and waited for an answer. Noticing the five stones on the ground, she snatched them up and added them to the bundle in her shirt.

"I would not do that," said the man with a tattoo on his cheek. He glanced at the other man. "His mind's destroyed. He can do little more than obey orders. Mine's damaged. Thinking is hard." The man reached into his coat and pulled out a handful of folded sheets of paper. Blood stained the outside and a hole ripped through one corner. The man handed it to her. "I took these because they reminded me of home. Our leaders were fools to banish Nalitran as they did. Now we suffer their folly."

Kyrie looked at the third Bound whose face had been destroyed. "He's not like you?"

The tattooed man shook his head. "Nalitran sent him to watch Mr. Rodgers. The High Lord will know something has happened to his man."

A thousand questions ran through Kyrie's mind. "I don't remember the other world. I only dream of it."

The tattooed man looked sad. "You must have been a child when they stole you. That could explain your limited memories." The man's face fell. "Your parents would have simply found your lifeless body when your soul was removed." He looked away. "I was a mother before my binding. They cared nothing for our gender or who we left behind." Tears fell from the man's face. "Now look at me."

Kyrie looked back at Tina and then toward the front of the barn. "Quiet." The sounds of a vehicle stopped. *This has gone wrong.* She pushed herself to her feet. She looked at the large men. They stared at her with uncertainty. "That could be the police or the Church of the Righteous Revenge."

The tattooed man looked toward the front of the barn. "You need to leave."

Tina sobbed quietly as she sat on the ground beside Michelle.

"Come with me?" Kyrie asked the men.

The tattooed man shook his head. "You know we cannot, which is why you did not make that an order." The man reached down and pulled a pistol from the bald man's body. "Order us to fight and then you destroy the stones. Free us." The other Bound took Mr. Rodgers' pistol from the floor and a fresh magazine from his former master's pocket.

Kyrie tried to expand her senses, but the pain made her weak. "That one. Where is his stone?"

She looked into the tattooed man's eyes and knew he did not know. She heard the front door of the barn burst open and could now feel several people coming in their direction. The hostility of their minds making its way through her exhaustion. "Damn it." She moved toward Tina and Michelle. *Stop them,* she thought to the stones.

The two men rushed toward the front of the barn. The repeated crack of rapid gunfire filled the air. Kyrie's eyes flew open. *That sounds like rifles.* She drew energy into herself, causing more blood to run from her nose. She bent down and lifted Michelle with one hand while she carried the stones in the other.

Tina screamed at every shot.

"Help me," Kyrie swore at Tina. The other girl snapped out of her panic just enough to take Michelle's other side. The three of them passed through the door and then Kyrie led the way to the trees. In the distance she heard the sounds of sirens.

Kyrie felt her own body suffering from shock and she barely reached their cover. Rapid gun fire continued inside the barn and she now doubted the police would make it in time.

Kyrie forced Michelle and Tina further into the trees and then set them down behind a large oak that shielded them from the barn. "You still with me?" She asked Michelle.

Michelle opened her eyes and nodded her head.

Tina continued her silent sobs. The loud gun fire ensured she did not reveal their location.

Kyrie wiped the blood from her face. *Where are the swords? Hurlington's men brought guns.* She focused on Michelle. "Where'd you hide it?"

Michelle understood Kyrie's meaning. "In the dirt under the big tree where we parked."

Kyrie looked at Tina. "Lay down as well." The blonde slowly complied, and Kyrie quickly covered them both with leaves and branches. "Don't make any sounds."

Kyrie pushed herself back to her feet and staggered away from her two friends. *The plan fell apart. Fool. You're a damn fool for letting them come. You should have known Michelle would follow you.*

She headed east along the side of the barn to the front of the building. Her hands trembled and she paused at a dead tree. *Rest. Sleep.* She shook her head and glanced over her shoulder, but she could see no one watching her. The stones felt like bricks and she looked for a place to hide them. Instinct drove her eyes upward and she spotted a decayed hole high up in the dead tree. "Just this one last thing," she told herself, then paused. *Find someplace safe to hide from Bishop,* she projected to the stones. Then with a deep breath, she drew in energy. Her body trembled as the stones floated up to the opening a dozen feet above her head. She collapsed to her knees as the energy left her.

Sirens and flashing lights drew her attention as three vehicles sped down the driveway and passed through her narrow field of vision between the house and the garage. She spared a thought for the Bound and wondered if they still lived. She had heard no weapons fire from the barn for a while and she doubted they had survived.

Gun fire suddenly erupted again from the barn, this time it peppered the police cars. Return fire came quickly. Kyrie dragged herself around the back of a tree. She could hear men running along the side of the barn, but had no energy left to deal with them.

More shots rang out, and from the sounds, she knew at least two men moved to flank the police. *You need them stopped.* She leaned around the tree and saw the men now following the south wall of the garage. She looked the other way to see if anyone else had come out of the barn. *No one in sight.* She used the tree to scratch her way to her feet.

The men at the garage had their backs to her and were over two hundred feet away. She wiped the blood from her face and pushed herself through the trees into the field. She clawed her way forward, demanding one foot to follow the other until she stood within thirty feet of the men.

One of the men, kneeling, took aim and fired his assault rifle around the edge of the barn. The other stood over the top of the first. Controlled shots rang out from the standing man's weapon. *You bastards should have brought swords.* Kyrie drew energy into herself, burning and searing her mind and flesh. She forced the rifle of the standing man downward and at the back of the one kneeling. The startled man fired into his companion and stumbled backward as the one kneeling fell forward in a heap.

Kyrie saw the man turn and focus on her. He brought the weapon around and pulled back the trigger just as she stepped behind a tree. Bullets thudded into the trunk and zipped past her. Blood poured from her nose and she felt her knees buckling under her. She could not sense the man, but after a moment, more bullets ripped through the narrow woods. She tried to breathe. *Accept it,* she told herself.

More gun fire filled the air and the man's rapid shooting stopped. She remained frozen in place, unable to move, even when she heard men yelling "clear" from the other side of the trees. No longer able to stand, she slipped down the side of the tree and onto the ground.

"Got one!" a man yelled from beside her. She turned her head and saw the officer pointing a gun at her. She closed her eyes and allowed darkness to fill her mind.

# Chapter 22

Kyrie woke up in an unfamiliar bed. The smell of chemicals hung heavy in the air. She tried to open her mind, but she found only pain.

She moved her left arm and winced as tubes weighed down her wrist. Her right arm burned where the Bound man's gravity wave had cut her. She knew she had healed some of the damage during the fight, but it remained a significant wound. She moved her arm and found a small clamp attached to one of her fingers on her right hand.

As her head cleared, she realized she was naked with only a robe on under the blanket. She tried to sit up, but found she lacked the strength. That also brought awareness to the various wires attached to her chest. *What is this place?*

Someone walked past the open door to the room and she called out. "Hello. Where am I?"

A woman in blue garments returned to the doorway and came into the room. "You're awake? I would have expected you to sleep longer." The woman brushed a hair from her face and came over to the side of Kyrie's bed. "How are you doing?"

"Hungry," Kyrie responded, the emptiness of her stomach became audible. "I need to eat something."

"I'm nurse Meg. Do you know what day it is?"

Kyrie shook her head and then looked out the dark window opposite the door. "The last I knew, it was Saturday."

"It is still Saturday night." The nurse came around the other side of the bed and pushed a button that caused the head of the bed to rise. "That better?" The nurse asked and Kyrie nodded yes. The nurse then examined Kyrie's right arm. "Doesn't look like there is a lot of bleeding through the bandage. It is fortunately for you that the slice didn't go too deep. I expect you'll have a scar, but it won't be too bad. We were more worried about the blow you must have taken to your head." The nurse pulled out a small flashlight, pulled back Kyrie's eyelids, and shined the light into her eyes. "No black eyes yet."

Kyrie tried to turn her head away.

"I'm just checking your pupil response."

"Michelle? The others?" Kyrie tried to sit up again.

"Your friends are okay. The one with the gunshot wound is recovering nicely. She won't lose the arm." The nurse put away the flashlight.

Kyrie allowed herself to settle down. "I was worried."

"I imagine so. The good news is you don't seem to have any signs of a concussion. Shock from blood loss, yes, but the blow that caused the nosebleed didn't do any other damage." The nurse forced a smile. "There are some officers that will want to talk with you now that you are awake." The nurse stepped away from the bed. "I'll get you some food while I let them know you're conscious."

Kyrie let out her breath. *For this to work, you can't run. Like you could if you wanted to,* she chided herself.

Several minutes later nurse Meg returned with a tray supporting a bowl of soup, a glass of juice, and a cup of pudding on it. Three officers followed the nurse into the room along with her aunt.

"Kyrie!" Her aunt pushed her way to the bed. "What is going on? If you have done something wrong, don't say anything and I will have Charles represent you."

The nurse pushed the button to raise the bed further. She then stepped back and let the three officers approach the bed.

"Good evening, Miss Landvik," the female officer said. "My name is Officer Marks. May I call you Kyrie?"

Kyrie nodded.

"What happened, Kyrie?" her aunt demanded.

Kyrie sighed. "My parents disappeared into the mountains because people wanted to hurt us. They hid, not to abuse me, but to keep me safe. When my mother died, and I came here, those people found me again, and then came after me."

"Do you know who these people are?" Officer Marks asked. "What they want?"

Kyrie wished she could read the emotions in the room, but her mind hurt too much. "Not much. Some church. I don't know who they are or why they fixated on me and my parents. But they called me a demon and wanted to kill me." Kyrie ignored the stunned expression on her aunt's face. "A van of men with swords jumped me and my friends on Thursday when we walked home from school. We managed to run and get away."

"And you didn't report it to the police?" her aunt demanded.

"The others wanted to, but the police, and everyone else, refused to believe my parents when they reported it all those years ago. My parents said a police officer was involved." Kyrie dropped her eyes and looked at the tray in front of her. "I convinced the others not to say anything. I told them I would run away to keep everyone else safe."

"And you trust us now?" A male officer with a mustache asked.

*Not in the least.* "The others convinced me that my parents had been wrong."

"Why'd you drive to Arkansas on Friday?" Officer Marks asked.

"Michelle didn't want me to run away. She wanted to convince me to come forward and report the attack and what I knew. But...I remained too afraid to do so. People had broken into my aunt's house and then tried to kill me with swords." Kyrie bit her lip. "I would've left Thursday night, but Michelle suggested we all go camping to get to someplace safe so no one would break into a house and hurt us. She wanted to convince me that running away would not solve anything."

Kyrie looked to each of the three officers. "She reluctantly agreed to take me to Arkansas. I wanted to go there because that is where my parents had been on vacation when this all started. I wanted to see if I could find out why."

"No one knows what they did in Arkansas!" Her aunt demanded. "The very idea. Stupid girl."

Officer Marks frowned at her aunt. "Ma'am, if you cannot be quiet, please wait outside."

"You will not question an underaged girl outside of my presence, unless you want to wait for my lawyer."

Officer Marks stood taller. "We need to establish what happened. She is not under arrest." She then turned back to Kyrie. "But not going to the police resulted in Tina Bruce's abduction. And your friend Michelle got shot."

Kyrie nodded her head. "Tina and Michelle had a fight at school on Thursday. She didn't see the attack, so we thought no one would go after her." Kyrie looked away again. "It was stupid of us."

Officer Marks nodded her head in agreement. "You should most definitely have come forward. We are trained to deal with things like this." She softened her expression. "How did you end up at that barn?"

"They used Tina's phone to contact us. We had no cell coverage at the campsite. When we went for food, the texts came in. They said they would kill her if we didn't do as they demanded. I knew they wanted me, so I thought if I turned myself over to them, they would let Tina go." Kyrie frowned. "Michelle wasn't supposed to follow me. But they saw her, and she got pulled in as well." She looked up at the officers. "I didn't want anyone to get hurt."

"It is a good thing your friend Becca called the police," the other male officer said. "Otherwise, you might all have ended up dead."

Kyrie looked abashed. "I thought I could handle it all on my own. My parents tried to prepare me to do that. I didn't consider the consequences."

"That stupid Robert Landvik," her aunt said. "He killed my sister and almost got my niece killed with the stupid things he put into her head." Her aunt shook her head. "Look at what I have to deal with."

Kyrie ignored her aunt and looked at the officers.

Officer Marks gave her a slight nod of the head. "We have been questioning the men that survived. They swear you are a demon. There is obviously a cult there. But it appears there were other people not part of the cult at the barn. And these people attacked each other. What happened there?"

Kyrie shrugged. She had no time to get a story straight between herself, Michelle, and Tina. *Partial truth and hope it works.* "I'm not certain. The man in the suit wanted my mother's brooch. He said it belonged to him. I think he broke into the house and stole all the jewelry."

"That bit of costume jewelry?" her aunt demanded. "Worthless."

Officer Marks spoke. "We found broken bits of costume jewelry in the barn. It did not appear to have any monetary value. However, what caused the men to attack each other? We are looking at the details, but it appears strange. A description of events will help."

"The man in the suit wanted to have all of us killed. I don't know why. Perhaps the men with swords hired him." She tried to shrug, but she winced at the movement. "I don't know. But after he took my mother's brooch, he talked about killing us. Not all of the men there appeared to be good with that. A man with a tattoo on his face objected, but the bald one wanted to do it. They started fighting and shooting. I had brought a metal bar and a machete with me from the garage. The bald man was going to kill us, so I hit him on the back when he fought with the others. I hit him a few times. One of the other men had the machete I dropped and used it." She looked away. "There was so much shooting and violence and yelling and screaming. I'm not sure of everything that happened." She looked back at the officers. "I did hit the bald man in the back so he couldn't use his gun."

"Someone with a gun shot him twice in the face," Officer Marks said.

Kyrie tried to look uncertain. "Michelle had been hit. I ran to her. The other guy had already untied Tina. Then more people with guns showed up and started shooting. I got Tina to help me get Michelle outside and into the tree line. I hid them and moved away so if the gunmen found me, they might not find the others."

Officer Marks looked at her and considered her statements. "We tested you for gunshot residue. Your clothes had some, but it was consistent with being in the area and not firing a weapon."

"I only hit the one man in the back to try and keep him from shooting others."

Officer Marks nodded her head. "Please, never do anything like this again. If you, or any of your friends are in danger, call the police. We are here to help."

"Exactly," her aunt said. "The fool things that are in your head."

Kyrie noticed the other two officers relax and she looked back at Officer Marks. "I will."

"We will have some officers stationed here to make sure you and your friend are safe in the hospital. The hospital security is also aware of possible threats. So, you can sleep well. We will track down this organization and arrest these people. We cannot have terrorists hunting young ladies."

"Thank you," Kyrie said. "When can I go home?"

The nurse stepped forward. "If everything is normal, the doctor will likely release you in the morning."

"And Michelle?"

The nurse raised a hand. "That I can't say. She had surgery for the gun shot. It may be a few days."

Kyrie nodded her head.

"We may have more questions for you," Officer Marks said. "If these men insist on going to trial, you will likely have to testify. Several people died at the barn and four officers sustained gunshot wounds as well. That will have every police department across the country willing to help."

"Just tell me what I need to do," Kyrie said.

The officers smiled. "Get better." They turned around and left with the nurse. Her aunt remained, but Kyrie dug into her food and tuned out her aunt's litany of complaints. They had removed Mr. Rodgers from the game, as well as several of Hurlington's men. She knew Nalitran would take a lot more work. *Keep taking out the orcs, when that is done, go for the dragon.*

# Chapter 23

Kyrie went back to school on Monday. Details of the armed assault at the barn filled the news cycles on Sunday and again on Monday morning. It even made the national news with the Church of the Righteous Revenge taking the bulk of the blame, though the anchors had few details on the organization. None of the news broadcasts mentioned Kyrie, or the others, by name, but the tone of the reports made them seem like gullible children.

Unfortunately, all their names turned up on social media and those posts quickly went viral. Kyrie did not need to read emotions and minds to know what her fellow students felt about her. She decided not to protest her intelligence. Her trip to Arkansas proved successful, and for the meantime, she could suffer the condescending comments, stares, and thoughts of others.

The students made few comments and even her teachers maintained a reserved distance. But their expressions and thoughts lacked kindness. *What is wrong is that your friends are suffering the same treatment.*

Neither Michelle, nor Tina, returned to classes on Monday. Kyrie had expected that of Michelle, but she wondered at the reason Tina had also stayed away.

After the last bell of the day, Kyrie waited just outside the school entrance to see if Becca, Aki, or Jake would decide to speak with her. She found the attention of the school security staff irritating. The idea that she would plan an attack, or cause trouble, meant they knew nothing of her.

Eventually, her three friends walked out of the school together. They saw her immediately and moved in her direction. "Hey," Kyrie said, offering both greeting and apology in a single word.

"Hey," Becca replied with a smile.

Aki let out a long sigh and shook her head. "My parents have forbidden me from hanging out with you. I'm not supposed to be grounded any more, but they still want me home after school and want me to check in every hour. So, I'm grounded. They think I lack any sense of good judgement."

"Sorry," Kyrie said.

Aki crossed her arms. "Not your fault. My decision to go with you." She huffed once and swallowed. "I haven't slept. I keep waking up seeing faces. The worst is when I see Steven Bishop's face. Knowing he likely knows who I am. And might know that I know the truth of him." She looked at Kyrie. "He won't let me live if he thinks I know." She hesitated. "I'm embarrassed about how emotional I got. I should have held it together better."

Jake put his arm around Aki's shoulder and pulled her against him. "You did fine, Aki. We all freaked out some."

Kyrie wanted to grin at Jake's protectiveness, but Aki's appraisal of the threat from Nalitran was accurate. "I think we have bought some time. Awan said Bishop's trying to appear legitimate. I think he will avoid reacting without understanding what we know for certain."

"I don't know." Aki pulled out her phone and showed Kyrie the screen. "The news caught wind of Rodgers' connection to Nalitran. They pressed Bishop on it this morning. He claimed he's got over ninety-thousand people working for him and cannot screen everyone personally. He felt bad about what happened, but he could take no responsibility as bad people show up all over the place." She looked at the screen and swiped to another page. "This came out an hour ago. The three captured church gunmen all managed to commit suicide overnight."

Becca shook her head. "I don't buy that."

Aki agreed visibly as she turned off the phone; a shiver ran through her body. "It's all bullshit. But the sheeple will believe it."

Becca swore. "Bishop must have done it. He certainly knows about us and he's got tons of money. Money that can make us disappear just like those men."

"I have money coming to me. Quite a bit, but Lars said my little adventure will make getting to it before my aunt does difficult."

"You called him?" Becca demanded.

Kyrie nodded her head. "I didn't reveal anything, but it would have been odd if I had not." She considered telling them about the nearly thirty-thousand dollars in Colorado, but she did not want to suggest another road trip so soon. *Besides, I need to get my stone and the stones Mr. Rodgers had first. I will need any information those Bound can provide to get at Bishop.* Aloud, she said, "I think we will need the money to deal with Bishop."

"How much?" Jake asked.

"Lars said about ten million."

Becca's eyes bulged. "Damn." She laughed. "Well, that's a good reason to call him."

Kyrie frowned; she could feel the desire coming from the others. "It's locked up in something he called a trust and I can't get to it." Kyrie changed the subject away from her money. "With Hurlington in the spotlight, I think the church is likely a bigger threat to Bishop than we are."

Aki leaned further into Jake and gave Kyrie a smile. "I hope you are right. And I hope they investigate how those men actually died."

*They look good together.* Kyrie lowered her voice. "He'll have to replace Rodgers eventually and that means letting other people in on the truth. If he does anything personally, that will draw more attention to his business."

"And his campaign," Aki said.

Becca shook her head. "I think this played into Hurlington's goals; some national coverage for his cult. The cops might find him, but you heard Awan, not even Bishop found him." Her face grew grim. "And that nut's got it in for you as well."

Kyrie nodded her head. "I won't ask any of you to get involved again. If I distance myself, they may leave you alone."

Becca flipped Kyrie off. "Screw you. I also knew I was getting into some deep shit when I agreed to go. I'm not going to just sit back and ignore this. I can't. They know we are all involved together. If you leave us now, it will sentence us to death." She moved a step closer. "Since Michelle is not here, I'll say it, don't split the damn party."

Jake nodded his head. "If it matters, I'm grounded as well." Jake smiled. "What pissed my parents off the most was that I camped out unsupervised with you girls." Becca and Aki laughed and he looked hurt. "I got the talk again." He shook his head. "I really don't want to discuss sex with my parents." The others cringed and he continued. "I will find a way to get out of being grounded so we can continue this. We have no other choice. Plus, we all like you."

Kyrie felt herself blush. "I appreciate it."

"I'm not saying this isn't your fault," Becca said with a smile. "My dad showed me the world had an ugly underbelly, but you've shown me things are worse than he ever imagined. It is a wake-up call I won't forget, and I know it won't forget me. But, I'd prefer to have a real mage on my side than be at this alone."

Kyrie looked around as the students continued to file out of the school. "I will keep working at my mother's papers. There may be more answers in the math."

"You got that all back?" Jake asked. "I was worried."

"The cops saw gaming materials and just gave it back to me," Kyrie ignored the security personnel looking in their direction. "Have you heard anything from Tina or Michelle?"

"Tina is getting counseling for being kidnapped," Becca said with a little disdain. "Not sure if she'll make it back to class this year at all. Michelle is home. She texted last night that she wants to be back in school later this week. The doctors expressed much surprise, and pleasure, with the limited amount of damage and how quickly she is recovering." Becca pulled up her phone and showed Kyrie a text. "She wants to thank you in person and also told me to make you promise not to run off." Becca rolled her eyes. "She sent kisses and hugs. She'd definitely not send those to me." Becca then pulled a small green stone from her pocket and slipped it to Kyrie. "I know you gave her the real one. I saw where she hid it and thought you might need it back."

Kyrie felt the connection to the stone the moment she saw it. She wrapped her arms around Becca, hugging her friend as a sense of relief washed through her.

"Hey, I didn't compel you to do that."

Kyrie continued to hug Becca. "Tell Michelle I won't leave. This is just the beginning and I desperately need all you guys."

www.ingramcontent.com/pod-product-compliance
Lightning Source LLC
Chambersburg PA
CBHW030656260626
47157CB00007B/2670